AND SEEK (NOT) TO ALTER ME

QUEER FANWORKS INSPIRED BY SHAKESPEARE'S
MUCH ADO ABOUT NOTHING

Duck Prints Press, LLC
Schenectady, NY

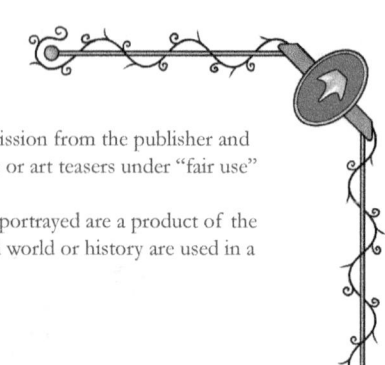

And Seek (Not) to Alter Me © 2024, Duck Prints Press LLC

Stories:
"Good Men and True" © 2024, Juno Caster
"Ruckus, Drama, and 2-Metre-Tall Penguins" © 2024, Era J. M. Couts
"An Office Ado" © 2024, Aria L. Deair
"Some Sparks That Are Like Wit" © 2024, Adrian Harley
"Much Ruckus" © 2024, R. L. Houck
"I Am For You" © 2024, Lucy K. R.
"Some Cupids" © 2024, Nickel J. Keep
"Dear Don Pedro" © 2024, Mikki Madison
"The Journal Of Don Pedro: Or, The Straights Are At It Again" © 2024, Nova Mason
"The Polyamorous 'Oh' " © 2024, Theo Neidlinger
"find ourselves unstuck" © 2024, nottesilhouette
"The False Sweet Bait" © 2024, Vee Sloane
"Hero's Moon" © 2024 , Theresa Tanner
"ASS[U]ME" © 2024, K. B. Vimes
"Can Virtue Hide Itself?" © 2024, Lyn Weaver
"A Skirmish of Wit" © 2024, Nicole Wilkinson

Art:
"Battle of Wit" © 2024, Aceriee
"Intimacy" © 2024, Cris Alborja
"Silver tongue" © 2024, Cris Alborja
"Melancholy" © 2024, Joshua Beeking
untitled art piece © 2024, Liz Brooks
"I Had Rather Hear My Dog Bark at a Crow" © 2024, Amy Fincher
"Masquerade" © 2024, Taylor C. Fischer
"Cottage Country Comic AU" © 2024, Joey Hazell
"The Sweetest Thing" © 2024, Alicia Matheson
"Taming My Wild Heart to Thy Loving Hand" © 2024, Pimmy Oldham
"Born Under Saturn" © 2024, Pallas Perilous
"Eat His Heart in the Marketplace" © 2024, Magnolia Porter
"Beatrice and Benedicia" © 2024, Jared Powell
"Hiro and Claudia" © 2024, Jared Powell
"Duly Noted" © 2024, Xanthe P. Russell
"Corkboard" © 2024, Casei Solus
"Beatrice (Disaster Bi)" © 2024, A. A. Weston
"Benedick (Disaster Bi)" © 2024, A. A. Weston

Front and back cover art © 2024, Gio Guimarães

Edited by A. L. Heard, Nina Waters, and Lacey Hayes. Significant contributions to the planning and development of this projects were also made by P. J. Claremore, A. Reilly, and Alessa Riel.
Print manuscript formatting by Hermit Writes.
E-book formatting by Nina Waters.

Published by Duck Prints Press, LLC
Schenectady, New York
duckprintspress.com

ISBN: 978-1-962488-21-1 (Paperback edition)
ISBN: 978-1-962488-23-5 (ePub edition)
ISBN: 978-1-962488-22-8 (PDF edition)

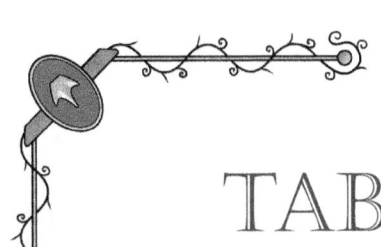

TABLE OF CONTENTS

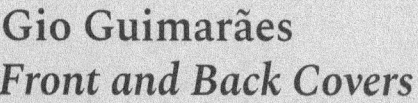

Gio Guimarães
Front and Back Covers

I started by looking for images showing the play with actors and the full set. My idea was to have the cover look like a stage, so I wanted the curtains, the stage itself, and the ornaments, like if the frame were the opening where we could see the actors in action. My research added the idea of the couch, the lights, and the purples and reds. Also, the idea was to dress each one of the actors in-scene with totally different costumes from different places and ages. And finally, I had the idea to add the little duck, as a little funny detail and also a signature!

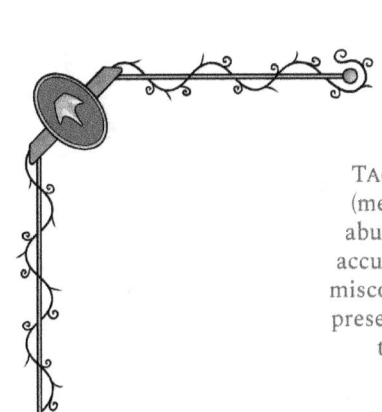

I AM FOR YOU

Lucy K. R.

When I was growing up, it was a joke in my house that my parents would out me to the military. Like most of the kids in my public high school, I was subject to frequent recruitment efforts. Once, my mother even answered the Navy's call with, "Oh, you don't want her, she's gay." But what was a fun joke to us was a reality for people who had dedicated their lives to an institution that counted on them to kill, but would kick them out for loving. Seeing Don Pedro as a military man with such a deep connection to Leonato in Much Ado About Nothing *brought to mind those Don't Ask Don't Tell days during which I grew up. From that framework I wondered: what would it look like to do anything for love?*

June 2003; the Governor's Mansion

If I were still a young man"—Leonato's voice is low, sheltered though they are behind rows of his father's books—"how would you woo me?"

"Ah," Don Pedro chuckles, flexing his left hand—always sore from the scar at the meat of his thumb. "If you were a young man, I would have to fight off your suitors with my cane."

"But you would be young too." Leonato notes Don Pedro's empty glass. A better host would fill it, but he's too busy enjoying Don Pedro's hand on his thigh, the warmth of his closeness, and the safety of the library. "Where would you even find a cane?"

"I suppose I would borrow one." Don Pedro's answer is light with amusement. "Surely some kind elder would lend theirs to such a cause."

"Would you lend yours today?"

"For love? In a heartbeat."

Love, he says, so easily. *Love*, in his rich voice, with the ever-lingering hint of Spain in his words. *Love*, as if Leonato is not already lost.

A breath closer, and they kiss as if they really are young again. Leonato's beard catches against Don Pedro's stubble, chaste affection giving way to bold desire.

Neither of them jolt at the sound of the door. They are old and battle-hardened. They know

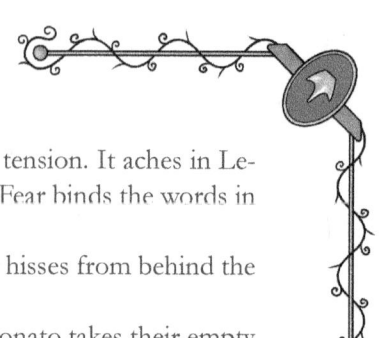

that secrets are best kept through calmness, that serenity hides more than tension. It aches in Leonato's chest to part slowly from their kiss. *One more*, he wants to whisper. Fear binds the words in his throat.

"Have you seen the way he looks at him?" one of the manor employees hisses from behind the shelves that hide them.

Don Pedro's hand twitches before he moves it from Leonato's thigh. Leonato takes their empty glasses to the bar. They listen by silent accord.

"The governor?" a second voice replies—one of his daughter's favorite maids, Margaret. "Of course! He's always like that when the general comes around. Brightens the whole house up."

"You don't think it's weird?" the first voice asks.

Leonato pours steadily. His heart pounds so hard that his pulse throbs down to his fingertips. Don Pedro's presence is a stable certainty—an anchor.

If they round the final row of books…

"What's weird about it?" Margaret has a sharp, repressive note in her voice. "A man's not allowed to have friends? Shame on you."

"It's not that! Never mind. Whatever."

"Not 'whatever.' Get your head on straight. The governor's had his share of heartbreak," says Margaret. Leonato flinches. "He can be as close as he likes with the general." Behind him, Don Pedro shifts his weight.

There's the sound of storming footsteps, then a muttered, "Can he?"

The library door closes behind them.

Don Pedro exhales. Leonato keeps his eyes on the too-generous pour of scotch, opening the freezer below the bar to add fresh ice to the glass.

"Leonato—"

"Thank goodness no one cares to read family history." Leonato gestures to the books sheltering them.

"Leonato."

The weight of how Don Pedro says his name has changed, but it's as heavy with love as ever. Leonato often wonders that no one else hears it—the way that light tongue frames the shape of him, as though he is a flavor to be savored.

"Forgive me," he says, returning with the drink and setting it down before his love.

He sits across the table this time rather than at his side. Don Pedro says nothing, but in his dark eyes Leonato sees pain.

What Leonato would give to beat that hurt back with a cane.

"How long," Beatrice asks, braced against the dining table with elbows locked, her head hanging low as though with exhaustion, "will these guests grace us with their presence?"

Leonato chokes on his tea and desperately tries to smother a laugh. Hero grins, unrepentant. She looks more like her mother each day, though the wicked amusement behind her sweet smile is hers alone.

"Beatrice finds Corporal Benedick intolerable," Hero informs him, and sends him a wink.

"A month or more," Leonato answers. The agonized groan that is unleashed upon him could not have been more wounded if he'd stabbed Beatrice with his butter knife. "Has the Corporal been so disagreeable?" He leans forward. "If he has made any untoward advances, or if you find him unkind—"

"Unkind? Untoward?" Beatrice's head snaps up, fire in her eyes. "Oh, unkind, no, *unkind* is not a word I would use. *Something* starting with 'un' or 'in,' but nothing involving *kind*! As for 'toward,' if only 'untoward' meant 'away' I'd welcome any of his advances in that direction!"

"Here she goes," Hero whispers, eager anticipation in her eyes.

Indeed, there she goes. He considers suggesting Beatrice avoid the young man, but he's certain that she would meet the suggestion with sharp-tongued scorn.

Besides, he doubts there's any cause to worry about Corporal Benedick. When Don Pedro introduced Claudio and Benedick as "brothers-in-arms" with one another, Leonato heard the truth: "here are a pair of lovers I'm entrusting to you. They are young, and we can give their fragile love shelter to grow in."

He leaves Beatrice still fuming to seek Don Pedro and share his amusement. He finds him on the veranda with both their other guests. He's patting Claudio's back while Benedick pouts, perched on the railing like a cat and ignoring them.

"Young Claudio would like permission to ask your Hero for a date." Don Pedro's voice is rich and easy, as if he can't see Benedick sulking over being thrown aside in favor of Leonato's daughter.

"Technically, Mr. Governor, sir," Claudio says, "I'd like your permission to get the General's help to ask your daughter for a date, sir. He, uh, offered."

"Boo," Corporal Benedick calls.

"I know Hero well." Don Pedro looks on the edge of laughing. "With the Governor's blessing, you'll have a date by sunset."

Leonato meets his eyes with confusion and sees the quiet pride there. Receives a small nod. "It's fine," that nod says, and more than that: "trust me."

He does.

"Go on, then." Leonato lifts a hand. "If you have Don Pedro's indulgence, you have mine, young man."

"Give me your phone, Claudio," Don Pedro says, a mischievous smile making his eyes sparkle.

Leonato knows well what a deft hand Don Pedro is with words of love. Before half an hour has passed, while Benedick is still sighing himself sick, Hero is won for Claudio through text messages alone.

Leonato waits for Claudio to flee in his delight, then approaches Benedick.

"All the best are eventually lost to marriage," he conspires.

He receives a cold smile from Benedick and a shake of his curly head.

"What does it matter?" he laughs. "There are always a dozen more. He's weaker than I thought, going doe-eyed within two days of meeting. If any woman were to hold my eyes hostage like that, I'd sooner gouge them out than be lost. Any man, too, for that matter."

"Hypothetically, of course," Don Pedro prompts, patience overwhelming in his measured words. *Don't tell*, his tone warns.

"Oh, the whole world is made of hypotheticals," Benedick agrees. "Just ask that Beatrice, she'll give you a whole list of things to wonder over. Things like 'how did she survive to near-adulthood?' and 'has no one yet been born who could make her hold her tongue?' I don't know how you live with her under your roof, good Governor."

Leonato lets him ramble. The spurned Corporal buries his heart under layers of scathing words, his scorn building a defensive wall. *Don't ask*, it says in the language of one too used to lying.

Don Pedro's room connects with Leonato's through the master bathroom. When he's not at the manor, their adjoining door stays locked, and the other room stands empty. When he visits, they lock the doors to the hallway and open the doors between them.

The cleaning staff often remark on how sharp the General's training must be, to make his bed so thoroughly every morning. It's like he never sleeps in it!

"Tell me how selfish I am"—Leonato tangles his hand in the waves of Don Pedro's salt-and-pepper hair—"to be jealous of my own daughter for having the pleasure of flirting with you."

"Do we not flirt enough?" Don Pedro leans into his touch. "It was not my finest work. I had to stay in character, you know, and Claudio is sweet but not overly gifted in speech. His strength lies in ardent truths plainly stated."

"And your strength?" Leonato twines their fingers together and lifts Don Pedro's knuckles into a kiss.

"You've felt it once tonight already," Don Pedro chuckles, mischief in his eyes. "Are you not worried?"

"For Hero? No. If you say the boy is good, then I believe you. I pity poor Benedick, though."

"Don't." Don Pedro sighs as Leonato presses a kiss to the scar on his thumb. It troubles him before rain, and the storm clouds are heavy outside the window. "Benedick is a callous thing. He throws aside conquests left and right; Claudio would have met the same fate. I believe no one is the challenge Benedick is hoping for."

"A challenge," scoffs Leonato, closing his eyes. "Who would want such a thing in love?"

"Good to know you're not here for the thrill of it." Don Pedro kisses Leonato's knuckles in return. "Normally I would urge Claudio to reconsider flinging himself into a new love, but I have seen your worry, Leonato. This will give the staff something new to talk of, the tabloids something else to capture."

"And your brother something new to fixate on," Leonato adds. "Why you had to bring him—"

"Because he is my brother. Excluding him invites more scrutiny, both from any watchful eyes and from Don John himself."

"How long until retirement?" Leonato presses the question into the skin where Don Pedro's neck meets his shoulder.

"A few years more." Don Pedro's fingers card through Leonato's thick hair, nails scraping over his scalp. "Pray this love will last so long…"

"Longer. Till death and beyond, gladly. I only wish I could make that official."

"Like this is fine," Don Pedro whispers. "The French say, 'a secret of two is a secret with God.'"

"I'm not sure I want him involved," Leonato admits, and splits into a grin when Don Pedro barks a laugh beside him.

In the sitting room the next day, Claudio and Hero are holding hands. They grin, conspire, and whisper, as thick as thieves. Hero waves the maids Ursula and Margaret over to join them. Leonato leans on the counter, watching with a raised brow. Mouths and minds are always busy in his house.

Leonato wonders why he keeps overhearing "Beatrice" and "Benedick," but he feigns ignorance until Don Pedro fills him in.

"Your daughter and Claudio have thought of a good game," he says as they wander through the governor's mansion gardens together. "They mean to get Beatrice and Benedick together with clever words and rumors. It should make for a lively month, don't you think?"

They walk so close that their knuckles brush, a subtle touch that fills his senses until they swing

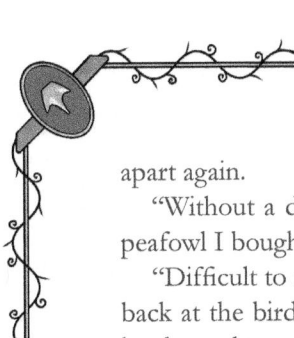

apart again.

"Without a doubt." Leonato laughs. "The two of them will make a bigger racket than those peafowl I bought for the garden. Surely you remember?"

"Difficult to forget," grimaces Don Pedro, who'd once leaned out Leonato's window to scream back at the birds in a rare glimpse of temper. "You have it right, though. In every way they are louder and prouder. If they set to crowing at one another, we'll hear of nothing else for *years*."

Meaning, Leonato thinks, that there will be no room for other gossip with those two at each other's throats. All in good fun, of course, and maybe ending with a suitable match. It seems possible that scorn added to scorn could equal affection, like taking two lefts in a maze.

If Benedick seeks "a challenge" in a lover, then he seeks Beatrice. If Beatrice seeks a sparring partner for her words, she will find it in Benedick.

Leonato will wish luck to all involved, but gladly stay to the side. They may clash while he treasures his own love in quiet secrecy. Like a rare and radiant creature born in the dark, his love for Don Pedro can only thrive unseen.

Hero's plan and the subsequent distraction ought to be enough to ease the fear in Leonato's chest. It ought to set his old heart at peace. However, one glimpse of Don John's cruel, knowing smile when they cross paths in the kitchen that evening is enough to make fear strangle him again.

That man will never be happy until Don Pedro is ruined. He cannot gain the lion's share of their family's glory or inheritance without finding cause for the general to be dishonorable discharged.

The only thing standing in his way is Don Pedro's impeccable record and pristine conduct. He is a man of honor and grace. There is only one thing that could destroy a career like his.

That "thing" nods to Don John with a forced smile as they exchange hollow pleasantries.

"Don't worry so much," Don Pedro says later, reaching for his hand in a quiet part of the garden.

Leonato shifts away from his touch unhappily. He cannot be calm when eyes and ears might be on them. He has heard too many stories of listening devices and hidden cameras. The chaff grenade that is Beatrice and Benedick's explosive collision has distracted the staff and their guests, certainly. But will it mollify one who is out for blood?

Blood is the first thing he remembers when he sees it. *Blood* is what he thinks of when he calls his daughter to the office upstairs: blood, and all its sources.

"It's not true," Hero says, trembling before his desk.

Between them, *The Dogberry Times* lies open. The font is garish, the paper cheap, the photo of Hero grainy but unmistakable. The headline screams:

REBELLIOUS WANTS TURNED STATEWIDE SCANDAL!
GOVERNOR'S DAUGHTER GONE WILD!

"Papa, you *know* it's not true," she repeats, a plea in her voice.

"Enough," he says, a thousand thoughts clustering in his mind. Outside, the storm clouds gather once more, just as the forecast had promised.

Of course I know it's not true, he wants to tell her. *You told me long ago that such things may never interest you. You confided your fear, and I heard you. Something has gone wrong, and your father will fix it.*

Instead he says, "I was warned by Don John himself, and by your own Claudio. Are they both liars?"

His voice is so cold he barely recognizes himself. If Don Pedro heard him using this tone, he'd laugh himself sick.

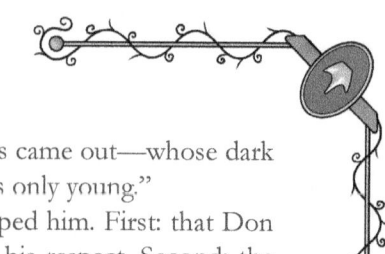

Don Pedro, who had pulled him aside to warn him before the tabloids came out—whose dark eyes had been full of concern— "Don't be angry at her, my friend, she is only young."

He'd almost spit with fury on Hero's behalf, but two things had stopped him. First: that Don Pedro is a good man who he loves and who deserves at the very least his respect. Second: the realization.

"Claudio, *Don John*, and I," Don Pedro had said of their impromptu spying. Don John, who would sooner swallow bees than spend quality time with his half-brother. His name is never stated in the article, but his cruelty is embedded in the very ink of *The Dogberry Times* headline. Leonato never suspected Don John would attack *his* reputation to wound Don Pedro. Now that he has…

Leonato won't waste the opportunity this presents. Beatrice and Benedick have played a good game, but their strange romance has only distracted from and delayed the inevitable. If Don John's bloodlust can be satisfied with Hero's shame…

She is young, he tells himself as he turns his back on her. She is young. She can take this wound and recover. If Don John wants to listen at a bedroom window and feed the words into the hellfire rumor mill, Leonato can only be grateful that it was *her* bedroom door Don John listened at and not his own.

"Papa, I don't understand. You know I wouldn't! Now Claudio won't talk to me, and my friends at school keep messaging—"

She circles his desk, reaching for his arm. He pulls away, and it breaks his heart.

"Thank the heavens your mother didn't live to see this," he mumbles.

He knows immediately he's gone too far. She answers him only with a sharp, wounded gasp. He does not watch her flee the room, but he hears the heaving sobs that tear from her throat long after she's closed the door between them.

She and Beatrice leave the estate that night. Ursula tells him they've gone as she drops two resignation letters onto the table before him—one for herself, one for Margaret.

He hasn't read them yet. He can't face their condemnation alone. He needs his lover's arms to remember the worth of this sacrifice. He needs to feel the always-tense muscles of Don Pedro's back and the way he shifts his weight into Leonato's arms. He needs to stroke the scar on Don Pedro's thumb and tangle his fingers in hair edging more toward salt than pepper. He needs to remember his beloved's vulnerability and melt into his comfort to cover the memory of Hero's sobs.

Relief pours through him at the sound of footsteps and the tap of a brass-tipped cane. But the Don Pedro who joins him in their secret place is grim-faced and stiff.

"Leonato." Don Pedro stands by the table staring down at him rather than joining him, or holding him, or resting his hand on his thigh. "Have you sent your daughter away?"

"Never," Leonato says, standing. "She and Beatrice chose to go."

"I'm aware." Don Pedro stays precisely in place—not quite at attention, but not standing at ease. "Beatrice told Benedick everything, and he reported to me."

"She confides in him now?" Leonato laughs, reaching toward his love. "What a satisfying end to their odd courtship."

Don Pedro steps away from Leonato's extended arm, and the separation aches in his chest like a wound.

"Leonato, speak plainly," Don Pedro insists. "Beatrice says Hero spoke of harming herself. What in the heavens did you do?"

"Harming herself?" Leonato's heart sinks, but he shakes his head. "It cannot be so. She is young and resilient; she will move past this."

Outside, raindrops battle against the windows of the manor, drenching his home and drowning

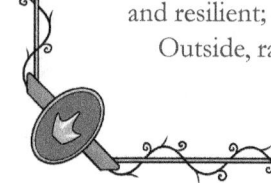

the garden. When the lighting flashes, it illuminates new angles of Don Pedro's face. It's a strange sight, made stranger by Don Pedro's frown. Thunder follows close on the lightning's heels.

"Leonato," Don Pedro says, and reaches for him. "You're better than this foolishness. What has happened, my love? What have you done?"

Ah, he is a weak man to the offer of Don Pedro's touch. They clasp hands. Already Leonato's harsh words rattle inside him. Already he aches from keeping even this small secret. He sighs, looks down at their joined hands, and strokes Don Pedro's knuckles. Leonato has always been a man who loves until it hurts. When he speaks, it is a confession.

"Whatever you heard, whatever photos were published, Hero had no part in," he admits.

Don Pedro balks. He doesn't draw his hand away, but his grip tightens on his cane.

"Will you not explain what has occurred, then?" Don Pedro's jaw muscles jump with disquiet, and Leonato itches to soothe him. Lightning flashes once more, so distant the thunder lags.

"Your brother's scheming, I suspect." Leonato hums, taking Don Pedro's hand and stroking his scarred thumb. It must ache, with all the rain. "He aims to wound you by association. But it's all fallen out well enough, hasn't it?"

"'Well'?" Don Pedro repeats hollowly. "You call this 'well'?"

Leonato nods. "Hero is strong, my friend. Do not be afraid. She will recover. Were she aware of our situation, she would gladly volunteer to sacrifice herself, I'm sure."

"Our— What has this to do with us?"

Leonato pauses. There is something wounded in Don Pedro's words. He lifts his gaze to Don Pedro's stricken face. He takes a breath then cups his beloved's jaw in his hand.

"If Don John is out for blood, let him take hers," he whispers. "I have lost a love before; I will not lose you as well."

"Leonato"—Don Pedro sounds so unlike himself; so grim—"tell me you've not wounded Hero for the sake of this secret."

"For the sake of a secret, no!" Leonato soothes, pressing closer. "For the sake of our lives. For your future! Only a few more years, and we will be free of it all. If this keeps you safe—"

"No."

"If *I* can keep you safe—"

"Leonato, my love—"

"—then I will do it!"

Don Pedro steps away. The pouring dark beyond the library window makes a statue of him, painted in artificial yellow light and dark grey. His stance is strained, and Leonato aches to reassure him. "How have I erred," Don Pedro says in a clear, cold tone, "for you to do such a thing? When have I made you feel that our love was worth such suffering?"

"I would bear any pain for you," Leonato swears, smiling.

"What pain do you think you've borne?"

The world freezes. Usually, Leonato watches with glee when Don Pedro raises his voice to fight in the name of righteousness. Never before has he been on the receiving end of his fury.

"Hero suffers in your place, and you seek praise for it," Don Pedro accuses. "Claudio and I became accomplices in an underhanded scheme to wound an innocent and you—you speak to me of bearing pain?"

"Don Pedro." Leonato beckons him closer, eager to explain.

"When did this start?" Don Pedro demands, holding his ground. "When did you decide you had to protect our secret at any cost? Even at the cost of your *child's* happiness?"

"Only temporarily," Leonato hurries to assure him, approaching Don Pedro and reaching to-

ward him. "It's only temporary. Dogberry is a hack, my friend—my *love*. No one will take his word at face value. It will blow over."

"It will not." Don Pedro replies in furious command. "You will fix it. If you love her, you will fix it. If you love *me*, you will fix it."

Leonato stares. He lets his hands drop slowly.

"It's a risk," he whispers. "Don John…"

"If he finds us out, he finds us out. If he tells, he tells."

Don Pedro's face has never looked so resolute. His dedication is desperately beautiful, and utterly devastating.

"I cannot." Leonato's arms fall limp at his sides. The driving rain is a steady white noise clamoring against the rioting confusion in his brain.

"Cannot what?" Don Pedro drops his cane with a clatter and grasps Leonato's shoulders, shaking him. His hands have always been so strong. "Cannot admit to your wrong? Cannot be inconvenienced?"

Leonato shakes his head, fumbling to hold his love's arms in return.

"I cannot lose you," he rasps, voice raw with grief.

The fury bleeds out of Don Pedro's dark eyes. His expression melts, furrowed brows tilting upward and snarling lips softening.

"My love"—Don Pedro's hands soften on his shoulders, no longer bruising and cruel—"whatever led you to believe that you would lose me?"

The power flickers. The storm rages. Leonato crumples under the force of a different storm all together, and Don Pedro holds him against the tearing winds.

"My love," he gasps, "my love, my love—"

"Shh," Don Pedro breathes in reply. "Here now, don't cry…my Leonato, there is still time. This can all be made well again."

He leans in and brushes their lips together. The touch is so electric that lightning flashes once more. Leonato sighs into the kiss, then realizes…

The thunder that should have accompanied the last lightning bolts never rumbled. He turns, suddenly freezing cold, toward the dark, storm-drenched window.

A figure on the balcony draws closer and waves.

"God," breathes Leonato in terror.

Don Pedro says nothing, his expression stony. When he moves forward to open the locked door, a dripping-wet Benedick steps inside, a plastic-bagged camera held tightly in his hand. His teeth chatter with his shivering, but there is vicious triumph in his expression.

"How now, Benedick?" Don Pedro asks him, low-voiced and calm. "Such a violent change of heart in one I would call kindred."

"General, whether you believe it or not, I have no interest in hurting you."

Leonato cannot speak. He has eyes only for the camera. Take it, destroy it, bribe him, fight him, anything but—

"I believe you, Corporal." Don Pedro says, unflappable. "Tell me what you want."

"It's not what I want." Benedick straightens his spine farther, fire in his eyes though he looks half-frozen. "Good Beatrice bade me send her salutations and her demands."

"Ah," Leonato chuckles, weak and breathy.

He turns to the small bar by the table and pours himself a scotch. When he sits, it is to see Don Pedro looking with pride upon the boy blackmailing them and Benedick checking his text messages to retrieve Beatrice's exact wording.

"My dear," Don Pedro says, his hands folded on the table they all sit around. "Please forgive your father if you can. Love makes us fools, and does not exclude cruelty."

"She has no reason to forgive, and he has no right to ask her to," Beatrice snaps before Hero can speak. There's a new issue of *The Dogberry Times* held in Beatrice's hand and a scowl on her face. Never has Leonato seen her so angry. The paper's headline reads, for all to see,

THAT'S NOT MY FACE...BUT THAT'S MY BODY!
GOVERNOR'S EX-MAID MARGARET TELLS ALL:
GENERAL DON JOHN DOCTORS DIRTY PHOTOS!

"And yet," Hero says in a quiet breath.

"Oh, do not yield so sweetly, dear cousin!" Beatrice moans. "Ask for more than the decency your so-called father should have granted you from the start! Margaret would have offered that retraction even without him forcing Dogberry to print it!"

"Indeed! Ask for a yacht," Benedick suggests helpfully, only to catch an elbow from Beatrice.

"A good many things seem clear now." Hero shakes her head, looking down at her hands. "I'm so sorry for Margaret. What an awful shock for her."

"Be more sorry for yourself!" Beatrice moans, putting her face in her hands.

"Better yet, be more angry at me," Leonato suggests, laying his hand on the table near her. Hidden from sight, Don Pedro slides a hand onto his thigh, squeezing. "In a better world, this man beside me would be a second father to you, yet in the name of my love for him I have done you harm."

"It's not as if I'm blind." Hero reaches out to squeeze his hand. "You've never looked at anyone but mom the way you look at him."

The hand on his leg squeezes tighter, and Don Pedro's cheeks fill with color. Leonato smiles at her proudly and takes a shaking breath.

"For whatever it's worth," Don Pedro tells her, offering his own hand, too, "your father already knew he was wrong. Even without your friend's intervention, we would not have let the slander continue, Hero."

Hero's smile is a fragile thing, so vulnerable it makes Leonato's chest ache, but she looks upon Don Pedro with love in her eyes. She takes his hand as well, connecting the three of them. Her phone buzzes, shaking the table—more messages from Claudio begging her pardon. He suspects that she will listen. She is so painfully kind.

"Your mother would be so proud," Leonato rasps. She clutches his fingers in return. "My Hero, I am a fool. She would be so, so proud."

"Yacht," whispers Benedick.

"Would that your needless words were *pennies* you could buy your *own* boat!" Beatrice roars in frustration.

Their relationship is not repaired. Their words now are merely a bandage on a wound, stopping the blood flow.

He dares to hope that in time the injury will heal without scarring.

That evening, Leonato stares out his bedroom window at the red sunset and the last wisps of the storm clouds.

"You never did answer your own question, my love," Don Pedro comments from the bed,

lounging half-dressed amid the linens.

Leonato swallows fear like ice. What has he forgotten? Hero's patient kindness has set them on the road to heal. Claudio's mournful messages have been answered with joking requests for a yacht. Beatrice and Benedick locked lips as soon as they thought they were alone. Don John has slipped away to avoid the defamation charges…Leonato must have missed something in all the chaos.

Dread sinking through him, Leonato closes his eyes, shutting out the view of the twilight sky, and forces himself to turn around. "Which question was that?" he asks, and opens his eyes to behold not another disaster, but the most beautiful sight he knows: Don Pedro grins indulgently toward him, not an ounce of malice in his sparkling eyes, and pats the space beside him on their bed.

"If I were a young man, how would you woo me?"

Relief makes Leonato dizzy. He sinks down to sit at his beloved's side and drops near-boneless into his embrace. Don Pedro's arms are strong and warm around him.

"Hm," Leonato whispers past a throat tight with emotion. "Peafowl, maybe?"

Don Pedro's answering laughter hangs bright in the clearing air between them.

Xanthe P. Russell
"Duly Noted"

The idea behind my work "Duly Noted" is a romantic comedy film adaptation of Much Ado About Nothing *set in the UK in the 1980s, with a specific focus on Beatrice and Benedick's relationship development. I thought it would be interesting to explore the frivolousness of the original story and its themes in what was quite a turbulent time (particularly for queer people). In my version of the story, Beatrice (who goes by "Bea") is a closeted lesbian and a bit of a prep, whereas Benedick (who goes by "Ben") is a trans woman and a self-identified punk. The two meet at a club owned by Bea's uncle and take an instant (dis)liking to each other. A big part of the original story focuses on hiding your true self behind a mask (both physically and metaphorically). In my story, Bea grew up in a Northern working class town, unaware of her connections to the wealthy Leonato until she was in her early 20s, and this sense of being an outsider is what makes her begin to open up to Ben (eventually). This also shapes how she deals with her sexuality, being uncomfortable both in the fact Ben annoys her, but also the fact that she's a woman. Ben hides behind the mask of being a "punk," embracing the androgynous style of the movement so she doesn't have to deal with being misgendered. She also boasts about being very anti-authoritarian, although she grew up in a well-off household, and has a turbulent relationship with her family. Overall, I wanted the focus to be that both character's are wearing "costumes" concealing who they really are, and only when they finally remove them do they finally begin to understand each other and begin to fall in love.*

TAGS: alternate universe, bipoc, character has a different gender than in the source material, college, epistolary, f/f, f/m, false accusations, fluff, friends to lovers, high school, meet cute, misunderstandings, mistaken identity, modern, past tense, pining, playing pranks, third person limited point of view

HERO'S MOON

Theresa Tanner

I am a high school science teacher. Putting the characters in high school meant daily exposure to inspiration! Margaret, Uranus's moon, is named for Margaret from Much Ado About Nothing, *and it's quite memorable for demonstrating the Kozai instability.*

My most dear, how I would love to debate with you for the rest of our lives! Your command of wordplay and the tools of rhetoric is beyond compare, and I would die a happy man to be slain by the sharpness of your wit.

I remain, as ever, your devoted servant.

Yeah. Beatrice hated it, thanks. Why this guy wrote like he was in a Victorian novel, she did not understand…although he hadn't initially, she remembered. The first letter had been so normal. Well, aside from the fact that it was a somewhat old-fashioned hand-written letter instead of an email or a DM—and the minor detail that she'd never even met this alleged "Benedick Johnson."

There was no way he was a real person.

Supposedly, he went to college with her cousin Hannah, who was sending the letters for him instead of giving him her address. That might be true, but if it was…how had he survived middle school with a name with two penis euphemisms?

The second letter had been weirder—and more personal, with specific details about her life. Nothing too stalkerish, at least; it was just weird. The third was even worse/better. They kept arriving, one per week, and the weirdness level kept getting higher. This one, the eighth, referred to her success in a debate competition the weekend before, where Beatrice and her partner Claudia Pedro won first place and advanced to the state competition.

How could a random stranger know so much about her?

They wouldn't, obviously.

Hannah was a creative writing major. She must have written the letters herself and sent them to Beatrice as a prank. Hannah certainly had the creativity, and Beatrice wouldn't recognize Hannah's rarely used cursive writing. It was a shame, really; if Benedick Johnson was real, she'd love to meet

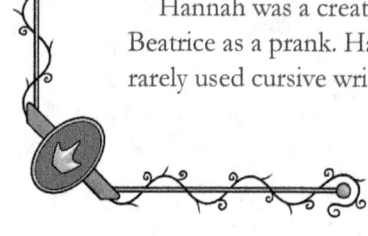

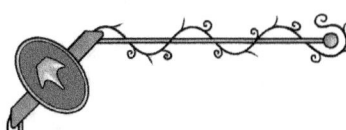

him and see if he was half as entertaining in person. Not that there was any chance he'd live up to the image in Beatrice's mind. It didn't matter. He *definitely* wasn't real. It was high time for Hannah to admit to the prank.

Beatrice looked over the letter one last time before she set it aside and took out a sheet of paper to write a silly response. Between the two of them, Hannah was the fiction writer, not her—but there was nothing Beatrice enjoyed more than a good argument. Poking fun at everything in the letter was a good way to kill some time. If nothing else, it was an excuse to respond in kind and practice the cursive writing that her grandmother had insisted she use for thank-you notes and such. With the state competition looming, Beatrice and Claudia had plans to meet for practice in Beatrice's room, so she had not-quite-forty minutes to mock the interesting imaginary man.

As soon as Claudia arrived for debate practice, she threw her phone at Beatrice with a groan. "It's hopeless, Bea. Hopeless. Why do I have to be so…so…cursed?"

"You're not cursed. No such thing as curses." Beatrice quickly tossed the letter she hadn't quite finished toward the trash, then picked up the phone. It was open to Hannah's Instagram, recognizable by her profile picture: a basketball hanging in space like a sun, with a tennis ball and a golf ball "in orbit" around it like planets. Beatrice had been avoiding Hannah's social media; she didn't care to find out Dick Boy was real and not a figment of Hannah's imagination. "What's my cousin got to do with anything?"

Another long groan, and Claudia tangled her fingers in her long black hair, pulling it ever so slightly. "She's so…perfect! I always knew there was never much hope. Only a fool's hope."

"Uh-oh. You're quoting Gandalf. This is serious." Beatrice looked more closely at Hannah's Instagram feed. The first picture was of the moon. That made sense—every full moon, Hannah took pictures and shared the best one, captioned with a fun lunar fact. Next post down was a picture of Uranus with a moon in transit, captioned *I wonder if Margaret ever gets tired of the jokes about mooning her dad?* "Who's Margaret?"

"I don't knooooooow," Claudia whined. "Don't you? You talk to Hero almost every day; I never get to talk to her anymore!"

"She's never mentioned any 'Margaret' to me." Beatrice kept scrolling. There were a couple other references to Margaret—a meme about being yourself even if everyone tells you you're wrong, captioned *Margaret my love, keep being weird, it makes you so special!* and a diagram explaining the eccentricity of an ellipse captioned *Margaret! It's you! You're eccentric!* "So the big deal here is what?"

"I've been in love with Hero since sophomore year when we were on the basketball team together and she helped me get good enough to move up to varsity!" Claudia wailed, as though Beatrice hadn't heard that at least twice a month for the past two years. She flopped dramatically on Beatrice's bed, knocking her stuffed dog onto the floor. "She said she didn't want to date until college, so I didn't say anything to her, and I wasn't going to until next year when I'm there too, but now there's Margaret."

Beatrice raised an eyebrow and switched to Twitter. Lots of references to Margaret there, too, continuing the theme of how weird Margaret was and how much Hannah admired her for it. "This doesn't sound to me like Hannah's in love. It's nothing like the love letters she's been writing to me."

Claudia's head popped up, staring at Beatrice with her head tilted to one side. "Wait, what?"

Oops. Beatrice's hand hit her face as she realized how it must have sounded. "That came out wrong. She's pranking me by writing letters that she claims were written by some 'Bent Dick' guy,

and trust me, her gushing about love sounds nothing like these posts."

"But if she's playing a prank on you, there's no reason she'd sound like she normally would. She might be hiding. And if it's not a prank, those letters aren't even by her!"

Claudia's logic was as solid as Beatrice expected from a debate star, but she was still wrong. "This sounds more like she's started writing a new story and is gushing about her main character. Margaret is probably some OC who's taking over her brain."

"But…Juan said that he's heard from Conrad—a friend of his at Hannah's college," Claudia whispered, "that Hero's always with some girl."

"First off, Hannah's made it clear that the Hero nickname makes her uncomfortable unless it's from a teammate. Juan wasn't on the basketball team, so he needs to stop using it. As for what Conrad says…so she's making friends." Beatrice shrugged. "Might be Ursula Ryan. They live on the same dorm floor, and they've got creative writing together. There's no way she's got a girlfriend she's never mentioned to me." On the contrary, every time Hannah called, she asked about Claudia and hung on every little detail Beatrice shared. Beatrice wasn't going to betray her cousin by telling Claudia that, but she could make sure that Hannah heard about the rumors going around and how upset Claudia was by them.

"If you say so."

Beatrice wanted to shake her. Who knew Hannah best, her, or Juan? Beatrice had nothing to gain by lying—even if Beatrice *did* lie, Claudia would learn the truth when Hannah brought a girlfriend home—but Juan did. If Claudia lost interest in Hannah, Juan had that much less competition, not that it mattered how much competition there was. Hannah preferred being alone to being with someone she didn't like, and Juan was a total jackwagon.

"Next question, why on Earth are you listening to Juan anyway? We don't call him 'the Bastard Prince' because he's a stand-up straight-shooter, you know. And it's definitely not because his parents weren't married, because who cares about that anymore?"

Claudia pouted. "I know he can be a jerk to people at school, but even if he lives with his mom, he's still my brother. He's always been good to me. Remember how he stood up for me when Borachio started spreading rumors?"

"And he's been trying to date Hannah for years," Beatrice said. "Maybe he sees a chance to break your heart so that you'll move on and he won't have to worry about you when the two of you go to college and he tries again." If Juan was feeding this line of crap to anyone else, Beatrice would be positive that it was to be a jerk. With Claudia, though…she did have a good point about Juan treating her well. Beatrice had forgotten about Borachio spreading rumors that he'd slept with Claudia. He and Juan had been good friends; by standing up for his sister and defending her reputation, Juan had put her above that friendship. "I guess it could be that he really thinks Margaret is Hannah's girlfriend and is trying to help you by letting you know you need to move on." Beatrice trusted Juan about as far as she could throw him, but maybe, just maybe, his heart was in the right place this time as well.

Hannah usually called Friday afternoons after her last class of the day let out. Most of Beatrice's friends were busy preparing for the football game, so it was the most likely time for her to be able to talk for an hour without someone interrupting. It was therefore not a surprise when Beatrice's phone rang at 4:30—a little earlier than usual, but even so, Beatrice was ready to answer.

"Hannah! What…" She trailed off as she took in Hannah's background. Instead of videocalling from her dorm or from the usual shady area in the park, Hannah was in a car, her tawny skin lit by

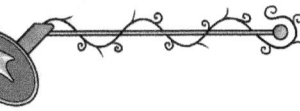

the late afternoon sun. Not her Kia, even—a vehicle Beatrice didn't recognize. "You on the road somewhere? Why call me now?"

"Surprise!" Hannah threw her free hand into the air. "I'm coming home for the weekend! I called to tell you to go to the football game. We'll meet you there."

" 'We'?" Beatrice blurted before it occurred to her that since Hannah was on FaceTime, she couldn't be driving; Hannah must mean the driver of this unfamiliar car. Maybe Beatrice had been wrong about the girlfriend thing after all? "Is that Margaret?"

A deep booming laugh came over the speakers, joining Hannah's tinkling giggles. "No, no, this is not Margaret. Margaret is tiny but not this tiny!" Hannah managed to get out as she caught her breath.

"Hey!" the driver squawked, followed by a more dignified, "I am not tiny."

"You're certainly not big! Didn't you tell me that your position in high school football was water boy because they thought you were twelve?"

The response came in an overly serious voice. "That was freshman year. By senior year, I'd been promoted to running back, I'll have you know." Hannah stared at the driver, lips twitching upward and one eyebrow raised; Beatrice wished Hannah would turn the camera so Beatrice could see this mystery companion. "…okay, because I was so small the other team had trouble hitting me, but still! I'm not tiny." They sounded less serious now, a teasing note slipping in.

"Anyway, not Margaret," Hannah concluded with a brilliant smile. "Is Claudia going to be at the game?"

"She's still a cheerleader, so I'm going with 'yes' on that. She'll be pleased that you don't have Margaret in tow."

"Wait, has Claudia got something against Margaret?" Hannah's laughter disappeared, and she frowned as she stared into the camera. "How could anyone not like Margaret? I could understand if she didn't care one way or the other, but does she really actively dislike Margaret to the point where you'd bring this up?"

The confusion was so genuine that Beatrice was seriously starting to wonder what Hannah's relationship with Margaret actually was. "Juan told her that Margaret is your girlfriend, and she's really upset about it."

"Oh, that's…shut *up*, you!" Hannah aimed a swat at the mystery driver of her mystery vehicle, sunny smile back in place. "That's great to know, thank you! I'm sorry she's upset, but it'll make things easier for me this weekend." There was a snort, and Hannah glared—the effect somewhat spoiled by her lingering smile. "I thought I told you to shut up."

"You did not, however, convince me that you have any sort of authority to make me. Funny how that works," the driver taunted. Oh, Beatrice already liked this person, whoever they were. "And I'm not going to sit here and get lectured on proper behavior by someone who just admitted to being happy to know that someone they call a friend is unhappy!"

Definitely liked this person. "Please tell me you're bringing your friend to the game?" Beatrice said. "I can't wait to meet them."

"See? Told you!" Hannah stuck her tongue out at the driver. "Yes, he's coming. You'll know him because he'll be the short guy fighting with me over who's paying for the tickets. You promise that Claudia will be there?"

"You know she will be, and I can't even warn her that you're coming because she's already busy with cheer stuff." Beatrice shook her head in admiration. Hannah was good at this. "See you tonight!"

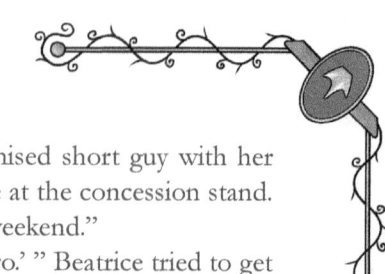

Of course, it wasn't actually that easy. While watching for the promised short guy with her cousin, she didn't see Juan before he was at her side as she waited in line at the concession stand. "Bea! You never come anymore! That must mean Hero's home for the weekend."

"She's not here to see you, so go away. And stop calling Hannah 'Hero.'" Beatrice tried to get away, but with the line, there wasn't anywhere for her to go without losing her place. She hoped that Hannah and her mystery friend would arrive soon. She tuned Juan out as he kept talking, checking in just enough to be sure that he wasn't saying anything important—or about Claudia— before zoning back out.

Juan stared in disbelief when she ordered three extra drinks and several different types of candy. "What's all that about?"

"Like you said—Hannah's coming. I know she still drinks Dr. Pepper, but she's bringing a friend. I didn't want to ask what to get him and spoil the surprise of greeting them with drinks and snacks. Almost everyone likes water, or at least drinks it." The look of shock on Juan's face was well worth deigning to explain herself to him.

"She's bringing a boy home from college?" Juan's entire body drooped. Beatrice couldn't help feeling a bit smug. "Did you know she had a boyfriend?"

"I heard rumors she had a girlfriend, actually. Nothing from her, though." For a fleeting moment, Beatrice thought she saw some guilt in Juan's eyes. Not enough for her to make a scene and try to force him to apologize to Claudia—Beatrice might be projecting—but enough for her to believe Juan had made a deliberate attempt to hurt Claudia. "You know, maybe spreading rumors about people is a bad idea. Oh, look, there they are!"

Juan followed her gaze toward the two people in the ticket line. Beatrice took a moment to study the boy with her cousin. Hannah hadn't been kidding: the boy with her really was short. His Afro added nearly a half-foot to his height, but Hannah still had at least four inches on him. His dark-brown skin contrasted with the bright yellow of his jacket. Overall, quite handsome, especially when he smiled.

"Good-looking, smart enough for Hannah to talk to, and—from the looks of things—not in the least intimidated by her. I'm all for him being her boyfriend."

"Yeah." Juan shoved his hands into his pockets. He left while Beatrice was gathering up her purchases, and Beatrice didn't bother to watch which way he was going.

Beatrice found her way through the crowd to Hannah and her friend, but Juan beat her to it. It would seem it had been too much to hope for that he'd given up and gone away. "Hero! It's so good to see you again!"

Hannah made a bit of a face at the nickname. "Hello, Juan. How many times do I have to tell you to quit calling me that?"

Juan shrugged. "At least once more?"

"Ugh. Go away." Hannah turned her back on Juan and started telling Beatrice and the cute friend a story about her partner for an astronomy project.

It took a bit of ignoring from the three of them before Juan got the point and slunk away. Once he was gone, Hannah's friend raised an eyebrow. "'Hero'? Obviously you hate it. What's wrong, is it sarcastic?"

"Nah…my junior year, our basketball team was really good," Hannah explained. "At the state tournament, everyone had counted us out after our team captain got benched, but I stepped up and rallied the team. They started calling me 'Hero' after we won the tournament. I don't mind it from my teammates, but it really gave me a lot to live up to, you know? I was so glad to go to college and get to be 'Hannah' again." Hannah flushed as she caught Beatrice smirking at her. "Okay,

Beatrice was nice; when I asked her to stop, she did. Mostly. When she wasn't just being a pain in the neck."

"Beatrice? This is…" The boy straightened up, lifting his chin as he held out a hand. "It's nice to meet you, Beatrice. I've heard a ton about you."

"And I've heard absolutely nothing about you," Beatrice said, staring down her cousin. "Not even a name. And I would shake your hand, but…" She gestured in a way that emphasized her armful of concessions.

"Oh! Right!" Hannah grabbed the Dr. Pepper and a bag of Fritos. "Benedick, she probably bought you stuff too. Grab whatever you want."

Now it was Beatrice's turn to freeze. Benedick? *The* Benedick? "Benedick the Epistler?"

"The one and only!" Hannah put a hand on Benedick's shoulder, giving him a gentle shove. "Dude. Quit staring like a weirdo and take your introduction gifts from Beatrice. Otherwise, I'm going to choose for you, and I'm going to choose the Reese's."

"No!" Benedick shook himself. "Are some of those for me?"

"Yes…what's this about?"

"I don't eat peanuts or peanut butter, that's all." Beatrice's eyebrows shot up, and she immediately began reading through the ingredients and cross-contamination warnings on the snacks in the hopes that there was something here he could have. Benedick huffed a soft laugh. "No, no, not…it's not an allergy or anything. There's nothing for you to worry about. I just don't eat them because I don't like the taste." He took the plain M&Ms and a bottle of water. "Thank you."

"You're welcome." Beatrice grabbed his hand to shake. "It's nice to meet you. Is there a reason you write like some weirdo from a hundred years ago?"

"Because it's hilarious!" Benedick winked, and Beatrice was very glad she wasn't trying to walk. She'd already admired his good looks, but the wink caught her completely off-guard. At least standing still, she couldn't lose track of her feet and stumble. "Hannah promised that you were enjoying the letters, even if your responses were kind of rude, so I kept having fun. Did she lie to me?"

"Well, someone did," Beatrice said, turning a glare on Hannah, who was suddenly fascinated with opening her Dr. Pepper. "I did enjoy the letters, that was true, but I thought Hannah was pranking me and you didn't exist. I never responded to them at all, let alone rudely." She paused and considered clarifying, but then decided that what she'd said was close enough to the truth. She'd never actually *sent* the responses she'd written.

"Don't look at me, I wasn't the one responding. How could I fake the postmark?" Hannah asked. "I sent the letters for Benedick instead of giving him your address, yes, but he wrote them all, just like I've been telling you. The answering letters sure sounded like your writing. I just thought you were being rude because that's how you are, and you didn't want to hide."

Benedick reached into the pocket of his jeans and pulled out his phone, unlocking it and opening the camera roll. "Look, I took pictures of all the letters you—or whoever—sent. Who knew about the letters, and knows you well enough to fool Hannah?"

"No one! I told Claudia about the letters yesterday, but she was the first person I'd said anything to. I can't think who could have seen them in my room, other than…" Beatrice tilted her head, thinking it over. Even her parents didn't go into her room. "Claudia's the only person who I hang out with in there. And, now that I'm thinking about it…she didn't seem surprised when I mentioned that Hannah was pranking me? Normally, she'd at least ask to see them…"

"You think Claudia…?"

Beatrice looked closer at the pictures. "It's Claudia's handwriting."

"But I'd recognize—" Hannah started to protest, but Beatrice interrupted.

"In cursive?" Beatrice paused until Hannah sheepishly conceded that no, she wouldn't, with a shake of her head. "I may need to beat some answers out of her."

Hannah took Benedick's phone from Beatrice, reading the letters for herself. Her gaze softened as she read, her smile growing huge. "Claudia's such a good friend. I can totally believe she wrote these pretending to be you." She handed the phone back to Beatrice.

Taking it, Beatrice scrolled through the photographs. The more she read, the more she realized what must have happened. There was, in fact, a huge difference between writing the responses out and just thinking them. If Beatrice had only thought them, these letters wouldn't have existed, and Benedick wouldn't be here, and—even if she'd never admit it to anyone else—she was really glad Benedick was here.

"Claudia wrote these," Beatrice explained. "Sort of."

" 'Sort of'?" Benedick asked, voice shaking a little. "So the girl I came out here to meet doesn't exist?"

"Well, I wrote responses to specific things in your letter with no intention of sending them, so I do exist, I promise. I'd scrawl out some answers, then crumple them up and throw them away," Beatrice admitted. "The 'sort of' comes from Claudia writing the filler to connect everything, and she must have been the one to send them." Beatrice returned Benedick's phone to him.

"Oh, thank goodness." Benedick offered Beatrice a shy smile. "So I came with Hannah to meet the girl who wrote the letters and ask her out. I completely understand if it's too soon for you, since you didn't even think I was real until a couple minutes ago, but I'd like to get to know you better. For real, this time."

"There's always a dance after the game. I've never actually been to one, but everyone says they're a lot of fun. We should go." Beatrice grinned. "As a date."

Hannah let out a loud squeal. "I'm so happy for you two! I knew you'd hit it off, but that was so quick! Soon it'll be my turn. Is it halftime yet?"

"They haven't even kicked off. But if we want seats, we'd better go find them." Beatrice led the way to the stands, and they managed to find three seats together close enough to the cheerleaders for Beatrice to get Claudia's attention and point out that Hannah was there. Claudia shot a puzzled look at Benedick, but there was no way to explain before another cheerleader called for her to get in position for a pregame cheer.

"So you played, huh?" she asked as she settled into her seat between Benedick and Hannah. "Did you like it?"

"Well enough to keep playing through senior year, not well enough to regret that I wasn't big enough for anyone to come recruiting. I was always more into the whole 'camaraderie with the guys' thing—oh shut up, *Hero*, not like that." Benedick thwapped her arm, but it didn't affect Hannah's snickering. "I didn't care about the game, but it was nice to be part of the team. Most of the time, anyway. Some of those guys I could have done without."

"By which he means that, when we met, he was with one of those old teammates, and he made a crude comment about my breasts and acted like I should be grateful he bothered to comment at all instead of being offended that he was a pig," Hannah clarified, and Beatrice shuddered. "We're friends because Benedick here told his friend he was being an ass and needed to either grow up or get new friends. Nearly kicked him to the curb when I found out he wrote you a love letter after watching that video of your play from last spring."

"In my defense, I wrote the letter with no intention of sending it. It was an assignment for a

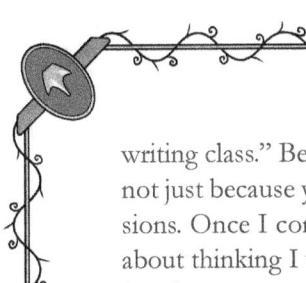

writing class." Benedick's lips curled into a half-smile. "I picked you because I admired your spirit, not just because you're gorgeous. Given how we met, I can't blame Hannah for jumping to conclusions. Once I convinced her that I was serious about wanting to get to know you but not serious about thinking I was in love with you, she stole the letter and sent it. I didn't know about it until I got the response."

That explained a couple things. Why that first letter had felt so generic, and why the ones she saved were different. "So basically, both our friends conned us into this…and now here we are?"

"That sounds about right."

"You know, I'm kinda glad this all happened. I can't wait to see what comes next."

"Me neither." Benedick reached out and took the hand Beatrice held out, giving it a squeeze.

It had been halftime for all of twenty seconds before Claudia made it up into the bleachers, plopping down beside Hannah. "It's great to see you! I'm glad you made it. Are you gonna come to any of the basketball games?"

"The plan is to come to all of the Friday games. It'll be easier now that Benedick and Beatrice are talking. He'll want to come too, so we can carpool."

"That's happening? Hooray!" Claudia smirked at Beatrice across Hannah. "I knew it was worth cobbling together those responses. Should've sent them yourself. You're an idiot, Bea."

"Forget me. You can tell me what an idiot I am later; you and Hannah have limited time to talk." Beatrice shot a pointed look at her cousin. "Hannah has something important to tell you."

Hannah cleared her throat, and Beatrice almost felt bad for her as she clutched her Dr. Pepper with both hands. "Your dad came into my restaurant when he was in the city last weekend, and he said you were mooning over me. At first, I thought he was messing with me—teasing me about my love for astronomy—but then I thought about it more and a lot of things from the past two years started adding up."

Claudia scowled, staring at the field. "I'm going to kill him. He had no business telling you that. I can take care of myself."

"You can, I know, but you might want to thank him. Now that I'm in college, I've been thinking about dating, and—"

"You found Margaret. I know." Claudia got to her feet. "I'm going—"

"Wait!" Hannah caught Claudia's hand. "We'll come back to Margaret—we will, promise—but Claudia, what I was going to say is that everyone I looked at, I was comparing them to you, and nobody measured up. I want it to be you. I want to *date* you!"

"So…Margaret?" Claudia sat back down, the fury and resignation in her eyes fading into hope. "Who is she?"

"I don't know what's going on with everyone assuming Margaret's my girlfriend," Hannah grumbled. "Margaret isn't even a person!"

"Wait, what?!"

"She's a moon. She's Uranus's only prograde irregular satellite, and I fell in love with her when my astronomy professor picked her as the example to explain the Kozai instability to us. Naturally, I was intrigued, and the more I learned about Margaret, the more I loved how weird she is."

"Oh." Claudia's russet skin always concealed blushes, but her slouch screamed embarrassment. "Then who's the girl you're always with?"

"My friend Ursula? Why would you think…oh." Hannah chuckled. "Of course. If you didn't realize Margaret was a moon and saw me with the same girl over and over again on social media…"

Hannah wrapped her arms around Claudia. "There's nothing romantic between us. You're the only girl I want." She paused. "I hope this doesn't cause problems with Juan. He's always had a crush on me, but...no. He's your brother, but he's not you."

Claudia leaned in, relaxing enough to giggle. "Juan will get over it." He would, Beatrice agreed, but he'd sulk for months first. No less than he deserved. "This is the best game ever! I wonder if the squad would notice if I just stayed here through the second half?"

"They'd notice," Hannah said. "If for no other reason than that your aunt's the sponsor. She'll notice you missing."

"Tia Antonia won't mind..." Claudia sighed. "...until she has to explain to one of the others why she's not giving me demerits for going AWOL. Fine. But I'm skipping the dance after the game unless you come as my date."

"Double date, then?" Benedick asked Beatrice.

"Hell yes, Bent Dick! That sounds *awesome*!"

"What did you call me?!" squawked Benedick.

Oops. Fortunately, Hannah and Claudia were both too busy staring at each other to laugh or contradict her, so Beatrice decided to bluff her way out. "Your name..."

Benedick raised an eyebrow, but let it go. Beatrice couldn't help but smile. He really was as awesome as his letters had made him sound. Claudia waited until the last possible second to return to the track, and Hannah didn't let go of her hand until she had to, which seemed promising for the future. That morning, Beatrice would never have guessed how things would go...this day could not get any better.

Jared Powell (Facing Page & Next Page)
"Beatrice and Benedicia" & "Hiro and Claudia"

These images originally came to be because Hero's part in the original play has always bothered me. I wanted to put her in a world where she could have agency, and what came to mind was the Golden Age of Piracy. In this world, Hero is free to do as she pleases and is proud of her body, in sharp contrast to the prim and fashionable Claudia. I've also given some intentionally confusing cues: is Hero a pirate, or is she innocent? Is Claudia apologizing, or is she being invited to join Hero on the high seas? That's up to the viewer.

Beatrice and Benedicia were easy to place in the same world as proud pirates who got tricked into admitting feelings they would rather have kept hidden just before a fight they couldn't avoid.

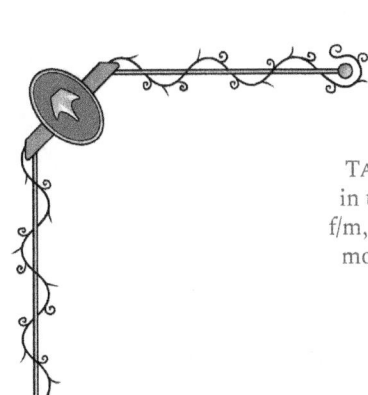

TAGS: alternate universe, character has a different gender than in the source material, everyone knows they're in love but them, f/m, false accusations, fluff, getting together, idiots to lovers, m/m, modern, office, past tense, pining (mutual), third person limited (alternating) point of view

AN OFFICE ADO

Aria L. Deair

One of my favorite parts of the Much Ado About Nothing *story is the chaotic Not-Courtship of Benedick and Beatrice. Between their friends attempting to match them together, their banter, and their complete disdain for love, it's a story we've all seen play out across many mediums, and I wanted to take a stab at it! First, by having Beatrice become Beauregard, and second, by bringing them into a modern office setting. This allowed me to keep my favorite elements, add a dash of Idiots-to-Lovers, and write a story that I hope will leave everyone smiling at the end!*

"Look at them. It's practically indecent."

Benedict hid his smile, barely, as Beau scoffed, tossing sandy, too-long hair out of his face. He needed another haircut. His eyes drifted to where Hero leaned into Claudio. "They look happy, Beau."

"Happiness looks good on everyone," Beau shot back. "You don't see everyone else envying them." He softened and lowered his voice, brushing his shoulder against Benedict's. "No matter how sickening, they do suit each other."

"It took Claudio far too long to fess up." Benedict snorted. He took another sip of the watered-down punch and leaned against the wall of his cubicle. "I was hours away from taking drastic action."

Beau fought down a smile. "Locking them in a closet?"

"Something like that," Benedict gave Beau a wink.

Beau sighed again as the couple smiled at each other. "Plans aside, do you know the worst part?"

Benedict raised an eyebrow and lifted his glass in toast to Claudio. "Other than punch that tastes like it once thought about having a flavor?"

Beau chuckled, ducking his head when a few people looked their way. "Other than the revolting punch, yes."

"Hmm." Benedict considered the glass and dumped it into the soil of the plant Antonio had

been attempting to keep alive for weeks. It kept dropping leaves on his desk. "Do tell?"

"You've heard about John transferring to Finance after the HR investigation into his behavior with Hero?" Beau didn't continue until Benedict acknowledged him with a nod. "Now that the situation is resolved, with Hero and Claudio finally together, our primary sources of gossip are gone." He sighed wistfully. "We'll have to go back to speculating on the identity of the yogurt thief."

Benedict smiled. "You do always love gossip when it isn't about you."

Beau primly took a sip of his punch and made a face, setting down the almost-full cup on his desk. "My one vice," he agreed, watching Benedict laugh.

"I still say my theory on Pedro being the yogurt thief is—"

"No, no, we're not getting into that," Beau held up a hand. "I have a meeting shortly, and I don't have time for what is, based on previous experience, at least a twenty-five-minute dissertation on the subject."

Benedict sighed and pouted, getting an eye roll in return. "I suppose things around here will be boring for who-knows-how-long."

"Knowing this office," Beau started, picking up his laptop and phone, turning to Benedict again, "it won't be that long."

Benedict narrowed his eyes. "You know something, don't you?"

Beau lifted his nose in the air. "No."

"Well," Benedict said, his lips twitching. He could see the tips of Beau's ears going red. "I'm sure it won't be long until we return to our—what do you call them? Our scathing observations."

"You know perfectly well I call them that, Benedict," Beau huffed, glancing at his phone to check the time.

Benedict grinned and fell into his chair. "I do enjoy them." He hit the power button on his computer. "If your meeting is upstairs, don't take the elevator. It'll be jammed with folks coming back from lunch."

Beau paused and looked at the elevator, then to the nearby stairwell. "That's a good idea. Thank you, Benedict."

"That's what you keep me around for—so you can continue to be early for every meeting and lord your timeliness over us all."

Beau turned back to Benedict in a huff. "I do not—"

"Don't be late," Benedict interrupted. Beau flushed in irritation and spun around on his heel. "One point to me for the elevator warning!" he called, laughing when Beau gave him a middle finger before stepping out of their aisle. Benedict waited until Beau was through the doors, then he added a tally under his name to the whiteboard hanging on the wall of his desk. Forty-seven to forty-nine. He was catching up.

After the meeting, Beau packed up his laptop as slowly as possible, but there was clearly nothing to be done. Hero hadn't given up and left; she was still waiting for him, still smiling as she had continuously since Claudio had put them both out of their respective misery. "Hero—"

"None of that, now; you're not going to out-stubborn me today, Beauregard," Hero said, tapping her nails on the laptop in her arms. "Not even your glare can ruin my good mood!"

"I'm sure," Beau said, then he stood and made his way to Hero. "After your display in front of the whole office."

Hero grinned, entirely unrepentant. "Which you were watching, so don't give me that! You and

Benedict, as always, whispering away in your private corner."

Frowning, Beau held open the door for her before leading the way to the stairs. "We were not."

"You were! Conspiring together as you always are." She sighed, glancing at Beau as they walked.

Hero was after something. Whatever it was, if Beau remained quiet, ignored the growing silence, she would eventually give up.

"Don't be like that." Hero bumped his shoulder with her own. When he still said nothing, she turned to look at him, then took his arm to stop them on the landing between floors. "We're friends, aren't we?"

Beau blinked in surprise, turning his full attention to her. "What makes you ask a question like that?"

She shifted on the balls of her feet, brushing a fleck of imaginary dust off her slacks. "I've been wondering if you talk to me the same way I do to you."

"I do." Beau tilted his head as he looked at her. It was clear she had more to say. "In fact, you often bemoan how much I talk about—"

"I'm not talking about work or office things, Beauregard," said Hero, pressing her lips together to make a thin line. "I'm talking about *you*."

Beau frowned, his shoulders hunching. "What about 'me'?"

Hero waved a hand at him. "Things like whether you're a cat or a dog person, why you only own six collared shirts—"

Beau stiffened indignantly. "It's efficient—"

"—and how long you've been in love with Benedict Dickson."

Beau froze.

Clearing his throat, he met Hero's eyes. "Pardon?"

Hero huffed. "You heard me, Beau. How long?"

"I— We're— I'm not in *love* with him! Hero, don't be ridiculous!" sputtered Beau.

"Ridiculous, am I?" Hero asked. She narrowed her eyes and lifted a finger. "Who drives you to work on rainy days because you don't own a car?"

"Benedict, but—"

"Who is the only one ever willing to get you coffee because of your monstrous order?"

Beau flushed, looking away. "It's not monstrous, and he-he…"

"Who do you dog-sit for regularly, despite being allergic and entirely unwilling to admit that to him?" Hero challenged.

With a sigh, Beau held up his hands. "Benedict has a specific schedule he prefers Riley be kept to, and Riley, for some Godforsaken reason, likes my house—"

"And," Hero said, brandishing another finger, "while this list could go on, my coup de grâce: who is the one person everyone in this office will go to when you are in a horrible mood, because none of us will go near you?"

Benedict had told him, repeatedly, he didn't mind! He'd even teased Beau about it. Called him "a walking storm cloud" in the fondest voice, his dark-brown eyes bright with laughter…

"See?" Hero said, laying her hand on Beau's arm. "In *love*," she emphasized. "How long?"

Beau stared at her, his heart pounding and cheeks flushed, then ducked away from the press of her hand, heading for the stairs again. "I don't know what you're talking about," he managed.

He made it back to his cubicle safely, without any more questions from her. An achy sort of relief settled into his chest when he realized Benedict wasn't there waiting for him.

In love. Beau scoffed and booted up his computer, his eyes darting to their One-Upmanship tally on the wall of Benedict's cubicle. He smiled and shook his head. They were kindred spirits,

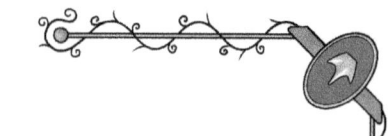

perhaps. They certainly weren't in *love*.

He pulled his eyes away from the empty desk, refocusing on the report in front of him. Completely ridiculous.

Benedict watched Beau head to the stairs, grinning triumphantly at their tally. Only two points behind. He'd have that by the end of the day for sure. Especially if he picked up coffee for Beau after his meeting—

The sound of a throat clearing jolted Benedict to attention, and he looked up to see their boss leaning against Beau's desk, both eyebrows raised. He fought down a grin and raised his eyebrows right back. "You want me to congratulate him, don't you?"

Pedro snorted. "I suppose that would be too much to ask from one of the two people in the office that considers themselves bachelors-for-life."

Benedict scoffed. "Claudio should be glad I didn't lock them in a room together to sort themselves out."

"I knew you were happy for him," Pedro teased. "But now how are you and Beau going to spend your afternoons? You always did call office gossip—"

"—cheaper entertainment than a cable package," Benedict finished, spinning in his chair to face Pedro properly. "We'll survive until the next drama-worthy discussion."

"It might be closer than you think," said Pedro. "The entertainment in the office is far from over."

Benedict glanced out across the floor, but it was quietly busy: murmured conversations, occasional phone rings, and the steady click of people typing. "What are you talking about?"

"I wonder," Pedro said dryly. He knocked on the cubicle in front of Beau's. "Claudio, any idea what I could be talking about?"

"Nope," Claudio said, rolling his chair into the aisle. "Unless, of course, you're talking about the number-one source of office drama for the rest of us."

Benedict blinked when Claudio stared at him. *Pointedly.*

"That is precisely what I'm talking about," Pedro said. He rocked back on his heels.

Benedict sighed and crossed his arms over his chest, glaring at Claudio. "You're going to lord this over me, aren't you?"

"For as long as I can," Claudio agreed. "Especially after all of the grief you gave me."

"You nearly transferred to Ireland to get away from the lady of your dreams, Claudio," said Benedict. "You deserve all of the grief I can give you and more." He looked between them. "All right, out with it. What office gossip have I missed?"

Claudio and Pedro said nothing, only stared at him with raised eyebrows. Benedict shifted uncomfortably. "Come on, please?"

Pedro tapped the side of Beau's cubicle with a considering hum. "I'm sure you'll figure it out eventually."

Benedict turned his attention to Claudio, but his friend had already slid back into his cubicle. With the two of them no longer watching him, Benedict turned to his screensaver, his eyes tracing the lines of pipes. What had he missed out on? Gossip that both Claudio *and* Pedro knew?

Benedict shook himself and stood up, heading down to the first floor of their office for coffee. The two of them were clearly joking at his expense. Stepping into line, he ordered for himself and Beau, glad when he didn't have to repeat Beau's order a second time. It was bad enough the first time.

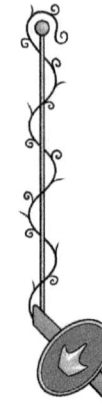

He picked up both coffees and took his time returning upstairs. If Beau was under-caffeinated after his last meeting, it might even earn Benedict another point on the tally board. Beau hated ordering his coffee so much that he jumped on any excuse to get out of doing it.

Whatever Pedro and Claudio had been teasing him about was only that—teasing.

Right?

A week and a half later, Benedict stood in the lunch line, exhausted, and, after being caught in the rain earlier, grumpy, listening to his coworkers gossip a few spots behind him. It was the only thing making the line bearable.

"Did you see? Did you see?"

Benedict did his best to pretend that he couldn't hear the conversation between Ursula and Richard.

"I did," Richard said, keeping his voice down. "You were right. He looked…like Beau was his personal hero."

Benedict blinked away some of the fugue that had settled over him. He should have listened to Beau and gone home earlier, but at least now he'd be able to share whatever this was with Beau and tease him about it. Beau hated being the subject of gossip.

Ursula sighed happily. "I thought they were going to kiss right then and there." She picked up a cupcake from the edge of the counter and put it on her tray. "It was wonderful to see; they're usually so private!"

Guilt crept up his spine. Did Beau like someone? Or did someone like him? Benedict approached the cashier, straining to hear more of their conversation as she rang up his lunch and Beau's. Buying lunch was the least he could do after—

"Benedict is a lucky bastard, that's for sure," Richard agreed. "How many boyfriends keep a spare suit in their locker?" He grabbed a cupcake for himself with a pleased hum.

Benedict stiffened, taking his card back from the cashier on reflex. Neither Ursula nor Richard had seen him. He ducked his head down, hurried out of the cafeteria and around the corner, and didn't stop until he could lean against a pillar on the other side of the condiments' table, his heart pounding.

Last Friday, Beau had picked up Benedict's dry cleaning from downstairs because Benedict had forgotten to take it before he left…and he'd continued to forget to take it all week. Beau had kept awarding himself points for it. Unexpectedly, it had come in handy today when Benedict been caught in a downpour between the parking garage and their building.

Beau had revealed the suit with a flourish worthy of a wedding gown, grin wide and grey eyes lit up with pride. He had…

Benedict shook himself. Once Richard and Ursula made their way out of the cafeteria, he picked up packets of dressing, croutons, and hot sauce, because Beau had no taste buds, and headed for the elevator, relieved to find it empty so he could relax.

Beau *had* rescued him that morning. Hell, Benedict hadn't even protested when Beau awarded himself five points for the whole mess. He'd earned every point.

But together? Them?

He stepped out of the elevator and headed toward their cubicles, meeting Beau's eyes as he approached. His heart ached to see his best friend's expression light up when he saw the peanut butter cookie he had bought him.

Benedict sank into his chair, focusing on his food, glad when Beau started talking about his last

meeting.

Shit.

Now that Hero had pointed out to him that he was "in love" with Benedict, Beau couldn't stop seeing things that weren't there. Like the way Benedict ordered Beau's coffee without teasing Beau about how much he hated doing it himself. Or how Benedict didn't argue as much over every point in their One-Upmanship competition. Or the way he kept catching Benedict staring at him!

Beau tensed and tried to focus on the presentation he needed to finish, but it was impossible when he could *feel* Benedict staring. Benedict hadn't typed a word in over six minutes. He let it go for another two, but after Benedict looked at him once more, Beau sighed and turned to face him.

"What is it?" Beau snapped, tired and wanting whatever this was to cease. "Tell me already."

Benedict blinked, taken aback. "You that stressed about your investment meeting?"

Beau tightened his fingers on his mouse and let out a slow breath. Pedro was counting on him to make this presentation flawless for their investors. It needed to be perfect, and Benedict knew that. "Is there something on my shirt? Or something wrong? You keep staring."

"I'm not staring," Benedict said, frowning. "What's wrong? Do you need coffee?"

Coffee sounded incredible, and he would have said yes, but he had to figure out what was going on. Beau shook his head. "No. What I need is to know why you keep looking at me so I can get you to stop and maybe finish my work."

"Beau…"

Beau glared at Benedict. "Whatever it is, get over it. I'm too busy for this today." He yanked open the bottom drawer of his filing cabinet and pulled out his noise-cancelling headphones. He connected them to his phone and turned up his music before refocusing. He needed to get this done!

More than an hour later, he hit save for the final time and tugged off his headphones with a relieved sigh, rolling his shoulders as he leaned back in his chair. A glance at Benedict's desk showed that he was long gone for the day, likely because Beau had made it clear company wasn't welcome. Beau slumped and blinked when he caught sight of the coffee cup and cookie beside his monitor.

The cup had a drawing of a thundercloud with a lightning bolt where the name would usually go. He wrapped his fingers around it; it was still warm, and the cookie had to be peanut butter. Beau's favorite, warmed up from the coffee, exactly how he liked it.

Swallowing, Beau took a long sip of the coffee, savoring the burst of caramel. Perfect, as always. He pulled the cup back, looked at the laundry list of adjustments on the small sticker, and clenched his eyes shut as he drank more.

Hero was wrong. It didn't mean anything.

They certainly weren't in love.

Opening the bag containing the peanut butter cookie, Beau broke off a piece and popped it into his mouth. Savoring it, he couldn't help the smile growing on his face.

It wasn't anything special. Benedict knowing his coffee order and favorite cookie didn't mean love.

Ursula warned him first.

Then Hero.

"Beau is on a rampage."

A righteous one, based on what little Ursula had told Benedict as she headed to another meeting. Turning the corner into their row of cubicles, he was unsurprised to find the section empty except for Beau's. The printed version of the presentation Beau had spent hours on was thrown across his desk haphazardly, some sheets fallen to the floor.

Benedict stopped in front of Beau.

"Don't. Say. Anything," Beau snarled. He glared at his computer, hitting the "enter" key viciously. "I don't need it from you."

Getting Beau to talk was always a matter of waiting him out, especially when he was this furious. He thought briefly of how this would look to Ursula if she were to see them, if it would make them seem even more like a couple, but he could worry about that later—after he got to the bottom of this.

Benedict leaned against the side of Beau's cubicle and looked at him, raising an eyebrow.

"Go away!" Beau snapped, glaring at Benedict. "Or do you have so little to do that you can afford to stand there while the rest of us—" He cut off and closed his eyes as he took a deep breath. Then another. "I'm sorry," Beau managed, his voice much quieter, looking up at Benedict.

Smiling, Benedict settled into the chair Beau kept for people who visited his desk. "You wouldn't have apologized so quickly to me a few years ago."

Beau acknowledged that truth with a sharp nod. "I'm not angry with you, Benedict." He looked down at the ruined presentation and continued, his voice softer, "I want John fired. Immediately."

"Excuse me?"

"You heard me," Beau's voice regained some of its previous fierceness. "I want him fired. I don't care that he just transferred to Finance."

Benedict shifted in his chair and hummed in consideration. "Why do you want him fired?"

Beau gestured to the scattered pages. "Incompetence. He cost us not one, but multiple investors, and risked putting the company in severe financial—"

"Beau," Benedict interrupted, keeping his voice soft, "you know it doesn't work like that."

Beau tensed, dropping his hands to the edge of his desk. "He blamed *my* numbers. He called *me* incompetent. In front of a dozen investors—in front of Pedro." He let out a breath. "If-if our friendship means anything to you, you'll help me get him fired, Benedict."

"All right." Benedict grabbed his laptop and booted it up with a quick flick of his fingers. "Where do we start?"

Beau blinked in surprise. The anger left him in an abrupt wash. "You'll…what?"

Benedict grinned, meeting Beau's gaze steadily. "You've asked for my help, Beau. Of course I'm going to help you." He paused, his voice softening. "I'll *always* help you."

Looking down at the mess on the desk, Beau swallowed hard. "I— Thank you." He blinked hard and cleared his throat. "Thank you, Benedict."

"You don't have to thank me," Benedict said. "You think I'm going to let anyone get away with calling you incompetent? I'm the only one in this office that gets to do that, and everyone knows it."

Beau let out a laugh, nodding. "You've got that right."

Benedict took Beau's hand and squeezed carefully. When Beau looked at him in surprise, he met his eyes steadily. "It's gonna be okay," he promised. "We'll figure it out."

Beau nodded again, took a deep breath, then squeezed Benedict's hand in return; Benedict nudging Beau's foot aside for more leg room under the table prompted a smile. "Let's get started," Beau said, his voice the tiniest bit hoarse, and not from anger.

"Farewell weekends, hello overtime," Benedict muttered, cursing when Beau returned Bene-

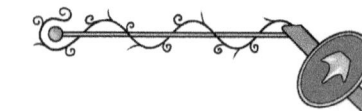

dict's gentle nudge as a kick. "Taking a point for that," he added, glancing at their competition chart. Judging by the slowly growing smile on Beau's lips, he didn't mind.

They'd done it. Together, they'd done it.

Beau looked at the folder on the desk in front of him. It was heavier than he'd expected. Twenty-seven pages of charts went into exquisite detail of his work and investment numbers; Benedict had made the data shine. Six pages highlighted their investment strategies, refuting John's claims bullet-point by bullet-point, followed by four pages describing the damage done by the doubt cast on his competence. All compiled over ten days of long nights at their houses, drinking far too much coffee and watching shows they'd never admit to enjoying.

A week and a half that had proven, more than anything else ever could, how in love with Benedict he was. Beau slid his fingers across the plain manila folder, the memory of Benedict's triumphant grin when they finished enough to make him shiver.

The folder was Benedict's love letter to the work Beau had spent the last six months doing.

More than once while working on it together, Beau had been astonished by the extent to which Benedict knew more about his work than Beau did himself.

In ten minutes, Beau would be presenting their findings to Pedro.

Unfortunately, all he could think about was kissing this morning's excited, proud grin off Benedict's face. Focusing was impossible. No matter what Beau tried, his mind was consumed with Benedict. Beau groaned and rubbed his face.

"What're you worried about?" Benedict asked, putting a cup of green tea down in front of Beau. "You're ready."

"What if this isn't enough data?" Beau asked, staring down at the folder, forcing his attention where it belonged. "I present all of this, and I get a 'thanks for your feedback' or something similar?"

"Pedro wouldn't do that," Benedict reasoned. "He knows how hard you've worked, and, in there, you've handed him all the details he needs to prove it to our investors, too."

Beau stood up from his desk and paced past Benedict, tapping nervously at his leg. "But what if it isn't enough?" he repeated.

"Then it isn't, but it's at least documented, and John will be someone else's problem."

Beau stopped in front of the window and leaned against it, exhaling hard. He could do this. He could. Benedict was right.

"Beau," Benedict called. "What else are you worried about? You know you're ready and—"

"I can't focus!" Beau snapped, pushing his hair out of his face with an annoyed growl. He turned on his heel and paced up the full length of the aisle, back to where Benedict was standing.

Benedict frowned and reached out to press his fingertips to Beau's arm. "What has you all spun up?"

Beau tensed, freezing in front of Benedict. "Nothing." He shook himself. "I'm fine." He reached for the tea that Benedict had gotten for him, because Benedict knew he preferred tea instead of coffee before big meetings so he didn't get too jittery. Benedict always knew.

Beau put the cup down.

"In love," Hero had said.

This was how Benedict loved people. Beau had seen him act this way toward Pedro. Even toward Claudio. Reassurances, support, and, when all else failed, small things that made a big difference.

Fuck.

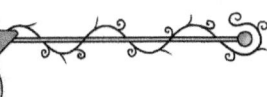

He *was* in love with his best friend.

Had been for who-knew-how-long.

"Fuck," Beau echoed the sentiment aloud, staring at the cup.

"Beau," Benedict soothed, stepping in closer to him again, tugging at his arm until Beau was facing him. "It's going to be fine."

Beau shook his head, groaning. "It's not, fuck, it's so not."

"It will be. Trust me."

"It won't be if I can't stop thinking about—" Beau cut off, his eyes wide. He yanked his arm away from Benedict, pacing toward the window. Mere minutes now until the meeting. He had to get himself under control.

"Talk to me," Benedict ordered. "You being all…like this…isn't because of the meeting."

Beau let out a frustrated breath. "It's fine. I'm fine."

Benedict frowned and moved beside Beau again. "Tell me what's wrong," he demanded. "I don't care what it is—tell me."

The steady, unflinching support, like *always*, had him snapping, rounding on Benedict angrily. "The problem? It's infuriating!" Beau stepped even closer to Benedict, glaring at the bastard who had the gall to stand one-inch taller than him and look perfectly composed while he was falling apart inside. "I'm in love with you. I am in love with you, Benedict, and I think you love me back, and as much as I want to focus on this meeting, all I can think about is you!"

Benedict stared at Beau, his breath catching. "You love me, too?"

"Too." Benedict said "too." Beau wanted to kiss him until he'd had enough time to process that single three-letter word. But he had no time. They had no time. "I have to stop thinking about *you* long enough to get through this meeting and—"

And…Benedict's lips were softer than he'd imagined.

Beau forgot how he'd planned to finish that sentence and relaxed, leaning in to gently brush their lips together. Behind him, there was a *whoop*, and an unmistakable cheer made him smile against Benedict's lips. By the time he leaned back, his lips tingling, to meet Benedict's dark eyes, there was no doubt in his mind.

Too.

Benedict loved him *too*.

"I get at least five points for that," Benedict whispered against Beau's lips. "At least."

Beau pulled him in for another kiss. Even if the smug bastard was right—Beau would put the points up himself—there was no need to let him gloat about it when they could be kissing instead. In fact, kissing Benedict was his new favorite distraction.

Benedict chuckled and pulled back enough to brush their noses together. "I know what you're doing," he whispered.

"Any objections?" Beau breathed back.

Benedict pretended to consider for a moment before he shook his head. "Nah. This is more important. You're more important."

The only thing Beau could do with an answer like that was lean in for another kiss.

"Well, at least Beau has a good reason for being late to our meeting."

Beau snapped back to their surroundings, their coworkers, their boss, and stepped back from Benedict, his lips still tingling as he turned to look at Pedro. "We, uh, we were—"

Pedro held up a hand. "Everyone knows, and I'm glad to see you two worked out your—situation."

Beau cleared his throat, reaching out for the folder on his desk. "Yes, sir. Could we go to your

office now?"

"Of course," Pedro looked behind Beau. "Benedict, you should know Claudio is going to mock you for *months* if you don't wipe that grin off your face."

Benedict shrugged. "Can't help it. Love's a good look on me."

Beau looked over his shoulder at Benedict, warm brown eyes making his heart skip a beat as Benedict grinned back at him and crowed, "Looks even better on Beau!"

The parting comment got him a middle finger from Beau, and Benedict leaned against his desk for a moment, looking at the whiteboard and tally marks. Instead of grabbing the marker, he took the eraser and wiped the board clean. In its place, he drew a heart with a storm cloud and a bolt of lightning in the middle.

There. Perfect.

Joshua Beeking
"Melancholy"

Considering how the play ends regarding Don Pedro, I thought it fitting to illustrate him with kind of an isolated, "put to the side" ambiance, and the sentence "You should get yourself a wife" at the end of the play is a sentence any aces* could find relatable, I think, regarding how pushy others can be toward aces/ aros.* It was an interpretation of the character I thought was most fitting, and the vibe was definitely to illustrate the struggles one can face being ace.

* Editor's Notes: "ace" and "aces" are common abbreviations used to refer to asexual people. "Aros" is, similarly, a common abbreviation used to refer to aromantic people.

TAGS: alternate universe, angst, bipoc, does drag, enemies to lovers, f/f, f/m, first kiss, fraught family dynamics, friends to lovers, gender non-conforming, homophobic language, homophobic violence (mentions of), in the closet, m/m, micro-aggressions (racist), misunderstandings, past tense, performer, period-typical homophobia, period-typical understandings of gender and sexuality, present tense, the 2000s, third person limited (alternating) point of view, united states of america, unreliable narrator

ASSIUIME: A QUEER LOVE STORY

K. B. Vimes

Inspiration: The inspiration for this story was spite in the face of unnecessary censoring and a lack of knowledge for the history of queer people. I hoped to illustrate that, historically, "queer" encompasses people who don't fit easily into simple boxes or standard LGBT+ groups, to send a message that we are here, we are queer, and we are going nowhere.

S*tage lights are going down. It's nearly time; the MC has finished announcing her, and it's a moment before the stage gets dark enough to let her take her place. She hits her mark, and it's on.*

"Sigh no more ladies, sigh no more.
Men were deceivers ever
One foot at sea and one on shore
To one thing constant never"

Bustychick Arnold always started her act with a song, and this time was no different. A song of heartbreak and sadness, tonight, to match her mood. Her best friend Claude had joined the rest of the guys in the unit on-base laughing about "men in dresses," and while she'd done her best to join in, Bustychick couldn't help but be heartbroken by it.

Her large, curly wig piled hair high on her head, far bigger than could have been managed without some serious hairspray or extremely twisty locks. It was bright pink, with a faux military cap pinned jauntily on top. Her hair didn't move as she swung her hips in time to the music, not made for the kind of subtlety other drag queens went for in their outfits. It reminded her of the helmets

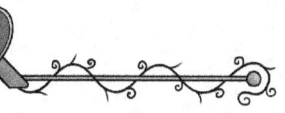

she wore in military life. Her outfit now, ironically, was as much a form of armor as that was.

A pink camouflage mini-dress sheathed her torso, the skirt flared out at her waist with layers and layers of petticoats and tulle. Her padded bra gave her an ample bosom; she was not particularly gifted in that department naturally, so her neckline looked best high to hide the space where the bra ended. Today, it was a mock-turtleneck halter top.

Her makeup was on point, contoured to hide her square jawline and sharp nose, with big eyes and high, painted-on eyebrows over her waxed-down real ones. Her pale skin was accentuated to the point that it looked clownish offstage but under the lights made her coloration just right, with blush high on her cheeks as if she'd been out in the sun. Bright-pink lipstick completed the look.

When the song ended, she breathed hard, smiling at her audience as they clapped and cheered.

"Now, now. I have some things to say before we end this!" she finally interrupted, and the crowd quieted. "How do you all like living in this town with its military base?" Bustychick asked, and was answered with loud boos. "I thought so! We all know how well the *military* treats us! Why, even just a hint of queerness can end a good man's career, as if we were all traitors to the cause!"

The jeering got louder, and someone in the back shouted, "Preach it, sister!"

"Don't Ask, Don't Tell might keep us in the military sometimes, but only under a cloak of shame! DADT was needed years ago, but now? Now it holds us back! A queer man deserves to be able to share his benefits with his male partner just like a straight man can!"

The crowd was riled up now, calls of "amen!" sounding from all around.

"And I, my dear family, have a secret." Bustychick knelt down, putting her painted finger to her lips as though she were going to whisper, and the crowd got quiet, leaning close. "Generals Pedro and John—the Big Wigs…even bigger than mine, honey." She patted her hair delicately and allowed the laughter to swim around the room. "Well, they'll be in town this week. What do you say we give them a show they won't forget?"

The crowd cheered, and she stood up. "We know not everyone can be there, but if we gather as many people as possible on that side of town for a good old-fashioned queer riot, maybe we can get something done in this town! Change some minds and *make* them listen to us!"

When the crowd went wild, she curtsied deeply, waved, and went backstage.

"Good show out there!" Lenora grinned from her seat in front of one of the mirrors in the back as she got her makeup on for her performance. The smell of powder and sweat was heavy on the air in the dressing room.

"Just getting them excited for you, girlfriend," Bustychick said, grabbing her bag and sliding into the curtained booth set aside for those who needed a little discretion. She closed the curtain and began removing the eye makeup and lipstick. The contouring would stay until she got home, the better to hide her face. As Benedick Padua—Ben, to those who knew him through work—he couldn't be seen at a place like this, but as long as she remained in her female persona, she could be seen anywhere. So she redid her eyes to something more delicate and painted her lips a little closer to her natural color. Then, she swapped her stage wig to one with long blonde hair; it blended in better with the Straights.

Stepping out of the backstage area, she waved at the other girls and headed into the bar area in front of the stage to meet her sister Margaret.

"So, how was it?" Bustychick asked, taking the open seat next to her at a small table in the corner.

"You did amazing," Margaret said, smiling widely and handing over a large, fruity mixed drink. "But are you sure you should be giving away information like that? Won't someone get mad and try to figure you out?"

Bustychick shrugged, taking a sip. "It'll be common knowledge in a couple of days, and by then no one will be sure who first said it."

"Still I worry, you know. You've done well for yourself in the military. I don't want you to throw away a good career." Margaret stirred her drink restlessly and sighed. "You know I'll support you through anything, and my husband feels the same, but your reputation and future is at stake every time you do this."

"What good is life without freedom?" Bustychick replied. "If I love who I choose, I'm risking everything. Any day now they could send my regiment back to Afghanistan, where I may die in the service of a country that would rather see my family live in shame and secrecy than enjoy the freedoms others take for granted."

"All right, all right, I get it." Margaret shook her head. "No need to soapbox. I'm your sister; I'm on your side."

They sat chatting for a couple more acts before Margaret began making the kinds of noises she only made when she was ready to go.

"Just one more act, Margie. General Disdain is on the schedule next, and I really want to see him," Bustychick said, looking at Margaret with pleading eyes.

"Okay, okay, put those big, brown eyes away. You know I can never say no to you. But after that, we go home. Borachio will have put the kids to bed, and I'd like to get some alone time with him before we fall asleep."

"Oh, honey, don't let me intrude on your 'alone time,' " Bustychick said with a wink. "It's not like you don't have two-dozen kids already. What are you going to name this one?"

Margaret stole the umbrella from Bustychick's drink and threw it at her with a look of mock outrage.

His makeup was flawless; he always triple-checked it before even thinking of coming onstage. It was contoured to square his jawline and emphasized his nose, with large, bushy eyebrows and highly defined eyes. His dark cheeks were highlighted with a metallic bronze, giving his skin a sparkle and shine. He hid his long, straightened hair under a gray, wavy wig that shone under the stage lights, with a large salt-and-pepper beard he'd designed to resemble Gimli's from the new *Lord of the Rings* movies. He wore tan suspenders with a white, glittery button-up shirt underneath, black slacks, and combat boots that added three inches to his height. As he stepped forward onstage, he used one hand to stretch his suspenders and spit to the side.

"Well, it's nice to see a crowd tonight!"

General Disdain bowed as the audience went wild.

"You know, I was just talking about you guys the other day," he said, pausing to let the crowd respond with cheers and whistles. "I was telling my soldiers—you all know the type. Rough, tough, *manly*…and ever so dull. Oh, there's a few bright spots in there, I know, but the straight ones…my God." The crowd roared with laughter. "Anyway, I was just telling them about how they could stand to brighten up their wardrobes a bit, add a little *color*, if you know what I mean. Maybe even some proper hygiene."

The audience cheered, shouting lewdness at General Disdain as he walked about the stage.

"They're all clowns, unfortunately, all sad faces and single tears. The military seems to draw such men. Their only gift is to devise impossible slanders against each other. Of course, Casanovas that they are, they all find it so amusing. Their commendations are not in their wit, but in their villainy. They *please* men…" He paused for emphasis again, his eyes sparkling. "…and they anger men, and

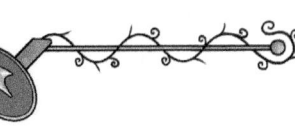

then those same men laugh at them and stand them up for target practice."

General Disdain smiled, returning to the front of the stage to continue his act. From there, he spotted Bustychick, and his smile turned genuine. Bustychick gave a wave and a wink, and he sent the wink right back at her. He'd have to catch up with her later.

As Disdain's act came to a close, Bustychick and Margaret joined the crowd in a standing ovation. General Disdain bowed and then motioned for quiet.

"Now don't forget, in addition to the protest Bustychick Arnold has so wonderfully supplied an opportunity for, we also have our on-going letter-writing campaign to protest the Defense Of Marriage Act. If you need help drafting a letter, talk to the bartender, who will direct you to those who can assist you. Thank you everyone! You've been wonderful!"

The sound swelled as General Disdain sauntered off the stage, and there was a brief pause for the house lights to come up while the show's staff set up for the next act. When General Disdain came out of the dressing area still in his stage outfit a few minutes later, Bustychick waved him over.

"Hey, darling, come sit with us," she said, offering him a sip of her drink.

"Don't mind if I do," he replied, sitting on her side of the table and accepting the drink, watching her as he suggestively sipped from her straw.

Bustychick fanned herself, maintaining eye contact until her sister kicked her under the table. "Oh! Honey, we have some letters for you. We can't risk them going out from our address, but the bartender said you could take them for us?"

General Disdain nodded with a smile and held out his hand. "Sure thing. How many do you have?"

"Three. Here's mine, and then my sister and her husband wrote separate ones."

Margaret cleared her throat when she was mentioned and nodded to General Disdain. "We thought more letters would be better. Is that okay?"

"It's perfect," General Disdain said, giving Margaret a grin. "If you can get anyone else in the family to write, bring those letters on in too. We'll be making weekly trips to the post office. Can we count on you two at the protest? I hear they're planning it for Friday."

"Sadly no," Bustychick sighed, stirring her drink. "I have to work that day, and I can't get out of it. Mandatory attendance and all that."

General Disdain reached up to brush her cheek and sighed. "Too bad. I was so looking forward to seeing you, my little angel."

Bustychick nearly swooned off her chair. She was sure the blush was showing on her ears, even if the makeup she wore was too heavy to show it on her face. "A-ah, well. Perhaps we can plan a performance together instead?"

"That would be lovely. Are you free—?"

Margaret cleared her throat again and stood up. "Unfortunately, I have to get back to my husband and the kids, and I'm Bustychick's ride. I'm sure you can arrange something through the manager, though."

It took a few moments more for them to extricate from each other, and Bustychick mourned the loss of General Disdain's touch, but Margaret was right. She *had* promised that they would leave after Disdain's performance. Hopefully next weekend General Disdain would be back. He didn't perform every week, but that made what time they did have together all the more precious.

For now, it was time to get back to her sister's house and back to her normal life.

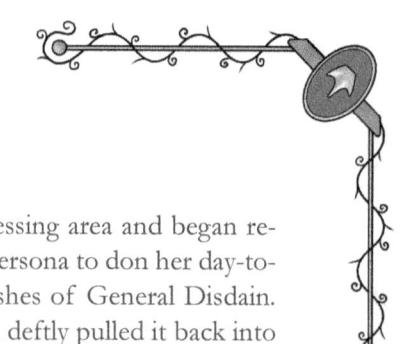

It was hours later when General Disdain finally went back to the dressing area and began removing his makeup. It was uncomfortable for him, discarding his stage persona to don her day-to-day self once more. Before long, Beatrice Messina emerged from the ashes of General Disdain. She brushed her hair out, getting rid of the tangles the wig had left, then deftly pulled it back into an uncomplicated ponytail. She carefully tucked her costume and wig into a plain duffle bag and slung it over her shoulder.

Beatrice wore a simple outfit—fitted jeans and a slim, black T-shirt—that her father despaired of. Leonato Messina was a proud, retired colonel who believed women should look, well. Womanly. Unlike her sister Hero, who wore mini-dresses and tights, Beatrice preferred outfits that weren't traditionally feminine. If she thought she could get away with it, she'd wear baggy jeans and band shirts purchased from the men's department. But her father would have a cow if she walked out of the house like that, so she compromised. General Disdain was her outlet, something her family knew nothing about, and it let her feel like she was "real" in a way her everyday life didn't.

The duffle went into the trunk of her car, where her parents and nosy sister never thought to check—Beatrice was careful to never give them cause to—then she headed home. If she had her way, she wouldn't still live at home, but her dad had insisted, and she couldn't argue with his points: since she was attending a local college, it made more sense for her to stay home and save money. If she moved out, she'd have to work a full-time job on top of taking classes. As it was, she worked part-time at a local grocery store to earn some extra cash—her parents only covered the basics. One night a week, when she could manage it, she came out to the bar and performed.

Sneaking into the house was the easy part. Getting past her parents' room at the top of the stairs was harder. She had to avoid the fourth stair: it would creak no matter how lightly she stepped. Then, she hugged the wall near the top of the stairs and around the corner; she knew better than to step in the center, where there were a few loose boards. She had to pause at the top of the stairs, checking for the sound of her mother's snores before she moved on. Finally, her own door hung low on the hinges and had to be lifted carefully to avoid it scraping loudly along the floor. But she'd had practice, and it was only a moment before she was safely in her own room with the door shut. She changed as quickly as she could and slipped into bed.

Home again, she thought as she drifted off. *Unfortunately.*

The next morning, Beatrice stretched as she went downstairs for breakfast, smelling the bacon and eggs from the top of the stairs. Her father had a rule that everyone had to be dressed for the meal, an annoyance not worth arguing over. He also had decreed years ago that *his* daughters would have "professional" hair, which to him meant that she had to go to a salon and have her hair straightened every few weeks and maintained in between; she mostly "maintained" it by shoving it in ponytails. She and her sister Hero had inherited their mother's curly 3b black hair and brown eyes. If she could have chopped it off, she would have, but her father felt that women should have long hair.

"I heard you come in last night," her father said as she sat down at the table. "What were you doing out at 2 a.m., young lady?"

"Studying," she said without missing a beat. "I told you I have a test on Monday. Ursula and I lost track of time."

"Humph. It isn't respectable, a woman staying out all hours of the night." He didn't say anything more, and she didn't either. They'd had this argument a hundred times, and it never mattered. He was stuck in the '60s, and nothing could bring him forward.

"Hey, Daddy, can Claude come over tomorrow?" Hero asked.

"We have church tomorrow," their mother replied. "You know that."

"I *know*. I meant, can he come to church with us and spend the afternoon here? He says the base chaplain isn't going to be there tomorrow."

"What is this world coming to, that our bright, young soldiers have to go off-base to get a proper Christian service?" Leonato growled. "Of course the boy can come here. Innogen will make sure he has a full stomach afterward, won't you dear?"

Their mother nodded as she finished serving everyone, then sat down. "I'd be happy to. Let him know if any of his friends are free, they're welcome to come along."

"All right! He might bring Ben, then. They're best friends."

Beatrice rolled her eyes. Hero mentioned that every time Ben came up, and the meaningful look Hero gave her made no difference. Ben was just another awful military man who believed awful things, and nothing was going to change Beatrice's mind. Hero sighed loudly, and Beatrice wanted to kick her under the table. She knew Hero wanted her to get along with Claude and Ben, but she had no plans to do so.

Honestly, Beatrice didn't understand what Hero saw in Claude, or what anyone saw in *any* military man. They were all alike, bigoted assholes who—

Beatrice closed her eyes, chewing her food slowly. It did no good to get angry when her dad was around. That would just end in tears. Probably hers.

There was a long silence as everyone ate and Leonato read the newspaper. It was shattered by a fist to the table. "That damn Shepherd woman is in the papers again. She needs to learn to shut up and be happy her dead son isn't shaming the community anymore. If some sexual deviant even fucking thought of touching me like that boy touched those guys, I'd kill him too."

Beatrice choked on her eggs, prompting her sister to pat her on the back until she stopped coughing. Their mother sighed.

"Language, honey. You know the girls aren't used to that kind of crudeness. You've upset Beatrice."

Thank God for Mom, Beatrice thought. As General Disdain, Beatrice had heard and used worse language than that, but she'd needed some excuse to cover her reaction. Even if her mom wasn't aware of what was really going on, her excuse was as good as any.

"May I be excused to the bathroom?" she asked, pushing her chair back. Her mother nodded, while her father simply grunted, going back to his paper. She escaped as quickly as she could before they could change their minds. She'd need to find a reason to leave for the rest of the day. Beatrice didn't think she could deal with her father again after that.

Sundays usually meant Ben spent a couple of hours sitting through the chaplain's service and then went back to work. Today was the odd day off, and Claude had invited him over to his girlfriend Hero's house for Sunday service followed by an afternoon at her family's home. On the surface, it might seem weird to invite your best friend along to your girlfriend's place, but Ben knew that Claude's girlfriend lived with her parents and sister. Having a friend along meant more opportunities to get Hero alone for some "quality time." Nothing too risqué, obviously, but maybe some necking. Ben had done this for Claude before, and he didn't really mind doing it again.

If only Hero's sister weren't so awful.

"So, how many civilians have you personally killed?" Beatrice asked Ben sweetly; Ben sighed.

"None that I know of."

" 'That you know of.' Hmmph. I've been watching news sources besides America's, you know. The local newspapers may be singing your praises, but the other countries are watching and judging us for this. We might've been attacked on 9/11, but now we're invading other countries for no reason."

Secretly, Ben agreed with her, but he didn't dare say that. He'd joined because he'd believed it to be a good cause; after two tours he was disillusioned about the whole thing. He'd seen too many things done in the name of Good and Justice that weren't good or just at all.

"I do what I'm told, ma'am."

"I'm sure you do. That's what the soldiers at Auschwitz said, too. When are we going to see you up on charges of treason?"

Hopefully never, Ben wanted to say, tugging at his dress shirt and looking around for an exit. It was bad enough that he was in men's clothing. He felt naked without the shaping undergarments he normally wore as Bustychick. He scratched at his collar and sighed. Wouldn't she be surprised if she knew he was at risk of that every day, but for his sexuality rather than for his conduct?

"And another thing—" Beatrice started until Ben cut her off.

"You know, I'm going to see if your mother needs any help in the kitchen. It's been lovely talking to you. Goodbye."

He heard Beatrice snort behind him, but she didn't stop him, Escape managed, he ducked into the house to find the kitchen, passing by Mr. Messina, who sat in the den watching a football game. Surely Mrs. Messina needed some kind of help. Anything would do, so long as Beatrice didn't wasn't there nagging him.

It was three weeks before the manager could arrange for General Disdain and Bustychick Arnold to do a joint performance. Bustychick had availability, but General Disdain had been out of touch for a while. The manager had assured her that this happened sometimes, that General Disdain sometimes wasn't able to get away for weeks at a time. Once everything was arranged, though, Bustychick asked if they could use the backstage area to practice their number. The manager gave his permission for Thursday night, with the performance on Friday, and promised to let Bustychick know.

It would have been easier, Bustychick thought, to give her General Disdain's number, but apparently his home situation wouldn't allow it. He wasn't the only one living a double life, so Bustychick swore she'd be there ready to go on Thursday and left the manager's office. She'd do her part to make this work.

General Disdain looked at his clock. It was 3:10 p.m., ten minutes after he and Bustychick had agreed to meet. Tapping his foot, he was beginning to wonder if Bustychick was even going to make it when a man in street clothes dashed into the backstage area, the hood on his sweatshirt up despite the heat of the day.

"I am *so* sorry I'm running late," he said, trying to hide his face as he hurried into the curtained booth. "My sister couldn't come and she's usually my ride and all my stuff is at her house and I didn't have time to get my base makeup on and—"

"It's fine, it's fine," General Disdain soothed, trying to figure out where he knew that face from. He'd only glimpsed it for a second, but... "It's only ten minutes, my love." Laughter came from behind the curtain, and General Disdain grinned. Then his eyebrows went up in shock as he put

two and two together. "The…the boy who always comes around with Hero's boyfriend…"

"Huh?" came from behind the curtain, starting to take on Bustychick's voice.

"Uh…just…thinking out loud, don't worry about it, dear."

If Bustychick is Ben…but that meant that Ben isn't anything like my father…he couldn't be…but what if…

General Disdain closed his eyes, the room's face-powder-and-sweat smell fading away as he thought back. Ben had never said anything terrible…not like Claude, who used the word "gay" as a pejorative regularly. In fact, whenever Claude or Hero had done so, Ben had winced. General Disdain distinctly remembered that now, because at the time he'd thought he perhaps was nursing a war wound or something. He'd thought it served the man right, to feel that sort of discomfort, but now…

And Ben had always been quick to change the subject when Beatrice's father had started in on an anti-gay rant. It hadn't always worked, stubborn as Leonato Messina was, and General Disdain remembered more than a few times, now that he was really thinking about it and giving Ben the benefit of the doubt, that Ben had excused himself to the bathroom when things had gotten really bad. But surely…

"Hey, you okay out there? You got quiet all of a sudden," Bustychick said from behind the curtain.

"Can you come out real quick? I need to talk to you," General Disdain said, scuffing his shoe and staring at the floor. He had to set this right.

"I don't have my face on yet. I'll be out soon!"

"I don't mind. I *need* to talk to you."

Bustychick's voice quivered. "I can't. I don't have my face on. Please, just a moment longer."

General Disdain cleared his throat as she took her wig off. "I'll take my face off, too. I think…I think we need to talk about something."

Grabbing a makeup removal sponge, Beatrice smeared her makeup until her unaltered face was visible. Then, she sat down and waited.

It took a moment, but Bustychick (*Ben*) finally peeked around the curtain and showed her face, partially covered by makeup but still unmistakable. Beatrice sighed.

"I'm so, *so* sorry. I…I didn't realize you…you're like me."

Bustychick's eyes widened, and she dropped the curtain, obscuring herself for a moment before she reached up and pushed it back fully, exposing the underthings she used to transform her body shape. "You're…Beatrice Messina?"

"Yes. And you're Ben Padua. And I'm an idiot. I just… Look, my father is ex-military. You know that. And he's just so…infuriating. If he knew about me… He hates queer people, and I just…I thought you'd be the same. You're friends with Claude, after all, and some of the things he's said…"

"I…" Bustychick gulped. "Claude doesn't know. He thinks I'm babysitting for my sister's girl's-night-outs, not that I *am* my sister's girl's-night-outs…"

"I get it. My sister doesn't know, either. I just… All those times you've come over, I've been awful, and I'm sorry."

"I haven't…I don't think I've been much better," Bustychick said, rubbing the back of her neck. "I can't imagine what it's like for you, living there all the time."

"Are we okay?" Beatrice rose and walked over to Bustychick, holding out her hand.

"Am I…still your angel?" Bustychick asked, staring at Beatrice's hand.

Reaching forward, General Disdain grabbed Bustychick's shoulder and pulled her into his arms. Warmth engulfed them, comfort and solidity within the embrace, however it didn't end there. With

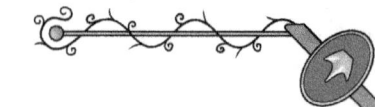

an eager sigh their lips touched, and a feeling like electricity shot between them, an explosive kiss. "Sugar, you will *always* be my angel. Now, get ready. We have a rehearsal to do."

With a blush, Bustychick nodded and sat back down to finish getting ready.

"My saucy bark, inferior far to his, on your broad main does willfully appear.
Your shallowest help will hold me up afloat,
whilst he upon your soundless deep does ride;
or, being wrecked, I am a worthless boat,
he of tall building, and of goodly pride.
Then if he thrive and I be cast away,
the worst was this: My love was my decay!"

General Disdain and Bustychick Arnold clasped hands and took a bow to the crowd wildly cheering for them. In the audience sat Margaret, cheering the loudest. Bustychick couldn't make out her words, but from the way her lips moved it was likely that she was suggesting they do something very crude in the dressing room. To the sounds of the standing ovation, General Disdain grabbed her around the waist and dipped her into a heated kiss. She swooned. What else could she do when a strong, handsome man like General Disdain did that?

When the Matthew Shepherd And James Byrd Jr. Hate Crimes Prevention Act was passed on October 22, 2009, General Disdain met with his father in his proper outfit for the first time, and Ben Padua stood beside him the whole time.

When DADT was repealed on September 20, 2011, Bustychick Arnold left the base wearing her proper outfit for the first time, and Beatrice met her at the gates.

When DOMA was overturned on June 26, 2013, General Disdain made an announcement at the club, and the party was unstoppable. Bustychick congratulated him with a kiss onstage.

And, on June 26, 2015, General Disdain got on one knee and asked a blushing, crying Bustychick Arnold if she would marry him.

Bustychick obviously said yes.

Stage lights are coming up. It's nearly time; the MC has finished announcing them and it's a moment before the curtains part. They hit the mark, and it's on.

Magnolia Porter
"Eat His Heart in the Marketplace"

Magnolia opted not to share the inspiration behind this artwork.

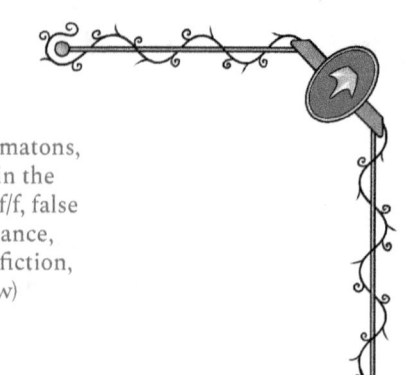

TAGS: alien, alternate universe, artificial intelligence, automatons, be gay do crimes, character has a different gender than in the source material, everyone knows they're in love but them, f/f, false accusations, genderfluid, genderqueer, interspecies romance, m/nb, mystery, non-human character, past tense, science fiction, tattooed, third person limited (multiple) point of view)

MUCH RUCKUS

R. L. Houck

I had just finished watching the entirety of the television series Leverage *shortly before starting "Much Ruckus," which is why I was inspired to include thieves in my story. From there, I drew on a lot of other favorites such as* Firefly, Cowboy Bebop, *and* Dark Matter *for the "Space Pirates" alternate universe. I enjoy reading about characters who have fallen out of grace, either by chance or by choice, and many of Shakespeare's characters are easy to place into those situations. Even with a large time jump forward, I wanted to touch on the themes of inclusion and diversity. While same-sex and interspecies partnerships are commonplace, there are still cultural differences in marriage practices and gender identification. And, regardless of how well people love one another, there will always be insecurity and misunderstanding.*

Messina Space Station, 04/16/3621, 14:02

"Hey there, gorgeous. Can I buy you a drink?"

B turned his head to scan the being who'd sidled up next to him. The human male winked salaciously, and B sighed.

"You could—but it would, ultimately, be useless. First, I'm a synthetic and can't consume organic matter. Second, this form doesn't have any genitals, so the whole concept of plying me with alcohol to 'get into my pants' won't work. Go away."

"Blending, B. Blending," Pedro said in a low voice from B's other side.

B whirled around and glared at his colleague, who leaned nonchalantly against the bar. "I've *been* blending! Probably too well, since this is the sixth person to proposition me. They all use the same boring line, too. Why can't they be more creative?"

"Well, you *are* standing in front of a bar," the prospective suitor muttered. "And you don't have to lie; there's no way you're a synthetic."

B looked over his shoulder, eyebrow raised. "I'm not lying. I'm a DI."

The man rapidly blinked, confused. Pedro leaned around B to offer an explanation before he could give a scathing retort. "Downloaded Intelligence—a rare offshoot of the Artificial Intelli-

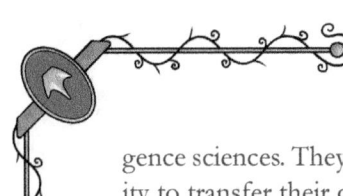

gence sciences. They do everything an AI can, but with a more human-like personality and the ability to transfer their consciousness into a synthetic body for short periods of time. A very realistic body. But, yes, completely synthetic."

Wordlessly, B opened a tiny compartment on the side of his neck to show off the inner workings of his body's mechanical wires and struts. The man's eyes widened.

He took a step back. "Goddamn." His voice was faint. "Your makers had no right to make you as hot as they did, girl."

B rose to his full height, eyes narrowing. "Girl? You think I'm presenting as a girl?"

Organics always made so many assumptions.

Pedro slid between them, placed a hand on the man's chest, and propelled him back several steps. "It's clear you've struck out here, my friend. Move along, all right?"

As the guy scampered off, Pedro gave B a warning look. "Stop it. Don't pick fights. Ben shouldn't be much longer."

Groaning, B collapsed onto the stool behind him. "I hope his transport gets struck by an asteroid and explodes."

Pedro glanced at B sidelong. "Do you still hold a grudge over the coding thing?"

"The 'coding thing'?" B stared at Pedro in astonishment. "I'm sorry, is that what you call trying to rewrite my entire base personality as a joke?"

"It wasn't your *whole* personality, and he *did* apologize."

"Oh, yes. That makes it all better," B said, rolling his eyes. He paused for a long moment before speaking again, voice lowered to avoid attracting unwanted attention. "You know, Hera and Claudia are so good at getting in and out of vaults undetected, there probably won't be a need for any more muscle. We already have you, and *I* can shoot. We don't need Ben for this job."

"Your range is limited outside the ship, B," Pedro replied. "How much farther could that body get than where we are now?"

B guiltily dropped his gaze to the grungy barroom floor—the man had a point.

Pedro continued, "Besides, the ship is getting glitchy. I need Ben as a mechanic almost as much as I need him as a gun."

B's eyes widened in outrage. "I am fully capable—"

"Pedro!"

A happy shout interrupted B, and Pedro turned in time to nearly be knocked off his feet by a laughing, broad-shouldered man: Ben. He notched his chin over Pedro's shoulder as they embraced, and his gaze immediately zeroed in on B.

Lips pursed, B slowly stood and crossed his arms over his chest. It gave him comfort to have even that small barrier between the two of them.

"So good to see you, my friend," Pedro said as Ben broke eye contact with B and stepped back from Pedro. "Thank you for coming."

"Of course! Anything for you, Pedro. Look who I found along the way!"

Ben stepped to the side and gestured to something behind him. Curious, B peered around Pedro's shoulder and gasped as he saw the reason for Ben's wide grin.

Before Pedro could voice a word of welcome, B rushed past and threw his arms around the petite woman who'd come to a stop just behind Ben. "Sister! I thought you weren't arriving until tomorrow?"

Hera giggled with joy as B picked her up and twirled her around. "I was, but I managed to catch an earlier flight—the same one as this ruffian. It's so good to see you, B. How has Dad been?"

"Oh, you know how he is," B said, putting Hera back on her feet. Hera leaned past B to greet

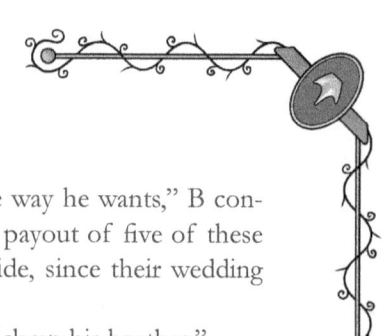

Pedro. He grabbed her hand and gave it a light squeeze.

"Complaining that Pedro won't let him stock the medical bay just the way he wants," B continued, "even though getting him everything he wants would cost us the payout of five of these jobs. Hey—where's your fiancée?" Shouldn't she have been by Hera's side, since their wedding ceremony was only a few weeks away?

Hera nodded toward Pedro. "Captain asked Claudia to sidetrack and pick up his brother."

Pedro subtly shuffled closer to Ben as B turned and glared at the Captain.

"Really, Captain? Jon and this one, both?" B snapped as he gestured at Ben.

"Hey now!" Ben protested. "I don't even get a 'hello' or a 'so glad you could take the time to help us'?"

"At least you're vaguely useful with a gun. And a wrench, I guess." B sniffed haughtily. "What can Jon do besides find ways to screw things up?"

"Wow. Thank you, baby boy. I think?" Ben turned and gave Pedro the stink-eye. "But I gotta agree with him, Cap. Why are we bringing Jon in on this?"

B glanced uneasily at Ben. It was unnerving how he always just *knew* how B was presenting, without ever asking. They hadn't seen one another in over a year and, apparently, Ben still possessed that skill.

Pedro sighed. "Getting into the actual vault where the titanium diamonds are kept will be the easy part. Getting into the building where the vault is—I need Jon for that. Or, specifically, I need one of his contacts."

"We're going to be relying on your *brother's* contacts?" B asked. "You brother, who tried to kill you a year ago? He nearly succeeded—do you remember that? Ben cried at your recovery bed."

It was one of the few times B had ever seen Ben's jovial playboy mask slip. It'd been an uncomfortable experience. B hadn't liked realizing Ben was an actual, caring human being.

Pedro shrugged, unconcerned. "I pulled through. And Jon didn't really mean it—things just got out of hand."

B bit his lower lip and looked over at Ben. They disagreed on practically everything except a mutual disdain for the Captain's brother. But, even their rare, unified front wasn't enough to sway Pedro. Before B could say anything further, however, Hera tugged his hand.

"Help me unpack? There are some details about the wedding I want your opinion on." Her eyes practically danced as she stared up at him. Despite his misgivings, B couldn't resist an ask from his sister. He nodded and let himself be dragged off, shooting one more worried glance over his shoulder.

The Merry War, 04/16/3621, 21:52

"That doesn't go there."

"It does." Ben was calm as he stretched his right arm up at an awkward angle to reattach the loose wire.

"All right, fine, it *does* go there, but it's not going to *stay* there." B's voice echoed slightly in the small room.

Ben grunted, feeling the plug pop almost immediately back out of the port he'd put it into moments before. Just to be obstinate, he tried to shove it in once more. It fell right back out again.

"Told you."

"Why haven't you changed this port?" Ben strained to feel around the edges of the socket. He jerked when a small electrical charge nipped his fingers. "Was that you?"

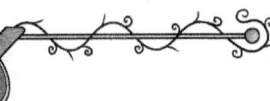

"What? No. I would *never*! And, because I can't reach it."

Ben paused, glancing over his shoulder at the speaker in the room's ceiling. B had put his body on its charging dock as soon as he and Hera had returned to the ship. It was harder to gauge B's meaning without seeing his facial expressions, but Ben had known the DI for years. He could garner much from tone alone and was *pretty* sure B had been honest when he said he hadn't shocked Ben. Though, the "never" part was a bold-faced lie.

"What do you mean, 'you can't reach it'?"

"My body's fingers—they're too short."

"Get someone else to do it, then," Ben retorted. "Get Leo."

"I don't want my dad working around a live circuit! He's a medic. What if he damages his fingers?"

"Oh, but it's fine if I hurt *my* fingers?" Ben removed his arm and examined the compartment. He sighed. He'd have to take the entire thing apart to reach the port.

"Yup," B said smugly. Ben rolled his eyes and pulled out his screwdriver, only to pause when he heard faint shouting. He cocked his head to the side to listen better, hand automatically going to his gun. "Is that Hera?"

"Yes—Claudia and Jon arrived half an hour ago. Ah, fuck. Jon's only been on board for a few minutes, and he's *already* causing trouble." B sounded distraught, and his distress was surprisingly motivating.

Ben tossed the screwdriver aside and pushed himself to his feet. "Do I need to shoot him?"

"Yes! No? I don't know. Hera's screaming at Claudia. Jon showed Hera images of Claud with another woman. But it's not...you can't see her face. *Ben*!"

"Yeah, yeah, I'm going." Ben ducked under the low ceiling of the doorway. "Where?"

"Kitchen. I'll meet you."

Moments later, Ben burst into the galley and took a second to assess the situation. Only Hera, Claudia, and Jon were present; Leo and Pedro were likely in their sound-proofed quarters, asleep at this late hour. Pedro would have been a calming influence, but Leo might have made things worse. He was extremely protective of both his biological daughter and B, who he'd illegally downloaded into the ship's mainframe shortly after Pedro had stolen The Merry War.

"Hey, hey, what's going on?" Ben raised his voice to be heard over the women's shouting. Out of the corner of his eye, he caught Jon smirking and trying to slip out of the room, but B appeared in the doorway and shoved him back inside.

"Ugh!" Jon glanced at B, his thin lips pursed in disgust. "I can't believe my brother still keeps this thing around."

"This 'thing' is about to kick your ass," B growled. His eyes burned with an unnatural light. "What did you do?"

"B, she—she cheated on me!" Hera rushed across the room and threw herself against her adopted sibling.

"Dear Gaia!" Claudia's crimson eyes narrowed as she glared at Jon. "I don't understand how you can believe this bastard's obviously fake pictures!"

Claudia practically vibrated in place, her hands clenching in and out of fists. Ben stood well out of her way, wary of what she might do. Claudia was known for her temper, though she would never direct it at Hera. No—Jon would be the more likely recipient in this scenario.

"It looks just like you! And you've done it before!" Tears ran down Hera's face.

"I cheated on you once. We were barely together!" Claudia shouted, her tail lashing at the air. "I've been with you, and you alone, since. I love *you*. I want to be *your*

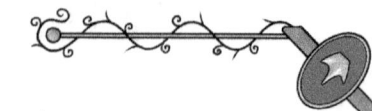

mate. Our ceremony is only weeks away. I've abided by those backward Pluotian engagement rules for the past 730 days, and for what? To ruin everything by fucking some whore who means nothing to me?"

"I don't know!" Hera wailed, burying her face against B's chest. B wrapped his arms around her shaking shoulders and growled at Jon when he made a *tsk*ing sound.

"Once a cheater, always a cheater," Jon said.

Claudia snarled at Jon's pious tone. A knife appeared between her fingers. Ben stepped in front of her, hands raised to show he was no threat. Not that he really cared if Jon were to have a fatal "accident," but if they wanted those diamonds, they needed him, so…

"Okay, okay, take a breath. Jon's an asshole. We all know that. Where are the pictures? Let's just prove they're fake, then we'll all get on with our night."

"They're not fake," Jon said smugly.

"I can literally rip you limb from limb. You know that, right?" B's tone went flat. "It would be my honest pleasure."

Hera was like a little sister to Ben, and seeing her upset made his chest hurt. Claudia had had his back in more than one fight. And B was—well, they had their differences, but he was still family. Jon had disrupted the group dynamic once again. Ben was sick of it and tired of playing peace-maker.

At this point, Ben was half-tempted to let B rip off a limb or two. It's not like they couldn't be replaced; Leo likely had a dozen in stock. An impromptu amputation wouldn't keep Jon from do-ing his part in the heist.

Probably.

"Not the best thing to do to your owner's brother, huh?" Jon raised an eyebrow.

"No one owns B," Ben said as he grabbed the tablet Claudia had gestured toward. She huffed and retreated to the opposite end of the room to pace in small circles as Ben flipped through the images.

His confidence wavered.

He wasn't an expert, of course, but the pictures didn't look fake. The Marvan in the images cer-tainly did look like Claudia. But, all females of her species had roughly the same height and build; it was only up close that one could spot distinguishing characteristics, like scars and such, between the bald, gray-skinned individuals.

"Well?" Claudia demanded after a long moment.

"Uh, B? I think I need your scanners," Ben said.

"You're joking!" Claudia came up to Ben's side and glared down at the tablet in his hand. "Those are obviously doctored."

"Here." Ben handed the tablet to B when he strode over. B flicked his right wrist, unspooling a thin cord that he quickly plugged into the device.

"B?" Claudia watched B's eyebrows furrow. "B, those are fake, right? They have to be fake, because that's *not me*."

B's face cleared. He detached his datacord and tucked it away. "They're real. The tablet hasn't been tampered with."

Hera let out a sob. They watched as she fled the room, cries echoing.

Jon turned back around as a door slammed in the distance. He shook his head at Claudia. "We have a job to do in two days," he chided. "Couldn't you have kept it in your pants a while longer?"

Jon turned on his heel and left as well, never one to stick around to clean up a mess. The image of his weasely smirk burned in Ben's brain. He wanted to go after Jon, but B grabbed his wrist.

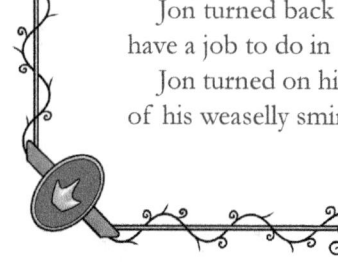

"You want something to fix?" He brandished the tablet and tossed it onto the table. "Fix this."

Then B strode off, no doubt going after his sister to comfort her. Once he left, Claudia turned to Ben and desperately shook her head.

"Ben, I didn't. I love Hera; I'd sooner cut off my own hands than betray her."

Ben considered the woman he'd worked alongside for years. "Swear it," he commanded.

"I swear on the blood of my mother, the blood of my father, and the souls of my ancestors. May they take my own soul if they find I have lied this day." A tear trickled down her right cheek.

Ben had believed her even before she'd sworn her people's most sacred oath, but hearing it certainly helped his conviction.

"All right. I'll figure it out."

The Merry War, 04/17/3621, 03:21

Hera wanted nothing more than to crawl into bed with B beside her like they'd done when they were young and still learning to use their limbs. But Pedro had a strict rule about B's synthetic body being at least fifty-percent charged unless there was an emergency. It was sweet B considered her enough of an emergency to break the rules, even a little.

With Ben on board, Pedro would likely be more lenient, but Hera wasn't about to walk down the hall and knock on his door to find out.

"Do you believe Claud?" Hera asked. B hovered in the doorway now that she was settled under the covers.

He hesitated before answering. "I want to. I mean, the pictures *were* real. But, Marvans pretty much all look alike, especially from behind."

"Claud's been so good to me all these years," Hera said. She wiped away a new trickle of tears. Had she been too hasty earlier? "I just can't believe it. At least, I don't want to believe it. Do you think Ben will be able to find something to support her innocence?"

"I hope so. I'll do a little digging of my own after my defrag. I can't have the fate of your relationship rest only in the hands of *Ben*." B crossed his arms over his chest with a huff.

Hera smiled softly at her sibling. "He's a good man, B. I've never understood the animosity between you two."

B sighed. "It's not animosity so much as it's—we just don't like each other." He shrugged uncomfortably as Hera raised her eyebrow.

"I've always rather thought it was the opposite, but whatever you tell yourself to help you sleep at night, I suppose," Hera said. "Which I'm about to try to do because, in a way, Jon's right: we've still got a heist in two days, and I'm a professional, damn it. Anyway, I'll check with you in a few hours, all right?"

Looking contemplative, B nodded and left. Hera shook her head, flicked off her bedside lamp, and buried her face in her pillow. After a moment, she moaned and flipped to her back. Claudia's familiar floral scent rose from the bedding, and Hera started sobbing again. Even the puzzle of B's and Ben's antagonistic relationship wasn't enough to distract her from the ache in her heart.

Who was she kidding? She wasn't getting any sleep tonight.

When Hera trudged into the dining area several hours later, it was with swollen, red-rimmed eyes. To her surprise, Ben was still there, hunched over the tablet and muttering to himself.

"Ben? Have you slept at all?" She trailed a hand over his shoulders as she made her way to the

coffee pot and started up a fresh brew.

"A little. Hey, can I ask you a delicate question?"

Hera turned and crossed her arms over her chest. "Uh, I suppose?"

"Where's Claudia's commitment tattoo?"

A faint blush rose in Hera's cheeks. "Neither of us have any tattoos."

Ben cocked his head and stared at Hera in silence.

She ducked, scuffing her foot on the decking. "It's on the underside of her tail—at the base."

He winced. "Damn. That's the most painful spot."

Marvans weren't supposed to tattoo themselves as a sign of their devotion to their mates until after the bonding ceremony, but Claudia had done so early. She'd known Hera still entertained the occasional doubt about Claudia's faithfulness.

Which, of course, had made Jon's evidence all the more painful.

"She never even flinched." Hera's voice was soft. Her hand unconsciously rose to the place beneath her left breast where her corresponding tattoo lay. "I cried the entire time."

"Maybe you were just emotional," Ben said.

Hera gave him a wobbly smile and wiped away a tear. Ugh. She was so tired of crying. "I was. You know me so well, Ben. Anyway, why do you ask?"

"Because I also know *Claudia*, and I thought she might've gotten inked early, so I kept looking over the images. I can't find a tattoo anywhere." Ben pushed the tablet closer to Hera. "This Marvan might not even *be* Claudia. Could you—?"

Hera turned her head away when she caught sight of an exposed gray thigh. "Please, Ben. No."

Not again. She couldn't look at those horrible pictures again—once was more than enough.

Fortunately, her brother saved her.

"What's going on?" B demanded as he entered. He stalked over to the table and loomed above Ben. Hera reflexively stepped forward, reaching out a calming hand.

"Brother, please—"

"—sister, now, actually," Ben interjected, giving Hera a quick, apologetic glance for interrupting.

Brow furrowing, Hera shifted her stare to her sibling for confirmation. After a long moment, B stopped glaring at Ben and sighed, nodding.

"All things considered, I wasn't feeling too happy sharing the same gender as Jon after his little stunt. I decided I didn't want to present as such for the foreseeable future," B explained, folding her arms over her chest.

Hera blinked in surprise, and her gaze ran down B's synthetic form. It was still draped in the matching flowy, green three-quarter length pants-and-shirt she favored regardless of gender presentation. But normally, when B decided she wanted to come across as feminine, she donned a wig of some sort. She wore none now and didn't hold herself any differently, so Hera didn't see how Ben could've known.

"How do you always know?" Hera wondered, half to herself, because Ben always knew, from the moment B had discovered gender and started experimenting. No matter how quickly B changed things up, Ben kept pace, even when everyone else was minutes to hours behind.

Ben shrugged. "I dunno, I just—feel it. Anyway, B, can you take another look at these? Hera said Claud has a commitment tat on the underside of the base of her tail, and I don't think I can see one, but—" Ben flinched as B dove across the table and grabbed the tablet, nearly hitting him in the face with her elbow in the rush to sit back down. "Okay, then. Sure, you take that."

Hera snorted in amusement as B got to work. She focused intently on the tablet surface, flicking through the pictures rapidly before unspooling a data cable and plugging in. The cord would

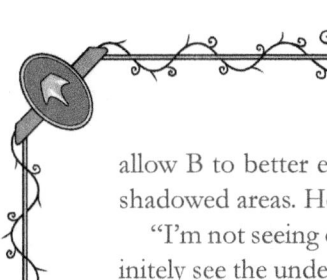

allow B to better evaluate the images pixel by pixel and extrapolate from what was visible in the shadowed areas. Hera held her breath, waiting for a verdict.

"I'm not seeing one either," B muttered. "Hera—" B's head shot up, her smile bright. "I can definitely see the underside of this Marvan's tail, and there is absolutely no tattoo. This is *not* Claudia!"

Hera's breath caught. "You—you're sure?"

"Absolutely positive. This is Jon being Jon again, preying on your insecurities and trying to cause trouble."

"And I fell for it." Hera's lower lip trembled. Tears made her sister's form blur. Hera swayed in place as she realized what she had done.

To her surprise, it was Ben who reached her first. Warm arms enfolded her and held her against a shirt that smelled like day-old sweat and gun oil. Her nose wrinkled. Human men were icky, but she appreciated the gesture.

"Hey, no, don't do that to yourself. Jon's a professional asshole, remember?"

A second later, B plastered herself to Hera's back and wrapped arms around her, too. Hera's chest warmed. Her sister must have truly loved her, because she was voluntarily touching *Ben*.

Even more amazingly, above her head, Hera heard B whisper a soft, heartfelt *"thank you."*

"Well, this is the oddest planning session I've ever walked in on."

Pedro's voice startled them apart. Ben stepped back enough for Hera to peer around his arm. The captain stood just inside the doorway to the hall, Claudia behind him, her crimson eyes locked on Hera.

The entire galaxy faded away as Hera gazed at Claudia.

"Hera?" Claudia hesitantly stepped around Pedro. Hera clutched her chest, feeling a sharp pain. Claudia was normally bold and confident. Yet, Hera's words yesterday had caused Claudia to approach as if she felt unwelcome.

"I'm sorry!" Hera stumbled toward Claudia, hand reaching out. "You were right. Of course. Of course, you were right—it wasn't you! I'm so sorry!"

She collapsed into Claudia's welcoming arms, burying her tear-streaked face against her mate's throat. Claudia's tail reassuringly wrapped around Hera's right thigh.

"Shhh, shhh, myloscha. I forgive you, my love."

Hera's knees wobbled in relief. She probably didn't deserve it, but she'd been given another chance by this wonderful woman. Hera wasn't going to squander it.

The Merry War, 04/17/3621, 10:02

"So, Ben knows?"

Hera had barely left Claudia's side since they'd reconciled, not that Claudia minded. Last night, she'd given Hera space and retreated to one of the open bunks at the other end of the ship. She'd kept her complaints to herself when B spitefully lowered the temperature in hers and Jon's rooms. If nothing else, she'd gotten to listen to Jon bitch at the DI for several hours.

"B, too. They won't tell Dad about the tattoos, either," Hera promised, squeezing Claudia around the middle.

Claudia hoped not. She'd already gotten an earful about the Marvan tradition and how "she'd better not think about dragging Leo's 'pure' daughter further into immorality." To Leo, it was bad enough they bunked together. Claudia and Hera had even kept to Pluotian tradition and not copulated for the length of their engagement.

Pluotians were so *weird*.

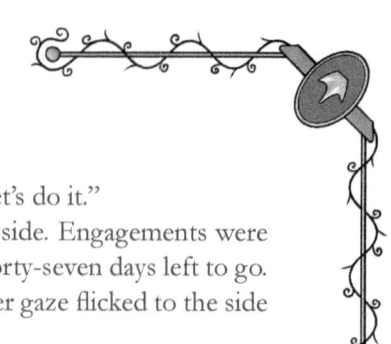

"I wish we could move up the ceremony," Claudia said wistfully.

Hera propped up her chin on Claudia's chest and bit her lower lip. "Let's do it."

"Just like that?" Claudia half-sat-up in surprise, Hera tumbling to the side. Engagements were supposed to last a full 777 rotations of the Pluotian sun. They only had forty-seven days left to go.

"I think it's far past the time I did a little compromising," Hera said. Her gaze flicked to the side in shame.

"Baby—" Claudia brought her hands up to frame Hera's face. "Culture is important. Family is important. I don't want to drive a wedge between you and your father, especially not so close to the end."

Hera stared for a long moment before shrugging and flashing Claudia a cheeky smile. "I think Dad's going to be a little more concerned with his other child entering into a relationship with a mercenary." Thank the ancestors there were privacy shields so the ship's AI wouldn't overhear conversations in crew quarters. Stunned, Claudia didn't resist as she was pushed prone again, and Hera flopped on top of her.

"I'm sorry—are you referring to B and Ben?"

"Yup."

"B—your sister? The artificial intelligence program who experiments with gender identity on a daily basis? And Ben, the self-proclaimed, life-long bachelor who's said on several occasions he doesn't believe in love? Those two? *In a relationship?*"

Hera tapped a nonsensical rhythm against Claudia's collarbone with her index finger, her body loose and warm where it was draped over Claudia's. "Ben is the only person who's ever truly understood B. We all know it, even B. She just doesn't want to admit it. Ben's only given up on love because he doesn't like sex. He doesn't think a relationship can work without it, so he's never realized what he's felt for B all these years has been love. They're perfect together; they just have preconceived notions of what a relationship should be."

She yawned and buried her face against Claudia's neck.

As Claudia's entire worldview rearranged itself, she stroked Hera's hair to soothe herself.

She supposed Hera was right…if Hera *was* right about certain facts, that is. She'd known the two far longer than Claudia had, and presumably had more insight.

"Do you think B loves him in return?" Claudia looked down and saw one mischievous brown eye sleepily peeking back at her.

"The lady doth protest too much, methinks," Hera said. "Now we just have to get them to realize how they feel about each other. Shouldn't be hard."

Knowing B and Ben, it would be *very* hard, but Hera was pretty stubborn herself.

"Nap first, though?"

"Mmm. Nap first," Hera agreed. "Then we need to figure out"—she yawned again—"what to do about Jon."

"Don't forget the robbery. It's the whole reason we're all here."

Hera's answer was a tiny kitten-snore. Claudia smiled, helplessly, at the top of her mate's head. There was a lot to do, but, for now, it could wait.

Nap first, after all.

HALL

Trixie

'a girl with a Star-Spangled heart

JOIN THE WAC NOW
Women's Army Corps
United States Army

GREETINGS from
COLUMBUS
MS
ARMY FLYING SCHOOL
Mississippi

Please join us for
BOOS & BOOZE
at our annual Halloween Party

SATURDAY | 31 | OCTOBER

The party begins at six o'clock
Hosted by the Leonatos
770 S Rosemary Ave

Dress in your best costume
for a chance to win a prize!

RSVP BY OCT. 20TH
561-650-0057

THE HONOR OF
YOUR PRESENCE IS REQUESTED
AT THE MARRIAGE CEREMONY OF

**CLAUDIA
AND
A SURPRISE!**

SATURDAY
11 / 05
TWO THOUSAND TWENTY SIX

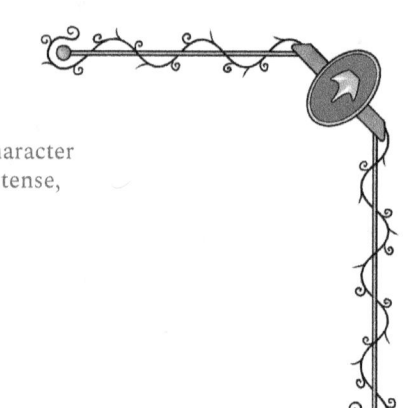

TAGS: alcohol use (casual), alternate universe, bisexual, character study, coming out, fluff, f/m, found family, modern, past tense, third person limited point of view, trans male

SOME SPARKS THAT ARE LIKE WIT

Adrian Harley

I've loved Beatrice and Benedick ever since I first encountered Much Ado About Nothing *in middle school. Naturally, I jumped at the chance to write them.* Much Ado *constantly talks about gender; as a nonbinary person, I too devote an unusually high percentage of my time to talking and thinking about gender (I in fact paused while writing this paragraph to read an article about gender). I wanted to explore how irreverent, jocular Benedick would approach gender today, and I wanted to tell a story about gender that encompassed the confusion and fun of knowing yourself and being known. Ben's coming-out journey is entirely imaginary, but I filled the piece with real things I love. I, too, am an Extremely Online Millennial. I was lucky enough to have a regular trivia night routine with wonderful friends while I lived in DC. The red-tailed hawk fact is one of my favorite fun animal facts to share, and I have a lot of those. And finally, my parents, in their early dating life, really did have a picnic to read poetry on rocks midstream.*

Casei Solus (Previous Page)
"Corkboard"

I knew I wanted to do a collage-style piece, and the story includes events for which there'd be pamphlets or invitations. I eventually settled on a bulletin board because of all the personal history and storytelling I could accomplish with it. Once I settled on F!Benedick* as the owner, I looked into their history to make sure I got that across. Then, of course, came the personal touches to give them a personality, likes, and dislikes—which is always fun.

* Editor's Note: this means "female Benedick"

Ben realized he was a guy after a normal Friday trivia night, which was deeply unfair. So many people had moving, or funny, or inspiring stories of self-discovery—which he knew before that Friday trivia night because he'd read a lot of them in his spare time. Y'know. Like good allies do.

But Ben's moment of piercing revelation, when the heavens parted and bestowed self-knowledge unto him, went like this:

The Know-Nothings, one of the best trivia teams ever to grace the stained wooden tables and murky atmosphere of Basement Bar, had just scored a hard-fought victory over their latest rivals, Shots Through the Heart. The Know-Nothings won by gambling ten points, the maximum possible, on the final bonus question, "The sound typically associated with bald eagles in American culture"—and here the trivia announcer played a screeching call, vaguely familiar—"is not, in fact, a bald eagle. What bird is it?" The correct answer, a red-tailed hawk, gave them a three-point victory over Shots Through the Heart, securing them the ultimate prizes: a ten-dollar gift card for Basement Bar, plus their pride.

The team clinked beer against wine against cocktail around the table. All six had made it tonight: Ben's old crew of Leo, Pedro, and Claudio, plus Beatrice and Hero.

"We're lucky Claudio is a birder," Hero said, smiling at Claudio and reaching across the table to squeeze his hand. Dating, if anything, had only intensified their sappiness. Unacceptable.

"You say that because you haven't been coerced into any 5 a.m. treks out of the city," Ben said.

"Like you have?" said Beatrice.

"I'll have you know that, in honor of our many years of friendship, I've accompanied Claudio on 5 a.m. birding trips not once, but *twice*," said Ben, tilting away from Hero and Claudio to give Beatrice his full attention.

"I'm astonished. Truly, you bear such hardships for your friends," Beatrice said.

"Constantly! When I lose to them at bowling tonight, it's because I want to protect their delicate egos," said Ben.

"And for all the things I've said about your ego—"

"—many things—"

"—I could never describe it as 'delicate,' " said Beatrice. "I've launched nuclear missiles at that thing, and it hasn't budged."

"We're in an arms race, and I plan to win," said Ben.

"I'd normally add a joke about toxic masculinity here, but, well…" Beatrice gestured with her rum and coke to Ben's whole self: plaid flannel, undercut, and all.

Ben thought, in that moment, *But I am a man.*

In the next moment, he thought, *Wait, no I'm not.*

And in the third moment, he thought, *Wait…*

And in the fourth moment, Pedro clapped him on the back and said something cutting about Ben's bowling abilities, as if Ben wasn't busy re-evaluating his entire existence.

By the end of that night, he wished he could blame his bowling score of 73 on the unprecedented amount of self-examination he'd performed throughout the game, but 73 was one of his better games.

Before Ben was Ben, and certainly before he suspected he was a man, he, Leo, Pedro, and Claudio had started the trivia night ritual together. They played under the name Never Gonna Give You Up—Claudio patiently explained the reference to Leo, who had always been a sixty-year-old man

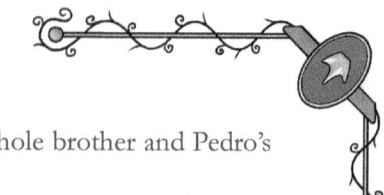

in spirit, even though he was only in his thirties. Sometimes, Pedro's asshole brother and Pedro's asshole brother's friends joined them.

They had many recurring opponents—Something Rotten reliably crushed literature rounds, and Midsummer Lovin' ran rings around everyone during the music round—but their sworn enemies were We Are No Men, a team of four people, presumably not men.

Other teams came and went, but Never Gonna Give You Up and We Are No Men remained fixtures almost every Friday. Team members came and went, too, but Ben himself attended nearly every week, as did one of the not-men. Tall, stately, looked like she knew the exact force needed to crack your skull with a slingshot and would have a great time doing it.

One Friday, the tall, stately one sauntered over to their table with a pitcher of beer and plunked it down for them.

"Consolation prize for your inevitable loss," she said.

"You could have thrown down a gauntlet and saved yourself the cost of a pitcher," said Ben.

"You want me to expose my gloves to this floor?" she said. "What have my gloves done to deserve that?"

So that was Beatrice. Always ready with a comeback. Always up for a battle of wits, though, as she put it, "Trivia is much more civilized than iocane powder."

The week after Beatrice's first direct volley, Ben bought a pitcher for her and her team. We Are No Men proceeded to trounce Never Gonna Give You Up, 160 points to 100 (other teams fell in between their scores, but those other teams were irrelevant). Ben stomped over to them after the match, carrying his mostly empty Guinness.

"Did you get the one about the top-selling video game console?" he asked.

"Yeah, Hero knew that one," Beatrice said.

"John said it was the Xbox 360. The Xbox! I can't believe the others listened to him!"

"You've got to watch out for those fake nerd boys," Beatrice said. "What did you think it was?"

"*I* had it right. Nobody believed me about the PlayStation 2. As if Claudio hasn't been deferring to my video game expertise since Ocarina of Time!"

"Ahh, so you *do* bring some value to the team. Shouldn't you be rubbing that in their faces?" said Beatrice.

"Oh, I've been doing that since that round ended. They're going to throw me in a dumpster if I bring it up again."

"You would prefer *I* throw you in a dumpster? I'm flattered," said Beatrice.

"As the smartest of my friends, I deserve only the most qualified dumpster-flinger," said Ben.

Life moved on. Leo got promoted, which meant he sometimes surrendered to the capitalist grindstone and worked into the evening. Pedro finally stopped pretending John was an acceptable addition to the group after John tried to convince Claudio that Pedro was stealing his girlfriend (John's motives for this remained unclear). Claudio went on date nights with said girlfriend until a mutually amicable breakup.

Trivia nights could get *really* small.

Ben's phone buzzed against the table, its screen bright in the gloom of Basement Bar. Ben sighed.

"Leo has abandoned us," he said to Claudio, the only other attendee. Claudio made a face.

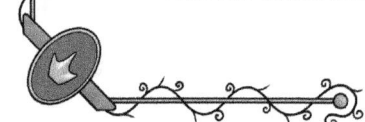

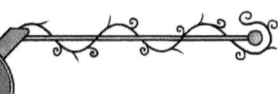

"Maybe we should call it a night? We could get dinner that *isn't* loaded tater tots."

"Your girl is still here," said Ben, gesturing to the closest end of the bar, where Beatrice and Hero sat. Claudio blushed. "You believe in these things called 'romance' and 'love,' and although I am proud to have no practical experience in the matter, I hear it works better if you actually talk to the woman."

"She's probably got someone! She's gorgeous! And you and Beatrice have your thing…I don't want to make it weird…"

Ben had been all set to talk about how Hero was *fine*, but not *impossibly* attractive, and it wasn't like all attractive people had preexisting romantic commitments. Then he registered what Claudio had said. "Our *thing*?" he asked.

"Look, I'm just saying, most of my girlfriends have been less excited by compliments than you two get about each other's insults."

"Maybe…and I say this as a friend, an honorary bro, a brother from another gender…maybe you're just bad at compliments, dude."

Claudio had no counter to Ben's keen observation. Or maybe he didn't reply because Beatrice and Hero had just arrived at their table.

Beatrice nudged Hero. "Speak, cuz."

Hero said, "Um…"

Beatrice sighed and said to the table, "She has a proposition for you. This was not my idea."

Hero found her tongue, looking at Claudio as if he was the only other person in this bar that still smelled like cigarette smoke a decade after the citywide ban on restaurant smoking. She said, "Since there's only two of us, and there's only two of you…well, trivia is more fun with more people, and we've known each other for a while now…maybe we could join forces tonight?"

Claudio said, "Absolutely!" without even a *second* of hesitation, like a golden retriever who had just seen God, and God was carrying a whole box of Milk-Bones.

"Great!" said Hero. Beatrice hip-checked her, and the smaller woman half-fell into the booth, catching herself so she sat upright and didn't quite tumble into Claudio. Not that either of them would have minded that, from the way they smiled at each other.

"I'll get us our drinks, Hero," Beatrice said brightly before heading to the bar.

Ben said, "I need another one," leapt up, and followed Beatrice, shoving his way through the press of people to stand next to her at the crowded bar, their arms against each other. When she deigned to look down at him, the bar lights reflected in her brown eyes looked like stars, like a summer night. He could get lost in them. Ben shook his head to rattle out those thoughts. Claudio must be contagious.

"Matchmaking? Romance? Right in front of my salad?" he demanded.

"It makes them happy, doesn't it?" Beatrice said. "Now to me, romance seems a bit like leaping off the Grand Canyon because you hear there might be pillows and fluffy ponies at the bottom. But they've been sighing from across the room since they set eyes on each other, and if sighing in closer proximity makes them as happy as I am on my own, let them have at it!"

"For once, something we agree on," said Ben. "Romance is for fools. You'll never catch me prancing around after some woman—some other woman—writing sonnets, or buying roses, or rhapsodizing about her beauty."

"Yes, you'd only look half as foolish as usual. Impossible," said Beatrice.

Once Hero and Claudio had started talking, wild horses couldn't have dragged them apart. In-

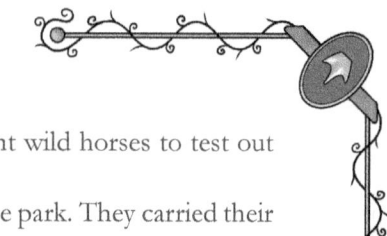

deed, early in their dating life, Ben even looked up whether he could rent wild horses to test out that prospect.

"Do you know what they did last weekend? They went on a picnic in the park. They carried their picnic baskets out to the rocks in the middle of the stream and read poetry to each other," Ben told the table, infusing his voice with as much disgust as it could hold. Leo, Pedro, and Beatrice were the trivia crew that night.

"People do those sorts of things when they fall in love," said Leo, as if he had decades more experience in the area than Ben rather than merely a few years.

"Another mark against love, if you ask me. It comes with such mandatory impracticality," said Ben.

"It's going to be hilarious when you fall in love," said Pedro.

"Ha. Ha. Politicians will be honest, Facebook will stop being evil, and fish will climb trees before you see me swooning over a woman."

"Speaking as the other representative of the gender at the table, womankind heaves a sigh of relief," said Beatrice. Ben had the briefest moment of discomfort—like a moth had brushed his leg, or a fly buzzed past his ear. Certainly not a moment to linger on. He had more important things to do: beating Beatrice at their rhetorical games and joining with his friends to beat everyone else at trivia.

After the unexpectedly introspective trivia-and-bowling night…after the long, introspective Metro ride out to his apartment, in a neighborhood where the one-bedrooms approached something like affordable…after completing the usual evening rituals of disrobing, re-robing, and washing up…after all that, Ben fell asleep in an instant. Understanding oneself was exhausting.

The next morning, he mused on the tiring nature of gender revelations, turning his usual wit to the matter. He'd built up a solid soliloquy, if he did say so himself (and he always did), when he froze, his hand stopping in the middle of brushing his teeth.

Who was he going to share his thoughts with? Who was his audience?

Who had he been picturing saying these things to as he narrated his own life?

He could tell his friends. They would be understanding. Anyway, he was already "one of the boys." (How many times had they said that? How many times had he gotten a comforting glow from hearing that?)

Ben nodded decisively at his reflection in the mirror. It was a good, firm nod. Manly. He rubbed his chin with the hand not holding his toothbrush.

He'd tell his friends, and things would go on exactly as normal, and nothing substantial would have to change in his blithe stroll through life.

Weeks passed.

He didn't tell them.

He lost count of the articles he read on transmasculinity. He joined a Reddit group. He checked out books from the library. He spent so long on name websites that diaper and baby store ads stalked him throughout the internet. Early in the haze of this process, he picked the name Ben, but he still went to four different name sites just to be sure. Just to be sure! He'd never been indecisive in his life! No, he picked a stance or food or outfit or bar and stuck with it. And if people made fun of him or looked down on him for it, he made a joke out of the whole enterprise but, crucially,

did not budge a fraction of an inch. That was his way.

With all the pep talks he was giving himself about decisiveness, he should have known that he'd end up coming out by accident.

He and Claudio were having a throwback-video-game Saturday: they played Halo 2, trash-talked each other, ate pizza, and generally tried to recapture the air of Claudio's parents' basement circa 2005, except with booze.

They were tied for the night, two and two. Claudio had taken an early lead, but had seemed distracted these last two rounds. Last kill, Ben had charged him down with an energy sword from clean across the map, right in his line of sight, yet *still* killed him. This time, Ben had the sniper rifle—not as suitable for Leeroy Jenkins shenanigans, but still satisfying.

Ben caught sight of Claudio.

Claudio had not seen Ben.

Ben began to aim.

"So…you're a woman," said Claudio, out of the blue, like that was a normal conversational opener.

"No I'm not," said Ben. And then said, "Shit." He moved his thumb to snipe Claudio and distract him, but Claudio paused the game. Ben glanced away from the screen, and, oh no, Claudio had his "sincere" face on.

"Are you being serious right now?" Claudio asked.

Ben had to tamp down his immediate, gut response of "Am I ever serious?" It was the hardest thing he'd ever done, and he would make sure Claudio appreciated that once they'd gotten this conversation out of the way. Instead, Ben said, "Yes. This isn't exactly how I planned to tell you."

"Thank you for telling me! I'm honored to know. What gender are you instead?"

"I'm a man. Uh. My name is Ben," Ben said.

"Ben! It suits you," said Claudio.

"I thought so. That's why I picked it," Ben said.

"If you need anything, I am always here for you. You know that, right?" said Claudio.

Ben felt the warmth of sitting by a fireplace on a winter day, like holding hot chocolate while swathed in blankets. He had no idea how to respond. So he said, "Thanks, man," and realized to his dismay that he was choked up.

"Anytime, *man*," said Claudio.

"Please unpause the game so I can snipe you," said Ben before genuine emotion could overwhelm him.

"Just one more thing. Who else are you telling?"

"I'm going to come out to the rest of the trivia team by Friday," said Ben, who up until that second had had no such plan.

"Great!" Claudio said, and leaned sideways to tug him into a one-armed hug.

Ben considered his options. "Wait, Claudio, you were going to say something. What was up with that whole 'you're a woman' thing?"

"Don't worry about it! I'll tell you later," said Claudio, releasing Ben and at last unpausing the game.

With a deadline now imposed, Ben turned his sights to Pedro.

Ben and Pedro were technically coworkers, though the labyrinthine structure and constantly expanding nature of their corporation meant they'd never once worked together. They'd met

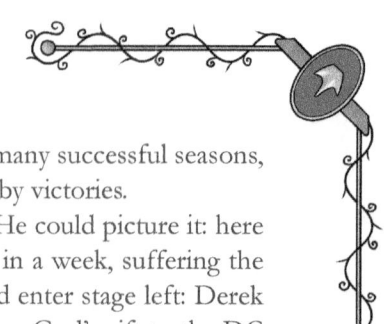

through the company softball team, which Pedro had captained through many successful seasons, if success was measured by beers drunk and good times had, rather than by victories.

Ben considered waiting until softball practice but dismissed that idea. He could picture it: here stands Ben, revealing personal truths about himself for the second time in a week, suffering the mortifying ordeal of being known. Here stands Pedro, sympathizing. And enter stage left: Derek from accounting, asking why he's not first in the batting order, as if he was God's gift to the DC intra-company softball league.

No. Ben needed to get Pedro alone. He proposed lunch.

On Tuesday, they met up and headed to the café on the first floor of their office building. The café charged $10 for a prepackaged turkey sandwich with "artisanal" printed on the label, but Pedro liked their salads, and Ben didn't fancy walking anywhere else in the swampy summer heat.

Ben grabbed a roast beef sandwich, the last remaining bag of potato chips that wasn't pretending to be anything fancier than potatoes in grease and salt, and the table farthest from other people. Pedro followed shortly after with a monstrous salad.

Ben jumped right in. He'd made his decision, damn it, and there was no point dithering now.

"So, I realized I'm a man. I'm trans."

Pedro paused with his fork halfway to his mouth.

"No kidding?" he asked.

"No kidding," Ben confirmed.

Pedro put down his fork. "That's wonderful! I'm so proud of you for understanding yourself like that. Self-knowledge is so important," he said.

"Did you start listening to those self-awareness podcasts Claudio talks about, then?" said Ben.

"What would you like to be called?" said Pedro, ignoring the question.

"Ben," said Ben.

"Ben! Great name, great name. I want you to know I'm here for you, Ben. Whatever you need."

"That's great," said Ben, who had no idea what he might need. "Thanks," he added. He took a large bite of his sandwich to avoid having to say more. Pedro was still beaming at him like Ben had hit a home run (or at least what Ben theorized Pedro's home-run expression would look like, as Ben had never had occasion to receive one of those).

"Who else are you coming out to?" Pedro asked.

Ben chewed his extra-large sandwich mouthful, regretting his stalling tactic of choice. Pedro smirked at the awkward moment, then attempted to hide his amusement. Ben wished he'd laughed. Once the sandwich bite was safely consumed, Ben said, "I told Claudio, and I'll tell the rest of the trivia team by Friday. And then. Uh. I'll go from there, I guess."

Pedro nodded earnestly. "Coming out is a process, I know. Let me know if you need any advice. Not that my being bisexual is the same as you being trans, of course. But it takes a lot of courage to share your authentic self."

Ben could only nod in reply. What was he supposed to say? He couldn't make a self-deprecating joke now, because now *Pedro* was being vulnerable and open. And Ben wasn't the most perceptive person, but, over the years, Pedro had dropped enough mentions of the awful reactions he'd gotten when people found out he was bi. So if Ben acted like coming out wasn't courageous…well, Ben may be an ass, but he wasn't *that* much of an ass.

But with humor taken out of Ben's toolbox of conversational tactics, he was left with only the rusted wrench of sincerity, underused and unfamiliar, and the screwdriver of deflection and small talk.

"How's work?" Ben asked.

To avoid another ordeal of people smiling understandingly at him, that night, Ben came out to Leo over text.

Ben

b

> Hey, man, so you know, I'm trans. I'm a man now.
> My name is Ben.

Ben set the phone aside. He sorted the mail pile he'd been neglecting. He cleaned his bathroom sink. He considered dusting his TV, and that's when he admitted to himself that he was avoiding his phone. He picked it back up.

Leo

l

> Ben Ben, I am so proud of you. 🎉🎊
> This is a brave thing to do. 🎊
> Please let me know if there is anything I can do to
> support you. 🫂

"Is this my life now?" Ben asked the empty air of his living room. "People being *sincere* at me?"

Ben typed "Thanks," thought about it, and added an exclamation point at the end. Message sent, he collapsed into his sagging corduroy armchair and pulled up Netflix.

His phone buzzed.

l

> In what situations should I call you Ben? And what
> pronouns are you using?

"Did he Google 'what to say to your transgender friend?' " Ben asked the TV.

On the TV, Nicole Byer said, "Hi, and welcome to *Nailed It!*" This did not answer Ben's question.

b

> I'm coming out to the trivia team. That's it for now.
> Dude pronouns.
> He/him
> In case you were about to google "what are dude
> pronouns"

l

> Ha ha have
> *ha
> Maybe! ☺

b

> Never change, Leo.

l

> You change as much as you want to make you
> happy! ☺ ✳ 🎊

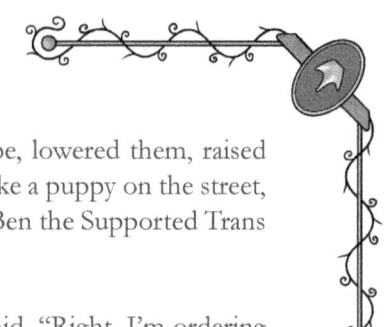

Ben stared at his phone for a long time. He raised his thumbs to type, lowered them, raised them, lowered them. He set down his phone. He felt…loved? But loved like a puppy on the street, loved without personality. Loved like a museum exhibit—this way to see Ben the Supported Trans Man!

But still, nonetheless, loved.

Ben reread Leo's last message again, gave himself a little shake, and said, "Right, I'm ordering cookies." He turned his attention to the amateur bakers who were doing their darndest to create underwater-themed cupcakes and failing spectacularly. He may have sniffled a little. But surely that was because he hadn't dusted the TV.

In theory, Ben could come out to Beatrice and Hero over text.

The problem was, Ben didn't text Hero. And although Ben texted Beatrice, their texts…well…

When the two teams had merged, they needed a new name. Hero had suggested "Pit of Voles." Ben had laughed…and Beatrice had too.

Beatrice understood a reference to fanfiction.net. Which meant…

"Oh! Did you write fanfiction back in the 2000s too?" Hero asked Ben, full of cheer, as if she was asking about something innocuous and charming.

"I plead the fifth," said Ben.

"Is your Pit of Voles account still online?" said Beatrice, a wicked gleam in her eyes.

"Is *yours*?" asked Ben, and the horror that came over Beatrice's face was all the answer he needed.

That night, Ben texted Beatrice for the first time. He sent a link to the oldest *Supernatural* fic he could find along with the message, "This you?" (He'd considered sending the *Very Secret Diaries*, but that would have implied that Beatrice was now a bestselling author, and he didn't wish to bestow that honor upon her.)

An hour later, he received a screenshot of the first lines of *My Immortal*, and the message, "This you?"

Since then, every couple of weeks, one or the other of them would text an old, ridiculous fic. And that was the entirety of Beatrice and Ben's text-based relationship. The last fic linked had featured Naruto and Sasuke as *Iron Chef* competitors (who, obviously, fell in love). Ben couldn't possibly follow that up with "By the way, I'm a man."

Trivia night rolled around, as it always did, given the linear nature of time. Ben still hadn't told Beatrice. Or Hero, but Ben figured her reaction would be "Claudio: Redux"—affirmative and kind because that was just how she was.

If Beatrice tried to be kind and sweet and mild and treat Ben like a glass vase instead of a person, Ben didn't know what he'd do.

Ben arrived at trivia first. His stomach jitters gradually increased as his friends arrived, one by one, but still Beatrice didn't come. He'd started with water instead of beer, and deeply regretted that decision as the minutes squirmed by like slugs. Just when the jitters were about to vibrate him out of his seat and into the air, Beatrice and Hero arrived.

Beatrice gave everyone an odd look. Ben noticed, for the first time, that his friends were sitting expectantly, looking at him.

Well. No turning back now.

He nodded his "hellos" to Hero and Beatrice.

He met Beatrice's eyes.

"So, I'm trans. I'm transgender. I'm a man," he said.

For a single moment, Beatrice's eyes widened in surprise. The dim lights of Basement Bar still looked like stars reflected in them.

And then she grinned her most satisfied grin.

"I should have known you were a man! Why, only a man could be as arrogant as you," she said.

Ben laughed and laughed and laughed in relief, stomach jitters taking flight and leaving without him.

"Only a man could so plague womankind," Beatrice continued, warming to her subject.

"Hey. Hey! Women love me. All women except you," Ben protested.

"Ah, but the depth of my disdain for you averages out, don't you see? It's an average of plague," argued Beatrice.

"Excuse me, Spiders Beatrice, you know what they say about outliers," said Ben.

As Hero and Claudio laughed…as Leo leaned over to ask Pedro what on earth spiders had to do with anything…as Beatrice readied her next volley…Ben basked in the glow of a normal trivia night. Everything and everyone was back in place, but even better than before, like an orchestra that had finished its warm-up, tightened strings, and tweaked mouthpieces, and now could create a precisely in-tune note. His friends loved him, and he loved them. He especially loved Beatrice, who'd never lost sight of who he was, who'd restored this perfect harmony.

And if he didn't come to some obvious conclusions about the nature of that love right away, well, surely he can be forgiven. It had been a trying week.

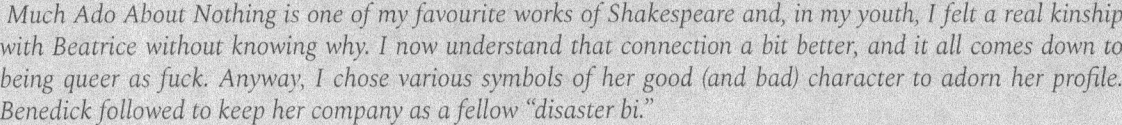

A. A. Weston (Next Pages)
"Benedick (Disaster Bi)" & "Beatrice (Disaster Bi)"

Much Ado About Nothing is one of my favourite works of Shakespeare and, in my youth, I felt a real kinship with Beatrice without knowing why. I now understand that connection a bit better, and it all comes down to being queer as fuck. Anyway, I chose various symbols of her good (and bad) character to adorn her profile. Benedick followed to keep her company as a fellow "disaster bi."

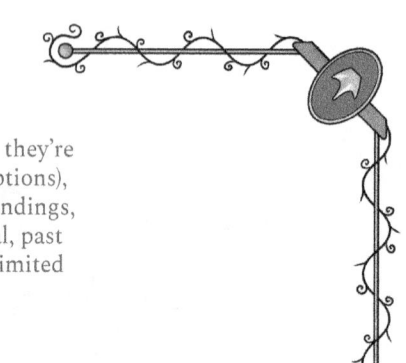

TAGS: berlin, bipoc, coffee shop, elderly, everyone knows they're in love but them, f/f, first kiss, fluff, food (graphic descriptions), genderqueer, germany, idiots to lovers, m/m, misunderstandings, modern, non-fanfiction story inspired by source material, past tense, performer, pining (mutual), theater, third person limited point of view, trans male, unreliable narrator

RUCKUS, DRAMA, AND 2-METRE-TALL PEN-GUINS

Era J. M. Couts

I wanted to write something set during current times, and I wanted it to be set in queer Berlin. I was a little unsure if I would be able to keep the characters IC*, and I also wanted to "recreate" the chaoticness of Much Ado About Nothing *but with a new, fresh feeling to it. Deciding to make my story about an amateur theatre group rehearsing the play instead of the main characters of* Much Ado About Nothing *was an early choice. Everything else from that point was due to the characters gaining life and making their own story.*

* Editor's Note: IC is a common fandom abbreviation that means "in character."

Jinji had a problem. He should've been paying proper attention to the rehearsal. He knew he should've. He was new to the theatre world, and he'd only run through his part twice, so his perfectionist nature yelled loudly in the back of his mind for him to focus, learn his lines, and make his theatre debut a splashing success.

Said perfectionist nature was, obviously, losing the war against his—whatever-it-was—that made him keep staring at fellow actor Pascoal instead of paying attention to the rehearsal in front of him. Jinji would love to be able to listen to his perfectionism; it had led him to great success in his studies and enabled him to deliver the level of execution he expected of himself, but his—whatever-it-was—was a lot more interested in memorizing the way Pascoal's hair flowed when he moved.

"Why, that's spoken like an honest drovier: so they sell bullocks. But did you think the King *would have served you thus?"*

Oh no, Jinji winced, his attention pulled from Pascoal to the other two men onstage.

Actually, Jinji had *two* problems.

"I *pray you*, learn your bloody lines before the rehearsal, Bren!" Carlo snapped, throwing his hands in the air, and Jinji mentally cursed. "You're always forgetting your words! We cannot rehearse like this!"

"If you would just follow the damn script even when I have *one* word wrong, maybe we could actually rehearse?" Bren crossed his arms defensively over his chest, his freckled nose scrunching as he frowned. Carlo's eye roll could be seen from the back of the theatre.

Jinji cursed again. There were days where he genuinely liked the amateur theatre group he'd joined, but there were others he wondered why he was wasting his time. It was ten past ten, and he could be doing something else. The smartest choice would be to study for the university exam he had in three days. Yet there he was, two weeks away from their play premiere, with his poor soul crying because a) he couldn't focus on his lines and b) two of their main actors spent the entire rehearsal time bitching at each other like fifteen year olds.

"I bet you a lokum cube they will stay at this for a good ten minutes." Brigit nudged Jinji gently, moving around on the old bench to make herself more comfortable. Her teasing smile made Jinji sigh.

Sitting next to Brigit, Hatice giggled. "Ten minutes? I say we will not have any more rehearsing to do tonight!" she said, stretching her legs in front of her. "I bet you two lokum cubes they will not even notice if we leave now."

"Am I the only one worried we won't be ready in time for the premiere?" Jinji eyed the ladies, with their light moods and high spirits, and tried not to frown. He was certainly the youngest in their theatre group; he was also—alongside the always warm, stunning, Jinji's "problem number one" Pascoal—the most recent to join. He didn't have much experience with theatre—or with any stage art for that matter—but his nature demanded he succeed. Shouldn't they be able to run the play from start to end when they were a mere 14 days away from the big night?

"You worry too much, pumpkin," Hatice said, and Jinji sighed again. She'd been saying that since the day he'd joined the group, three months before. "Your generation seems to be built to worry! Our grandkids are the same. Always worrying about one thing or another."

"You will have worry wrinkles by the age of twenty-five if you keep frowning like that," Brigit warned, nudging him again. Carlo's cursing onstage grew so loud it nearly drowned her out. "And then, when you get to our age, you will look like our rescued Sphynx cat!"

"No, but for real," he said, trying not to laugh at the way Hatice squeezed her warm-ochre cheeks together, mimicking how their cat looked. "Our Claudio and Benedick fight every single time they're onstage together, and we've never done the entire play in one go. I'm the villain, but they're the ones ruining this. How are you not worried?"

"Maybe we should cast Carlo as Beatrice instead of you, Brigit. They would be perfect!" Hatice suggested, letting go of her cheeks and returning to her somehow-mischievous-yet-oh-so-innocent old-lady smile.

"Those two have known each other for years and always find one thing or another to argue about." Brigit looked at the men onstage with what Jinji almost thought was fondness. There, Carlo walked dramatically around, cursing, while Bren moped and frowned. Between them, looking from one to the other as if watching a tennis match, was "problem number one," and the main instigator of "problem number two": Pascoal. Brigit giggled quietly. "Don Pedro, Prince Charming, Pascoal is quite dreamy, isn't he? I understand Carlo and Bren fighting for his attention."

"But Pascoal Prince Charming is a sweet toasted mushroom that does not really get the drama

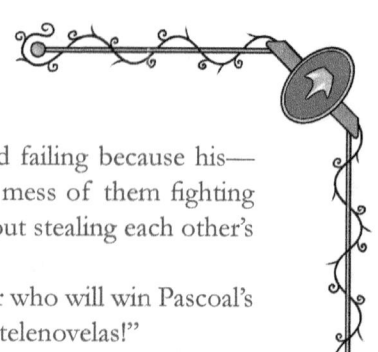

here," Hatice said. Jinji snorted loudly, trying not to look at Pascoal (and failing because his—whatever-it-was—kept prompting him to stare). Hatice continued, "This mess of them fighting over Pascoal is more entertaining than the time Carlo and Bren argued about stealing each other's leather costumes for Folsom!"

"I bet you a lokum cube they will start some ridiculous competition over who will win Pascoal's heart!" Brigit's enthusiasm was almost contagious. "This is better than the telenovelas!"

"Which reminds me—we are missing a *Tatort* episode." Hatice smiled softly at her wife. "Shall we leave these silly boys here and go home?"

"You're leaving already?" Jinji asked, glancing at the stage in the vain hope that their fellow actors had finished fighting. "What about the rehearsal?!"

"Oh, pumpkin, you will not be able to get anything other than profanities from Carlo's mouth for the rest of the night," Brigit said as she and Hatice stood and got ready to leave. As a courtesy, Jinji rose as well.

"You might get some things in, but I sure *do not* want to stay here to watch that!" Hatice snorted loudly before she stretched to her tiptoes to pat her hand on top of Jinji's head. "Don't get in trouble with those three sillies."

"But…" Jinji mumbled as they waved goodnight and walked away, "what about the play?"

Almost two years ago, Jinji had met Hatice at the tea-shop-slash-bookstore she owned at the center of Berlin's queer district. He'd walked in with a gigantic dark cloud over his head, shoes wet from the fresh snow, and sat at a table in a corner, staring at nothing. Those first few weeks living in a new city, his head had felt like exploding, a little too much of everything pressuring him.

He'd barely noticed when a small, tulip-shaped glass of a dark, rich liquid was placed in front of him, along with a dessert plate full of lokum cubes. He blinked, trying to find his voice.

"I haven't ordered yet…"

"This one is on the house, pumpkin," Hatice had said, as if talking to her own grandson. "It will brighten your spirit a little—hopefully enough to shoo away that gloomy aura over you."

It had. For a brief moment, it had.

There, he'd met Pascoal. One day, when Jinji had felt like shit again, and the world had seemed dark and hopeless, and his eyes were so blurred with tears he couldn't read his notes for an upcoming exam, Pascoal had randomly sat in front of him and said: "The colossal penguin was like 2 metres tall! Can you imagine how freaking adorable a penguin that big would be?!"

"A 2 m tall penguin is a freaking Godzilla wannabe. How is that adorable!?" Jinji had blurted, a mix of confusion, concern, and absurdity washing over him.

Pascoal had looked at him with stars in his eyes and the universe in his smile, warm as the summer sun, fresh as the first gust of air after a long winter and said, "We should be friends!"

Denying Pascoal anything was impossible, Jinji soon discovered. Pascoal was the type of person who made others feel comfortable just by being beside them. He was caring by nature, warm, and somehow brought a sort of zen-ness to the environment.

So Jinji had come back the next day, and Pascoal was there, welcoming. He came back the day after that, too, and—as expected—Pascoal was there as well. Jinji came back after he'd completely shaved his head and bought a bright-pink dress. He came back in a wig and heels. He came back in combat boots and after he'd tried to grow a beard. He came back when he had nothing on his mind and when his mind felt about to burst. He came back when he felt himself, when he felt like someone else, and when he wasn't sure who he was at all.

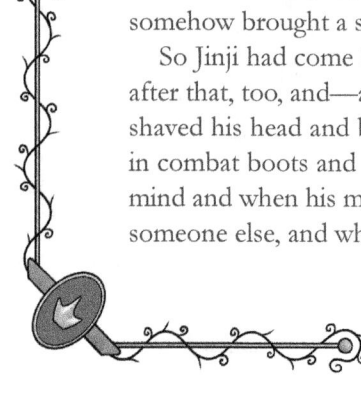

And, every single time, Pascoal had greeted him with warmth and an honest smile. From the counter, Hatice would sneak them one little lokum cube each.

In an eternity that felt like a blink of an eye, Pascoal and the tea shop had made Jinji feel like he was, finally, home. Once, he'd been horrified at the idea of standing out. He'd forced himself to comply with the heteronormative pressure surrounding him, afraid of being *judged* for who he was, judged for even daring to question that he might be anyone other than who those around him pre-determined him to be. But here, in this foreign city, no one gave a damn about who he was or what he was wearing. Here, people were so used to the weird and the weirder that he was just another fish in a multicoloured pond. Here, he could be whoever he wanted to be! He could experiment, explore himself; he could *discover* who he was and be *seen* for who he was.

Jinji would have never thought he would be at home in an old tea shop with a walking animal-fun-facts encyclopedia and two eighty-year-old ladies, with English as the common language of their recently formed found family. Yet there he was. His new friends were as unique and particular as Jinji, and finally he felt like he'd found somewhere he belonged.

Then, he'd met Carlo. Brigit and Hatice were part of an amateur theatre crew and, every now and then, they would organise meetings for their crew at the tea shop. Jinji usually missed them—the meetings happened during his classes—but one day Carlo stayed behind after the meeting, and they finally had a conversation.

Carlo was fun, dramatic, and always exaggerating things, with a sharp tongue and a twisted sense of humour that no one laughed at. He was the one who suggested Jinji join their theatre crew.

"We're looking for new actors for our next play. We're doing Shakespeare! Much shorter, of course, nobody's got time for three hours of blah blah blah nonsense!" he had said one evening, pacing around the books area. "We haven't finished the casting—we need two more people. Wanna join us? We need young blood!"

"Stop talking like an old man, Carlo. You are barely in your thirties!" Hatice intervened as Jinji looked down at the Shakespeare play Carlo had dropped on his lap. "But he is right, pumpkin. You could join us. It will be fun!"

"Well," Jinji had mused, grabbing the play and reading the first few lines of *Much Ado About Nothing*. "It can't be bad, right?"

Except it was.

With 13 days until the premiere, Carlo and Bren argued about the masks they needed for the masquerade ball scene. Pascoal asked if he could have his blue-pink-and-white pin glued to his Don Pedro mask. Brigit and Hatice giggled while trying on their own costumes.

With 12 days until the premiere, Bren got angry about the lack of emotion in the way Carlo said "*Yet say I, he is in love.*" Pascoal got distracted by a beetle on the wall ("Jinji, did you know beetles chew their food?"). Brigit and Hatice tapped Jinji's head and offered him more lokum cubes.

With 11 days until the premiere, they argued because Bren had decided to be theatrical and throw himself in Pascoal's arms during Claudio and Hero's wedding scene. Pascoal laughed, picked him up, and twirled him around while Carlo screamed at the top of his lungs and Jinji ignored the sting from his—whatever-it-was! Hatice decided to mimic Bren and throw herself into Brigit's arms, then they exploded in giggles again. No more rehearsing for the day.

With 10 days until the premiere, Jinji was losing it. No one in the group was taking the play seriously, his perfectionist nature was howling in frustration, and he was so done with it. So done!

"But doesn't it bother you?!" he interrogated Pascoal at the end of the night as they walked

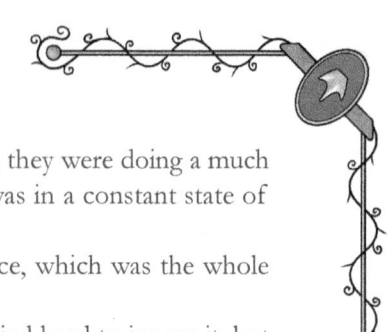

together to the bus station. *Much Ado About Nothing* was a long play. Sure, they were doing a much shorter version since they were only a crew of six (plus a director who was in a constant state of mild anxiety), but they still had a solid hour of play to present.

"Doesn't what bother me?" There was always a smile on Pascoal's face, which was the whole reason for the chaos with Carlo and Bren.

Jinji's "problem number one" was that Pascoal was hot as fuck! Jinji tried hard to ignore it, but damn! There was only so much Jinji could do when a demigod in a human body *smiled* at him. Pascoal's face was so symmetrical and beautiful, Jinji caught himself getting lost in his soft dimples and the high planes of his cheekbones. Branding Pascoal as Jinji's "problem number one" was not an exaggeration.

And, as if "problem number one" wasn't enough, Hatice convinced Pascoal to join the theatre group, and "problem number two" was created.

Jinji was sure he'd seen Bren have a heart attack the first time Pascoal grinned at him. And, because Bren had been having a moment, Carlo—*obviously* by accident—bumped into Pascoal and spilled coffee all over his white T-shirt. Pascoal, zen, beautiful, peaceful Pascoal, of course, had then removed the stained T-shirt to reveal sculpted muscles and flawless bronze skin and the faded lines of his top scars. Fighting back a blush, Jinji had looked away from Pascoal's statue-like body, because *bloodydamnhell!* As he had looked away, he could have sworn he saw the moment something snapped inside Carlo and Bren's brains (while Hatice's phone mysteriously played a song about it "becoming too hot in here" or something). Carlo and Bren's arguments had become a regular feature of rehearsals immediately after that.

Forcing his mind back to reality, Jinji frowned at Pascoal. Their bus was still nowhere to be seen.

"Doesn't Carlo and Bren's constant fighting bother you?" Jinji asked. He was sure he'd have worry lines on his forehead by the end of rehearsals. He really would look like Hatice and Brigit's cat. "We haven't even been able to rehearse the whole play yet."

"They're such good people!" Pascoal exclaimed with a happy look on his face. Jinji tried to stop frowning. He'd had a feeling talking with Pascoal about his worries wouldn't prove successful, but he had to try. Brigit and Hatice were clearly okay with the mess that their rehearsals had become, and Carlo and Bren were so deep in their own crap they didn't even see the problem. Pascoal seemed like Jinji's last hope to do something about it.

"Listen," Jinji started to explain. The blush attacked his face again as nervous bubbles popped in his stomach. Pascoal's face was close to his, because that was how Pascoal talked to people. The definition of personal space was clearly different from culture to culture. Not that Jinji minded, really, just…blushing turned his brain into pudding, and his—whatever-it-was—was far too excited by Pascoal's proximity. "10 days from now, we have a one-hour play to present to almost 300 people, and we haven't done the whole play in one go without any arguments."

"We've done all of the scenes at least twice," Pascoal shrugged casually. "You're worrying too much. Carlo and Bren are very passionate about the play, and they want it to be perfect. I'm sure they will be amazing on the premiere night!"

"But with all their fighting?" Jinji asked again. He didn't understand why everyone was so chill about this.

"Ah, Jinji," Pascoal said, dropping an arm around Jinji's shoulders and pulling him into a half-hug. Jinji's cheeks flushed, and he was sure his heart was running a marathon. "Breathe! Have some fun! It will be fine. After all, everyone has a lover's quarrel at one time or another!"

"W-wait," Jinji muttered, trying to gather the brain cells scattered by Pascoal's charm. "Lover's quarrel?!"

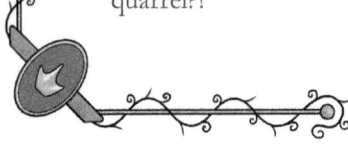

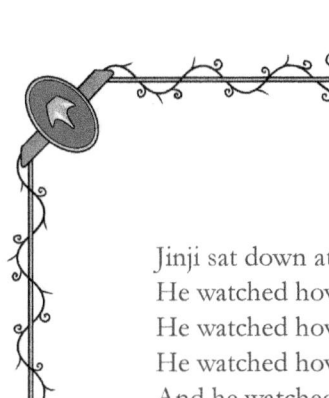

Jinji sat down at the next evening's rehearsal and simply watched.

He watched how Carlo ignored Pascoal until the moment Bren walked in.

He watched how Bren looked hurt that Carlo kept staring at Pascoal like a dazzled teenager.

He watched how they pined over each other whenever the other wasn't looking.

And he watched how each seemed to force themselves to get Pascoal's attention.

"They cannot be that stupid…" Jinji muttered, palms pressed together on his nose, staring at the men in front of him. "Are they that stupid?!"

"Yes," Hatice chuckled, glasses perched on the tip of her nose as she re-checked her lines. "My great-grandchildren are smarter than those two, and they are toddlers."

"Love has funny ways of showing itself," Brigit giggled, watching the new fight that had broken out onstage. Pascoal was, somehow, shirtless again. Jinji was, once more, blushing furiously while trying really hard not to stare (and failing).

"But they could just, you know, talk about it instead of trying to—what? Make the other jealous by flirting with Pascoal?"

"Oh, yes, communication! Communication is the most important thing you will never really find around here, pumpkin," Hatice said, closing her play book and looking at the men onstage. "Maybe we should write a script about this and sell it to a TV channel. It would be a great telenovela!"

"What if we tell them about their feelings?" Jinji suggested. "I mean, if they don't realise it themselves, then maybe we can just tell them?"

"We tried," Brigit confessed with a sigh. "It didn't work."

"So we just let them be," Hatice said, shaking her head. "One day they will see it for themselves."

"What if we make them see it?" Jinji suggested. "Because they're ruining the damn rehearsals and will ruin our premiere if they don't stop this stupid bullshit! We could create a situation which forces them to figure it out, no?"

"Very Don Pedro of you, Jinji! Are you trying to steal Pascoal's role?" Hatice laughed, shaking her head again. "Well, we did hope he would fix Carlo and Bren…"

"Excuse me, what? How?!"

"Pascoal likes stage arts, and he's so lovely to everyone. We thought he would be a great addition to the crew," Brigit said. "It was also pretty obvious that, because he's drop-dead gorgeous, either Carlo or Bren would swoon. We thought maybe that would drive them to confess their feelings for one another, but we didn't think it would be this dramatic."

"We will accept suggestions on how to fix this if you have any." Hatice looked at him with amusement.

"So this is all your fault!" Jinji complained, and Hatice's gasp was worthy of one of her favourite telenovelas.

"I have no idea what you're talking about, pumpkin!" Brigit said in a high-pitched voice. "Absolutely no idea. No idea at all!"

The thing was, Jinji didn't really have a plan. He just wanted Carlo and Bren to stop arguing so they could run the play from beginning to end in one go *before* the premiere night. It was so obvious that the two men just needed to figure their shit out, stop flirting with Pascoal, and be happy together. He was sure it was also obvious to Hatice and Brigit. The issues with his "problem number two" were: a) Carlo and Bren and b) Pascoal.

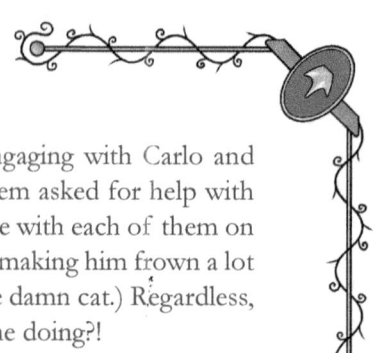

Because, Goddamn Pascoal, brilliant and beautiful, was, of course, engaging with Carlo and Bren. If one of them leant against him, he supported them. If one of them asked for help with their costume, he helped them. Damn, Jinji was sure he'd seen Pascoal alone with each of them on what looked like dates! (His—whatever-it-was—was very upset about that, making him frown a lot more than he should if he wanted to stand a chance of not looking like the damn cat.) Regardless, Pascoal knew Carlo and Bren were into each other, so what the heck was he doing?!

With eight days to go, Jinji arrived to rehearsal earlier than usual and found Pascoal staring at a pocket mirror. He focused on not combusting just because of Pascoal's existence and sat next to him on the bench.

"Would you call this a beard?" Pascoal asked, leaning in Jinji's direction and pointing to his own face, while—weirdly—frowning. It was so out of character, Jinji blinked at him. "I wouldn't call this a beard."

"Growing a beard is hard, man. Mine still looks like rat hair," Jinji said, trying to be comfortable with how close Pascoal's perfect face was to his. "The good thing is I don't have to shave every day."

"I've been on T since I was 16, and the only hair I can grow is on my butt!" Pascoal groaned, and Jinji choked. Of course, he was suddenly imagining Pascoal's naked butt! "I guess I'll ask Santa for a full beard. I was a good boy this year!"

Then Pascoal winked at him—in a completely chill and totally cool, yet slightly flirty, but not too much, way—that left Jinji's heart on the floor.

And *Oh fuck!*

Oh no, fuck, no! Jinji thought, his body burning with warmth and care and *want*, heart beating faster than a sledgehammer because *fuck!*

So that's what his—whatever-it-was—actually was! *No, no, no!* The last thing Jinji needed was to be heavily crushing on "problem number one" that was the main trigger for "problem number two"! His life was complicated enough; he seriously didn't need a "problem number three" on top of all this!! Okay, okay, he could handle this. He could handle this! He'd ignore it, pretend it never existed, so it would eventually disappear. All would be well. He cursed mentally, took a deep breath, and turned his attention back to Pascoal.

"You need to do something about Carlo and Bren," he blurted, desperate to change the topic. "They keep getting into these fights they pretend are about you, when they're actually just trying to make the other jealous. And they don't seem to be able to break the cycle. So *you* have to do something!"

"But this isn't about me?" Pascoal said, looking confused. He put his pocket mirror in his back-pack and crossed his muscular arms around it. "They need to figure themselves out."

"They've both been hitting on you since the day you walked in and dazzled them with that smile," Jinji pointed out, as if it wasn't the most obvious thing ever. "If you just refuse them direc—"

"Who's been hitting on me?!" Pascoal interrogated, curious eyes staring at Jinji.

"Wha— Carlo and Bren," Jinji answered, raising an eyebrow.

"They are *not* hitting on me. They're crazy about each other!" Pascoal said with a Goddamn amused expression.

"Oh hell, no! You cannot be that dense!" Jinji gaped at him. No, no, no, Pascoal was a sweet toasted mushroom, but that didn't excuse him being this clueless. It was so obvious! Everyone could see it! There was no way he would— "They've been all over you! Throwing themselves in your arms, demanding your attention, grabbing any chance to get you shirtless so they can ogle

your hot-and-perfect body!"

"Oh…" Pascoal's expression went from "toothpaste model" to "deep thinker."

Jinji was so tired. How could Pascoal not see what was happening right under his nose? How was Pascoal so damn dense? Sighing again, Jinji turned to face his friend only to have his heart skip a beat when he found Pascoal's trademark breathtaking grin aimed at him.

"You think I'm hot!" exclaimed Pascoal.

Fuck!

"I…what?!" Jinji almost screeched, his face turning into a hot tomato. Pascoal was *still* very, very close! "Not the point!"

"Totally the point! I've been trying really hard, but you're difficult to read, you know that?" Pascoal said, his dazzling grin fading into a ridiculously calm, soothing expression. Jinji cursed mentally again, and once more for good measure. He was suddenly aware of all the points where his body was touching Pascoal's: the side of their sneakers pressed together, the tiny contact at his right knee, his elbow softly leaning against Pascoal's forearm. And Pascoal was there, too close for what Jinji could call "casual" contact, dreamy eyes staring at him as if searching for something, as if hoping for an answer to an unasked question.

Oh, fuck!

"*That* is not gonna fix *this* problem!" Jinji exclaimed, trying his best to ignore the massive heat crackling under his skin. "We need Carlo and Bren to—"

"That *is* gonna fix the problem," Pascoal had the audacity to practically purr. He was right there, so close, yet distant enough to give Jinji an escape. So hopeful, yet respectful enough to not push too hard. So clearly mesmerized, without trying to claim what he set his eyes upon. "If Carlo and Bren are hitting on me to make the other jealous, and I happen to suddenly, casually, show up with a new *boyfriend*, that would fix our rehearsal issues, no?"

"I…" Jinji started, but he trailed off. Pascoal was *right there*, being his stunning self. He *was* actually saying what Jinji thought he was saying, wasn't he? Did Jinji even have any arguments against it? Did Jinji even want to have any arguments against it?! He swallowed dry, nervous. "I guess…it might?"

"It definitely will! So, I just need to go and find a boyfriend!" Pascoal said, leaning against the wall behind them, his eyes sparkling at Jinji. "As I see it, we have two options: either we get me a date to bring to the tea shop tomorrow at six, where they'll see that I'm taken, or," he paused, making sure Jinji's full attention was on him before his dazzling smile returned, "*or you can just kiss me now.*"

"Oh, fuck me!" Jinji covered his face, hoping that his tawny complexion wouldn't be as red as the autumn leaves, an explosion of damned butterflies flapping around like maniacs throughout his stomach. Pascoal's knee was still solid against his.

"Later," Pascoal laughed, and Jinji could hear the endearing nervousness in his voice. "If you want, of course."

"I— Like— Why is it— *Ugh!*" Jinji was an intelligent young man yet, somehow, Pascoal simply existing next to him made his brain into penguin food and his words as eloquent as a roasted sweet potato.

"Fuck," he muttered, passing nervous fingers through his hair before smoothing his hands over the shaved sides of his head. He breathed, closed his eyes for a moment, and turned to Pascoal. "Problem number one" might have just solved itself, *and* "problem number two" with it. "Date, tomorrow at six, at the tea shop."

"You and I?" Pascoal asked.

"Yeah," Jinji agreed. "You and I."

He did kiss Pascoal, the next day, after their date, as the rainbow colours of Berlin's Nollendorfplatz Station reflected brightly on their faces.

And damn! He should have done that the moment Pascoal asked him about 2-meter-tall penguins.

When Pascoal walked into their rehearsal and told Carlo and Bren that he and Jinji had finally gone on a date, both men exploded in happy cheers and congratulations, confusing the heck out of Jinji.

"Well, pumpkin! It was about time you figured out he was so hopefully crushing on you!" Hatice told him the day after. Jinji gaped at her. Brigit nodded in agreement and sneaked a lokum cube into his palm before he could say anything.

Apparently, Carlo and Bren had been aware of Pascoal's crush on him. Each had decided to be "extra" to help Pascoal win Jinji's heart, without telling anyone about their plan; accidentally, they'd tricked each other in the process.

"Well, we thought it was obvious, and that you were a bit dense, Jinji," Bren told him six nights before their premiere. "I mean, Pascoal can't take his eyes off you. How could you not see it?"

"You could have told me?!" Jinji turned to Brigit and Hatice as if the old ladies had somehow betrayed him.

"We tried!" Hatice giggled. "You were too busy blushing to notice."

They did their first full run of the play four days before the premiere. And, on the big night, the show went off without a hitch.

As the curtain closed and the ovation started, Jinji's heart couldn't be more relieved.

So Jinji breathed, tired and content, as he stepped onstage alongside Carlo and Bren, held hands with Hatice as she kissed Brigit's cheek, and smiled when Pascoal's warm arm curled around his waist and pulled him just a little bit closer.

And, together, they stepped forward for their curtain call.

Pimmy Oldham
"Taming My Wild Heart to Thy Loving Hand"
Pimmy opted not to share the inspiration behind this artwork.

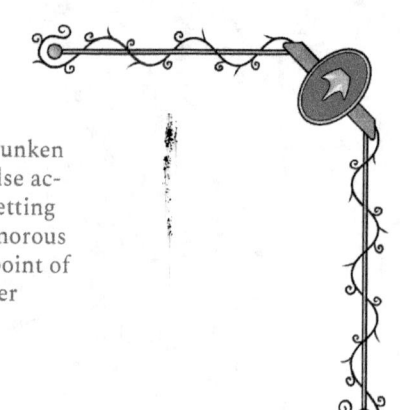

TAGS: alternate universe, angst (minor), bipoc, bisexual, drunken confessions, epistolary, established relationship, f/m/m, false accusations, food (graphic descriptions), friends to lovers, getting drunk, getting together, modern, past tense, pining, polyamorous relationship negotiation, polyamory, third person limited point of view, twosome to threesome, unreliable narrator, writer

DEAR DON PEDRO

Mikki Madison

When I was invited to contribute to this anthology, I had never read or seen Much Ado About Nothing, *so I watched the '90s filmed version with Kenneth Branagh as Benedick, Emma Thompson as Beatrice, and Denzel Washington as Don Pedro to see if I could get some inspiration for my story. One of my absolute favorite scenes in the entire movie was the one between Beatrice and Don Pedro when he proposes to her and she turns him down. It was just so sweetly played between the two of them, and I found myself wondering how it could work out. By the end of the movie, I'd decided that whatever I did, it needed to end up with Benedick/Beatrice/Don Pedro.*

Dear Don Pedro,

I screwed up big-time. A "friend" of mine told me that my best friend's girlfriend was cheating on him and showed me what looked like rock-solid proof. Obviously, I went and told my best friend...only to find out later that this "friend" was lying and had fabricated the proof he was showing me. So now I've wrecked my best friend's relationship over something that wasn't even true! He was all set to marry this girl, too, and I completely blew it. How can I fix this?

- Fucked Up in Frankfurt

Dear Fucked Up,

I hate to tell it to you, man, but there may not be a way you *can* fix it. Unfortunately, real life doesn't come with an undo button, and this situation depends entirely on how forgiving your best friend and his girlfriend are feeling.

The best thing you can do is apologize to both of them and make it very clear you know you were in the wrong. Then pray they're both in a forgiving mood.

You might also want to kick your other "friend" to the curb, if you haven't already. If they'd lie about that, who knows what else they're lying to you about?

- Don Pedro

"Are you going to join us for dinner anytime soon, or are you going to sit there on your computer all night?"

Pedro glanced over to where Beatrice was hanging over the back of the couch. "I'm working, Bea."

She pouted, but she didn't try to touch his computer; Pedro was grateful for small miracles.

"Come on. I know for a fact your deadline isn't until tomorrow afternoon." She jerked her head toward the kitchen, where Benedick was mixing up a truly gigantic bowl of spaghetti and marinara. "You can stop working for an hour and have a conversation with your friends."

"You know she's not going to let it go until you decide to be sociable," Benedick said. "She's never learned to take no for an answer."

Beatrice rolled her eyes and shoved off the couch to saunter over to her husband. "And just *why* might I do that, hm? Might it have anything to do with certain other people in this room who are too stubborn for their own good?"

Benedick caught her hand and kissed it. "No idea what you're talking about, Bea, my love."

She yanked her hand back, but her cheeks flushed, and she was obviously suppressing a smile. "You're incorrigible, and I don't know why I love you."

"You love me *because* I'm incorrigible."

Pedro sighed, shut his laptop, and stood up to join them in the kitchen. They were his best friends; that they'd even started dating was about seventy percent his fault, but it was always a little sticky when they got flirty. "Fine, fine, I'm coming to the table. Are you happy?"

Benedick threw an arm around his shoulder. "Rapturously."

"Deliriously." Beatrice hugged his other side. "We hardly ever get to see you anymore. You're busy all the time."

Pedro gently extricated himself and sat at the small, round table they'd picked up at a yard sale for $25. "You know how it is. You're newlyweds, and I've got a new job."

"We've been married nearly two years." Beatrice plopped down in the seat to his right, her knee knocking into his. "That hardly counts as 'newlywed' anymore."

"And you don't have a new job so much as you have the same old job for a new company. Well, new paper, anyway," Benedick pointed out as he sat on Beatrice's other side. "You've been writing that advice column since we were in college."

"I'm surprised you're arguing the 'newlywed' point," Pedro said, sidestepping the comment about his column. "Most people would say the newlywed stage lasts for at least three years."

Benedick shrugged and poured them some wine. "But Bea and I have known each other for ages and spent most of those ages bickering. We were an old married couple before we ever got married."

That was the damn truth, and it was one of the reasons Pedro had decided to set them up in the first place, no matter how much it had hurt him to do so. Besides, Beatrice had already made her feelings about Pedro clear, and after everything that had happened with Hero…well, he was just happy they were all still on speaking terms.

Beatrice patted his shoulder. "Besides, we like having you over here. You shouldn't be such a stranger."

That was also true. He *shouldn't* be such a stranger, not with Benedick and Beatrice, but it was difficult for him to spend as much time with them as he had before they'd gotten married.

"Pedro?" Beatrice asked, eyes filled with concern as the silence stretched a beat too long. "Is

everything all right?"

He shook himself out of his thoughts and back to the present. "Sorry. I'm over-thinking the letters."

She squeezed his arm. "The letters will still be there when dinner's over. You can spend a little time talking with us."

Benedick grinned and passed the Parmesan. "Maybe we can help you answer them."

Pedro nearly choked on his wine. "No, no. I remember how that went the last time, thank you very much."

Benedick waved a hand at his wife. "We have Bea to help us now!"

"She's the one I'm worried about!"

Benedick and Beatrice both laughed wholeheartedly, and Pedro loved them both so much his heart ached.

They were happy. That was really all that mattered, in the end, wasn't it?

Dear Don Pedro,

A few years ago, I told my best friend I had romantic feelings for her, and she turned me down. I accepted the rejection and we continued being friends, but I admit, my feelings for her have remained romantic in nature even though I know that's not a possibility.

Recently, though, it seems like things have changed. It really feels like she's flirting with me whenever we're hanging out: sitting closer than usual, touching my arm/hand/hair, etc. She's even put on perfume the last couple of times we've gone to dinner together. If it weren't for that previous rejection, I would have made a move already, but since she flat-out told me she didn't want to date me, I'm hesitant. Should I make a move, or respect her previous wishes?

- Mixed Signals in Miami

Dear Mixed,

It doesn't matter what signals you think she's sending you now; your friend gave you a pretty clear one when she turned you down. It's on you to respect that. If she's changed her mind about you as a romantic partner, it's on her to let you know.

Maybe you should consider jumping into the dating app pool. There are plenty of people out there who haven't previously rejected you, and meeting up with a few of them could help you get your mind off your friend.

- Don Pedro

Pedro had confessed his feelings to Beatrice their freshman year of college, about three days after she and Benedick had had a doozy of a fight and well before they'd actually started dating. Well, maybe it hadn't really been a confession; he'd ridden the line between truth and teasing on the chance she turned him down. Which she did, gently and kindly, and in such a way that Pedro never doubted she meant it when she said they'd be better off as friends.

"I would need another boyfriend for the weekdays, because I never see you then," she'd told him. "I'm lucky to get a glimpse of you even on the weekends."

Much as the rejection stung, Pedro had accepted it gracefully and set about finding her a boyfriend who *would* be good for her. Said boyfriend turned out to be Benedick, and the plan to get them together had succeeded beyond Pedro's wildest dreams.

He'd been happy for them. He still was. Really.

But that didn't change that he felt like a third wheel around them, watching two people he was half in love with be besotted with each other. This was his punishment for what he'd done to Beatrice's cousin Hero, he was sure of it.

"You've been awfully quiet today," Beatrice said as they walked down the sidewalk between their houses. She and Benedick had bought one down the street from him after they'd had enough of apartment life. "Penny for your thoughts?"

"The paper says they're worth more than that," Pedro joked.

She swatted his shoulder. "You know what I mean, you twit."

"It's all right, Bea. It's just work."

She frowned. "Is it really?"

"*Yes*," he said, and hoped it sounded reassuring. "I've had a few questions lately that have hit too close to home, that's all. It makes me a little melancholy, but it'll pass."

He cringed inwardly at the admission—Beatrice *did* read his column, after all—but those letters were at least a week or more away from being published. She'd probably forget this conversation by the time she read them.

Beatrice worried her lower lip. "I suppose you don't want to talk about it?"

"No, not really."

She didn't press, thankfully, and they walked on in companionable silence.

"You know, I've always wondered why you forgave me," Pedro said, forcing casualness into his voice.

She didn't pretend she didn't know what he was talking about. "Because Hero did."

Her admission sank his heart. "Is that the only reason? If she had decided not to, would we even be talking right now?"

"Did you still apologize?"

He blinked. "What do you mean?"

"In this hypothetical world where Hero didn't forgive you for helping your degenerate half-brother spread the rumor that she cheated on Claudio to the *entire* student body, did you apologize as eloquently and genuinely as you did in the real world?"

"…yes?"

"Then yes," Beatrice said simply. "Yes, I still would've forgiven you. Yes, we'd be talking right now." She knocked her shoulder against his. "One mistake shouldn't condemn you for life, especially when you realize it's a mistake."

Pedro took her hand and squeezed it. "Thank you."

Beatrice rewarded him with a blinding smile and wrapped her free hand around his upper arm. "No need for that, Pedro my dear. But if you're feeling particularly grateful, I wouldn't say no to a batch of your snickerdoodles."

He laughed, relieved. "That can be arranged."

She didn't let go of his arm for the rest of their walk, and Pedro had to remind himself not to read anything into it.

Dear Don Pedro,

My friend and I have been best buds since we were teenagers, and I'd always thought we were both straight. But about three months ago, he came out and told me he was bi. No big deal, right? He's my best friend. Of course I'm going to be supportive.

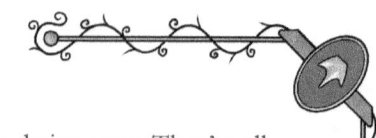

But the problem is that now I get really uncomfortable when I see him dating guys. They're all total players, just looking to get laid then move on. My friend is way hot, way awesome, and deserves *way* better than that. How can I make sure he finds someone good enough for him?

- Wingman in Wyoming

Dear Wingman,

The way I see it, you have two options. One, you offer to help your friend find guys who are looking for the same thing as him in a relationship...*if* he's even looking for a relationship right now. For all you know, he might *want* to play the field, in which case, more power to him and remind him to use protection.

Two, you can date him yourself. Because that vaguely uncomfortable feeling? Might just be jealousy.

- Don Pedro

"This is by far the most boring thing we've ever done together," Benedick said.

Pedro dunked his brush in the paint tray and went back to carefully cutting-in the bottom edge of the wall. "Oh, I don't know about that. We had Mrs. Heller for World History junior year."

Benedick barked a laugh. "Fair enough. But I have to say, I think I'd rather listen to one of her rambling lectures than paint another room in this house."

A fixer-upper is fine! Benedick had declared earlier that year, after he and Beatrice had been house-hunting for six months to no avail. *It'll be nice to get something we can make our own! A little paint, some new flooring, it's fine.*

What they'd ended up with was a house that needed paint, flooring, windows, cabinets and counters, and a couple bathrooms. In the roughly eight months they'd owned the place, they'd managed to get the flooring, the cabinets and counters, and one of the bathrooms fixed. In between projects that required actual contractors, Pedro was helping them. This weekend's project was painting the third bedroom in the house, which Benedick and Beatrice were hoping to turn into Benedick's office.

"You're the ones who picked a fixer-upper," Pedro reminded him. "There were plenty of homes that didn't need any work."

"Yes, and they were all above our budget or well outside this neighborhood." Benedick jumped off his ladder to load his brush again. "A few weekends of painting is a minor trade-off. Even if it is boring as shit."

"You didn't *have* to move to this neighborhood." Pedro leaned back to see how far he had to go to reach the corner of the wall. More than halfway done. Good. His knees were killing him. "There were plenty of other nice neighborhoods you looked at."

"Yeah, but then one of us would've had an hour-long commute." Benedick jabbed the brush in his direction, dripping a bit of grey paint on the shower curtain liners they'd used in lieu of actual drop cloths. "One way. No thank you."

Pedro laughed. "Well, that would be a deal-breaker."

"Of course it is, Mr. 'I've never worked a real office job a day in my life.' " Benedick went back to carefully painting along the edge where the wall met the ceiling. "After you've spent two hours a day trapped in traffic jams, you'll *also* only consider locations that allow you to shave that time in half. Not to mention, this is *your* neighborhood."

Pedro raised an eyebrow. "Are you saying proximity to me was a determining factor?"

Benedick tossed a grin over his shoulder. "It did lend a certain weight to the decision. Although

if I'd known I'd spend the next year repainting every damn room in this house, I may have reconsidered."

"I thought it was a 'minor trade-off,' " Pedro shot Benedick's words back at him. "Just a 'few weekends of painting.' "

"I…you…shut up!"

They went back to painting in—well, not in silence, since Beatrice had helpfully set up the speakers nearby so they could play music while they worked—but back to painting without talking, and Pedro considered the new information.

He hadn't realized that this being *his* neighborhood had played a part in their decision. He had thought it had just been a bonus, and more for him than them.

The knowledge made warmth curl in the pit of his stomach; he squashed it down. They were his friends. They liked to spend time with him. That was all it meant, nothing else.

A new song came over the speakers, instantly recognizable: the first one Benedick and Beatrice had danced to at their wedding. Pedro smiled at the memory.

"You know, Pedro, I've always wondered," Benedick said. "How come you haven't dated much the past few years?"

Ah, *that* question. Pedro sighed. "I haven't wanted to, that's all. What brought that to mind?"

"The song." Benedick nodded to the phone. "You've always wanted a relationship. When I got married, I told you that it'd be good for you to get a wife. But you haven't dated since we got out of college. If I didn't know better, I'd say you were avoiding it."

Pedro shrugged and kept his focus on the paint. He was very nearly done with this wall. "I like my life the way it is, and I haven't much felt like shaking that up."

"Mm-hmm."

Benedick didn't sound convinced, but Pedro ignored it. It wasn't a lie, but it wasn't the entire truth, either.

It felt disingenuous to date when he was in love with two other people. At some point, he'd get over them, and he'd be able to move on, to actually be interested in pursuing a relationship, but right now, he wasn't there. And it wouldn't be fair to whoever he dated.

But he absolutely couldn't tell Benedick any of that.

"Well, if you ever do decide to dip back into the dating pool, let me know," Benedick said. "I can think of three women off the top of my head who'd be great for you."

"Only women?" Pedro said.

Benedick turned to him, eyebrow raised assessingly. "*Really?*"

Pedro wanted to kick himself. *Why* had he said that? It wasn't that he hid his bisexuality; it was more that it hadn't come up and he hadn't seen much reason *to* bring it up. Not because he was worried about their reactions—Benedick and Beatrice would be supportive as always—but because *he* didn't find it particularly important, especially considering that he wasn't actively dating.

"Well, in that case," Benedick continued, "I can think of a few guys, too." He grinned. "Something else we have in common, then."

Pedro blinked at him. "What, really?"

Benedick nodded. "Probably seventy/thirty, if I had to guess, but the thirty percent is definitely there. Gives Bea and I something to talk about."

Pedro laughed. It was a better reaction than continuing to stare, gobsmacked, at his long-time best friend. Of all the things he didn't know about Benedick even now, he hadn't expected *that* one to be on the list. "As though you two don't have enough to talk about, you have to add in men you both find attractive?"

"Of course." Benedick wiped his hand on his shirt, smearing paint along the edge. "You'd be surprised how often we agree."

"I'm afraid to ask who made the list," Pedro said.

Benedick winked. "Alas, my dear Pedro, that list is not something I'm at liberty to discuss without my darling wife's permission."

"Ooo, *darling* wife?" Beatrice leaned on the doorframe, her arms crossed and a smile dancing in her eyes. "Have you done something to get in trouble?"

Pedro jerked at her sudden appearance and sent a line of gray paint up the wall, narrowly missing the tape-covered outlet.

"Jeez, Bea!" Benedick covered his heart with his free hand. "Some warning next time!"

"I heard my name and thought you might need something." She glanced between them. "But I seem to be mistaken. What trouble *are* you getting into?"

"None!" Benedick looked to Pedro with something akin to panic. "Pedro, tell her we were just talking and that I've done nothing wrong."

"Quite the opposite, actually," Pedro said. "He's refusing to break a confidence of yours until he can discuss it with you."

Beatrice grinned. "Good man." She scanned the room and nodded approvingly. "You've made good progress. Are you ready for lunch?"

"Not just yet." Benedick climbed back on the ladder. "We're almost finished with the cut-in and then, what do you think, another half hour for the first coat on the walls?"

Pedro leaned back on his heels and considered. "Probably. Should go pretty quick with the two of us. Maybe forty-five minutes altogether."

"All right," Beatrice said. "I'll finish up in the guest room before then."

Benedick bent over the edge of the ladder and kissed her on the cheek. "You are an angel among women, Bea, my love."

Pedro went back to finishing his section of the wall. Really, he'd never expected his first attempt at matchmaking to go so well.

Or that it would end up hurting him so much.

Dear Don Pedro,

Two friends are dropping *major* hints that they'd want a threesome with me. On the one hand, they're super hot and I'd absolutely go for it. On the other hand, they're two of my closest friends, and won't sex mess up our friendship? What should I do?

- Tempted In Tallahassee

Dear Tempted,

Nothing's wrong with sex between friends, as long as everybody's clear on the boundaries and expectations. Be sure you all communicate up front and don't give into the urge to hide things for the sake of keeping the peace. Good luck, and be sure to enjoy yourself.

- Don Pedro

Pedro sat up gingerly, pressing the heel of his hand to his forehead in an effort to quiet the pounding there. This would be the last time he let Benedick and Beatrice talk him into having "just one glass" as a celebratory nightcap. Granted, after finishing the home office two weeks ago and

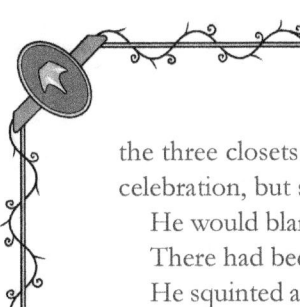

the three closets this weekend, they'd finally painted everything that needed it, so it was a worthy celebration, but still.

He would blame the wine.

There had been a lot of wine. It would make a good scapegoat.

He squinted and looked around the darkened room. It took him longer than it should've to realize he was not in his own bed. It took him even longer to realize he was in Benedick and Beatrice's bed. *With* Benedick and Beatrice.

And, he noted, he was wearing remarkably less clothing than he should be in this situation. Zero clothing, in fact.

Hell.

He was *definitely* blaming the wine.

Pedro scanned the room for his clothes, but it was nearly impossible to see anything with the curtains drawn so tight. The light around the edges told him it was morning, but it wasn't enough to see by or to gauge the time. He cautiously eased out of the bed, feeling at the floor with his bare foot to make sure he didn't step on anything, trying not to make a sound. Benedick and Beatrice seemed to be asleep, and he wanted to keep them that way.

He found his phone on the dresser, battery dead, and he groped around the piles of clothing on the floor looking for his underwear. Hell, even just his pants would do. He could come back for the rest later.

His foot landed on something sharp; he fell to the ground with a muffled curse and a very loud *thump*.

Benedick and Beatrice both sat up in bed, Benedick swearing like a sailor while Beatrice flipped on the lamp. Pedro covered his eyes at the sudden light, which sent his headache skyrocketing.

"Pedro?" Benedick's voice was thick. "What the hell are you doing on the floor?"

Pedro was grateful the heat on his cheeks wouldn't be visible. "Tripping." He searched for what he'd stepped on and grabbed the offending object: a shoe. "Over Beatrice's stiletto, apparently."

Beatrice winced. "Sorry about that. I wasn't thinking about where those were landing."

A dim memory of the shoes getting flung across the room surfaced, and Pedro's cheeks heated further.

"What are you doing stumbling around in the dark, anyway?" she asked. "You could've turned on a light."

"You were both asleep," Pedro said. "I didn't want to disturb you."

Benedick scrubbed a hand over his face, his blond hair sticking up every which way. "Ah, hell, it's too early for this."

Beatrice peered at her phone. "It's nearly ten."

"Still too early," Benedick said, and he turned back to Pedro. "Were you sneaking out?"

Pedro groaned inwardly. "I told you, I was trying not to wake you up. I was being polite."

Benedick scoffed. "Who gives a shit about being polite? We fucked last night, and now you're trying to leave without saying anything?"

Beatrice swatted his shoulder. "*Benedick.*"

"What?! What are you hitting me for?" Benedick gestured at him. "He's the one sneaking off like he's ashamed of us!"

"He could be going to make breakfast!"

"Bea, if he were going to make breakfast, he'd have said so."

Pedro covered his face. "For fuck's sake."

"Am I wrong?" Benedick challenged him. "Tell me I'm wrong and I'll apologize, and *I'll* go

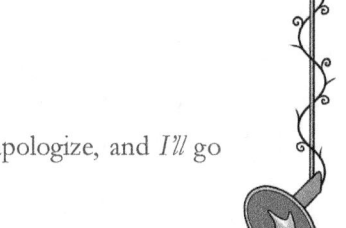

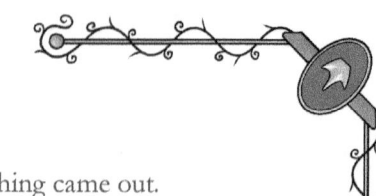

make breakfast."

Pedro opened his mouth to lie, to make some kind of excuse, but nothing came out.

Benedick cursed again and threw off the covers.

Beatrice grabbed his arm. "If you two start fighting in the middle of our bedroom, I will be *very upset.*"

Benedick glowered. "We were already fighting. I'm just continuing it."

She narrowed her eyes at him, and then turned her attention to Pedro. "Why?"

" 'Why' what?"

"Why are you sneaking out?"

There were a lot of answers to that question. Because spending the night with them had been a bad decision brought on by too much wine. Because he didn't want to ruin his friendship with them. Because, no matter how this morning-after conversation went, it wouldn't end well for him, and Pedro had a foolish desire to try and protect himself from at least some of the hurt that was bound to follow.

"Because it seemed like the prudent thing to do," he said finally. "On all parts."

Beatrice's face fell. "Oh. Well. If that's how you really feel, then."

Pedro rubbed the back of his neck. He felt like he was missing something, but between the headache and the heartache, he'd be damned if he could figure out what it was. "Well, it…it has to be, right? This"—he gestured between them—"it was just a one-time thing for you, wasn't it?"

"That depends," Benedick said. "Was it for you?"

Pedro swallowed hard. The safe answer was *yes.* The truth was so much more complicated. He'd happily do it again, but he couldn't—not if it was always going to be "them" and "him" in the end.

Beatrice rested her hand on Benedick's arm. "It wasn't for us," she said quietly. "Or at least, we'd prefer it not to be. And it wasn't just sex, either, before you bring that up. But if this isn't something you want, you should tell us now."

" 'This'?" Pedro repeated, dumbfounded. He couldn't really believe his ears.

"Oh please, don't pretend you don't understand what I mean," Beatrice snapped. "This isn't easy for us, either, you know."

"You…but…" Pedro sat there, trying to put his thoughts into some sort of order. "You're married. You turned me down. I didn't even know Benedick *liked* men until two weeks ago!"

"I turned you down? That was years ago," Beatrice said. "And, might I remind you, I didn't say *no.* I specified that it would have to be a triad. That's not a rejection. It's a qualification."

Pedro was certain he was gaping like a fish, but yes, he remembered exactly what Beatrice had said. *I would need another boyfriend for the weekdays.* "You were serious."

"Of course I was serious." She smiled at him tentatively. "I had thought that was part of why you were throwing Benedick at me. I didn't realize until after we'd gotten married that you'd given up."

"Yes, I gave up! You said no! I thought you did, anyway," he amended. "I wasn't going to keep pursuing you when you'd said you weren't interested."

Benedick rubbed the corner of his eye. "As fascinating as this dive into the past is, I would really appreciate it if we could clear up what's happening *now.*" He looked at Pedro. "Is this—the three of us together, I mean—something you want? If not, it's okay, we can just continue on as we were. But…"

He trailed off, letting the rest of the sentence hang in the air.

And really, what was Pedro to do? He stood on the edge of a precipice. If he took a single step forward, everything would change. But on the other side of that step was everything he'd ever

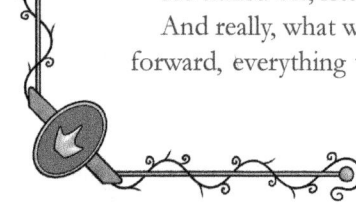

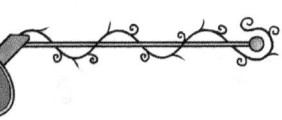

wanted.

And, apparently, it was what Benedick and Beatrice wanted as well.

So perhaps it wasn't really that complicated after all.

He finally spotted his boxers a few feet away, and he yanked them on, grateful to no longer be having this conversation naked. "I should go make breakfast. As an apology for all the confusion this morning. And then…" He took a deep breath. "I suppose I'll join you back in bed, if that's all right with you?"

Beatrice tipped her head to the side. "Is that a 'yes' to our proposal?"

His heart was pounding like a bass drum, from excitement or fear or possibly both. "It's a yes."

Beatrice jumped out of bed and threw her arms around him, and Benedick wasn't far behind. Pedro hugged them back, fiercely, still not processing that this was his life now. That the three of them were now…well, the *three* of them.

"I think you should come back to bed now," Beatrice said. "Breakfast can wait."

"A fantastic idea," Benedick said. "Isn't she full of fantastic ideas?"

Pedro laughed and let his two best friends—whom he'd loved for so long—drag him back into bed. "She really is."

Dear Don Pedro,

I've been friends with a married couple for ages and, to make a long story short, we're embarking on a polyamorous relationship and I'm *freaking out*. I love them both so much, and I'm so scared of screwing it up. Any advice for making sure I don't ruin the best thing that's ever happened to me?

- Anxious in Albany

Dear Anxious,

Believe me, I understand that feeling. Embarking on a new relationship is always a risk, and no matter how much you love each other, there are going to be rough patches. There are rough patches in any relationship. But here are some tips for weathering those:

Be honest.

Don't be afraid to have those hard conversations.

Know your boundaries, and make sure your partners know them (and vice versa).

Always, always, always let them know that you love them.

Best of luck to you, Anxious. If I know nothing else, I know this: it's worth it.

- Don Pedro

Joey Hazell (Next Pages)
"Cottage Country Comic AU"

Many adaptations have shown how well the drama of Shakespeare pairs with the messiness of young coming-of-age stories, and I personally love reading about the kind of dynamics that come about with clunky friend groups. This past summer I had also really been missing spending quality time down by the lake. So I combined these elements together in my imagining of the Much Ado cast. Seven young adults stuck together in a cottage for the summer—what drama will they get up to?

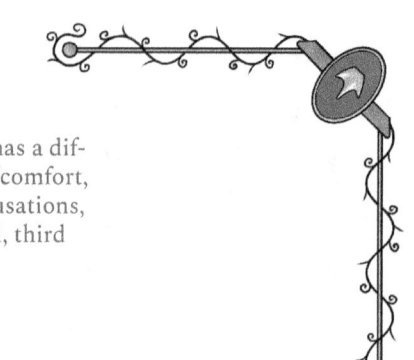

TAGS: alcohol use (casual), alternate universe, character has a different gender than in the source material, emotional hurt/comfort, established relationship, executive assistant, f/f, false accusations, m/m, modern, mystery, office, past tense, security guard, third person limited point of view,

GOOD MEN AND TRUE

Juno Caster

I set out to write a simple, modern take on the play—replacing the lords and masters with CEOs and lawyers, and turning Claudio into Claudia—but as I started outlining my story, and as I rewatched Kenneth Branagh's movie adaptation for inspiration, I found myself drawn to other characters—namely, to Verges and Dogberry. An odd pair—easily transformed into an explicitly queer one. I had already decided, at that point, to tell things from Margaret's point of view: since she wasn't one of the protagonists, I could use her to focus only on a few key characters and events, thus allowing me to keep the story short. Put it all together and—voilà! In this version, the plot unfolds, more or less, as it does in the play, though seen from the wings. And, through rewritings and editing, Margaret's character has solidified and gained agency at the same time as she has found, in Verges and Dogberry, the friends and allies she needed. I have grown very fond of this little trio—and I hope the readers will, too!

Margaret was earlier than usual that morning. She walked up the few steps to the entrance of the office building, fishing her keycard out of her purse. But when she swiped it at the front door, the reader flashed red, not green. She tried it again; again, the reader flashed red. She rang the buzzer then stepped back to stand in full view of the security camera. A few seconds later, the door clicked open.

She entered the lobby frowning down at her card. A familiar voice called out her name in greeting, and she raised her head to see a brawny, middle-aged man clad in a uniform this side of too tight grinning at her from the security desk.

"Oh! Hi, Dogberry."

Years of working the night shift had permanently ringed Dogberry's eyes and washed out his skin, making it look sallow under the fluorescent lights, but his whole face crinkled pleasantly as he smiled at her. His hair hadn't lost its luster; like his beard, it still grew dark and thick with barely a hint of gray in it.

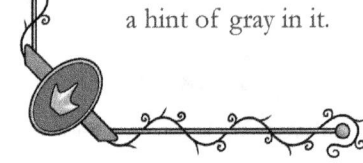

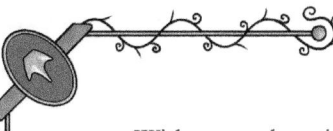

With an apologetic shrug, Margaret held up her card.

"I don't know what's wrong with it," she explained. "It just wouldn't work."

"Of course it wouldn't," he said. "It's too early. You can only access the building outside business hours using a permanent employee card; that temporary one you've been relying on won't cut it."

"I see." She nodded sheepishly and slipped the card back into her purse. Her employee card had been missing for days. She should have reported it lost and requested a new one as soon as she realized it was gone, but that would have meant going to Ursula, their office administrator, and enduring one of the scathing lectures she was notorious for. Instead, Margaret had asked Dogberry for help, that he'd given her in the form of her current temporary card.

She'd been quite sure, initially, that she had merely misplaced her own card and that she'd soon find it again. Now, she wasn't so sure, but each passing day made it harder to face Ursula.

Her thoughts—and her rising anxiety—were interrupted by the chime of the elevator at the far end of the lobby. Out stepped Verges, carrying two steaming paper cups. Upon noticing Margaret, he raised one to her in greeting, the gesture careful and measured. The slightly acrid smell of vending machine coffee wafted after him as he walked past her to bring Dogberry the second cup.

"Thanks, dear."

Next to his partner (in every sense of the word), Verges appeared deceptively unremarkable. He didn't possess Dogberry's muscular bulk; instead, he was tall and wiry. His uniform fit him perfectly, and while it was a little creased from having been worn almost a whole shift through, it still looked as neat as the rest of him. He always kept his hair close-cropped, his cheeks clean-shaved; he would have looked austere were it not for the way his blue eyes shone, gentle and observant, from behind his silver-rimmed glasses.

He smiled at Dogberry, who was making a show of savoring his first sip of coffee, then turned his attention to Margaret.

"You're looking very sharp."

"Thank you."

"Today's the day, right?"

"Today's the day."

Margaret lightly ran her fingers from her temple to the back of her neck, over the dark curls she'd pulled into a tight bun. Her hand brushed one of the lapels of her blazer and tugged at its bottom hem on the way down. It was the nicest one she owned, a deep-red silk-and-cotton blend that felt nice and cool to the touch. Not for the first time since she had left her apartment that morning, she wondered if she hadn't overdone it—but today *was* a big day, the biggest of her career.

She glanced at the gleaming lettering adorning one of the walls. *Messina.* Leonato's success had etched his name in gold, literally and figuratively, long before Margaret had joined the company. Today, however, it was Hero, Leonato's daughter, whose brilliance was to be on display—and Margaret, as her assistant, would have the privilege of standing at her shoulder.

It had been a long time coming—months and months of planning and meetings and protracted proceedings. The evening it had all started, though, stood out in Margaret's memory. Well, one particular moment did. The rest of it—the big fancy venue, the self-congratulatory speeches, the tuxedos and the evening gowns, the glasses of champagne and the platters of delicacies—was barely more than glittering bokeh.

Don Pedro's belated arrival had been heralded by a swell of murmurs and exclamations. He'd just come back to the country after sealing a huge deal overseas, and everyone had fallen over

themselves for the opportunity to pay him court. Within earshot of Margaret, who had been craning her neck to get a glimpse of him, someone had asked: "Who's that next to Don Pedro?"

Someone else had let out a disbelieving huff.

"You don't know? That's his brother John. Well, *half*-brother. I'm surprised he's here. He never comes to these things."

Margaret had heard about John—about how he'd tried to quit the family business and succeed on his own, but mostly about how he'd failed and subsequently been forced to return to the fold. If not for his brother's generosity, he'd have faced bankruptcy, maybe even jail time. Rumor had also had it that, instead of being grateful, John was resentful. Once Don Pedro's party had come into view, the sour expression on John's face had Margaret believing all the worst she'd heard whole-heartedly.

"No, not him. *Her.*"

"Oh! She's his new protégée. I heard she played a big part in getting him that deal. She's just made one of those lists, you know, one of those '30 Under 30' things? Wait, they're coming over."

Don Pedro's booming "Leonato!" and the resounding clap of his hand on the other man's shoulder had brought what had seemed like the whole room's attention to their little group. John had stood back and graced them with a mere stiff nod while his brother and Leonato had exchanged pleasantries. Don Pedro had paid his compliments to Hero, who had smiled and responded in kind, but her attention had kept drifting to the woman at Don Pedro's shoulder. That woman, in return, had looked as enraptured; and, as soon as Don Pedro had mentioned her name, she had stepped forward and extended her hand—not to Leonato, but to Hero.

It had been a bold move, but Claudia Fiorentino, Margaret would come to learn, was a bold woman. Hero had eagerly grasped her hand—and, in a sense, hadn't let go of it since.

Soon after that night, Hero had called both Beatrice—their sharpest legal advisor and Hero's closest friend—and Margaret to her office. They would be working on a new project: a joint venture that would pull Hero out from under her father's shadow and secure Claudia's position and reputation.

And today—

"What time's the conference?" Verges asked.

Today, they were finally going public.

"Eleven," Margaret replied. She caught Dogberry's quizzical look—there was still a while to go before then—and added, "I just want to make sure everything's in order before they get here."

Verges nodded. "Well, don't let us keep you, then."

Just as the doors of the elevator were closing behind her, Dogberry's voice boomed across the lobby, echoed by Verges's more temperate baritone. "Blow them dead!"

"Blow them *away.*"

"Same thing."

Later that day—so much later that it wasn't even technically the same day anymore—those same two voices stirred Margaret awake. She raised her head and uncrossed her arms, wincing at the stiffness in her neck and shoulders, then blinked, trying to adjust to the surrounding darkness. She was in her office, adjacent to Hero's, but she had left the door open, and Verges and Dogberry's conversation carried easily over the open bullpen area that took up much of the otherwise silent, empty floor.

She was exhausted. What little sleep she had managed to get, slumped over her desk, hadn't

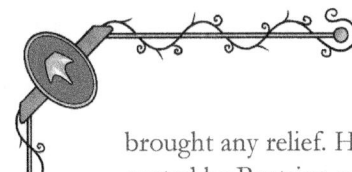

brought any relief. Her eyes felt hot and puffy, her throat parched. Hero had long gone home, escorted by Beatrice, while Margaret had offered to stay behind—somebody had to, after...after...

"I'm not saying she did it," Verges declared. "All I'm saying is that I don't see why Don Pedro and Ms. Fiorentino would make up something like that."

"Well, I don't either, but it simply can't be true!" Dogberry retorted.

There was a pause, then Verges spoke again, his tone low and placating. "Look, let's just check on Margaret first. She'll know more about this than we do."

Their footsteps drew nearer. Margaret quickly pulled herself together to face them as best as she could, but once they came to the door, their eyes only met momentarily before both night watchmen noticed the state of her office. Shock passed over their faces as they took in the empty filing shelves, the gaping drawers, the dangling cables.

"The investigators," Margaret explained. "They came and took everything."

The story was all over social media and the news already. Pictures of Hero at recent events, bright and confident, overlapping dark, blurry shots of her quickly and covertly exiting the building earlier that day, after the press meeting was abruptly canceled, to disappear into the back of a company car. Videos of Don Pedro and Claudia leaving the conference room, John trailing behind them, refusing to stop and make further comments—and then quotes from their company's official statement in which they condemned Hero and congratulated themselves for severing ties with her. On top of all that were a barrage of headlines associating Hero's name with words like *fraud*, *scam*, and *corruption*.

In the morning there'd be more. Reports, articles, think pieces, all of Hero's life laid bare for anyone and everyone to dissect and try to pinpoint exactly where and why she had gone wrong.

Margaret's chest heaved with a sob. It came as a surprise—she hadn't thought she had any more tears in her. Dogberry came closer and, after a moment's hesitation, put a hand on her shoulder. It was heavy and warm, and Margaret felt so brittle and so cold that she hunched over and broke down. Dogberry's hand moved to cup the back of her head, squashing her half-undone bun, and he held her close while she cried.

"She's innocent," she eventually managed. "She's innocent."

"I'm sure she is." Dogberry's voice rumbled deep in his chest; it felt like his words were reverberating through her. "You know her better than anyone. I'm sure it's all a miscontraption."

She couldn't help herself. A laugh—barely more than a hiccup—escaped her. Dogberry shifted, presumably to glance back at Verges, because next came the gentle correction: "*Misconstruction*, dear." Then, to Margaret, just as gently: "Come down with us. We'll get you some tea, and then I'll ask Seacoal to drive you home."

She sat back and nodded. She wiped her face and ran her fingers through her hair, though it was disheveled beyond anything a passing touch could repair. Dogberry's hand moved down to her arm to help her up and remained there to guide her until he and Verges had her settled in an office chair they pulled up behind the security desk.

Verges disappeared through a door marked "Private" that Margaret had never paid attention to before. Some sort of back office, she supposed. She kept staring at it, unfocused, as the weight of the day started pulling at her again. Dogberry had stepped away to call Seacoal, their new watchman-in-training, and ask him to bring one of the company cars around— "No, not right now, finish your round first."

He came back as Verges returned with—to Margaret's surprise and relief—a proper ceramic mug. She took it and inhaled deeply. The tea was too hot to drink, but at least it *was* tea, steaming and smelling of chamomile, rather than the vile cardboard-tasting hot beverage that the vending

machine upstairs dispensed.

"What happened?" Dogberry asked.

Margaret looked up at him, then at Verges. What had happened? She wished she knew. The whole sequence of events kept replaying in her head like a disjointed film reel she couldn't make sense of. She recognized the characters in it, and the setting, but the plot was incomprehensible.

She opened her mouth, closed it, opened it again.

"I have no idea," she blurted. "I really don't."

Word by word, she forced herself to describe it all to them—and still she couldn't understand any of it. Claudia refusing to sign the contract they had drawn up to seal the collaboration between their companies. Claudia accusing Hero of having deceived them all for her own profit. The shock and disbelief on everyone's faces. The swell of protests, rising and rising and rising until Don Pedro himself had intervened, claiming that they had proof and declaring that Hero's fate was out of their hands. John, terse, nodding to his assistant Borachio before standing up and informing everyone assembled for the conference that the investigators were on their way.

Finally, Margaret couldn't go on. She thought about Hero—brave, brilliant, beautiful Hero—watching Claudia leave the conference room and collapsing into her seat, pale and distressed, and she felt the pinprick of fresh tears. She swallowed them along with the rest of her tea—which had grown cold by then, not that it mattered—and, glancing toward the entrance, asked, "Is Seacoal getting here soon?"

"He shouldn't be long now," Dogberry replied, "but—"

Verges squeezed his partner's arm and then picked the mug out of Margaret's hands.

"I'll put that away. Text Seacoal, let him know Margaret's ready to go."

Dogberry took out his phone and started typing out a message.

"How did you know I was still here?" Margaret wondered.

"Your keycard," Dogberry said. "You didn't check out."

She frowned. "But it's a temporary one. It could've been someone else, couldn't it?"

"Well, who issued it to you? I know which ID's yours."

"Oh. Thank you," Margaret said. "For…"

And, just like that, she choked up again. Dogberry squeezed her shoulder.

"Aye, don't you worry. It'll all get cleared up in no time." His phone chimed; he glanced at the screen and added, "Look, Seacoal's here. He'll get you home safe. Try and get some rest, all right?"

"I hope I'm not waking you up," Verges's text began. *"Would you be able to visit Dogberry and I in the Messina lobby tonight?"*

He needn't have worried. Margaret hadn't had a full night's sleep in weeks. She suspected Hero hadn't either, though they hadn't seen each other recently. They had both gone on leave; Hero denied having done anything wrong, but she cited concerns for the company while the investigation (which, she was certain, would prove her innocence) was still under way. And, since Margaret had been working so closely with her, Beatrice had advised her to do the same.

It was well past midnight, but Margaret wasn't in bed. She was sitting on the floor of her living room, her back against the couch, her knees folded under the coffee table. Her laptop was precariously wedged on the few inches of tabletop that weren't piled with papers—personal notes, articles she had printed out, files Beatrice had shared with her. She'd reconstructed the case against Hero, but she hadn't been able to deconstruct it—yet.

There *were* some discrepancies with the times and dates of what the investigators regarded as

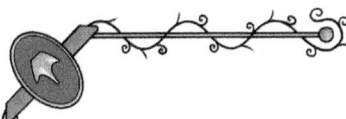

"suspicious activities" on Hero's part, but Margaret couldn't prove anything—except, it had turned out, her own possible guilt by association.

"Of course we've already checked the logs," Beatrice had retorted when Margaret had gone to her. "But even if Hero's keycard wasn't used at those times, yours was."

"But it wasn't me! I told you I lost it. It must have been someone else!"

"You didn't *report* that it was lost. Otherwise, it would have been deactivated once you had been issued a new one. Don't you see that Hero's defense can't do anything with those logs? They would be torn to shreds in court! You say you've lost your card—but we can't prove it! The prosecution will say it proves, at best, that you're naïve and incompetent and Hero manipulated you; at worst, that you knew what she was doing and you helped her do it. Now, which version do you prefer?"

Margaret had argued that Verges and Dogberry could attest to her losing her card, but Beatrice had promptly countered that as well. "Why would you drag them into this mess? They haven't followed protocol either—they'd be in as much trouble as you!"

Margaret sighed. Well, she wasn't going to crack the case tonight. She might as well go and see why Verges wanted her to come by the office.

Verges's and Dogberry's twin expressions of concern when she stepped into the lobby made Margaret wince. She had done her best to freshen up, but when she had left home, her face in the mirror had still looked taut and ashen.

Verges gestured for her to join them behind the security desk. Dogberry was at the computer; there were a couple of screens in front of him displaying images from security cameras inside and outside the building. Verges got up from his seat and went to stand behind his partner.

"Sit down," Verges told her. "We're going to bring this to M. Messina first thing in the morning, but we wanted you to see it first."

Dogberry picked up something from the desk and handed it to her.

"We've found your keycard."

Margaret took it and looked it over. It seemed normal, exactly how it used to be. She glanced at Verges and Dogberry, uncomprehending. She didn't want to get them in trouble, so she had heeded Beatrice's advice and hadn't even mentioned the matter of the keycard to them. So what had made them invite her here, in the middle of the night, to discuss precisely this? How was this a matter for Leonato?

"Someone left it at reception," Dogberry added. "On *that* day."

"Seacoal only noticed it yesterday," Verges explained. "Since you were on leave, it'd been put aside. Still, we ran it through the system to make sure it hadn't been used."

Dogberry opened up a spreadsheet on the computer. He scrolled through the file and then stopped and tapped at the screen with the tip of his finger. "And here's the thing—the logs don't match up."

Margaret looked closer. She didn't know what most of the data on the sheet meant; the first two columns were just times and dates going back a few weeks.

"See these? They're all after you told us you lost your card."

His words jolted Margaret.

"I did! I did lose it! These aren't— I didn't—"

"We know," Verges said.

"No, you don't—" She took a deep breath then started over. "I've already mentioned the logs to Beatrice, but we can't do anything with them because I didn't report that I lost the keycard. There's

no way to prove that I wasn't the one who used it—or worse, that *Hero* didn't use it to cover her tracks."

Verges and Dogberry stared at her.

"Yes, there is."

"What?"

"There is a way to prove it wasn't you." While Verges spoke, Dogberry pulled up another computer folder. "Security footage is automatically deleted after thirty days," he explained, "so we don't have video for all these dates, but we do have this."

Dogberry clicked on one of the files. The recording was bluish and grainy, but it was clear enough for Margaret to make out the faces of her colleagues as they paused to swipe their keycards and unlock the front door. It was a little before nine, according to the timestamp, and people kept coming in for the day.

Margaret wasn't one of them. She did recognize someone else, though, someone who should have had to ring the buzzer and wait to be let in—but didn't need to, because, somehow, he had a keycard.

"That's Borachio," she said. "John's assistant."

"That's who used your card."

She pulled out her phone and opened her work calendar—the one she shared with Hero. She clicked on the day in question and then tilted the screen toward Verges and Dogberry.

"I wasn't at the office that day. We didn't come in because Claudia invited us out for breakfast before a meeting we had scheduled with Don Pedro and John." She paused. "They knew we weren't there. Do you think Claudia…? No, wait, that was Borachio on the video. John, then?"

Margaret slumped into her seat. She couldn't have stood up if she had tried. It was too much to take, too much to comprehend. She looked at Verges and Dogberry; they watched her, silent, unmoving, letting her put together the pieces of what she knew and what they had just shown her.

It must have been John. Although both he and Don Pedro had been overseeing Claudia and Hero's project, he'd never shown any enthusiasm for it, never given any input. He had made excuse after excuse to avoid meetings, preferring to send Borachio in his place. The few times he had to show up, he appeared to simply endure it, grim and silent.

And now, he was being heralded as the company's savior for seeing through Hero's schemes and bringing them to Claudia's attention. His past mistakes had been forgiven, his debts cleared, while Hero's reputation was in tatters.

Margaret's hand, the one that wasn't still holding her phone, clenched into a fist so tight that her fingernails dug into her palm.

"That bastard!" she hissed.

Verges squeezed her shoulder. "We've got him now," he said. "We've got him, and we'll get justice for Hero as well."

Margaret slipped off her high heels and kicked them under the desk before sitting in her chair with a sigh. Even with the door closed, the cacophony from the party still filled her office, but she was in desperate need of a breather. She threw her head back and closed her eyes, immediately regretted it when the room started spinning, and then opened them again and sat up when she heard a knock at the door. The room spun even worse, and she eyed the bin in the corner—she could probably make it there in time if needed.

The door opened, and Verges entered. He raised both his eyebrows and the two Champagne

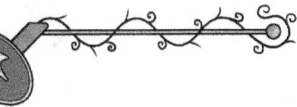

flutes he was carrying, and Margaret grinned at him.

"I hope we're not intruding?"

"Not at all."

He stepped in, followed, of course, by Dogberry, who had brought a third glass and a full bottle of Veuve Clicquot. He put them both on the desk and took one of the seats opposite Margaret. Verges made to take the other one, but Dogberry tugged him onto his lap and held him there, clasping an arm around his waist. Verges's subsequent chiding was rendered quite ineffectual by his settling down and handing Dogberry one of the flutes he'd held—he even managed not to spill a single drop of Champagne in the process, which was a testament to his reflexes, or perhaps just to his being used to Dogberry's antics.

They made quite the picture dressed in suits instead of their usual uniforms. Leonato had given them the night off and invited them to celebrate Hero's official return to the company; he had also, from what Margaret had gathered, offered them a substantial bonus for helping clear his daughter's name.

It was nothing less than they deserved. Although Margaret's dizziness hadn't dissipated, she picked up the flute of Champagne they had brought her and clinked glasses with them. She could still manage a celebratory sip, if nothing else.

"What about Claudia?" Verges asked at some point. "Will Hero go back to her?"

"Back to working with her? Yes."

Margaret left the rest unsaid. Claudia had made public apologies and announced that she would be quite happy to collaborate with Hero once more. It'd been good PR for both of them, but, privately, it would take much more than that to repair their relationship.

"And John? Any news?"

She shook her head. Borachio had pled guilty to fabricating evidence against Hero and agreed to testify against John in exchange for a reduced sentence, but John had fled the country before charges could be brought against him.

"Well, whether they get him or not, that's not for us to antagonize over," Dogberry said.

Verges laughed and kissed his partner's temple. "Agonize, dear."

"Yeah, that's what I said."

Margaret picked up the bottle and poured the last of the Champagne in Verges's and Dogberry's glasses. She raised her own flute, which was still almost full, and declared: "Here's to karma getting the bastard—and to us helping!"

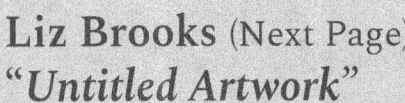

Liz Brooks (Next Page)
"Untitled Artwork"

Liz opted not to share the inspiration behind this artwork.

@lizzybizzyart

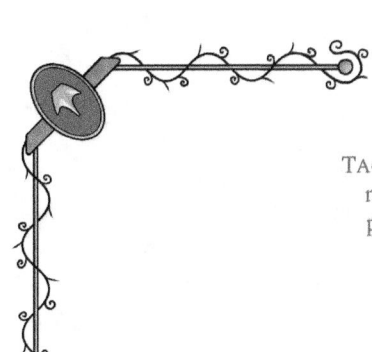

TAGS: angst (minor), bipoc, f/f, fantasy, magic use, masquerade, non-fanfiction story inspired by source material, piercings, polyamory, present tense, royalty, sexual harassment (mild), soldier, third person limited point of view

A SKIRMISH OF WIT

Nicole Wilkinson

My approach to writing "A Skirmish of Wit" was to take inspiration from Much Ado About Nothing. *Rather than transform the existing characters, I plucked what I felt was the most important theme from the work and included several notable elements while applying those to my original characters. For me, the greatest takeaway from* Much Ado About Nothing *is that sometimes, a falsehood is a necessary means to an end. I chose a wlw poly relationship which uses clever interpretations and some magical misdirection to ensure the three women can have the marriage they choose.*

It's hot in the ballroom.

There are too many people and, despite the wide-flung windows, the lack of a breeze makes the interior tepid and muggy. The air is thick with the stench of colliding perfumes, overly sweet foods, and spicy-tart wines. It's hard to say which is louder, the conversation or the band, as if the two are in competition to see which will first ruin the ears of those present.

Strings of bright fairy lights crisscross above the dancers, twinkling merrily in imitation of stars. Sprays of lily-and-waxflower bouquets decorate every table and spring from every sconce. The ballroom is a riot of color, garish and mesmerizing, which is all part of the appeal.

The official Courtship Masquerade has yet to begin, but there are as many dancers swirling around the ballroom as there are revelers partaking of the food and drink. Rae need only glance through the nearest window to see where the party has spilled out of the manor into the courtyard and the gardens, and farther still. Lanterns flicker in the fading sun, lining the lane toward the city square where even more citizens have gathered, and where another band is tasked with playing an identical tune.

It's a night for a great many things: promises and possibilities, hopes and dreams. Because the Masquerade can be attended by anyone regardless of their social status, it's not uncommon to see unexpected matches arise from it. Rae wishes she could feel that same hopeful joy, but the weight of what she must accomplish tonight keeps her too grounded.

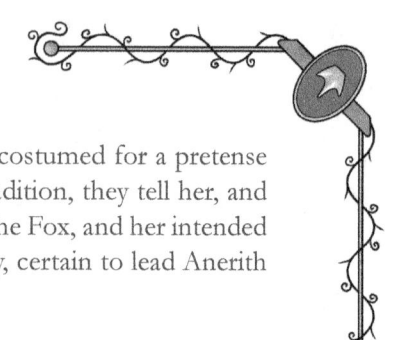

Rae stands on the dais with her mother and father, all three of them costumed for a pretense of anonymity, though they're easily recognized as the royal family. It's tradition, they tell her, and tradition must be heeded. Rae, as the named heir, must bear the mask of the Fox, and her intended shall be costumed as the Raven—two animals of clever wit and creativity, certain to lead Anerith into a bright tomorrow.

The ballroom is sweltering.

Rae is parched. Her feet swell in the confines of her heels, and her lower back aches. She's grateful for the mask that obscures everything but her eyes from view. She doesn't have to bother with a plastered-on smile or pretend civility. Her hair has lost the battle against the humidity, frizzy auburn waves erupting around the strap of the mask and over her shoulders. Even without the mask, people would recognize her distinctive curls.

Rae waits, fingers tangled together in nervous knots, wishing she had something to occupy her besides anxious fidgeting. She tries and fails to resist the urge to scan the crowd, seeking her lovers in the swirl of patterns and masks and colors.

Hyacinth lingers near the balcony doors, the black feathers of her raven mask nearly blending with the shadows of the drapery and with her dark, glossy curls. She holds herself with a calm poise Rae envies.

Madeline is by the buffet, tucked behind a potted plant. There are mounds of cupcakes within her reach, and Rae wonders how many she's already consumed. Thankfully, the brilliant red-and-yellow feathers of her mask make her easier to spot; otherwise, her short stature would be lost to the crowd. She's costumed as a songbird, but that's merely a pair of illusions cast by Rae's own hand. As far as she can tell, no one has noticed it to be a ruse.

"It's not going to work," Madeline had fretted but a few hours earlier. She'd glared at their costumes, at the heavy silks and masks that limited their visibility. Every inch of her muscled frame had been tense with displeasure.

Madeline takes their safety seriously; being unarmored and unarmed in the midst of a fraught situation had forced her usually sunny façade into a twist of discomfort.

"You're both at least a head taller than me," she'd pointed out, and though her observation hadn't been wrong, it was nothing a little magic couldn't fix.

Magic couldn't make Madeline's stout, muscular frame physically match the tall reediness of Hyacinth's nor the soft-and-round curves of Rae's, but it *could* convince curious eyes that there were other, more interesting things to observe. It wouldn't survive a curious touch, but no one would be touching Madeline without her permission regardless.

Madeline had gnawed on her worry, while Hyacinth had been all logic. "Over half the attendees will indulge in illusion if only to seem more desirable. There will be so much spellcraft in the air, no one will notice a minor transmutation."

"This will work," Rae had assured Madeline. She'd taken each of their hands in hers, tried to warm Hyacinth's chilled fingers, and had swallowed a wince as Madeline had squeezed back a touch too strongly. "I love you both, and this *will* work."

Rae had believed it then.

She believes it still.

Rae runs through the expected sequence once more, if only to calm herself. There are four stages to the Dance, excluding the Call inviting anyone to join, and Rae has divided them accordingly. First, Hyacinth will accompany her during the Proposal, then Madeline will take Hyacinth's place for the Intent. When they reach the third stage, the Consent, Rae will find Hyacinth again. Finally, when the Dance culminates in the Promise, she'll reunite with Madeline.

By the end of the Dance, there will be no confusion about whom Rae has chosen. The Fox will have both of her Ravens. Her parents won't be able to refuse them, not after the Dance.

This will work.

The song comes to an end with a vibrant flourish from the violin. The dancers swirl to a stop, politely clapping. A few exit the dance floor, flocking to the buffet for refreshment or seeking a breath of cooler air through the patio doors. Most remain to join the Dance. Attendees not participating in the Dance form a makeshift circle for those who will.

The sun has set, the stars have risen, and now the most treasured part of the Masquerade can officially begin.

A long, slow trill fills the air: the opening strains of the Courtship Dance rising above the chatter as the lone clarinet plays the Call to Court.

Rae's shoulders itch. She's too aware of her parents staring at her back. She glances at them, her head dipping deferentially.

Mother gives her a hard, warning stare. Father is as cold and still as stone.

This is the deadline they've given her. They want her to choose, or they will make the decision in her stead.

If she wishes to lead Anerith, Rae must obey its traditions and select a spouse.

Rae respectfully lowers her gaze—concession. Mother's approval, shaped as a thin smile, is barely visible beneath the sharp lines of her owl-themed mask. Grey-and-white feathers frame a face that hasn't softened for Rae in years.

Rae's lips twitch into a smirk they can't see.

She takes a deep breath and descends among the other romantic hopefuls. The anticipation filling the room stems from far more than only Rae's own jitters. Many who could never join hands at any other time will woo tonight. Those hoping to meet someone new, perhaps make a love connection, will also join the Dance.

What better test of love is there than to know one's partner not by their face, but by their energy? Their poise? Their Dance? At heart, that's the purpose of the Courtship Masquerade: to test the familiarity of lovers and see if they are well and truly matched. For those not already spoken for, there's no opportunity more charged with potential than when two strangers learn one another's rhythms, their identities concealed beneath the guise of their favorite creature.

A masked dancer intercepts Rae—they're neither Hyacinth nor Madeline, no, she knows this dancer only too well. Icy, blue eyes glitter at her from behind the gem-studded mask that can only be described as a rainbow snake if Rae is feeling kind, which she isn't. It's garish and hideous, and there's only one man who would proudly wear such a mask and so boldly accost her. Rae's grateful the Fox mask hides her frown as her belly roils with disgust.

"Lord Airy," Rae greets him with the kind of politeness years at court have taught her. "I have no desire to dance with you."

"I present myself as an escort only," Airy says, smooth and insincere. He wears a half-mask, his mouth visible, his mustache neatly trimmed and bobbing with each word.

It doesn't escape Rae's notice that he's approached her within view of her parents, who would be more than pleased if Rae took his hand. Yes, he's a snake rather than the Raven, but a mask can be swapped easily enough if she wished him to.

Rae would *never*.

"Surely, in all our years acquaintance, you can spare me the Call?" Airy asks with a genteel bow, offering his palm to her. Unfortunately, this *is* within the etiquette of the Dance's commencement. "Unless you'll reconsider declining my previous proposal, in which case it's not too late. We could

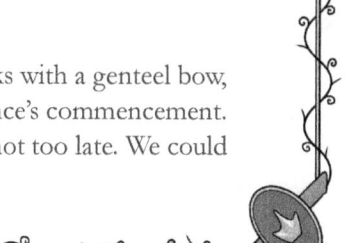

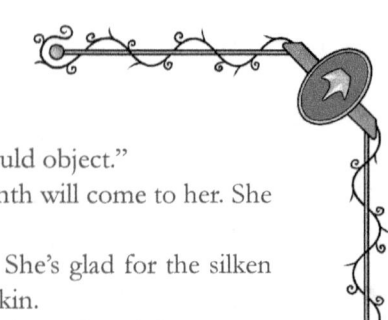

continue our embrace through the next movement. I dare say no one would object."

Rae grits her teeth but doesn't risk a glance through the crowd. Hyacinth will come to her. She need only make it through the Call.

She rests her fingertips across his palm, as loathe as she is to do so. She's glad for the silken gloves of her station. This would be worse if she had to touch his bare skin.

"Milady honors me," Airy simpers, and he guides her to the center of the gathered dancers.

More woodwinds join the lone clarinet, building the Call to Court with each successive instrument.

"Politeness is as politeness does," Rae says.

Airy smiles and hums as he lifts their clasped hands and rests his other hand on her waist. Wisely, he curls his fingers on her clothed hip rather than over the tempting slit of bare skin created by her gown. She returns the gesture by placing her hand over his: rejection in all but voice.

His lips twitch into a frown, then smooth into neutrality. "Word is that the Fox will be choosing her Raven tonight," he says as she steps forward, forcing him to defer and let her lead.

"I cannot be held responsible for whatever rumor you may have caught on the wind," Rae replies. She can't risk him figuring things out. She focuses on the Dance, on keeping Airy off balance, rather than seeking Hyacinth. That he's stolen her attention thus only irks her further.

The low, building cadence of a drum joins the woodwinds, marking the halfway point of the Call to Court's introduction. Other dancers swirl around them, a blur of faces masked in a variety of styles and colors, too many to count.

Airy's hand tightens around hers, a muscle in his jaw twitching.

"Am I mistaken? My apologies." He gestures across the dance floor with a lift of his chin. "Then I suppose it's no worry that she's dancing with a wolf right now."

Rae doesn't look. To do so would only buy into whatever tripe Airy is attempting to sell, whatever seed of discord he wants to sow in some vain attempt at revenge. Airy has never been one to take rejection lightly or with grace.

"She's free to do as she wishes, as am I," Rae says. Lightning crackles in her eyes, sparks casting shadows through the sockets of the Fox mask. She pushes forward, backing Airy away from her, forcing him to rely on her lead. "And I do *not*, nor will I *ever*, have any interest in snakes."

She shoves him to the rising crescendo of a flute and spins away, her hand outstretched, desperately hoping Hyacinth will come to her rescue. A rapidly trilling flute signals the shift to the first movement, the Proposal, and her fingers hang in the air, waiting. If a stranger dares take her hand, Rae will unleash a storm.

Fingertips press to hers, warm despite her gloves, and Rae smiles behind her mask. Raven feathers flutter in the corner of her eye, and Rae spins into Hyacinth's embrace as the Proposal thrums through the night.

Their hands clasp, right to right, as they face opposite directions and glide in slow circles, as Hyacinth asks with their Dance if there's mutual interest between them. Rae answers by interlacing their fingers, keeping her free hand tucked to her body to demonstrate her disinterest in other courters. If anyone tries to insinuate themselves between Rae and Hyacinth, it will be a grave breach of conduct.

Their eyes lock through their masks. Hyacinth's expression is hard, but her anger is not for Rae. "I will flay him," she hisses, too low for other ears. "He will be nothing when I am done."

"Airy will get his," Rae murmurs, projecting soothing calm. "Don't let him rattle you. This is going to work."

"I know," Hyacinth says, eyes at last softening with all of the love Rae knows she carries. "He

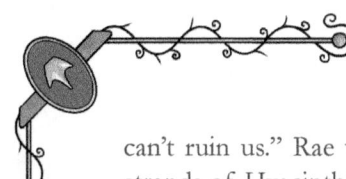

can't ruin us." Rae wishes Hyacinth could see her smile, wishes she could stroke the escaping strands of Hyacinth's bouncy, dark curls. She squeezes Hyacinth's hand instead.

"No, he can't," Rae agrees.

Hyacinth draws in a steadying breath, her gaze flicking past Rae as the Proposal crests and lingers. "Madeline is behind you."

"Good."

A lone, spiraling flute player slows the melody until more join to build the tension. Rae pulls away from Hyacinth, half-turning to seek Madeline. The Intent rises with each additional instrument, and Rae finds her awkward songbird behind her just as Hyacinth said, trying desperately not to look out of place.

Rae loves her clumsiness.

She takes Madeline's hand, dissolving the illusory mask as she does, and the bright feathers ripple away to reveal a second Raven, black and iridescent in the fairy lights. Someone gasps, and a few dancers lose their rhythm, heads swinging left and right as though trying to place where the new Raven has come from. Hyacinth vanishes into the fray, away from Rae and Madeline, gone but not far.

Madeline rests her hand on Rae's waist, erasing the lingering impression of Airy's touch, and Rae mirrors the placement of her hand, correcting at the last moment to account for the extra height of the secondary illusion.

Their Intent to Court projects to all as they interlace their fingers, palms pressed together, Madeline's grip a touch stronger than necessary. But, then, she's always had trouble softening her grip. She's built to protect, a warrior from the tip of her feet to the top of her head. Rae often teases that Madeline was born with a sword in her hand and a shield on her back.

"I'm so nervous." Madeline's fingers tremble, and Rae suspects she'd feel the slick of sweat if it weren't for her gloves. "I hope I don't trip."

A dancer she is not, but Madeline has grace. On the battlefield, in the training ring, she's a sight to behold. She's agile and dexterous, and if she can wield a sword like fine art, then surely she can dance.

"You're doing great. Our lessons paid off," Rae soothes. She dares tip her head a little closer than propriety allows. "And if you fall, I'll pick you back up."

Madeline chuckles. "Yes, but Hyacinth will never let me live it down." Her attention flicks away, scanning the crowd. Always on alert, their soldier. "I will kiss away his touch later, promise."

"Were we in a different time, I'd let you take your blade to him, but alas," says Rae.

"Don't tempt me with a good time," Madeline grumbles, and she squeezes Rae's waist, the force of her grip sending a thread of warmth through Rae's belly. "Count it down for me? I don't want to miss our cue."

Rae smiles, heart bursting with love, and, under her breath, she counts the steps of the Intent as the Dance glides into the third movement: the Consent.

She gives Madeline a nudge, and they turn away from each other—by the rules of the Dance, this is their chance to choose a new lover should they wish—and for a moment, Rae fears Airy might try to intercede again. But no, there's Hyacinth, beautiful in her raven feathers, taking Rae's offered hand. She pulls Rae close, their bodies mere inches apart, and Rae surrenders to her embrace.

Their hands interlace—right to left, palm to palm—and Hyacinth's other hand curls against the small of her back, a welcome weight. Rae rests her free hand along the back of Hyacinth's shoulder, silently refusing anyone who might try to make Rae an offer.

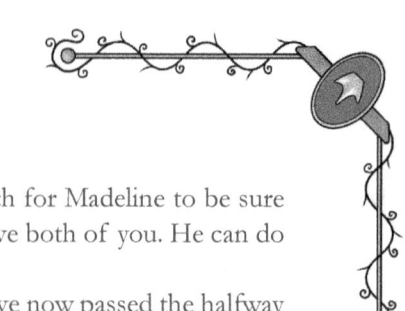

"Airy's watching," Hyacinth murmurs.

"Good." Rae keeps her gaze on Hyacinth, resisting the urge to search for Madeline to be sure her worried warrior hadn't tripped and fallen when they separated. "I love both of you. He can do nothing about it."

Her heart's in her throat, pounding so fast it echoes in her ears. They've now passed the halfway mark of the Dance. Surely, people have noticed that there are two Ravens. Rae, Madeline, and Hyacinth had been relying on the chaos of the Dance to keep people confused, but Rae's not foolish enough to think their ruse will work for long.

Sure enough, she can hear the whispers:

"Are there two of them?"

"I can't tell. They keep moving."

"Is that allowed?"

"I don't know."

Worry clutches Rae's heart. If the crowd has noticed, Mother and Father certainly have as well. Their stares have been smoldering between Rae's shoulders all evening. Her only consolation is that they will never dare interfere with the Dance.

Hyacinth squeezes her hand. "We're yours," she says, presumably reading Rae's disquiet. She presses her forehead to Rae's; though their masks ruin the intimacy of the gesture, Rae still greatly appreciates it.

Rae breathes in and out slowly, dragging in the scent of Hyacinth's familiar perfume and the echo of the promise they've made: all three of them, or none at all. Woe be unto anyone who tries to demand otherwise.

Drums join the trilling flute chorus, and, for the last time, Rae twirls away from Hyacinth, reaching for Madeline in the press of bodies. She glimpses Airy only briefly before Madeline shoulders into place, their fingers tangling and their bodies pressing as close as possible. The Promise rises sweetly around them as Rae's free hand rests on the nape of Madeline's neck and Madeline's hand presses between her shoulder blades.

"Whatever happens, we'll figure it out," Madeline whispers, her palm hot against the bared skin of Rae's hip. "I have a sword, and I'm not afraid to use it."

Rae chuckles through the lump in her throat. "It won't come to that. I promise." She presses her cheek to Madeline's and looks toward the dais.

Mother looks triumphant, smiling broadly, her hands clasped demurely in front of her. Father has moved closer to her, but there's nothing in his posture to suggest anger. They've assumed she's made her choice, which means they haven't figured out the ruse.

Hope swells within her, riding the coattails of her relief.

This is going to work.

The Masquerade Dance peaks with a dazzling clamor of woodwinds and drums, building to a glorious finale. Rae spins Madeline in her arms, and bends her into a dip, pressing their foreheads together. Madeline grins up at her, red-cheeked and breathless, as a loud cymbal clangs the final note.

For a moment, all is still and quiet. Rae stares into Madeline's eyes, sure Hyacinth must have already moved into position. She breaths heavily, sweating profusely beneath the layers of her gown and the thickness of her mask. Anxiety clings to her, a miasma thicker than the humidity.

Applause ripples through the ballroom. Cheers and whistles celebrate the end of this year's Courtship Masquerade, though the night is far from over.

Rae straightens, squeezing Madeline's hands before releasing her, letting Madeline ease into the

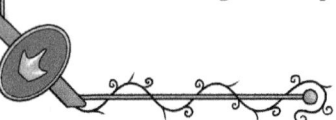

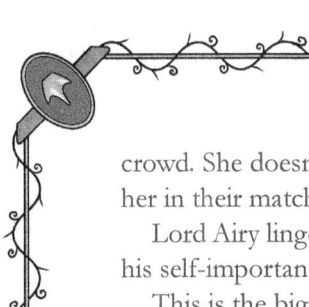

crowd. She doesn't let herself look back as she returns to the dais, to her parents staring down at her in their matching bird-of-prey masks.

Lord Airy lingers at the periphery of her vision, smirking and uncomfortably close. The reek of his self-importance makes her stomach churn—or maybe that's her nerves.

This is the biggest risk Rae has ever taken. And the most important.

Mother lifts her hands and silence falls, expectation thick in the atmosphere. The Courtship Dance is for everyone—commoner and noble alike—but, as always, nobility comes first. Who the heir-apparent will choose to wed is the highlight of the evening and must be addressed before anyone else can lay their claims on each other.

The Dance is always a show, but tonight it's a performance of the highest order. The nobility and the peasantry have no idea what's truly at stake. An ultimatum has been laid at Rae's feet; here and now, she must make a choice that will impact more than the identity of Rae's future spouse.

"Tell us, daughter, who your Dance has chosen," Mother says, her voice carrying easily through the ballroom—no doubt enhanced by spellcraft. She's always been one for a bit of drama. Perhaps Rae inherited it from her.

Rae lifts her chin. "Like all my kin before me, the Fox has danced with the Raven, and the Raven owns my heart." She presses her palm to her chest, a gesture of the solemn vow she's both offered and accepted. "We are promised."

Mother smiles.

Father says, "Then let the Raven step forward and take the hand of their beloved."

Those assembled turn, murmuring, searching the myriad of masked faces for a raven. Rae holds her parents' gaze, chin raised. Both her hands hang ready at her sides, but if her mother and father notice, they don't react.

Rae only knows Hyacinth and Madeline have both emerged from the crowd by the gasps.

"I knew there were two!" one attendee hisses gleefully.

Mother's eyes widen. Father's hand drops to the hilt of the sword at his hip before he presumably remembers where he is and tucks the hand behind his back.

Hyacinth's cold fingers slide into her right hand; Madeline's grip is painfully firm on her left.

"The Raven accepts the vow of the Fox," they say in tandem. "We are one."

Mother's hands form fists; Father rips away his mask, a storm brewing in dark eyes the same shade as Rae's own. She and her father have so much in common; up until recently, she'd been proud of that.

"What is the meaning of this?" Father demands. Crimson creeps up his neck and onto his face, making it blotchy beneath the carefully applied concealer.

"I have chosen my spouses through the dance, as you asked of me," Rae says with feigned innocence. Her hands are cold and slick with sweat, but she presses on. "As tradition dictates, we are bound by the promise we have made."

Mother still hides behind her mask, as though the gleaming owl—a paragon of wisdom—lends her words weight. "It is meant—"

"—for consenting parties," Hyacinth says, and she removes her mask, holding it in her free hand. She's using That Voice, the one that always means victory in the judgment halls. "I believe you'll find the sacred texts place no other restrictions."

Ripples of agreement surge through the crowd behind them. The Dance was witnessed, they tell each other. The Fox knew the Raven, they whisper. Did you notice there were two? Does it matter? The Fox accepts both of them.

Each murmured approval strengthens Rae's shoulders.

Her parents rule Anerith, but the people have a voice which doesn't go unheard.

Rae smiles behind her mask.

"By the dictates of the Courtship Masquerade, I will marry my Ravens," she says. "Or do you break tradition and deny my engagement?"

Gasps precede a sweeping silence.

Madeline removes her mask, letting it hit the floor with a dull *thump*. Rae drops the minor illusion, and Madeline shrinks to her natural height, her shoulders broadening and straining the seams of her costume. Her free hand rests on the hilt of her sword, now peeking through the feathers of her elaborate cloak.

Unmasked, they are a study in contrasts: Hyacinth tall and stern with dark curls and dark skin, bookish and brilliant and a force to be reckoned with; Madeline a danger in her own right, rippling with muscle, scarred from battle, her hair brown and undercut, the metal of her eyebrow ring catching the fairy lights.

Rae stands between them, aristocratic in her carriage and equally firm. She could not and would not choose between Hyacinth and Madeline. Neither would she abide by an arranged marriage. They'd studied the tomes, the stories, the numerous recountings of the numerous years of the Courtship Masquerade.

The Dance has no precedence for a polyamorous relationship. But there are no laws forbidding it, either. Where the law isn't explicit, there is leeway which can be bent, according to Hyacinth.

Rae squeezes her lovers' hands and waits.

Mother takes a quiet breath and removes her mask, lips forced into a smile that doesn't reach her eyes. It's the same cold look she'd offered when she first gave Rae the ultimatum, when she'd proven deaf to Rae's begging and pleading for compassion or compromise.

Her parents have been as statues, refusing to bend. They'd thought they could break Rae in the end.

Tradition is the backbone of Anerith, Mother had said, *and if you hope to rule this city one day, you will abide by it.*

Tradition, as Mother said, must be followed. So Rae found a way.

Mother speaks, flat and angry, "Tradition will, of course, be upheld. I do not object."

"Well played, daughter," says Father. He dips his head, though his eyes never drop from hers. "I cannot object. The Fox will marry her Ravens."

The crowd behind them erupts in elation—restrained clapping by the nobility and sheer enthusiasm from the common-folk lucky enough to win the raffle to attend. A low growl tugs Rae's attention; when she turns to investigate, she sees Lord Airy spin away from them and shove through the crowd.

Two battles have been won tonight.

The band strikes up a celebratory tune. Soon, romantic hopefuls of noble birth will step forward to announce their engagements, and they'll be followed by the commoners later still, but this moment is Rae's, and Madeline's and Hyacinth's.

Rae can't stop grinning. She can feel her feet again, her heart's still beating, and Madeline and Hyacinth are hers.

Nothing can separate them now.

Madeline yanks on her hand and pulls her down into an embrace, throwing her arms around Rae's neck. "It worked!" she says, planting kisses all over Rae's mask. "I can't believe it worked!"

"I knew it would," Hyacinth says, gentler as she extracts Rae from Madeline's over-strong grasp and lifts Rae's fox mask away. Her eyes glitter with triumph. "We won."

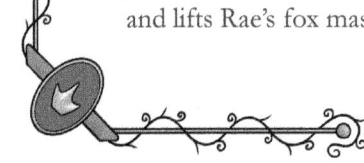

"Yes, we did." Rae's thoughts twirl, dancing between the sheer joy of their success and the sudden veer away from a cliff of anxiety.

Hyacinth kisses her, fierce and celebratory for all that it's chaste, and Madeline throws her arms around both of them. Their bodies tangle, costumes a hindrance, but it doesn't matter. Madeline laughs as she rises on her tiptoes, stealing a kiss from Rae, then from Hyacinth, and back to Rae again.

Rae feels like she can breathe for the first time in weeks.

There will still be many conversations. Her parents' displeasure hangs over her like a dreary cloud, but they can no longer object. They've given their blessing in front of every noble and commoner assembled for the Dance.

Rae can marry Hyacinth and Madeline both.

The rest, they'll manage as it comes.

Alicia Matheson (Next Page)
"The Sweetest Thing"

I think love stories between two people of the same gender are so beautiful, so I really loved recreating "Ben and Bee" as two men. In Shakespeare's day, a woman in theater would be painted with her shirt open to prove she was female, since women were typically portrayed by men. I wanted to do the same for Bee and paint him with his shirt open to show he is male, and I chose the color red to represent the characters' passion. I included Ben's bouquet of snapdragons because they are the flower that means "deception," which is a big theme in the play.

In Mine Eye
he Is The Sweetest
That Ever I
Looked On

Alicia Matheson
2021

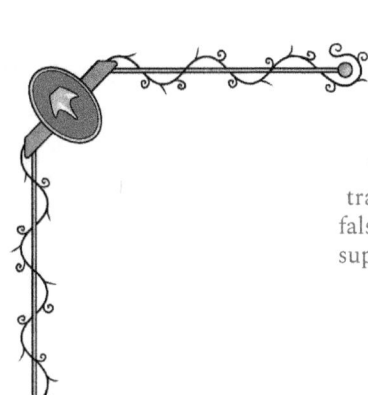

TAGS: alternate universe, angst (minor), bisexual, creature transformation (cat), emotional hurt/comfort, engineer, f/f, f/m, false accusations, friends to lovers, meet awkward, modern with superpowers, past tense, secret identity, superhero, third person limited point of view

CAN VIRTUE HIDE ITSELF?

Lyn Weaver

In the original version of Much Ado About Nothing, *Ursula is not a particularly important character. Some people don't even remember that she exists. But the first version of Much Ado that I read—a social media/band AU* hosted on Tumblr—featured Ursula as a mean lesbian who acted as a much-needed emotional support to Hero, and I fell in love with that interpretation of her. Of course, there's usually more to someone than simply being mean, a lesbian, and liking a girl, so when I had the chance to write my own Ursula, I knew I had to give her something else to feel strongly about. This ended up being superheroes. Write what you know, I guess. Hero being a hero flowed from there, and the two girls ended up on a collision course lined with laser guns, silly costumes, and a dash of social commentary. I think it turned out well.*

* Editor's Note: AU stands for "alternate universe"

The first time Ursula fell in love, it was in the middle of a supervillain attack. One moment, she was walking home from school, wondering why she bothered going to class if the teachers were just gonna fanboy about superheroes the whole time. The next, the bridge she stood on was hit by a bolt of energy: Cloudrunner's blasts were devastating to inanimate matter but didn't damage living beings. It passed through her, but with a horrible noise, the concrete under her feet gave way.

She grabbed the nearest crumbling edge just in time to keep from falling as Cloudrunner's white, ruffled form soared overhead, energy building around his arm. A second figure, with a dark suit and ominous full-face helmet, swooped around him—the Bastard, the city's most dangerous supervillain.

For Ursula, the real danger was Cloudrunner's blast. "Don't shoot!" she shouted.

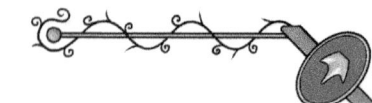

He slung the bolt without looking down. The Bastard dodged; Ursula couldn't. She clung to the bridge and waited to be sent plummeting into the icy water below. For Cloudrunner to realize his mistake. For someone to save her.

"Hold on!" a voice called, and the sky filled with light.

Ursula refused to squeeze her eyes shut. Even as tears dripped from her eyes, she watched as the approaching light took on a woman's shape.

No, not a woman. A girl, barely Ursula's age. Crackling energy danced over silver armour. Had she—absorbed the blast?

"That was close. Are you all right?" The girl reached out an arm. Ursula flinched. "Sorry, is it too bright?"

As the glow dimmed, Ursula could make out colours again. The broken bridge had been scorched black, but there were no burns beneath where the girl hovered inches above the ground. Long, dark hair bobbed around her shoulders as though she were underwater. Behind a domino mask, her eyes were whiskey brown and terribly warm.

"Is that better?"

"Yeah," Ursula rasped, still holding on. "Who…?"

"I'm Hero. And I'm a hero."

"That's terrible."

The girl in gold—Hero?—laughed. "It is, isn't it? But that's my name!"

"You shouldn't give it out." Ursula glanced up. "The Bastard was right there."

"It's also my hero name!"

"Well, that's just uncreative."

"It's meant to be funny. A hero should be able to make people smile, right?"

Ursula prepared a cutting remark, saw Hero's smile, and coughed instead. "Shouldn't you be chasing the Bastard?"

Hero drooped. "I'm…not exactly a combat hero. I just absorb energy. Clau— Cloudrunner and Soldier B have it handled."

"Soldier B isn't even here!"

She wilted farther. "He and Bea must be arguing again. I can fly you somewhere safe?"

Another burst of light overhead. "That would be nice."

Hero was smaller than Ursula had thought, but she lifted Ursula effortlessly. She smelled like the air after a storm, and her might made Ursula's mouth go dry.

When they touched down on a rooftop, Ursula finally got a decent look at the battlefield. "This fight would be over if you were out there!"

"No way." Hero gave Ursula one final squeeze and let her go.

"Way. The Bastard isn't watching his back. Anyone could take him out while he's distracted by Cloudrunner. Here." Ursula rummaged through her bag and pulled out a prototype laser gun. Hero stiffened but said nothing. Ursula smirked and handed it over. "If you can't shoot energy, use this. It's set to stun. This button shoots, this one recharges for the next shot."

Hero bit her lip. Another burst of light cracked across the city, and her jaw firmed. She raised the gun and fired once—a miss—twice—a hit—three times, another hit, sending the Bastard spinning.

Ursula made the mistake of looking away from the explosions and froze.

Hero's smile was blinding. "It worked!"

Ursula's throat was too dry to speak. She nodded instead, unable to look away.

Hero lowered the gun and handed it back. "We should get out of here. Come on. I'll fly you

home."

Just like that, Ursula fell in love.

Ursula was kind of offended that she'd fallen for a superhero. She didn't even like superheroes. Yet here she was, sitting at her desk in her cramped, dark room, surrounded by the remains of discarded projects—and her laser gun, which had been enshrined in a place of honour—daydreaming about a hero named Hero. Disgusting.

She'd been collateral damage before. This was the first time Cloudrunner had shot at her, but she'd had a few other near misses. Once, the Don had ordered the Bastard to kneel with his Compelling Voice while over Ursula's rundown high school. The Bastard had been wearing ear plugs. Ursula hadn't been. She and the rest of her class had blinked and found themselves on their knees.

It'd been the single most terrifying experience of her life. She'd always been inclined to tinker, but she'd only started building weapons after that.

She kicked at a piece of scrap metal under her desk. So what if the heroes had just been careless? When one had superpowers, one couldn't afford to be careless—not when mistakes destroyed people.

Hero had saved Ursula when no one else had noticed her. Was that why Ursula couldn't get Hero out of her head?

A smile so bright. Eyes so kind. Just thinking about her made Ursula's cold, dead heart flutter.

The hunt for Hero began not out of gratitude, but self-preservation. Maybe if Ursula could see Hero again—reassure herself that her saviour was just another careless fake—her stomach would stop twisting in knots.

It'd been easy to find Hero. There weren't many girls as beautiful and even if there were, Ursula still would've recognized her smile.

Hero Messina was also sixteen. She attended a fancy school for rich kids—the kind that let daddy buy good grades, not the kind that pushed kids into breakdowns. She was also, obviously, a superhero. Even if Ursula hadn't spotted her grin in the huge photo of her splashed over the school's website, Hero did a terrible job hiding. The photo linked to the school newspaper, which linked to Hero's socials. They were full of gorgeous selfies taken mid-flight.

The descriptions said she was standing on tall buildings. Ursula called bullshit. No one could perch on an open-roofed skyscraper while keeping both Town Hall and the observation tower at their back at such a photographic angle. Hero had taken the pic while pretending to crouch, the tower level with her perfectly plucked brows. She was giving the peace sign.

Of course she was giving the peace sign.

"What a loser," Ursula sighed. "I've gotta meet her."

Maybe she could transfer to Hero's school? No, she'd never get into a school that judged one's family tree instead of entrance exams.

Well, whatever.

Ursula spun her pencil around her fingers and plotted how to "accidentally" bump into the girl of her dreams.

The hero of her dreams?

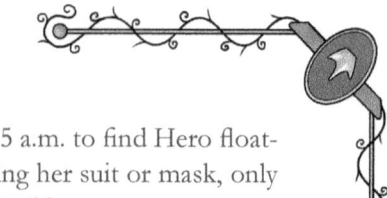

After two weeks of planning, Ursula stepped out of her apartment at 5 a.m. to find Hero floating about twenty feet above the tree in her front yard. Hero wasn't wearing her suit or mask, only a long white dress that glimmered in the gathering dawn. Her exposed cheekbones—

A loud meow echoed in the morning air. A black cat the size of a German shepherd crouched on a branch, eyes gleaming.

"Come on, Bea." Hero gestured encouragingly. "It's not that high. You can jump down."

"Rrrr," said what must've been the shapeshifting superhero, Black Cat. Well, ex-superhero. Black Cat had last appeared on the news several years ago where she'd called Soldier B some hideous names, scratched up his pretty face, and then transformed from a cat-woman to a full-on cat to make her escape.

Was Black Cat a villain now?

"If you slip, I'll catch you!"

Black Cat stayed where she was and glowered at Ursula over Hero's shoulder. "Rrrreowr."

"What do you mean you can't jump if someone's watching? Nobody's awake, Bea."

"Is that so?" Ursula deadpanned.

Hero froze in mid-air then whipped around, cheeks flushed. "H-hello there, person I have never met!"

"Hello yourself, Hero." Ursula emphasized the name to distinguish it from the word. "Nice to see you again. Do you make a habit of saving girls stranded in high places?"

"I, uh—I'm not sure what you mean." Hero belatedly tried to cling to the same branch Black Cat—or Bea, apparently—sat on. "I'm just a totally normal girl climbing a tree after my totally normal cat!"

"Well, it's too late now." With a huff, Bea became mostly human-shaped save for her flicking kitty ears. Her hair was the same shade as Hero's, but wilder. Her lips were pressed into a scowl even before they'd reformed. "Cat's out of the bag."

"Bea!"

Bea grimaced. "Your feet aren't even on the tree, Hero. Hey, innocent-bystander-Hero-definitely-hasn't-met, you wouldn't happen to have a ladder handy?"

Ursula grimaced back. Just because she lived alone didn't mean she was a real adult. "I'm a high school student, why would I have a ladder?"

"Does your landlord—?"

"I do have an anti-grav gun though. Hang on, I'll get it."

Both Hero and Bea looked shocked when Ursula came back, multi-colored anti-grav gun in hand. The gun kinda looked like it'd been made by a balloon clown, but it worked like a dream. Bea flinched when Ursula pulled the trigger and remained stiff as she was lifted off the branch in a sphere of wobbly gravity. Only when her feet were safely on the ground, and Ursula had turned the gun off, did Bea relax.

"That's so cool!" Hero kicked off the tree and flew down.

Ursula coughed and looked away. "It was nothing. Why were you in my tree to begin with?"

"Well, you see—"

"Hero," Bea said sharply. "Not in public."

Hero drooped. "But—"

"You could come inside if you want to talk." Ursula tried not to sound eager. "I don't have parents." Thanks to The Bastard's villainous debut. "And my place is soundproof. The neighbours got sick of hearing explosions."

The heroes shared a glance, then nodded.

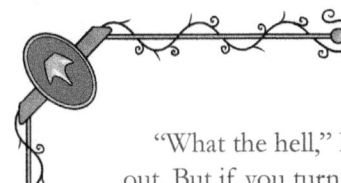

"What the hell," Bea sighed. "You helped Hero before, and it's not like anyone else will hear us out. But if you turn out to be a supervillain, I'm going to scratch your face off."

Ursula scowled. "Abusing your authority?"

"It was a joke. Lead the way."

There weren't enough chairs in her room for all three of them. Ursula had gone on a huge engineering binge after Hero had brought her home; now, bits of machinery filled the place and there were scribbled-on sticky notes stuck to every surface.

She sacrificed her rolling chair to Hero and hopped up on the counter. Bea followed suit. For a long moment, they just looked at each other, waiting for someone else to speak.

Finally, Ursula took the plunge. "So?"

"We're not here as heroes." Bea said firmly.

Hero nodded. "We're here because Benny hurt Bea's feelings."

"He couldn't hurt me if he tried!"

"You were crying, Bea."

"I've never shed a tear in my life!"

Ursula cleared her throat. "Who's Benny?"

"Soldier B." Bea spat his name like a physical blow. "You know him. Everyone does."

Oh. Him. "He almost ran me over once. Didn't apologize."

Bea threw her hands up. "He's the worst! He convinced me to date him for three months in high school. Biggest mistake of my life."

Hero squirmed. "Look, I know he's made mistakes, but he's changed, Bea! Or…he's trying to change. For you."

"Too late. He had his chance."

"No, really!" Hero protested. "I heard him talking to Cla—Cloudrunner—about how much he regrets breaking it off with you."

"Excuse me? I broke it off with him!" Bea hissed, but she couldn't quite meet Hero's eyes.

"He realized how wonderful you are, Bea. He knows he screwed up and wants to make up for it."

"Really?" Ursula asked. "That doesn't sound like any boy I know."

Bea snorted. "He's 18 and off the junior team, so he thinks he's a man now. Apparently, men must make up for the mistakes of their youth."

Ursula made a face. "That really doesn't sound like any man I know."

"It's true!" Hero smiled shyly but couldn't stop fidgeting. "He told Claudio, who told me. Then Bea overheard me talking about it. They talked, he came on a little strong, and Bea was so embarrassed she got stuck up your tree."

One question, in particular, stuck out to Ursula. "Why were you meeting him at, like, 4 a.m.?"

"Early morning patrol!" Hero yawned cutely. "Crime never sleeps."

"Unfortunately, Hero's not a morning person." Bea's yawn showed significantly more teeth. "Neither am I. Goddamn Benny sure is, though. We need someone on our side who can match his energy."

"Yeah. Someone creative and passionate, who can keep up with us and keep us pointed in the right direction. I'm still pretty new at this 'hero' thing. I mean, it's been in my family for generations—"

"Hero, don't—oh, forget it." Bea stared up at the ceiling. "We're so bad at secret identities."

"Don't worry," Ursula told her, idly taking the anti-grav gun out to tinker with it. "I won't tell anyone. Never been into the hero scene."

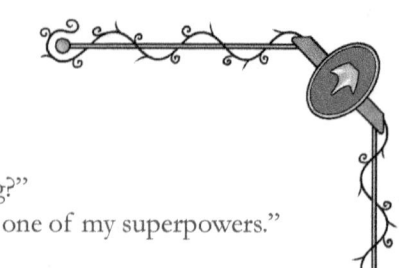

"Too bad," Hero said. "I think you'd be good at it."

Ursula laughed. Then she realized Hero was serious. "Are you kidding?"

"We worked well together. Besides, I'm a good judge of character! It's one of my superpowers."

"I'm bad with authority. Can't take orders for the life of me."

"Well, Hero and I were thinking of striking out together," Bea noted. "Forming our own girl group. I won't have to look at Benny's face all the time, and the boys can get things done without Hero mooning over Claudio all day."

Hero blushed, and something in Ursula's stomach twisted. "Bea! We aren't that bad!" She glanced sideways, seeking out Ursula's gaze. "I really do think you'd be a great addition to our team. Do you have a summer job lined up? Maybe you could hang out with us for a few weeks! Or a month! Or forever!"

Ursula raised her hands. "I'm not superhero material. No connections in the industry. And smiling for the camera gives me hives."

"That's fine!" Hero bounced out of the chair. "I can do all the smiling!"

Bea huffed. "Whoever gave you the gravity gun thinks you can do it."

"I built it myself."

Hero's eyes went huge and starry. Oh no. Ursula's one weakness.

"Wow, really? That's amazing, Ursula!"

"All the more reason you should join us." Bea didn't miss a beat. "You can build all sorts of things without worrying about getting permits. One of your weapons took the Bastard down in one shot. I definitely want that on my side."

No way in hell. Ursula set her jaw. "There's absolutely no chance you're going to drag me into this superhero bull."

Three weeks later, Ursula stood in a shiny new laboratory as an official sidekick. She hated that she didn't hate it. The girls *had* split from the main team, so it was usually just the three of them. Hero's father the Lionheart and the Don stayed busy elsewhere. Unfortunately, Soldier B and Cloudrunner kept dropping in.

At least Soldier B was Bea's problem. Cloudrunner was Hero's, which made him Ursula's by proxy.

"It's good to have you on board," he said, all tousled dark hair and flashing eyes. He was, objectively speaking, very handsome, but Ursula kinda hated his smug face.

"Thanks. It's good to be here." In a real lab with real gear, not just the hand-me-downs her parents had left her.

"The Lionheart put a lot of resources into building this place." Cloudrunner slapped the nearest machine. Fortunately, it was turned off, so he didn't get a burst of gamma radiation to the face. "I'm glad to see it's going to someone who understands its value."

Hero perked up from behind him. "Don't worry. We'll take good care of the base!"

Cloudrunner nodded absently. "It's been a while since the team had a good tinkerer. I'm looking forward to seeing what you can contribute."

Last time Ursula checked, she was on Hero's team, not his. "I'm thinking I'll start with better detection programs. Built into a protective visor, maybe, with an aim assist so those energy blasts of yours are always on-target."

"That'd be a big help."

Yeah, Ursula bet it would.

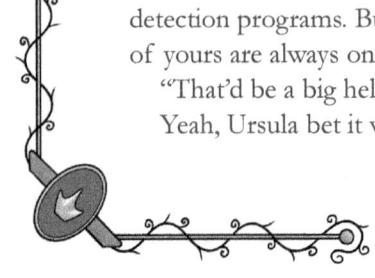

Cloudrunner cleared his throat, glanced sideways at Hero, then looked back at Ursula. "Please don't take this the wrong way, but I really appreciate the level of thought you're putting into this. Most people don't really see us heroes as people. It's easier for them to hold us up as idols than treat us as friends."

Ursula crossed her arms. "You'd better not be hitting on me."

"I'm not! I just—wanted to thank you."

"Thank Hero for convincing me to give you a chance."

Cloudrunner winced. "Sorry. I didn't know you were on that bridge."

"That's why I'm making you better gear instead of stabbing you while you sleep."

Cloudrunner laughed and spent a few more minutes watching as Ursula bustled around and made the lab her own. He didn't acknowledge Hero, who bobbed in his wake. The starry sheen in her eyes made Ursula's heart skip a beat even as her stomach churned. Finally, he turned around and gave Ursula a friendly goodbye and Hero a quick nod. He didn't even check to see if Hero was following before he left.

The second the door closed, Hero sighed and floated onto the counter. "Cloudrunner's taking extra patrols, so he can't stay around. He's so brave."

Ursula grunted into the microscope she was setting up. "Or maybe he's just trying to make up for being an ass."

"He did apologize. And his aim is so much more accurate now."

"Yours is still better. You're a better hero all around."

"Now you're just being silly!" But Hero was smiling, and Ursula's stomach filled with butterflies. For a moment, all was right with the world. Of course, that feeling didn't last.

"Thank you, Ursula. I don't have a lot of friends."

Ursula's heart didn't break in two, but it sure felt like it did. "Yeah," she managed. "Friends."

"Best friends?" Hero asked hopefully, and damn it, they'd known each other for maybe a month and Ursula already couldn't deny her anything.

"Yeah. Best friends." It was fine. Ursula didn't need a functioning heart, anyway. "Is that why you two haven't been going out together? Extra patrols?"

Hero wilted. "…no. He's always busy. He spends a lot of time with my dad, talking about the future of the team."

"Won't you be leading with him?"

"I'd like to." Hero kicked her legs into the air. "But that's still a ways off. Bea thinks it's good for us to find our footing as separate heroes."

"You don't?"

Hero lowered her eyes. "I wish he'd at least take patrols with me."

"Hey." Ursula waited until Hero looked up again before she smiled. "If you're lonely, my lab door is always open. Unless it's closed for safety reasons, in which case we can talk through the intercom."

Bright, golden light bloomed around them. "Thanks, Ursula!"

The nice thing about having her own lab was that Ursula could go into proper multi-day engineering binges without risking someone calling Child Services. She was 18 hours into a cold-fusion reactor when someone knocked on her door.

"Just a minute, Hero!" she called. "I'm in the middle of something."

"Ursula, come out." Soldier B's voice. Not Hero's.

"Why are you here?" Ursula demanded.

"Please. Hero and Bea need you."

She put the project into suspension, slipped her lab coat off, and ran through decontamination protocols. Soldier B stood costumed in the hallway, mask off, pitch-black circles under his eyes.

"What happened?"

"You didn't watch the news today, did you?"

"No."

"Just come with me," he said. "Bea will explain it better, anyway."

Ursula followed him to the living room, where Hero usually spent her time playing video games, painting her nails, and waiting for Cloudrunner to drop by. She wasn't there now. Instead, an enormous black cat paced back and forth.

Bea flowed into human form when she spotted them. Her ears stayed pinned back. "I'm going to kill him. He's ruined everything."

"Who?" Ursula jogged forward to put herself between Bea and their visitor, sliding off her safety glasses. "What did he do? Do you need an alibi?"

"Claudio. He told the press she cheated on him with a villain. Said she shared all their secrets with the Bastard—had pictures of her screwing a known henchman and threw them at the news crews."

A trickle of dread went down Ursula's spine. "Her…who?"

"Hero, of course! Who else could it be?"

Ursula's glasses clattered against the floor, but she could hardly hear it over the ringing in her ears. "Where is she? What the hell did he do to her?"

"She's in a holding cell. I already posted bail, but they aren't letting her out for 72 hours." A deep, animal growl. "She didn't do it. I don't care if she doesn't have an alibi!"

Behind them, Soldier B bowed his head. "I know."

"She would never." Ursula's chest ached. "She loved him."

Bea nodded sharply. "I'm going to kill him."

"Good. I'll be your alibi."

Soldier B pressed his lips together. "Might be tricky. Last I checked, he was locked up in our team's secret base. He and the Don changed the security codes, so you girls won't be able to get in. They knew how you'd react."

Bea lashed her tail. "Ursula, how long will it take you to build a death ray to destroy the whole building?"

"About a week. We should break Hero out first." Every second they spent talking was another Hero suffered in jail.

"Yeah," Soldier B said heavily. "Give me twenty-four hours to get her out legally. If I can't pull it off by then, we'll have to break her out."

Ursula spent the next day chugging energy drinks and working on a very dramatic, very lethal upgrade to the laser gun she'd once lent Hero. Bea described Cloudrunner's weaknesses while pouring over the horrific press conference he'd thrown. Every couple of seconds, she hit pause and jotted something down on her phone.

"Evidence. For when Benny comes through."

"*If* he comes through." Ursula slotted the gun's power cell into place.

"He will."

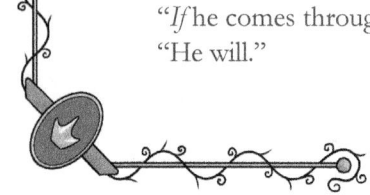

Despite the certainty in her tone, Bea's eyes went wide when Soldier B paged the base's intercom three hours before his one-day deadline.

"I brought her home. Let us in?"

The two of them dropped everything. Bea checked the security cameras, while Ursula raced for the door. Soldier B looked almost the same as before: tired, disappointed, and with a grim cast to his boyish features. Hero, though…

Bea herded them inside. Ursula wrapped Hero in thick blankets and pressed a mug of hot chocolate into her shaking hands. Hero didn't seem to notice. Her gaze was distant, even when Ursula hugged her and settled her onto the nearest couch.

"I vouched for her innocence," Soldier B said. "When that didn't work, I took her into my custody. She can't leave the base until the investigation is over. One of us will have to stay with her at all times, while the others get to the bottom of this."

"I'll do it." Ursula glanced over her shoulder. "I'll keep her safe. No one will get through me."

He smiled faintly. "I'll hold you to that."

Just like that, "Soldier B" became "Benny" to Ursula. He and Bea glanced at Hero, then went into the other room. Ursula stayed on the couch and waited. "Sorry." Hero's voice was rough, her eyes red and swollen.

Ursula hugged her. "Don't apologize."

"I have to. You're going to be attached to this. What they say about me, it's going to affect you too—"

"I don't care. Don't apologize."

"But I—"

"You are the best thing that's ever happened to me. Before I met you, I was spinning my wheels, wondering why I bothered doing anything. I didn't believe in heroes. I didn't believe anyone would help me if I was in trouble. You changed all that." Ursula softened. "You saved me, Hero."

Tears gathered in Hero's dark lashes. She sniffed loudly and buried her nose in the hot chocolate. "…it's cold."

"I'll get you a new cup." Ursula moved to stand, but Hero grabbed her hand and refused to let go. "Hero?"

"It's okay. I'll drink it."

"Cold hot chocolate? That's a travesty. If it was meant to be cold, they'd call it 'cold chocolate.'"

"It's okay," Hero repeated. "Because you made it for me."

Despite everything, Ursula's cheeks burned. In the other room, Bea and Benny traded affectionate threats—most of them aimed at Cloudrunner. Hero leaned against Ursula's side. She had bony elbows, her hair hadn't been washed in a while, and she was agonizingly perfect.

"I'm sorry," Ursula said in a rush. "If I'd known—"

"How could you know when I didn't? I was the one dating him." Hero looked down. "I thought I'd marry him when things with the Bastard settled and my dad was ready to name Claudio as his successor." Every word was another needle in Ursula's heart. "I was going to step down from heroing. Focus on our family, like dad wanted. I was looking forward to it, I think. I wasn't *not* looking forward to it, anyway. I would've been a good wife."

"You'd be an amazing wife, but you're also an amazing hero. If Cloudrunner can't see that, the problem is on his end."

"I thought I loved him, but now I can't feel anything when I think about him. Isn't that terrible?"

"No." Ursula squeezed tighter. "It's human."

If Ursula could build a suit of armour around the fragile look in Hero's eyes, the spark slowly coming back to life, she would.

Hero was almost asleep on Ursula's shoulder when Bea slammed the door open. "It was the Bastard!"

"Shh!" Ursula hissed. Too late. Hero froze beside her.

For a long, terrible moment, there was nothing but fear in those dark eyes. "Bea?"

Bea pulled the two of them into an awkward hug. "We can fix this, Hero. We figured it out."

Benny stumbled in looking like he'd been hit by a very excited truck. "Bea found evidence that the person in the photos isn't Hero. I remembered a low-profile career criminal who can swap objects—or people—in images. The guy isn't exactly a threat, but he's great at blackmail. And frame jobs, apparently. The Bastard broke him out of jail around the same time you joined the team."

"That bastard," Ursula breathed.

"Exactly."

"Why?" Hero asked softly.

Bea laid her ears back. "Who cares? It's probably something stupid."

"I want to know why he did…all of this."

"Then we'll drag it out of him at the court hearing. Right, Benny?"

Benny petted her head. "Right, Bea."

The two of them headed out. Hero and Ursula watched the confrontation on TV. Getting the Bastard's side of the story was easy—the hard part was making him stop monologuing to the cameras.

Supervillains: almost as ridiculous as superheroes.

Paraphrased, he'd used his falsified pictures to ruin Hero's image in the superhero community and, since she was from a hero family, her civilian life. When her friends and family turned against her, he'd planned to drive her into the pits of despair, then send some minions to finish her off and make it look like a suicide. Then, he'd reveal that she'd been innocent all along. Brilliant plan.

The Bastard's motivation was less brilliant: he was still pissed Hero had shot him with Ursula's gun. That impressive level of pettiness didn't save him from Bea's claws or Benny's super-speed punches.

Hero watched from the edge of her seat, tiny sparks jumping around her clenched fists. Ursula sat beside her, upgrading the gun that'd kicked everything off.

Well, not quite. It might've been Ursula's gun, but it was Hero who'd shot it. She'd been magnificent. She was always magnificent. Even right now.

Maybe especially right now.

Onscreen, the Don and the Lionheart eventually appeared with apologies, but Cloudrunner didn't.

"He must be running late," Hero murmured as the Bastard was slapped in cuffs.

"He's afraid to show his face," Ursula countered.

"I want to hear his side of the story."

The misery in Hero's voice was too much to bear. Ursula turned the TV off. "The Bastard's finished, your dad knows you're innocent, and our friends are gonna be occupied for the next few hours. You wanna move to the lab and help me finish this death ray?"

A shaky smile. "I'd love to."

Tinkering always soothed Ursula's nerves, especially with Hero cuddled up on the stool behind

her, chin on her shoulder. Hopefully it was doing the same for Hero.

"That can't be comfortable. Do you want me to get you a pillow or something?"

"I'm good."

"You fall asleep like this, you'll get a crick in your neck."

"If I fall asleep, I'll start floating."

Ursula paused. "Really?"

"I always wake up on the ceiling."

"Sounds adorable. I'd love to see that." As soon as the words were out of her mouth, she knew she'd made a mistake.

"Oh." Hero went still against her. "You like me. That, um, explains a lot."

"Please, just forget about it."

"I don't think I want to." Hero turned Ursula's stool around. For the first time since everything had fallen apart, she was glowing. Her hair swirled as she leaned in for a kiss.

When she pulled back, the whole room was filled with light.

"Sorry, is it too bright?"

"No," Ursula said, "you're perfect."

Hero's smile was brighter than the sun.

Pallas Perilous
"Born Under Saturn"

Contemporary productions often add a twist to Don John's interactions with his flunkies (the drunken Borachio and subservient Conrade) by casting Conrade as his lover. A same-sex pairing certainly adds some extra heft to Don John's outsider angst.

I thought it would be more interesting, though, to keep Conrade as his lover but show that the source of Don John's envy of all these almost-happy couples is not based in heteronormativity—hey, the whole anthology is queer!—but in lack of any real human connection. I recast Conrade as an android (mandroid?), one of just two crewmembers on a spaceship of war commanded by Don John, piloted by Borachio.

The rest of the cast enjoy the sunny afternoons of the planetary surface below, while Don John remains self-exiled in orbit above, spying on their romantic frolics from cold, empty space.

Also, I like purple.

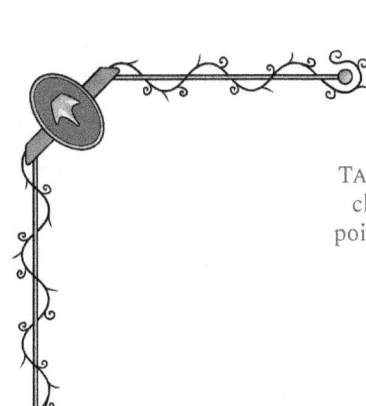

TAGS: alcohol use (casual), aromantic, asexual, canon compliant, character study, epistolary, f/m, false accusations, first person point of view, mistakenly believed dead, misunderstandings, past tense, present tense, wedding

THE JOURNAL OF DON PEDRO:

OR, THE STRAIGHTS ARE AT IT AGAIN

Nova Mason

I absolutely love experimenting with different voice styles when writing. Digging into something first-person, using Shakespearean language, was definitely a challenge. It was also incredibly fun! I wanted to play with the idea of an "outsider" to the two main couples, someone who knew enough to understand what was happening and to be invested in it but who wasn't one of the four lovers. Don Pedro was an obvious choice. I originally thought the story might be letters to Don Pedro's male lover, but decided to go with a diary from an ace/aro* narrator instead. I feel like it gives him a motivation to write things down as he tries to figure out what the heck is going on. Making sure to increase the amount of ace and aro rep in the world was also a motivating factor!

* Editor's Note: "ace" is short for "asexual" and "aro" is short for "aromantic."

The Sixth of July

Ah! We have arrived, whole, at the lodgings of the generous Signior Leonato. We were here but a minute when Benedick and his enemy, Beatrice, renewed their ancient quarrel, and only another 'fore a shine grew in Claudio's eye for the young Hero. Everyone is in good spirits. Even my morose brother seems in a fine mood. Benedick, too, for he is happiest when quarrelling.

The full moon has come and gone too many times since last we visited fair Messina; the stars have shifted to something unrecognisable. Such fortune that I do not need the heavens to know the city. I know it by something in the air—a sweet scent coming in through the window, a full jug

heavy with wine on my desk, and everywhere laughter and merriment.

Merriment for all but Claudio. He has it, true, but his is of a serious nature.

Alas, poor Claudio, so struck by Cupid's bow he cannot speak before his beloved. Ne'er did he show fear on the battlefield. Yet when it comes to love, he requires aid. I, immune to those arrows of affection, offered to speak, masqued, on his behalf this evening. No lady nor man shall affect my voice, and I am glad to offer him this service. He is a fine soldier and shall make a fine husband.

Husband. What a strange thing. I suppose it is the natural way for most men, though never for me. Benedick claims it unnatural and jests about the indignity of husbandry. Yet, though he may disdain romance, he certainly can, and will, speak much of a woman's beauty. I suspect, then, that his nature is different from mine. Otherwise, why should he low and crow so much? Bravado, perhaps? Fear? I wonder. Dare I suspect my friend a brash liar? Perhaps Benedick only speaks of disdain for being so yoked when he truly so desires.

Ha! I suspect that is the truth of it. The boor distains wit, and the stoic turns his nose up at sentiment. It may be nature for a man to decry what he fears he cannot accomplish. Benedick is no coward. Yet, I detect a certain air of horror in him when it comes to nuptials. Well. I have no such fear of man, nor woman, nor any person. Perhaps in assisting Claudio with his trepidatious tongue, I may find an opportunity to aid Benedick as well. For well I may have no romantic inclinations of mine own, I admit a certain weakness for intrigue. If all men must have a folly, let it be said mine is an interest in my comrades and in their romances. I will see them all wed and myself a lonely bachelor. I aim to meddle myself deserted.

Ah, I only wish I had more insight into my brother's melancholy. I know him to be an intelligent man. When he does speak, he shows wit in his observations and yet he does not appreciate the measure and music of a good banter. He speaks not of love nor sentiment, not even in japes. Perhaps this time of rest and leisure will allow me a chance to learn more of his nature. And, on that, I must make a disguise of my own nature for this masquerade.

The Seventh of July

Such an evening we had! Sleep is far afield, where even the best scouts cannot spot her. The music comes in the window yet: a lively dancing tune. I doubt not that some revellers continue in their festivities. Though I have retired to my room, there is wine still in my cask. This moment is for savouring. I will search once more for slumber when the music ends.

Poor Claudio! To believe I had wooed Hero for my own. He does not know me well enough, yet, to know it is outside my nature. Even apart from my own romantic disinclination—to believe me capable of such a disloyal act! I remind myself that lovers do not maintain cool hearts, and their passions are easily inflamed. Bachelor though I am, I have no desire to place horns upon any man's head—particularly so dear a companion as Claudio.

And Beatrice was in unusual form tonight. Her words can draw blood. Though she defends herself as a creature of mirth, her barbs cut not only others, but also her own spirit. She seemed toss'd like a boat in a storm, first lamenting her lack of any proper suitor and then rejoicing in it. Though she and I have spoken of marriage many times past, she again declined a friendly arrangement.

Too costly! Ha!

What cost to Beatrice? What price for her to have the matter settled? The cost to her would be only a chance to wed for love. I have known Beatrice since we were but babes, and I know her heart. Her jests about losing love are a sign, clear as the stars tonight, that her woes are severe. Though she would ne'er admit it, Beatrice needs a happy match. It cannot be me, convenient

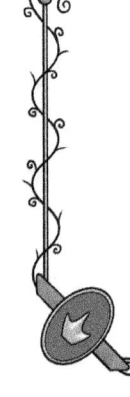

though it would be to release myself from the relentless expectations of bachelorhood.

Well, if I cannot throw off the scent of the wedding hounds by a marriage of my own, then I shall have to throw them on the trail of another. Luck is with me, for Beatrice proposed two targets for Cupid's bow: my brother, and Benedick.

I confess I am not confident of my brother's adequacy for the task. She finds him handsome, but I know not his inclinations for love. I do know Benedick. He rails against the sacrament and the very notion. I believe his fiery passion against it can be diverted to flow a less resistant direction. Leonato, Claudio, and Hero have joined my cabal and each vowed to assist. With luck, Leonato will gain not only a son but also a promised nephew before the wedding bells ring on Monday.

The music fades. I suspect light may break o'er the horizon before I sleep, but a soldier cannot fight without rest. Rest I must, and release the pen that helps me coalesce the matters of my brain and heart. Even now, as I take my evening's last dip into the ink, I envision plans in my mind's eye.

The Twelfth of July

Fate has a strange way of things.

Claudio and I have worked on our Benedick, and I have no doubt we will hook his heart to Beatrice's. But Claudio! My poor Claudio.

I thought my brother uninterested in the well-being of my companions. I was wrong. He told us of Hero's licentious ways to save my dear Claudio from horns. Antlers, by the sounds of it. I pray that, when we attend to her window tonight, we shall see no man enter.

I do not understand what might drive Hero to such an action. Is Claudio not sufficient? Is he not handsome, and witty, and full of charms? Ah, but the heart and the mind and the humours do not always move in concert. Is it not so that sometimes, when man is full, he continues to eat something appetising? Or, when man has not thirst, he yet drinks wine?

Wine, perhaps, is more likened to love. Tempting to some who like its taste, even when they are not thirsty or have been made mad by its effect. An overabundance can make one sick.

The Thirteenth of July

I have seen it. Zounds! Though I swim in it, I keep encountering the bottom of this cup. Wine! Yes, wine must be like to love, for I drink it now despite its lost flavour.

Cheers to sickness. A toast to regret.

The Fourteenth of July

The wedding was to be today. Hero feigned ignorance to the point of a swoon. Hero! Only last evening, we saw and heard such things at her window that all the casks and barrels in Messina could not erase them. There was no such weakness in her then.

I ne'er saw Claudio so inflamed as when he detailed Hero's sins. Even Beatrice grew pale and fretted about.

Claudio has sworn off love. He will never be a husband.

Ah, if I could remake the time since our arrival! My days meddling in love are finished. I will set my mind towards less risky pursuits. Perhaps I shall hunt boars.

If anything is to be salvaged from this mishap, 'tis that I have learnt the true nature of my brother. He is a quiet man, but it has become clear to me he values honour above all else. He

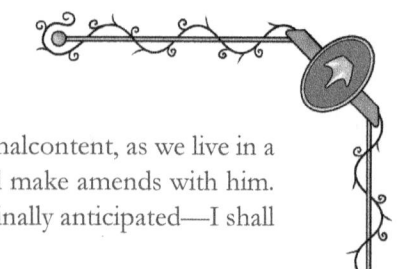

seemed near sick to even speak of Hero's impurity. No wonder he is so malcontent, as we live in a world where so many beautiful things are befouled by hidden rot. I shall make amends with him. When we have arrived at our next destination—sooner, I think, than originally anticipated—I shall make a proper elevation of him.

Yes, we should depart sooner. Poor Leonato! He must act as host while he has only just found out the vile truth of his daughter's wicked ways. I must allow my men to collect themselves, and then we shall make haste away.

Ay, my men! Benedick! Now I fear I have led him astray. If demure-seeming Hero was capable of such a betrayal—no. I know Beatrice. I only pray he is not so diverted by his own affection he is unable to provide amusement and companionship for Claudio, who will so desperately need what merriment Benedick can provide him.

The Fourteenth of July

The villain. The cur! To think that only this morn I vowed to dignify the bastard! Reunited as brothers after such a time apart, and he chose this course. I have sent men after him. A man cannot keep his brother, but I can and shall arrange for a gaoler.

Alas, Hero. The shock was fatal; she never recovered from the faint. Her wedding veil shall become a burial shroud. Alas, Leonato, who has lost a child. His only daughter! We japed and mocked his loss and his infirmity. I console myself that he still has a brother and niece to care for him. I cannot make recompense. Naught can replace his Hero.

Benedick had the right of it before the proof. And Claudio is to marry Benedick's beloved Beatrice! Oh, how Claudio and I abused him 'fore we knew! Not a single soul shall have a happy ending of this.

As a youth, I oft lamented that I did not feel love as other men do. I felt the fool for not understanding their games. As I grew wiser, I accepted that at least love could not turn me a fool. Yet Cupid has come in, not with a bow, but a cannon, and snared me in the blast.

The Fifteenth of July

Cast off our lamentations and mourning garb! We were tricked not only by my brother, but by that Hero who—along with her relations—conspired to teach us the truth through the mask of funerary garb. I must forgive her wiles when they result in such a happy end. Claudio and Benedick, married men! Rather, the friar married them: Claudio to Hero and Benedick to Beatrice. My soldiers are now cousins, and must cease their quarrel. Ha! I am sure they will begin again before we depart Messina, if not before the sun sets. I do not suppose, however, that it will come to swordpoint during the honeymoons. And should they draw, Hero and Beatrice are well-equipped for the management. Hero to soothe, and Beatrice to redirect Benedick's temper.

They are all suited and shall make a happy family. 'ere long, I suspect the family will increase. I shall be the happiest doting Godfather, if they will have me.

I may not love man nor woman, but I love. I love! A match well-made; a wedding feast; friends; and merriment. These I cherish and hold dear; these I shall protect, and so long as I have them, I will be the happiest of men.

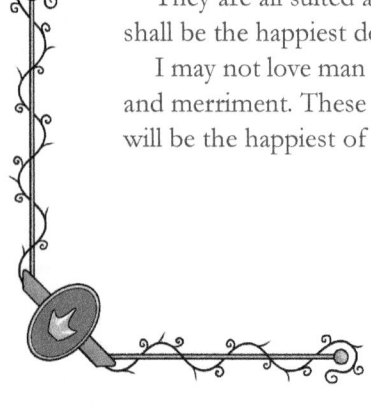

TAGS: alcohol use (casual), alternate universe, character has a different gender than in the source material, everyone knows they're in love but them, f/f, f/m, first kiss, friends to lovers, historical, homophobia (internalized), homophobic language, meddling friends, past tense, period-typical homophobia, period-typical understandings of gender and sexuality, pining (mutual), the 1940s, third person limited (multiple) point of view, veteran, world war ii

SOME CUPIDS

Nickel J. Keep

I've always wanted to write something historical, and with the theme for this anthology being a timeless Shakespeare piece, it felt like the perfect opportunity to take that leap. I chose to set my story post-World War II, wanting to keep with the "return from the war" theme in the original material. The 1940s weren't the friendliest of times to members of the queer community, and something that always stuck out to me about that time frame were the tragic lesbian love stories. So, I chose to focus on subverting that period-typical narrative—Bea is very aware of how women in love are treated by society. However, I wanted to break that cycle, and have Beni fight to bring them a happy ever-after.

Beatrice stood in the doorway of Hero's room, watching over her beloved cousin. He was curled up and closed off, lying quietly in his bed. His placidity was a stark and alarming contrast to his usual behavior and personality, and it broke Bea's heart.

"How is he?" Benivida's voice startled Bea out of her vigil, causing her to jump. "Or is that a stupid question?"

"There are no stupid questions, Beni." Bea wiped the tears from her face before turning around. "Just a stupid person asking them."

"I'm not sure I deserve that, but I'll let it slide." The taller woman stepped closer to Bea. Her olive skin glowed in the candlelight, and, for a brief moment, Bea allowed herself to stare. Beni frowned as the distance between them diminished. "You've been crying."

"I figured that would be obvious. My cousin is heartbroken, and my heart breaks for him." She shook her head and turned back to watch over Hero. "The pain he feels, I feel."

Beni rested her hand on Bea's shoulder. "Neither of you deserve the hurt you're feeling. Please, tell me what I can do for you?"

"Is murdering Claudia off the table?"

"I think that goes without saying, Bea."

"Then there's nothing you can do to help." To distract herself, Bea futzed with her shirt collar, adjusting the wide lapel, then readjusting it. "Hero didn't do what Claudia accused him of."

"I've known Hero most of my life, Bea. I know he wouldn't. But I also don't know what Claudia saw. I wasn't with her; I was talking to your uncle."

Bea looked over her shoulder at Beni. She wanted to snap at her, wanted to yell at her for choosing Claudia over Hero. Yet, when she couldn't find malice in Beni's warm, hazel eyes, Bea took pause and considered her words. "Perhaps someone who is as fond of Hero as I am would be able to uncover the truth. They'd be able to right this wrong. And, in so doing, they would certainly endear themselves to me…"

"And if, on the off chance, they were already dear to you?" Beni's hand slid off Bea's shoulder.

"You assume there's anyone I hold dear outside of my family, Benivida." Bea repositioned herself and looked up to Beni. "But if they were someone that I cared for immensely, then, well…who knows?"

"Who knows, indeed." Beni gently squeezed Bea's shoulder, then left.

Bea watched until Beni was out of sight, then she shivered. While Bea tried to chalk her reaction up to a breeze blowing through the open window, deep down, she knew that the room's warmth had left with Beni.

"Connie, can you please tell the rest of the group what you've already told the constable?" Beni rested her hand on the other woman's shoulders but kept her eyes locked on Bea.

"Do I have to?" Connie fidgeted with a handkerchief as she squirmed under Beni's hand. "Matthew can confirm just as much as I can."

"Matthew is also Hero's servant and confidant. One could argue that he would lie for Hero," Beni leaned down and whispered in Connie's ear. "Lady Joan isn't going to come in and help you hit the silk. She'll cut the lines and let you plummet."

Connie turned her head quickly, and the blonde curls pinned to the top of her head started to fall loose. Her usually bright-blue eyes were dull; Beni almost felt bad for her. Connie choked back a sob as she shook her head. "Joan's my gal."

"Then why would she tell you to climb all over Hero, then go and sleep with Matthew? Hmm? You were in cahoots with her. You just didn't know it." Beni stood back and looked at the expectant group. "Go on and tell 'em, Connie." When Connie adamantly shook her head, Beni walked in front of her and hooked a finger under her chin, forcing her to look up. "It's easier to just repeat yourself and get out of this predicament than it is to throw your life away for a woman who will never love you back."

The words appeared to hit Connie hard, and her resolve came tumbling down. "I didn't sleep with Hero." She slumped in the chair, her face slipping loose from Beni's grasp. "I didn't sleep with Matthew, either. Joan told me that she'd make all my dreams come true if I flirted with the boys. She said…" Connie hesitated. She focused on the handkerchief in her hands, running her fingers along the embroidery before continuing. "She said to make it look good, to get the boys all riled up. But I swear—I didn't sleep with them. I couldn't. My heart belongs to Joan."

Beni patted Connie's shoulder then crossed her arms over her chest. She glared at Claudia; Claudia sank into her chair. "The constable's out looking for Joan. Pedro's going to send her back to the mainland and ban her from the Isle."

"What have I done?" Claudia hid her face in her hands. "I should've listened to Hero."

"You think, you daffy broad?" Bea snarked. "You had people shouting his innocence at you, but

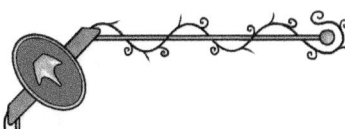

still you believed Joan. Granted," Bea paused and looked at Beni. "Benivida should have warned you about the first rule of the Isle: don't trust Joan."

"I didn't think Joan would be here!" Beni countered. She moved out of the constable's way as he came to collect Connie. "Neither did Pedro! As far as we knew, she was still on active duty. Besides, how I was to know that she was still hung up on Hero?"

Bea stood up and quietly smoothed out her skirt. "Well, at least you figured it out eventually. I take it you want a cookie?"

"I was offered different motivation to figure out the truth, Bea." Beni waited until Connie was out of the room before walking over to the other woman. Bea's long brown hair hung disheveled around her shoulders, and her alabaster skin showed the telltale redness of tears. "I'm armed with the truth, and I'll take Claudia to task."

"How does that help Hero heal?"

"Hero's name is cleared, and I'll drag the damn apology out of Claudia myself." Beni reached for Bea's hand, only to find it snatched away. "Bea?"

"You really think you've earned a reward? You haven't finished righting the wrong." Beatrice turned and stalked from the room, leaving Beni to plan out how to finish making things right.

"I'm so glad I get to do this." Claudia sat in Hero's lap, running her fingers through his dark brown hair. "I messed up something major. I almost lost the best thing that's ever happened to me. And it took everything they could do, including turning Connie against Lady Joan, to prove that I'd made an error in judgment. As Bea put it, what a 'daffy broad' I was!"

Hero shrugged, his smile steadfast as he held Claudia close. "I told you—when I first saw you, I was smitten." He stole a look over at Matthew. "Not going to let you live down that you confused me for Matt, though."

"Yeah, yeah. It was dark. And Connie had been flirting with you all night. I jumped to conclusions, and I screwed up." She leaned in and playfully kissed Hero's cheek. "I'll apologize as many times as you need me to."

"I *am* a dreamboat, thank you very much, Hero." Matthew poured himself some more barley wine. "That said, let me reiterate that I'm sorry. I should have known what Connie was doing. I should have spoken up. But I didn't realize that it was me that you'd seen."

"You're golden, Matthew. Connie came around. Everything worked out all right in the end." Claudia looked at Beni; she was staring over the horizon by her lonesome. "Which brings me back around to my original point."

"Getting Beni and Bea together?" Hero followed Claudia's gaze and frowned. "Bea and I have known Beni for a long time. And I'm pretty sure that Bea has loved Beni just as long."

Matthew nodded in agreement. "It's obvious that Benivida feels the same way. I noticed right off when your father brought me on as your servant. Those two have only ever had eyes for one another."

"Wait. You said that Beni and Bea have been in love for years. But since Beni and I got here with Lord Pedro, they've either ignored each other or been at each other's throats. Has it always been like this?"

"Yes," Hero and Matthew responded at the same time, but only Hero continued. "When they're alone? Or think they're alone? They act completely different. That said…" Hero paused to take a drink of his wine. "I think they're trying to protect one another."

"From people who would disapprove of them knocking boots? Did they not see how open

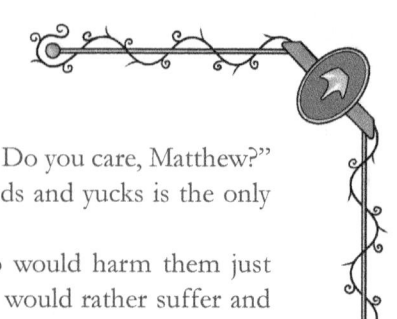

Connie was with her affection toward Joan? You lot clearly wouldn't care. Do you care, Matthew?" Claudia looked at Matthew, who shook his head. "So, the fear of fatheads and yucks is the only thing that's stopping them? Just ignore the fuddy-duddies!"

"It's not that easy, Claudia." Hero frowned. "There are people who would harm them just because they love one another." He nodded toward Bea's balcony. "She would rather suffer and love Beni from afar than do anything to put her at risk. And, I venture to say, Beni's the same way about Bea."

Claudia shook her head. "What a pair of cockeyed broads." She stood up, nearly throwing Hero off-balance as she got off his lap. "We're going to fix this. Beni is my dear friend, and yours. I've grown rather fond of Bea, too, and you two are in her corner. The best repayment for helping us love freely and fiercely is to make sure that they can as well!"

"You picked a firecracker, didn't you, Hero?" Matthew leaned back and shook his head, smiling. "I'm in if you're in. They got me off the hook as much as they did you."

"Well, then." Hero looked between his friend and his fiancé. "I guess we're in cahoots. What brainchild are you cooking up, Claudia?"

"I am so glad you asked…"

Beni awoke early to head into town. Being back on the Isle was both a blessing and a curse. Beni missed the smell of the sea air, but Beatrice was here. Beni missed her family terribly, but Bea was here. The way that she felt at peace when she walked the long-familiar streets filled her heart with joy. Yet her heart would stop and break anytime she saw Bea.

"Wait up, Beni!"

"Claudia?" Beni stopped and turned around, her eyebrow raised in confusion as Claudia ran up to her. "What are you doing up so early?"

"Is it a crime to want to spend time with my dear friend?"

"The sun is barely up." Beni crossed her arms over her chest and looked Claudia over. By some miracle, Claudia was awake, dressed in a blue, cotton popover dress. "Who are you, and what did you do with Claudia?" Beni turned and continued to walk, not letting the unplanned interruption stop her.

Claudia laughed as she reached Beni's side. "It's me, you booger." She looped her arm through Beni's. "We haven't spent much time together, just the two of us, since we got here. And if having the opportunity to spend time with you means waking up like I'm on the day shift rather than the swing? So be it."

"I suppose it's safe to say you've never been a morning person?" Beni's shoulders relaxed as they made their way down the street. "How did you survive on the front?"

"Coffee. When Pedro introduced it to me, I thought it was a gift from God." Claudia laughed. "One could ask how you're a morning person."

"Easy—that's how life is on the Isle. My family owns several fishing boats. We had to get up early to catch the fish, clean them, and bring them to the monger."

"Which part did you do? Sorry if I'm prying, but you never really talked about home while we were serving."

Beni sighed, stopping before looking over at her friend. "I signed up for the war to get away from home. Being a nurse sounded better than being here." The "*sounded better than pining after Bea, anyway,*" part was best left unsaid. "Everyone works in the family business. I was a fishmonger when I was a kid. Then, when I was old enough, I was taught how to clean the fish. But that didn't

last long because we lost one of my cousins overboard, and they needed another body to replace him."

"Hold on. Let me get this straight. You actually worked on your family's boats? I thought fishing was a man's job?" Claudia held up a finger to keep Beni from interrupting her. "Don't get me wrong—I'm glad your family knows that a woman can do as good a job as a man. But that's unheard of in most places."

"Yeah, well, I guess I've always been a bit of a tomboy. I was the only girl of my generation in the family, so I had to keep up." Beni started walking again, practically pulling Claudia by their entangled arms. "Why are you so curious about my life all of a sudden?"

Claudia cleared her throat. "We're in your hometown. Seeing you in your element made me realize how much you've kept from me."

"You never asked."

"And you never said." Claudia took in their surroundings. "Where are we going, exactly?"

"The port. To see my family. I haven't formally visited them since I've returned. Been busy, you know…I somehow got roped into fixing someone's love life." Beni let out a sigh, remembering Bea's plea to help clear Hero's name. "I guess they get to meet my newest friend."

"I must say, I'm glad to be your patsy if they're going to give you grief."

Beni snorted. "You were gonna be whether you came with me or not."

"Wise guy."

"You know it." Beni carefully untangled her arm from Claudia's as they stopped in front of a vast, sprawling manor. Unlike the other houses they had passed, the manor exuded wealth. From the ivy that clung to the white-washed bricks to the elaborate wrought-iron railings, the building stood out in stark contrast. "We're here."

"Beni!" Claudia stared at the majestic mansion. "This is your family home? You grew up here?" Shaking her head in awe, she examined the house. "You gave this up to go to war? How sauced were you when you made that decision? How lucrative is this fishing business?"

"Yes, it's the family home." Beni sighed. "All of them live here. Parents, aunts, uncles, cousins. Even as big as it is, there's a family member in every corner." She paused. "You gonna think of me differently now that you know where I'm from?"

Claudia shook her head. "No, but I'm trying to figure out what else I don't know about you."

"If you don't know that you don't know it, then how do you know you're missing anything?" Beni stood at the door and let out a hesitant sigh before knocking.

"This is your home, and you're knocking on the door?"

"I…may not have left on the best of terms. My family loves me and they worried about me, but that doesn't mean they like me or have forgiven me for leaving." Beni lifted her chin and squared her shoulders as the door opened. "Smile, Claudia."

"Bea?"

Beatrice looked up to see Hero standing next to her. Despite his size and aloofness, he certainly had a way of sneaking up on people.

"Penny for your thoughts?" he asked.

"Am I only worth a penny?" She shook her head and smirked as she patted the sandy shore next to her. "Or is the going rate a penny for each thought?"

"If it were a penny for each thought, you'd bankrupt the Isle, cousin." Hero sat beside her and pulled off his shoes. He dug his toes into the sand, copying Bea, then faced toward her. "How

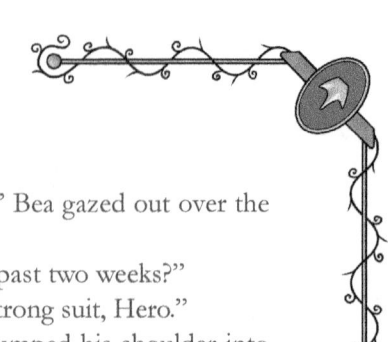

about you start talking, and I'll cut you off before I go belly up."

"I'm proud of you for not risking the financial demise of our home." Bea gazed out over the water. "Where do you want me to start?"

"How about explaining why you've been so happily miserable for the past two weeks?"

Bea laughed fondly, yet with a hint of severity. "Tact was never your strong suit, Hero."

"My charisma and good looks make up for what I'm lacking." He bumped his shoulder into Bea's. "Come on. This is about Beni, right? Her being back has been both the best and worst thing for you."

"You're not as charismatic as you think you are. Especially not with the gobbledygook you're spouting." Bea rested her head on Hero's shoulder. "I didn't think she'd come back."

"Yet here she is. The same Benivida we've known our entire lives." Hero rested his head on top of Bea's; she smiled. "You know you wear your heart on your sleeve when it comes to Beni, right?"

"And you know how hard I've worked to make sure my feelings aren't obvious." Bea sighed, knowing where this conversation was headed. "If something happened to her because I slipped up? Because I'm a freak?"

Hero shot up, knocking Bea askew. "I don't ever want to hear you call yourself that again."

"And if someone else calls me that?"

"Then they get a knuckle sandwich. Simple as that." Hero wrapped his arm around Bea's shoulder and pulled her into a hug. "There are people who don't understand it, Bea. There always will be. But you are who you are, and who you love doesn't change that."

"While I'm glad you're in my corner, Hero, that doesn't mean the rest of the world is. There are cruel bastards who hurt people like me because they don't understand. Because they're taught by someone else that my love is a perversion." Bea cleaned her hands on her shirt before wiping away the tears that had started to fall. "I don't even know if Beni cares for me. Even if she doesn't…what if someone hurts her because I love her?"

"I mean, you're a special kind of stupid if you think she's not in love with you. But would you rather suffer in silence than let your heart follow its own path? You're a lot of things, Bea, but a coward isn't something I'd have put on that list."

Bea bristled. "This isn't a new conversation for us, Hero. Why do you keep pushing it?"

"Because you make a point of taking care of everyone else. Who takes care of you?" Hero waited a moment, but when Bea didn't respond, he continued, "You took care of your father until he passed. You help me take care of my father. Damn it, Bea, you take care of me!"

"And I can take care of myself!" Bea pulled away, staring in shock and awe at her cousin. In all their years, he had never questioned her, never raised his voice at her.

"No—no, you can't. Or, at least, you don't." Hero pinned her with a pointed finger, and she snapped her mouth shut on a reply. "Sure, you get your meals. You go swim. You do the things necessary to live. But do you actually feel alive? Because I hate to be the bearer of bad news, Bea, but from where I sit? You don't live except when Beni is around. These last two weeks are the happiest I've seen you in the past two years."

"That's a bold claim, Hero."

He laughed and nodded. "It is. But I wouldn't make it if I couldn't back it up."

"When did you become so bold?"

"I had a good teacher." Hero held his arm out and tugged Bea back in. Side by side, they watched the sea. "Even if she doesn't practice what she preaches. Crazy dame."

Bea laughed and poked Hero's side before settling against him. "Yeah, well, if I'd known it would turn you into a pain in the neck?"

"You wouldn't change a thing."

"Everything's set," said Matthew, taking a seat across from Hero. "Claudia's got Beni, and Bea should be walking out any moment." He looked toward the manor, watching for Bea. "You sure this is going to work?"

"Yeah, I am." Hero leaned back in his chair and kicked up his feet. "Some Cupid kills with arrows, others with traps." He stole a glance over his shoulder before looking at Matthew again. "Did Claudia tell you how long she'd be?"

Out of the corner of his eye, Matthew saw Bea and gave a slight nod in her direction. "She said she'd be coming before too long. Something about the conversation she was having with Beni."

"Oh?" Hero, catching Matthew's cue, raised his voice. He pulled his feet off the table, sat up, and leaned forward. "Anything fun going on there?"

"Apparently, Beni's been having a hard time being back on the Isle." Matthew did everything in his power to not look toward Bea as she approached. "Something about unrequited love hurting."

"Wait. Beni—Benivida—is in love with someone?"

"That's what Claudia said." Matthew smiled softly when Bea quickly hid behind a bush. "Beni went home yesterday, and Claudia tagged along. Beni's family's hounding her, asking her if she's found a fine young soldier to bring home. She said no, and, per Claudia, stayed quiet for the rest of the visit. When they were leaving, Beni apparently said that while she knew that someone would ask that question, she'd hoped they wouldn't because she didn't want to lie to them."

Hero replied, speaking a little louder than he had been previously, "So does Claudia know who Beni is in love with?"

"Who doesn't know? But she confirmed it—heard straight from the horse's mouth that Beni's in love with Bea."

"I don't know if I should tell you to close your trap, or if I should smoke out all the information you've got." Hero jabbed a finger at Matthew. "You're telling me that the dame my cousin's in love with is in love with her too?"

No longer trying to hide, Bea walked closer, her expression twisting in confusion.

"I just told you. That's what Claudia was able to confirm from—" Matthew stopped abruptly, pretending that he'd just noticed Bea with a polite acknowledging nod in her direction. He play-acted obliviousness in response to the look on her face. "Didn't expect you out here yet! Everything all right? Need me to get you something?"

"I…" Bea watched Matthew carefully; he squirmed in his seat under her scrutiny. "I think I misheard you. You were talking about Beni?"

"Who else?" laughed Hero. "You know that Beni went home yesterday? Claudia went with her. I'm not sure if that was her first time back since she was discharged, but if it is, it took her long enough to get there."

"When would she have had a chance?" Matthew noted. "Between her getting Lord Pedro situated in the Governor's Mansion then dropping everything to help Bea clear your name?"

"She's been back on the Isle for two weeks. Beni's had to have returned home before yesterday," said Bea, taking the seat between Matthew and Hero.

Hero shook his head. "Other than to sleep and help Pedro when he needed it? Beni never left your side, Bea." Hero paused, looked at Matthew, then looked at Bea again. "How much did you hear?"

"More than I was supposed to, I'm sure." Bea turned to Matthew. "I don't know whether to yell

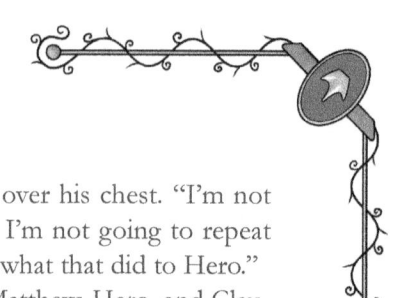

at you for being a gossipmonger, for lying, or for both!"

"Excuse me?" Matthew sat up straight in his seat, crossing his arms over his chest. "I'm not lying, and I'm not spreading gossip! Claudia told me—you know what? I'm not going to repeat myself again and have you accuse me of something I didn't do. You saw what that did to Hero."

Bea at least had the grace to look ashamed, not that it was a part of Matthew, Hero, and Claudia's plan for her to feel that way. She sat quietly for several moments, then reached for the bottle of barley wine that sat in the middle of the table. Taking a glass, Bea poured herself a drink and slowly downed it.

"I don't like where you've gone, Bea," Hero said, reaching for his cousin's glass. "The moping, the drinking? This ain't you. You're filling a hole with the wrong things."

"We had this conversation yesterday." She set down her glass, pouting as Hero took it away. "Matthew, since we didn't, I'll tell you what I told Hero. You can't just share a secret like that. Are you trying to get her hurt?!"

"What? No!" Matthew exclaimed, trying with a desperate, slack-jawed look to communicate that this was Hero's moment to chime in and help. "Beni's family."

"Then what aren't you getting about this?" Bea pointed between the two of them. "I won't ever deny how much I love Beni. I love her with so much of my heart that there's none left to protest my feelings. But I won't risk her. I won't say those words to her, no matter how much I want to. If the wrong person were to hear?" Bea reached over, snatched her glass back from Hero, downed the contents, and set the tumbler on the table. "I'd rather believe she doesn't love me than risk her safety."

A shuffle behind Bea caused both Matthew and Hero to look up quickly. Beni tumbled out of the underbrush, with Claudia rushing out behind her. She was staring at Bea's back, her expression shocked.

"Believe what you will," Beni announced, "but know: there is nothing in the world that I love as much as you." Bea startled and turned; she and Beni came face to face as Beni approached the table. Smiling sadly, Beni continued, "Do you honestly think that I don't? Or do you think that I can't protect myself or you?"

"I think that's our sign to go," Matthew whispered to Hero. The men carefully rose, trying not to disrupt the long-needed conversation. Claudia waved them down the path, away from Beni and Bea, and they followed her to another part of the garden where they would be able to keep an eye on the pair.

"Well, Bea?" Beni offered her hand, but all Bea could do was stare. Beni's eyes were boring into Bea's very soul, and an unfamiliar—but very wanted—warmth spread through her chest. She looked at the outstretched hand and hesitantly took it, allowing Beni to pull her to her feet. "Do you truly believe I don't love you?"

"I may have dreamed that you did. That you do. But I never dared hope." Bea stared at their clasped hands. How many times had she imagined her fingers entwined in Beni's? Bea swallowed harshly to keep the threat of tears at bay, to keep the butterflies in her stomach from escaping. "I'm afraid I'll wake up to find that this has been a dream."

Beni ran her thumb over Bea's knuckles. "Is that why you've been so subdued of late? Your insults and snark haven't had the bite that I've grown to love over the years."

"You enjoy my insults? You're insane."

"Maybe. But, to be blunt, this?" Beni pointed between herself and Bea. "There's no world

where we both exist that you and I have a calm and peaceful courtship. We're too bright for that. We fan each other's flames and push the other to be their best. Or, when it comes to insults, our worst." She brought Bea's hand to her lips, turned it over, and softly kissed Bea's palm. Then, as if encouraging her to hold the kiss close, Beni closed Bea's fingers, curling them as though she grasped something. "I'll keep yours safe if you keep mine."

Afraid to look up, Bea kept her focus on Beni's hands holding hers. "Keep what safe?"

"My heart."

Bea smiled softly, her own heart beating a tattoo. "Always."

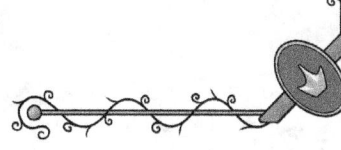

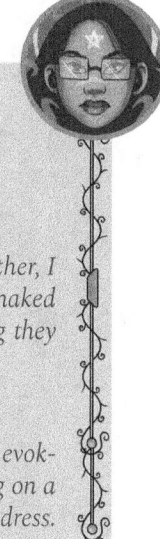

Cris Alborja (Next Pages)
"Intimacy" & "Silver tongue"

Intimacy (Benedick and Beatrice piece): Even though in the original story they are tricked into being together, I wanted to do a very intimate piece, referencing another painting by Dante Gabriel Rosetti. They are half-naked and kissing alone at dusk time. I used warm colors to represent the intimacy and mutual understanding they have.

Silver tongue (Beatrice-only piece): [This piece] was a reinterpretation of a Dante Gabriel Rosetti painting, evoking the first scene of the Much Ado About Nothing *movie when Beatrice is reading poems while sitting on a tree branch. I pictured her as a strong-featured woman, similar to Rosetti's, wearing an immaculate white dress.*

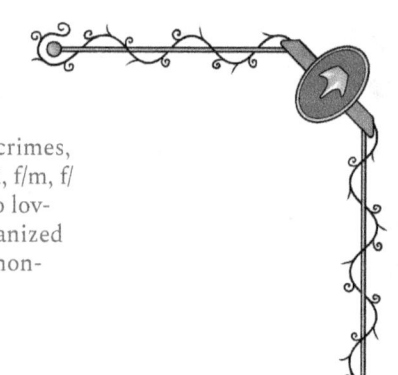

TAGS: alcohol use (casual), alternate universe, be gay solve crimes, character has a different gender than in the source material, f/m, f/ nb, false accusations, first person point of view, friends to lovers, genderqueer, historical, mystery, noir, non-binary, organized crime, past tense, private detective, the 1950s, violence (non-graphic descriptions)

THE FALSE SWEET BAIT

Vee Sloane

I knew that I wanted to move the characters into a noir setting almost immediately. The snappy dialogue and witty flirtation from the original made it feel like a very natural genre for them to land in. The idea of two private investigators working together on a case created the potential for both romance and intrigue!

It was the done thing to have plants in your office. All the best private dicks had them. Big, fake plants that caught the dust and made dismal offices look less dingy. I didn't have a secretary to wipe down plastic leaves, nor did I have the taste for them. Instead, I had one small pot on the lone windowsill. A pitcher plant with its graceful stream of yellow-and-pink furled leaves delicately fluted open to welcome in weary insects, then slowly sip them down.

Hero had bought it for me, the little deadly thing, when I first opened the business. Now, two years and too-few visits later, she sat at the edge of my guest chair, avoiding a crack in the vinyl. She was as pressed for the day as a crisp suit. She'd even done perfect victory rolls in her full, dark hair.

"It's business hours, Bunny." She'd taken me off guard by coming, and even as I sat behind my desk, I felt as if it was I who'd arrived unannounced.

"You're the only one that still calls me that, you know."

Her laugh tinkled like bells. "Your nose doesn't twitch as much these days."

I smiled, because what else could I do? "Did you need something?"

"For you to come to my engagement party tonight."

"Oh no." I pointed a finger at her. "You promised. Just the rehearsal and the wedding."

"Please, Bea." She sat even farther forward, nearly tipping out of the chair. "Not as a guest. I need to employ you."

"You? What for?"

"There's been a threat against my life." She looked down at the ground. "Some old enemy of Claudio's. I thought it was silly—they sent one of those cut-up ransom notes like out of a story—

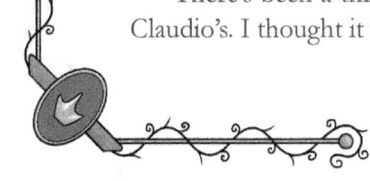

but Claudio thinks it's real enough."

"But not credible enough to call the police?" I asked dryly.

On paper, Claudio was a small business owner who'd struck it rich. He'd met Hero when she was waitressing between auditions. A meet-cute, for the cute. But, adorable small business owners didn't have death-threat-level enemies, and I'd had my suspicions about Claudio for a while. Hero would make a nice moll for the up-and-coming gangster.

"You know how private he is." She flashed me big doe eyes. "He said Benni will be there; I guess I could ask them?"

"That pretentious so-and-so?" I scoffed. "What are they going to do? Take notes and hope for the best?"

"I thought you liked how they handled the McBride case? You said they had style."

"Style, but no substance." I flushed. That'd been a comment made after far too much Champagne.

"Claudio is hiring some security too, but I'd feel better if you were there."

"Of course I'll be there." I'd decided before she'd finished asking.

"Good," she breathed out. Crisis averted, she smiled. "Oh, I brought you some lunch!"

A smart tweed suit and, as a concession to the occasion, a string of my mother's pearls would have to do for clothes. I kept to flats. Never knew when I'd have to run.

Claudio's estate was outside the city, but I had a good car and the desire to speed. I arrived before the bulk of the fashionably late and parked myself, scandalizing the valet. The estate was the kind that had a fancy name and rose out of the cliff face like a fairy-tale castle. At night, it shone like a golden beacon.

I took my time heading up, refamiliarizing myself of its entrances and exits; all the places a shady character might hide.

So, naturally, I found one.

They stood in the lee of the kitchen door, half-hidden by a jasmine bush. The white flowers bent around them as if to hide their lean form. They were dressed to the nines in a beautiful silk suit the color of the night sky. Cufflinks caught the starlight, and the moon caught the sharp angles of their cheekbones as well as the gleaming, black coif of their hair. All beauty and grace in one Benni Padua.

What an asshole.

"What are you doing here?" I barked, pleased when they fumbled with their fussy little notebook.

"I was invited." They were the very picture of polite confusion. "And what are you doing here, Her Private Eyeness?"

"Doing the job you should be, apparently." I held myself taller, taking advantage of the bare inch I held over them.

"What job?"

"Claudio didn't tell you about the threats?"

"No, no he did not." Their brow wrinkled. The confusion seemed genuine enough. Benni wasn't much of a liar for someone who made a living the way we did.

"Then maybe I shouldn't."

"You already half have. You might as well."

"And let you scoop my fee?"

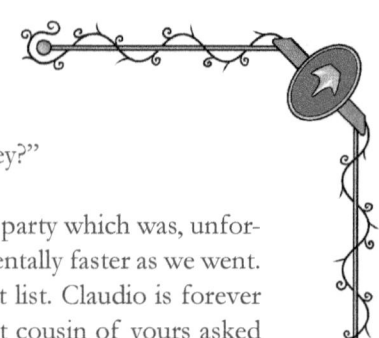

"You, The Right Honorable Bea, are actually taking your cousin's money?"

"Don't pretend to know me."

"I don't have to," they said breezily. They moved to the entrance of the party which was, unfortunately, the way I had to go, too. I kept pace, despite them moving incrementally faster as we went. "Let me guess, then: you didn't originally intend to come? I saw the guest list. Claudio is forever leaving out important relations. But, at the last minute, that flibbertigibbet cousin of yours asked you because of these threats?"

"Or, I just like parties."

"Lies don't become you." They snorted. "You must know there's a full security detail here tonight? No one could even sneeze without getting snot on a uniform."

"That's disgusting." I stifled a laugh as one such uniform wearer gave a disgruntled look at the suggestion.

"But accurate. So, you're here to be Hero's security blanket?"

"No." But, yes—probably. I'd realized around the time I'd put on the pearls. Hero always looked so composed. It was easy to forget she was only nineteen and surrounded by occasionally vicious socialites. Claudio had security. Beefy, angry security. Hero only had her wits. "I'm here to make sure nothing happens."

"Nothing at all? It's a party." They set their hand lightly on my forearm, barely the suggestion of a touch.

"May I see your invitation, please?" a stiff-looking bit of muscle asked as we crossed through the front door.

Benni waved their invitation about. "Miss Leonato is my guest."

"I'm on the list," I said sharply, but they were already guiding me away.

"Hero will make her entrance shortly. Why not get an hors d'oeuvre or two in the meantime, hm?"

It would make more sense to circulate and get a feel for the crowd, but the grand dining room and its attendant sitting room were already full of the social elite giving my poor tweed suit the eye. I let Benni lead me to a shadowed corner where tray-laden waiters bearing dainty bites were starting to emerge.

"I heard you solved the Roberts' kidnapping." They plucked down two Champagne glasses from a teetering pyramid of them and handed me one. I wouldn't drink, but a prop couldn't hurt.

"It wasn't much of a brain teaser. The boy had holed up with his lover in a pied d'terre. He staged the whole thing to cover the rent. Left a paper trail a mile long. You got the Zoo Thief."

"Oh, I had an advantage." They flashed a silver-screen smile. "The supervisor was in such a state after firing you, he left me alone in his office for nearly an hour. I read every piece of paperwork on his desk and had it solved before he came back."

"He didn't fire me. I quit," I growled. Suddenly the Champagne looked more tempting. "After he insulted me."

"Don't you want to know whodunit?" they asked wryly.

"No," I lied.

The string quartet that'd been playing swelled, and the happy couple appeared atop the grand staircase. There was Claudio in a white linen suit, as crisp and easy as a summer breeze. Hero wore pink, a frothy affair that threatened to swallow her. Claudio's enormous gift of engagement jewels hung around her neck and from each ear. She'd confided she hated them, but wore them to please him. They were heavy and too encrusted with gems to be pretty.

"She's getting her duds made at a higher-quality rag seller," Benni murmured. "Claudio must

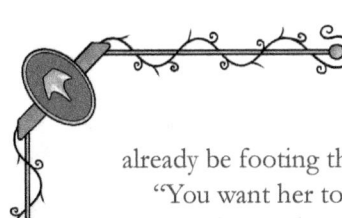

already be footing the bills."

"You want her to pay for this life on tips?" I hissed.

Hero beamed at the crowd, descended gracefully, then merged into their midst like an old pro. I watched as she smiled and complimented the guests, loosening up the room. Claudio detached from her and embedded himself with a group that looked like they'd all been cut from the same cloth. They each wore impeccable suits and, worse, their hair was slicked with a pound of pomade. Businessmen, all of them. What business was left entirely up to supposition.

"Aren't those your friends, too?" I glanced away to Benni.

"Mm." They sipped their Champagne.

Hero drifted closer and alighted at my side.

"Nothing suspicious so far," I told her. "Except for this one."

"Hello, Benni," Hero laughed as if I'd told a great joke.

"Hello to you, too." They saluted with their glass. "Congratulations on your nuptials. May all go to the gallows looking so happy."

"Oh, you." Hero wrinkled her nose. "What do you have against marriage?"

"Only everything," they said amiably.

"They strive to be contrary," I assured her. "Ignore them."

"I didn't know you two were so well acquainted." Hero's hand fluttered up to her necklace, adjusting it minutely.

"It's a small world."

"Smaller, still, when your cousin insists on scooping every case in a ten-mile radius before a poor bum like me can hoof it there."

"Not all of us have the entire city council in their pockets to point them toward the money cases."

"Now hold on there—"

"Is that the time?" Hero glanced at the grandfather clock. "Excuse me, I must speak with the chef. Claudio was specific about when dinner should begin."

She stepped through the door, and her voice trilled for a moment before it closed.

"You surely don't think I'm bribing people?" Benni sounded wounded.

"I think you have an awfully convenient way of showing up to high-profile cases."

"I can't help who my friends are and that they call me in a pickle, *Your Eyeness*."

"And I can't help that I drive faster than you. It's an unfair world."

Hero re-emerged and gave me a grateful smile before she eased into the crowd. This time, they turned to her warmly, flowers to her radiant, pink sun.

"You never did tell me what the threat was," Benni followed her with their eyes, too.

"Claudio has a lot of enemies."

"We're talking about the same man? Claudio wouldn't hurt a fly."

"A world of difference between a fly and a pocketbook," I said dryly. "Apparently—"

The lights cut out, and the screaming started.

"Hero!" I charged forward. The heavy, metal flashlight I kept in my purse, which often doubled as a weapon, now lit the tipsy and confused crowd. A second beam joined mine. Benni stood at my elbow.

I found Hero slumped and lost in the volume of her dress. For a brief, horrifying moment, I thought she was dead. Then, I made out the thin sound of her beginning to cry. Her shoulders shook, and her wretched sob cut through the crowd.

"Oh, Bea, that horrible necklace." Her hands wrapped around her neck. A red line cut down

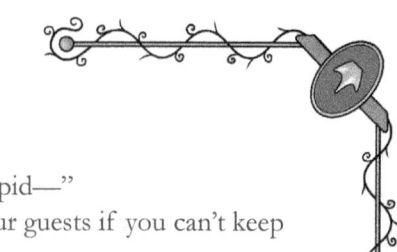

both sides of her pale skin. "They ripped it off of me!"

"You lost it?" Claudio emerged from the shadows. "You careless, stupid—"

"Claudio," Benni snapped, "don't make an ass of yourself! See to your guests if you can't keep a civil tongue in your head!"

Hero's crying redoubled.

"Just the fuse box, everyone!" one of the waiters called out, "Please sit tight and it'll be reset shortly."

Less than a minute later, the lights jumped back to life. Claudio had composed himself. Gone was the anger and in its place, a doting fiancé. He knelt at Hero's side.

"I'm sorry for snapping at you, my love. You must've had such a shock." He simpered.

Hero reached for him, wrapping herself up in his arms.

"They almost strangled me getting it off. I'm lucky the clasp gave out before my throat did."

"Bea, would you please take her upstairs?" He looked up at me. "It won't do her any good to sit here, hysterical."

"Of course." I offered Hero both my hands. "And once she's settled, I can come back down and help."

"No, Benni's here." He waved me off.

A frown had settled on Benni's generous lips. Their eyes met mine with a frisson of understanding. Something was rotten, and we were going to get to the bottom of it.

The grand staircase wasn't so grand when I was climbing it to help my crying cousin retire to a guest room. Someone had ripped hard at that ugly, heavy necklace, leaving dark marks on her neck.

"I want to clean this out, but I need to take a closer look," I explained over her hitching sobs. She gave something like a nod.

Aside from blood and torn skin, there wasn't a lick of evidence. No convenient hairs or fibers. They'd taken it off without touching her skin.

"Do you remember who was near you when the lights went out?"

"I was talking with Denny." She sniffled, taking my offered handkerchief and a deep breath. "His date was there too, but I don't know him."

"It's a place to start. Did you hear anything?"

"I was screaming too much." She hung her head. "I'm sorry. I've made a mess of things."

"Hero—" I couldn't pretend at my job anymore and folded her into a hug. The ridiculous dress crinkled and stabbed at me, but she clung back.

"Claudio will never forgive me."

"Then he's a fool. He knew there were threats, and he should be grateful they wanted the necklace instead of your life."

There was a knock at the door. I was surprised to find Benni on the other side. They had their little notebook out, spidery letters scrawled on the open page.

"Anything?"

"Some." They stepped inside and closed the door. "How are you, Hero?"

"I've been better." She put on a game smile. "But I'm alive."

"First step, kiddo." They gave her a wink and turned back to me. "Security is patting everyone down. The attendants say none of the cars are missing and all the staff are accounted for. Whoever swiped it is still on the grounds."

"They probably ditched it somewhere so they could come back to get it."

"Likely," they agreed. "Hero, do you know how much that necklace was worth?"

"Oh, I don't know." She wiped her eyes. "Claudio doesn't like to talk about money, but I know there are a few diamonds in it, and some good rubies."

"Could've just been for the money," Benni muttered.

"Why do it so publicly?" I frowned.

"He usually keeps them in the safe," Hero offered. She touched her ears where the matching earrings still hung, then took them out carefully. "He should lock these back up."

"Was anything else taken?" I asked.

"So far, nothing. One guy thought his wedding ring was gone, but turned out to be wishful thinking—he had it on his other hand."

"Seems like a lot of trouble for one necklace. They've gotta pry the gems out to sell it safely."

"People make those kinds of mistakes, though." Benni frowned. "So, what're you thinking?"

"Thoughts."

"C'mon, we're working on this together. Aren't we?"

"It's us or the coppers…"

We shared an understanding look. The cops in our city made more money looking the other way than finding clues.

"Hero, I need to snoop." I turned to her. "Do you want me to send someone else up to keep you company?"

"I'll call for Tabby." She gave me a watery smile. "Claudio is paying her overtime tonight, she might as well have an easy hour of it."

The maid would do; she and Hero were friendly enough. I didn't know the woman, but didn't have time to run background checks.

As soon as Tabby was on her way, we were off.

I headed for the back stairs, the ones that descended into the working guts of the estate. "Here's the thing. I'm thinking a hit like this—it has to be someone familiar with the place. Two even. One to blow the breaker and the other to do the grab."

"Seems sound. Plenty of temporary staff tonight. It could even be some of the guests."

"If I were them, I'd definitely ditch it and retrieve it later."

"Right."

The service hallway at the bottom of the stairs led us to the now-empty kitchen. A sumptuous feast had been ready to roll out. In one corner stood a shiny, new oven. Guess they'd needed two for a night like tonight.

"Who benefits from stealing that particular necklace?" The food smelled good, but dinner was the last thing on my mind. The breaker box was likely in the basement, and I wanted a look.

I found the stairs behind another door.

"You think it's Claudio," Benni accused.

"I didn't say that." I headed down. The light was on, a bare bulb that seemed incongruous with the opulence upstairs.

"Because you wanted to make me say it," they accused.

"He's probably got that thing insured out the wazoo." We clambered around a collection of suitcases and sheet-shrouded furniture to reach the breaker box. "And Hero might think the sun rises and sets on his shoulders, but he doesn't give her the same credit."

"So, what? He gets engaged to her and sets up a party just to steal a necklace that already belongs to him? Come on, Lady Eyeness, that's a thin limb you're going out on."

"Just the kind of thing a wannabe criminal would come up with."

"Very clever, except he doesn't need the money."

"Doesn't he? Doesn't anyone who gets in too deep?" I examined the breaker. "Do you know anything about electronics?"

"Enough to know anyone could throw some switches and make the world dark."

"Great. Fingerprint it?"

"If the thief was smart and got in like you think, they could've just as easily been the one to turn things back on. Or worse, we'll wind up arresting a helpful servant."

"Right." I turned and almost stepped on Benni's shiny shoes. When had they moved in so close? "Let's check for hidey holes."

"Good plan." They smelled unreasonably good—peppery and sweet all at once. Threads of brown laced through the green of their irises.

I squeezed past them, toward the stairs. There was no time for this.

We had work to do.

Splitting up might've made more sense, but with the thief still at large, and likely still in the manor, we stuck together. We tossed a few rooms downstairs; the spots someone could've easily tucked a necklace into and then blended back into the party during the short stretch without lights. Nothing. Not even spare change between the couch cushions.

"Could've chucked it into the bushes." Benni leaned out a window that'd been cracked to let the perfume of jasmine in. "Hope your flashlight has fresh batteries."

We wound up muddied to our ankles with our hair full of leaves a short time later. Benni's hairdo suffered more than mine, collapsing like a soufflé to droop around their face. It was, distressingly, even more appealing.

The shrubbery provided interesting fodder: a few lost bits of underclothing, probably from parties gone by, and evidence of a large raccoon population. But, not much else.

"Nothing." Benni kicked at the last shrub and sent a cascade of dried leaves flying around our feet.

The back door opened with an abrupt *bang*, and we careened for the cover of the shrubs. We collided, and their face was unceremoniously introduced to my bosom.

"Sorry," they whispered, attempting to extricate themself without making more noise.

"What was that?" A deep voice shot through the night. The beam of a flashlight crossed the sidewalk. It would've been nearly impossible for them not to see us, but it must've been our lucky night.

"Raccoon," another voice offered, stepping into the beam to reveal a very shiny pair of loafers. They searched no farther.

"This night is all wet," Deep Voice grumbled. He must've lit a cigar, judging by the smell.

"You said it." Shiny Loafers spat onto the sidewalk. "You think we'll still get the coin?"

"The dame's still alive, isn't she?" Deep Voice scoffed.

"She's in a locked room! What were we supposed to do?"

"Ask yourself what we can still do, knucklehead. Maybe it won't be exactly what he wanted, but we'll get the job done."

"I don't like it."

I clutched at Benni, probably holding their wrist a little too tight, but they didn't make a sound, only turned their hand to meet mine palm to palm.

"Me either. She's a looker, it seems a shame." A flick of sparking ash bounced by. "Come on,

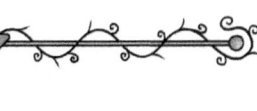

let's find a spot to lay low."

A shuffling, and the door banged closed again.

I said a few words that could've peeled paint.

Benni's eyes widened. "That's some vocabulary."

"What are the odds someone steals from her and someone else wants to kill her on the same night?" I stepped out of the bushes. The night had gained a chill. "They've got to be related."

"Maybe." Benni had a leaf in their hair. After a moment's hesitation, I reached out and plucked it off, letting it flutter between us as their nose crinkled in thought. "Let's follow. Best lead we have."

Tailing them was easy to say, harder to do, in the milling, angry crowd that filtered out the front door. Claudio, a little rumpled and wide-eyed, found us before we could find the thugs.

"No one knows anything, Benni, not even Denny, and he was looking her in the eyes when the lights went out!"

"You got a nose for liars now?" Benni snorted. "Did you get the cops on the horn?"

"Benni—" He blinked. "C'mon, you know I can't do that. Not with the side business."

"What side business?" Now there was the cold gumshoe I knew from cases, frosting out Benni's "polite socialite" mask in seconds.

"Not now." Claudio's eyes cut to me. I stared him down, eager to match Benni's professional ice.

"You shouldn't let the crowd go," I said into the silence.

"I can't keep half of the city council and the cream of society locked up here."

"You damn well can, you wet sock!" Benni snapped.

"I'm going to get Hero," I decided. Let them bicker. I didn't know if the goons would really wait for bedtime.

"She's staying the night." Claudio frowned. "She's had a fright. I wouldn't make her take the long ride out now."

"Now he's sweet." I rolled my eyes. "Someone got by your great security and nabbed a necklace, who's gonna stop someone from killing her?"

"Killing her?" Claudio blinked wetly.

"Get out of my way." I pushed past him up the stairs. Footsteps sounded behind me.

Hero's door was closed and, for the space between the heartbeats it took me to open it, I imagined the worst.

She still sat on the bed, eyes less tearful and dress smoothed back to pretty perfection. She gave me a weak smile when I stepped in.

"Pack up your things. You're not safe here."

Bless Hero, she didn't ask any questions. She was on her feet and collecting her purse in a second.

"You should come to my place," Benni said from behind me. "If they're really gunning for her, they'll know where you live. We'll take separate cars. I'm on Fifth and Brewster—the ugly building—apartment five."

"You don't have to do that," I protested.

"I think I do," they said gravely. "Claudio gave me the fast low-down on his side business. I should've known."

"It's hard to see the people we love clearly." I touched their shoulder. "I'm sorry."

"Not your fault."

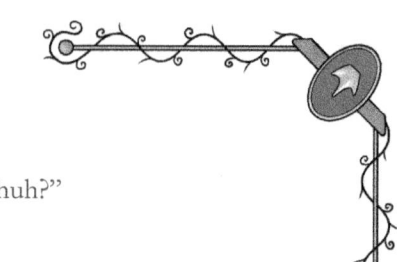

"I want to go," Hero said softly.

"I know." I put my arm around her shoulders. "Let's blow this joint, huh?"

Claudio was nowhere to be seen. The security detail he'd hired seemed more interested in soothing upset party-goers than monitoring who left. We slipped right by. The parking attendant was surrounded, and we easily slid past and got into the car. Hero was quiet the whole ride, her eyes on the mansion until it disappeared over the horizon.

The apartment building was as ugly as Benni had promised, but their place was the kind I wished I had—homey with dark woods and overstuffed couches. It looked like someone who lived there gave a damn.

Benni gave Hero their bed, then sat down heavily beside me on the couch. We looked out the window over the glittering city.

"I don't get any of this. What's the end goal?" I stole a glance at them. "Why a theft and a murder? What's he got to gain?"

"You seemed ready to condemn him earlier." Benni's voice was as soft and rumpled as their hair. We were sitting closer than I'd realized.

"I'm not going to accuse without facts."

"You're a good detective, Bea."

"You're not half-bad yourself."

After a moment's hesitation, I let my head rest against their shoulder. Their lips touched my forehead.

"When the dust settles, can I buy you dinner?" I asked.

"I hoped you'd ask."

We talked about the case a little more, but it'd been a long night, so we dozed off just that way. I woke before them with a crick in my neck, but couldn't make myself move. Every inch where our bodies pressed together was warm, the air around us scented with their pomade. When they stirred, I reached for their hand and we tangled our fingers together in the cool, grey light of dawn.

"Oh, I couldn't sleep a wink!" Hero called from the bedroom, and we sprang apart as if electrified. We had a somber breakfast, all still in our wrinkled clothes from the night before.

"I think I want to go home for a few days," Hero said. "Just to rest a little."

"Your mother would like that," I said, relieved. A rural location would keep her out of harm's way.

Benni drove her to her apartment and I, tired but ever diligent, returned to my office. I sat at my typewriter and tried to put together a few thoughts.

Why would Claudio steal his own necklace? Who else would want to? And what had he done that would provoke a hit on Hero? Who benefited from any of this?

I gave up and turned to my window where I gazed blankly out into the street. A fly buzzed by and landed on the lip of the pitcher plant. Poor soul, that was the end of it.

The pitcher plant!

I sat up as if electrocuted.

An extra oven in the kitchen might overload a circuit breaker, if plugged in at the right moment. Two people wouldn't be needed then—just one.

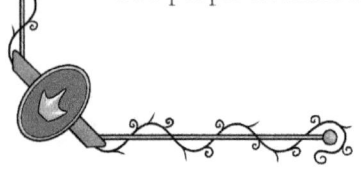

I didn't have the train schedule, so I had to hope it hadn't come yet. The situation called for the demonic driving that'd always been my weapon in a clutch. A train pulled in just as I arrived at the station. Dashing through the crowd, I ignored protests and resorted to shoving. Hero was about to board, Benni's hand offered up to her for balance.

"Hero!" I called out, and she turned. Her mask of sadness dropped away as she met my eyes. She smiled, slow and catlike.

"Sorry, Bea," she sing-songed as I got closer. She took a step up onto the train, her summery dress floating around her.

"Why? How?" I pulled up short.

"You know what kind of man he is." She sniffed delicately. "How he treated me—talked to me. He deserved a little humiliation. And I deserve to be compensated. As to the rest—"

"The rest of what?" Benni looked between us, bewildered.

"If I was going to do an elaborate scheme, I thought it'd be nice if you got something you wanted too," Hero said. "I knew neither of you could resist a good mystery. Be good to each other."

"But the necklace?" Benni had apparently caught on, eyes narrowing. "Where did you put it?"

"It's amazing what a good seamstress can do." She laughed. "Never underestimate the power of a needle—or a few hard-up actors that like gangster movies. Sorry to give you a scare, but I had to be sure you'd get me out."

"I'm not sure I forgive you," Benni said coolly.

I reached down and took their hand. "Me neither."

"So be it." She sighed. "I'll write."

Neither of us tried to stop her. Maybe we should've, but we weren't the law, just two PIs watching a train pull out of the station.

"What now?" Benni asked when the noise and smoke had passed.

"Lunch?" I suggested.

"You know, I am a little hungry."

We shared a turkey club at a diner. Benni had picked it, and it must've been their regular joint. The waitress greeted them by name, anyway. Jazz played softly on the radio, and Benni captured one of my legs between theirs while we sucked down black coffees.

"Excuse me?" A nervous young man stopped at our table as we were considering a slice of pie for dessert. "Are you Benni Padua?"

"Depends who's asking," they said warily.

"I was told you could help me find a person. My niece. She went missing a few weeks ago."

Our eyes locked. Benni lifted an eyebrow, and I smiled over the rim of my cracked mug.

"We can help. Have a seat, kid, and let's talk money."

Maybe I'd get a desk at Benni's place. I bet it had a big fake plant, and space for a partner.

TAGS: didn't know they were dating, everyone knows they're in love but them, farmer, farmer's market, genderfluid, getting together, modern, non-binary, non-fanfiction story inspired by source material, polyamory, present tense, seattle, third person limited point of view, united states of america

THE POLYAMOROUS "OH"

Theo Neidlinger

The original idea for my piece was a romantic comedy of sorts—hence the title and attempts at humor—but as I wrote more, it mellowed. Really, the setting is the focus of the story. The characters are wonderful, and the storyline is cute, but I think what will draw readers in is the description of the heat, the din of the market, the arrangement of the produce. As a queer farmer myself, it was easy to write about LGBTQ+ people at a Seattle farmers market! And it's a pleasure to give readers a piece of that experience.

Working the U-District farmers market has a few distinct advantages over working the one at Capitol Hill. It's full of people busily grocery shopping, rather than people tipsily meandering after brunch. The farm's chalk-lined spot is ninety-percent shaded, rather than in full sun. And, best of all, their box truck stays parked right behind their two tents. There's no rush to unload everything, move the truck, and hustle back in time to set up before the early birds descend.

The biggest downside, in Harper's opinion, is that the last hour of the U-District market drags. By one in the afternoon, the cordoned-off street is pleasantly warm, most customers are drowsy

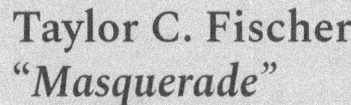

Taylor C. Fischer
"Masquerade"

Taylor opted not to share the inspiration behind this artwork.

145

from lunch, and the steady thrum of her farmers-market energy has fizzled into a slow-blinking civility that's much harder to maintain.

Diagonally, across the U of their green-and-yellow checkered tables, Bea's by the tomato starts, hip cocked as she idly prunes suckers and drops them to the pavement. Tomatoes are Bea's favorite plants, and the only ones they brought with them for which the starts need tending. There's nothing else to do but wait until it's time to count the till.

Harper stands behind the cash box and tries not to zone out as people trickle by. It's not that she's tired, exactly. "Tired" is a word she's always associated with being physically drained. Sure, her feet hurt a little, and it's been almost a full day of work, but it's her mind that's fuzzy and checked-out, not her body.

Wheels rattling on the asphalt announce Mrs. Matthews as she trundles her little cart over. Her dress today is particularly colorful: a glorious ombre that's orange at the shoulders, red at the waist, and dark blue-black at the hem. It's a little at odds with her white Nike sneakers, but Harper would never judge someone for their practical footwear.

As usual, Mrs. Matthews starts her skeptical perusal with the rainbow chard, which is right on the end next to Bea and the tomatoes. Her scarlet lipstick scrunches as she frowns severely at their bright, colorful bunches. It's Harper's theory that Mrs. Matthews wants to like chard (because it's so pretty, and it's guaranteed to match her outfits if she were ever to put any in her cart), but she simply doesn't, and that's deeply, aesthetically offensive to her.

"Hey Mrs. Matthews," Bea drawls, wiping her green-stained fingertips on her jeans, "what can I get for you?"

Mrs. Matthews pulls her sparkling, white shawl tighter around her shoulders with one hand and points regally with the other. "Are those fresh?"

The chard, slightly limp from being on display for hours, is not upset by her tone; neither is Bea.

"Harvested just yesterday. You know we pick everything Friday morning."

"Hm." Mrs. Matthews narrows her eyes and huffs, dramatically betrayed as ever, then moves along to the green curly kale. Behind her back, Bea rolls her eyes at Harper with fond exasperation.

"Hi there!" The new voice is chipper and smooth with a hint of an accent Harper can't place. She's pulled on her muted customer-service smile before she's fully turned.

"Hello! How can I…help you?"

Hands tucked into worn, brown overalls. Lightly tanned skin. Long, brown hair that curls into ringlets, tucked behind ears lined with piercings. A soft, earnest smile. Huge, grey eyes with starry, white striations that make Harper itch to paint them.

"I was just looking at your stuff," they say. They have dimples. *Dimples.* "You've got a nice variety! Is any of it overwintered?"

There's a long moment where Harper doesn't even vaguely recall what the term "overwintered" means, her mind hung up on whiskey-colored freckles and how she'd gently dot the canvas to capture them. Then:

"Yes!" Suddenly, her spark of energy is back, flustered and warm, zapping the last-hour-fuzz from her brain. "Some of the kale, and the rapini. It's cauliflower rapini! Looks a bit funny, but it's pretty tasty."

"Well, if you're recommending it, then I'll have to try it." Their head tilts as they deliver a devastating wink. "I'm Cloud. It's nice to meet you…?"

"It's nice to meet you too!" Harper says with her sunniest smile. She blinks when Cloud's smile just widens, showing off adorable buck teeth. "Oh! I'm Harper." Heat rises in her cheeks and on the back of her neck.

Cloud bites their lower lip and twists their hands in their pockets. "I work at Merry's"—they nod to the side, down the street toward a tent with a banner that reads "Merry Orchards ~ As merry as the day is long" in bright-purple print—"if you'd like to trade?" They're looking up at her through their eyelashes. Their very long, very beautiful eyelashes.

"Sure! Yes! I'd love to trade. Um—" For the second time, Harper can't seem to remember anything remotely useful. All her thoughts are along the lines of "cute" and "wow" and "pretty."

As if sensing her panic, the warm, familiar weight of Bea's arm wraps around her shoulders. "Hey, sorry to interrupt. Did you keep any greens in the truck? Mrs. Matthews asked for our spicy mix."

Harper slumps into Bea's side with relief and weakly pats the back of Bea's hand where it rests on her bicep. "Yeah, there should be some in the back. Black tote, on the left."

"Thanks," Bea says and smacks a kiss to Harper's temple.

Harper focuses back on Cloud, feeling more capable of coherent thought and decision making now.

"Sorry about that," she says, and asks what the orchard has this week. Turns out, they've got some Rainier cherries left, which is exciting because she hasn't eaten any yet this season. Cloud doesn't wink again, but Harper is at least eighty percent sure they were flirting with her.

Which is why it's so surprising when they return to their tent and she sees them immediately folded into the arms of another worker. There's hair petting. It doesn't look platonic.

"What is it?" Bea asks when Harper sighs deeply, all the breath leaving her with a rush of disappointment. Mrs. Matthews has made off with her spicy mix, Hakurei turnips, and Tuscan kale (forgoing the chard, as she always does), and no other customers have stopped by.

"I thought they were flirting with me." As she watches, Cloud pulls back from the hug and gets a forehead kiss, further confirming her suspicions.

"Maybe they were." Bea shrugs and nudges her with a hip so she can reach the till and start counting.

Harper sighs again.

Well. If they weren't flirting, maybe she's made a new friend!

The following Saturday is unseasonably hot, the temperature record-breaking for June in Seattle. Sweat drips down the back of Harper's neck while he tries, once again, to get the lettuce heads to stay upright so that they won't flop over and expose their browning, nubby butts. Bea has scurried off to trade with the cheese lady at the other end of the market, because she is an abandonous traitor who holds nothing in her heart but evil.

"Hello," someone says, drawing Harper's attention from the equally treacherous lettuce pile. In a startling moment of déjà vu, he turns and finds himself stunned.

The speaker looks nothing like Cloud. He's darker and bigger, the muscles of his shoulders straining the soft cotton of his T-shirt. His hair is short and curly over a smooth undercut. There's a vertical barbell in his right eyebrow, and he's raising that brow, probably because Harper has just spent five full seconds staring without saying a single word.

"Hi! Hello," he says belatedly, and hopes in vain he doesn't look as dumbstruck as he feels.

Thankfully, the beautiful market stranger seems more amused than off-put, judging by the smug quirk of his full lips and how his eyes crinkle at the corners. "I think my partner Cloud traded with you last week? They wanted me to tell the cute farm girl that the rapini was delicious." He holds out a hand to shake. "I'm Ben."

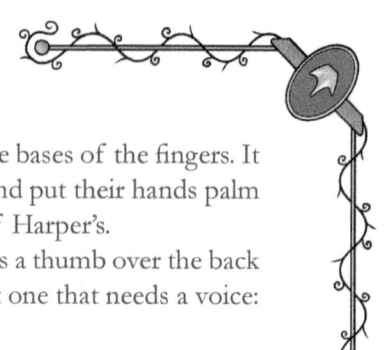

Ben's hand is warm and damp when Harper takes it, calloused around the bases of the fingers. It also dwarfs Harper's completely. If they were to stretch their fingers out and put their hands palm to palm, Ben would be able to wrap his fingers completely over the tips of Harper's.

"G-good! I'm so glad they liked it," Harper manages to stutter. Ben drags a thumb over the back of Harper's wrist. It scatters almost all of his thoughts, leaving behind just one that needs a voice: "I'm a cute farm boy today, though."

He's braced for a reaction. People usually have one. Maybe they have questions, or they offer an awkward "oh wow." If they're not on board with it, they might scoff or roll their eyes. Worse, sometimes.

Ben doesn't react in any of the ways Harper has come to expect. Instead, he looks Harper up and down once, squeezes Harper's hand, and says, "The most beautiful boy at the market. Your chard is gorgeous. I love the red-and-orange leaf in the mix."

The feeling of Ben's thumb on Harper's wrist lingers after he lets go, as do his words. Harper's never had someone just…roll with his gender before. Even his friends asked whether he was FTM when he first told them. It's difficult to wrap his mind around this simple acceptance and move on but, thankfully, if there's one thing Harper can talk about, it's vegetables. Even if his brain isn't online yet, he can babble about chard.

"Thank you! That's my favorite, too, the one that's red in the middle and orange on the outside? I call it the 'sunset chard.' I was so sad—the cucumber beetles got to that bed and we had to till it in. Nobody wants to buy chard with a bunch of holes in it, even if it tastes just the same and the colors are still gorgeous. We didn't lose the kale though!" He chuckles weakly; he may be babbling a little too much. "We've always got kale."

"I'd take some kale." Ben's voice is the rumbly sort of deep that makes Harper shiver. Honestly, as far as Harper's concerned Ben could take some of whatever he'd like. "We still have cherries, if you want any, and we also brought the season's first apricots."

Trading. Yes. Ben is here to trade. He's not here to take some of anything. Well, to take some vegetables. Only vegetables. Nothing else that is currently under the tent. Because Ben has a Cloud. A partner, who is a Cloud—

"I have Gouda!" Bea, the light of Harper's life, goddess among mortals, squeezes around the back edge of their tables and hoists a white paper bag aloft like a prize. It is a prize, really: Gouda is a favorite. "And I refilled your water bottle, which you didn't even notice was gone because you don't drink enough water."

She sets Harper's "pansexual" water bottle next to the cash box with a *thud* then climbs into the back of the truck.

"Thank you!" Harper calls after her, then takes a quick, stabilizing breath before saying to Ben, "We'd love some apricots." Of course they would. Apricots are, objectively, delicious, and Bea adores them.

"I'll bring some over, then." He tilts his head, eyes flicking to the truck and back again. "She seems lovely. Maybe the four of us could go out sometime?"

"The four of…yeah! That would be great." It really would be. Harper is the only reason Bea ever goes out, and it's been forever since he's dragged her anywhere. She's long overdue. "Maybe we could go see a movie? Or there's this new restaurant a friend of mine just opened, I'm sure they'd love to have us in. It's all fancy pizzas. They even order some of their ingredients from our farm!"

"Sounds perfect." Ben's smile seems the littlest bit confused, or maybe thoughtful. There's a small furrow in his brow. But he doesn't ask anything else, so Harper doesn't mention it.

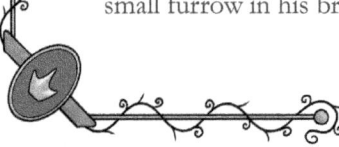

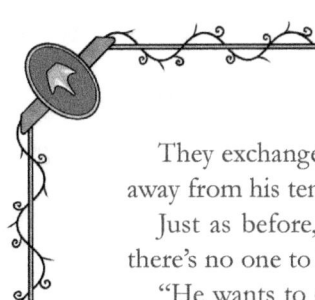

They exchange numbers and, once again, Harper is left watching a beautiful human being walk away from his tent and into the arms of another beautiful human being.

Just as before, he releases an audible sigh from deep in his gut. He might pout. If he does, there's no one to know.

"He wants to get into your pants." Bea's voice sounds right next to Harper's shoulder, and he nearly jumps out of his skin.

"Jeez! Warn a guy! I almost died." He rubs his chest, looking at Bea with a wounded expression.

She does not appear impressed. "I'm just saying. He was absolutely trying to vibe-check you. I think he wants to get in your pants." If she had bubblegum, she'd be popping it.

Harper looks back toward Merry's. "Pft. No, he doesn't. He's got Cloud."

Bea shrugs. "I stand by my statement," she says, and wanders over to the plant starts, taking up her post.

It's ridiculous, of course. Ben and Cloud are clearly together. Neither of them were flirting with Harper, today or last week. They were just looking for more queer people to hang out with, because what queer person isn't looking for more queer friends?

That's all it is. They're just being friendly.

Tomato crates are the least aesthetically pleasing, yet most practically functioning, object Harper has ever beheld. They're rectangular, flat, and tan, with little lines of vertical holes that provide excellent ventilation. Sturdy black handles swing over the top and matching horizontal divots line the bottom so they stack and store like a dream.

Naturally, Mrs. Matthews regards them with the utmost disdain. Still, she endures their plastic audacity. Probably because the tomatoes are gorgeous: plump and ripe, their colors ranging from dark red to hot pink to honey yellow. Bea holds the tomatoes up, one after another, for her to inspect. Each time, Mrs. Matthews squints at them for a moment then purses her lips and shakes her head minutely, as if they've fallen just short of her exacting requirements.

Harper, meanwhile, continues the conversation he'd been having with Bea before Mrs. Matthews moseyed over. "Bea, they thought we were *together*." It's been more than a month since Harper last worked U-District and less than two days since that little revelation: that Ben and Cloud thought Harper and Bea were a couple. "Can you believe that?" He looks to Mrs. Matthews as if she'll sympathize. Predictably, she purses her lips again, blinks once, then shakes her head at him precisely as she has for each of the tomatoes.

Bea just snorts. "We don't exactly look alike."

She's not wrong. Bea's always been darker, with her deep-brown eyes, thick, black hair, and skin that tans faster than anyone else's in the family. By contrast, Harper has wispy, honey-colored hair and hazel eyes that look more green than brown in most lighting. He and Bea don't really look like family, let alone like close family.

"I guess, but I dunno, it still feels silly. They could've just asked? But instead, they assumed we were together. It took ages for them to figure out we're cousins."

"Yes, it's wild," Bea deadpans, holding up a beautiful pink oxheart, which Mrs. Matthews finally nods her approval of. "Who in the world makes assumptions about the nature of a relationship based on watching how two people interact? I can't *imagine* anyone ever doing that."

"How much do I owe you?" Vegetables obtained, Mrs. Matthews is ready to leave, already fishing out a pink-sequined change purse. Her nails shimmer pink-red as she opens the clasp.

"Fourteen dollars and thirty-two cents"—Bea leans forward and winks—"but for you I'll make

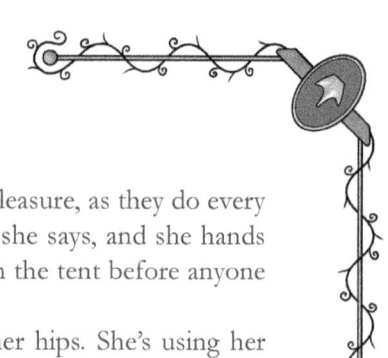

it fourteen."

Mrs. Matthews rolls her eyes, but her lips twitch with something like pleasure, as they do every time Bea knocks a few cents off her total. "Fourteen even, then," is all she says, and she hands over the cash then snaps her purse shut. She's rattling her cart away from the tent before anyone can accuse her of sentiment.

"Harper." Bea straightens up and faces Harper with her hands on her hips. She's using her "time to realize the obvious" tone. "My favorite person on this whole planet. The only reason I ever willingly leave the farm for non-work-related things. Remind me, how often do you talk to Ben and Cloud?"

Harper can't look her in the eye. He looks at the garlic instead and starts sorting it by size. "Not every day," he mumbles.

Bea's never had an issue cutting through bullshit. "But you talk to them most days?"

"Maybe." Absolutely.

"And what have you talked about?" She asks the question like she knows the answer, because she does. Harper tells her everything.

Still, he humors her, albeit reluctantly. "Lots of things. How the farm is doing, whether the smoke will be bad this year…"

"…gender and sexuality, queer representation, capitalism, and the deep, soul-crushing reality of climate change," Bea finishes for him. Harper can feel her stare on the side of his head. She *tsks.* "I'm just saying, that's not the kind of thing you talk about with people you aren't interested in romantically."

That's just so false that Harper has to correct her. "Literally every queer person we know talks about gender and sex and stuff within the first week of getting to know another queer person. I can totally talk about all those things with someone and have a completely platonic relationship with them."

"What do you talk about when you're romantically interested in someone, then?"

"I dunno. Family? Future plans? What I want to do. Where I want to be. What my favorite places are, because I want to share them. I'd make a lot of plans, too, just to spend more time together…" He trails off, staring at a garlic head as if it's suddenly gained the power of speech and told him one of life's fundamental truths. "…fuck."

Bea doesn't say anything, but her silence is extraordinarily smug as she opens the till to start counting.

The thing is, Harper has talked about all those things with Ben and Cloud. He's made plans with them every week. He's shown them the spot by the river that runs next to the farm where the trees are so dense, and the water curves so sharply that it feels like a pocket universe separate from the rest of reality. They know about the hill with the plum trees on top where he and Bea used to go and get stoned in high school, always right before school started again when the plums were ripe for picking. They know Harper's mother died in a car accident when he was little, and that his father is just starting to date again. They know how happy it makes him, how proud he is that his dad is looking for love.

Harper is so deep in thought, he doesn't realize, at first, that someone has come up to the table beside him.

"Hey, gorgeous." Ben's voice hits the back of Harper's ear like a caress and sends shivers all the way down to his toes, making them curl in his boots.

"Rude!" Harper exclaims as he turns around, puffing up in mock upset. "What have we said about startling me?"

"That it's rude. You never told me to stop though." His smile is roguish. His eyes sparkle.

"Well." There's no real protest Harper can voice without lying, so he deflates, then smiles and rolls his eyes. "All right, fine, you win. What veggies do you want? I saved you yellow squash! It's not even that dinged."

"Whatever you've got the most of left."

Harper nods and walks around to the other side of the tables, grabs a brown bag and starts filling it. "There's a little cauliflower if you want any? And one monster tomato nobody dared to buy."

Ben shakes his head. "Cowards."

"I know! Who doesn't want more of a tomato? Ridiculous." He hands Ben the bag when he's through, not having waited for an answer about the cauliflower. There's no reason for Ben not to take some. They're beautiful purple-heads, and Harper knows for a fact Cloud loves purple food. "What am I getting in return?" Harper leans forward, hands on the table, face upturned expectantly, smile teasing.

"Pluots." Ben full-on smirks at him. "They're Cloud's favorites." He mirrors Harper, leaning over so they're in each other's space. "Super sweet." His eyes flick down to Harper's lips and then back to his eyes. "Just a bit messy."

"Hah." If Harper were a fictional character, there'd be steam pouring from his ears. As it is, he hears a faint, distant ringing. "Sounds great!" His voice is much higher-pitched than intended. "I could definitely take those."

Ben's eyes glitter as if they're laughing at Harper. "I knew you could," he murmurs, and hands over a white paper bag.

He walks away before Harper can pick up his jaw, much less find a response.

As soon as Ben is out of earshot, Harper starts babbling, "I like them. It's not platonic. I like them in a not-at-all platonic, entirely romantic way."

Bea closes the till with a snap. "I am always right."

The following market is hot, even for August. They're in the middle of a second record-breaking heat wave, and people are grumpy about it. Babies fuss in their strollers, crying more than usual, and dogs pant with their tongues lolling out as they trot alongside their owners. The morning is so hectic, Harper feels like she doesn't have time to breathe until three hours have passed and she's blinking at her shockingly empty water bottle. For once she might be drinking as much water as she should.

When the foot traffic finally eases off enough that she can think again, her mind drifts and gets stuck on the argument she'd had with Bea in the truck on their way over. After Harper's revelation last week, Bea insisted Harper was, pretty much, in a relationship with Ben and Cloud already. So, Bea proposed, Harper should talk things out with them and make it official. Harper insisted that just because she had feelings for them didn't mean they returned her feelings. Ben and Cloud were in a relationship already. It would be absurd for her to be in a relationship with them, too, especially without knowing she was.

The afternoon goes slower as the temperature rises from hot to scorching and people retreat to find air conditioning and ice water. The produce looks sad, but there's not much of it left, really, so it's fine. Everyone came to shop in the morning because they knew what the afternoon would be like. Even Mrs. Matthews had come early.

Bea's started consolidating their display onto two tables instead of four by the time Cloud walks up and sets a bag on the table by the till.

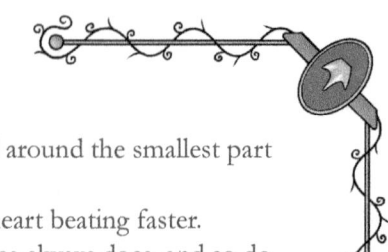

"Hey you," they say, and pull Harper in for a hug, their arms wrapped around the smallest part of her waist, squeezing tight. "He or she today?"

"She," Harper says, feeling incredibly seen, her ears burning and her heart beating faster.

Cloud isn't the only person who checks in with her about pronouns. Bea always does, and so do most of Harper's friends, but it's especially good coming from Cloud. Casual, and understanding, and "right" in a way that settles into Harper's belly like a perfectly portioned meal.

"All right, gorgeous." Cloud raises one hand to ruffle her hair where it's short in the front. "We still on for tonight?"

She's due to hang out at Ben and Cloud's apartment for a movie night. Harper hasn't ever seen *But I'm a Cheerleader* and that fact is, apparently, outrageous and unacceptable. The possibility of cancelling plans with them has never occurred to her before. Why would she pass up the chance to spend an evening with people who make her feel so comfortable? But this time, she hesitates for a split second, wondering if she should back off. Let them live their lives without complicating things. They don't need her bringing romantic feelings into something that is obviously platonic.

Cloud's arm settles back around Harper's waist, warm and familiar, and the answer she wants to give is pulled out of her mouth before she can stop it.

"Yeah, of course."

Harper has never put any weight on how easily they touch each other. She's always been a strong proponent of platonic intimacy, and she and Cloud are both tactile people. Touching this way doesn't have to be romantic, no matter what Bea says.

"Great. I brought you pluots again, since you liked them so much last time." Their smile is buck-toothed and adorable. "See you tonight, love."

Cloud squeezes her waist again, as tight as before, right around her lowermost ribs where the compression feels best.

They lean up to kiss her cheek, soft as a flower petal. Their nose brushes her cheek as they pull back.

Then they practically skip back to Merry's tent.

Harper stares after them. She's never heard them call anyone but Ben "love." They use endearments all the time, sure, but "love" has always been a special thing. Something reserved for Ben and the kind of relationship Cloud has with Ben.

It's possible, maybe, perhaps, that in all of her insisting that her relationship with Ben and Cloud is platonic—with all of the assumptions she's made about what they want from her—she's been a bit of a hypocritical idiot. She blinks and turns to look at Bea.

Bea is giving her the "see?" look with one eyebrow raised

"Polyamory," Bea says, making a rainbow motion with her hands.

Harper blinks again and looks back at the tent where Cloud and Ben are chatting. Cloud bounces on the balls of their feet. Ben looks up, over Cloud's shoulder, and gives her a wave. Harper waves back.

Then, what Bea said clicks in her slow-as-molasses brain. "...*oh.*"

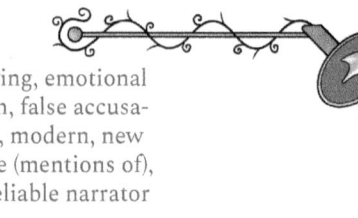

TAGS: abuse (past), alternate universe, angst, asexual, bullying, emotional abuse (mentions of), emotional hurt/comfort, epistolary, f/m, false accusations, first person point of view, found family, high school, modern, new zealand, panic attacks, present tense, ptsd, recovery, suicide (mentions of), therapy, third person limited (multiple) point of view), unreliable narrator

FIND OURSELVES UNSTUCK

nottesilhouette

nottesilhouette opted not to share the inspiration behind this story.

66

"Why did you do it?"

"Shouldn't I be asking you that?"

John shifts awkwardly on his feet, shuffling straight into startled shame at her sharp response. He hasn't cut his hair since he ran away weeks ago, and his curly bangs flop over his eyes now. It makes him look like a sheepdog, which seems fitting, seeing how sheepish he is to be talking to her. "I'm sorry, Hero. I'll answer, if you want me to, it's just—you didn't ask, and I didn't want to push my excuses on you. Not you, not after everything. But you weren't asking, so I thought maybe I'd ask for some answers, if you're willing."

Hero leans back against the porch step and squirms as the wood cuts into her back, then ignores the way John's concern glances over her and winces away. The party where they've both ended up is still throbbing around them, the bass thumping to a steady, solid beat.

"Why are you even here?" She doesn't say it to be mean. The way her voice falls flat and her gaze cuts to the road ahead, she's sure he wouldn't know it.

"Same reason I thought you were, I guess. Senior year. College apps are in. What else do I do with my free time?"

Aceriee (Previous Page)
"Battle of Wit"

As I was looking for inspiration for the piece I came across a book illustration depicting Benedick and Beatrice by Norman Mills Price and I wanted to try and convey the emotion captured in the piece. Ultimately I ended up doing my own spin on the original illustration by taking the pose and setting and making it my own.

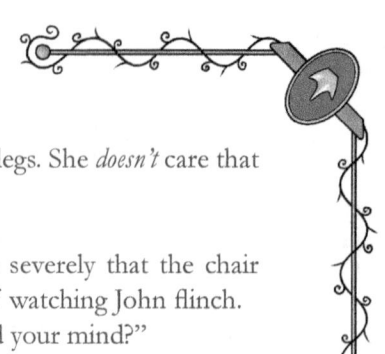

heartbeat pounding in her ears. Two seats away from her, John swings his legs. She *doesn't* care that he's here, she tells herself. She doesn't.

"You never answered, by the way."

Hero nearly jumps out of her plastic chair; she startles backward so severely that the chair screeches against the floor's linoleum tiles. At least she has the pleasure of watching John flinch.

"Answered what?" she asks. "You haven't exactly spoken. Should I read your mind?"

He flinches at that, too. "I just meant—at the party last week? You never answered my question." Hero stares at him until he rushes to add: "You don't have to! I just figured, you never said you *wouldn't*, so I'm trying again…"

"You never even told me what 'it' is."

"Right!" John is jumpier than Hero's seen him in months, back to the squirrely boy who'd shrunk away at every glance once the truth of his actions came out. "Uh, well, that is—um—why did you…" John pauses, squirming. "…forgive me?"

Hero squints at his tapping sneakers and bouncing leg. He'd gotten over this, she thought. "I don't hate you, John Donaldson. I don't care enough about you to hate you."

"You should."

"I should care about you?"

"N-no!" This time it's his chair screeching metal legs over tile. "You should hate me." When Hero doesn't respond beyond a blank look, he adds helpfully, "I hurt you."

"No, you didn't."

"To humiliate my half-brother, I set Robbie up in your room with some blonde girl." So helpful of him to remind her of exactly what happened, as if she's not sitting in the waiting room of the counselor she sees because she can't forget. "I made sure Pedro and Claudio were looking through that window when it happened. I encouraged them to confront you, and now half the school thinks you're—" He has the good sense to cut himself off there, perhaps *helped* along by Hero's withering glare.

"You dragged Ben along too, didn't you?"

John nods, tentatively, as if he suspects she's setting a trap a trap.

"Ben, who's known me as long as Pedro has, who was as much a brother to me as Pedro was, saw a blonde girl in my room fucking Robbie, and yelled at the cameras to stop filming when Claudio screamed at me at my own birthday party. When Robbie cheated on Meg, his *girlfriend*, she blamed Robbie and believed me. Beatrice skipped school for days and left Pedro, the Goddamn class president, with three bruises and a black eye because she's my cousin and best friend. You fucked up, John, but you didn't fuck it up with me."

"If it weren't for me—"

"If it weren't for you, I'd have spent months longer dating an abusive asshole lurking under a pretty face. Claudio didn't trust me, plain and simple. Hell if *I* know why. You didn't make him scream at me in front of half the school—he *chose* that. All you did was show him something he was far too ready to believe."

John mulls over her words as she lays out the choices people made and the ones they could've made. "I ran away, though. Without ever knowing why I'd done it, you forgave me—even held a vigil to convince me to come home."

"It was hurting people to have you gone, John Donaldson. You don't actually stop hurting people by running away. You do not exist alone in this world."

Furious insistence chokes her voice—does he remember who he is? He is John, his mother's son, and a Donaldson, Peter's brother. To forget one name is to forget all he's done.

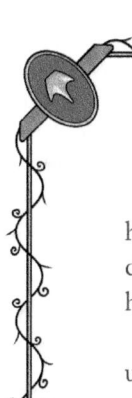

"So you always do what's best for everyone around you?"

Hero's chest clenches. Her vision swims. There's a weight on her shoulders that sinks claws into her heart and yanks down past her stomach. Everything around her sways and fades in and out of darkness. Her clothes are too tight, or too itchy, or too much; they turn into prickling needles across her skin until she scrabbles at her arms to get the sensation to stop.

"Hero Duke? Dr. Francis is ready for you. Please bring your worksheet in. Note that I've scheduled you for another appointment in two weeks on April 30th. John, she'll see you right after." The receptionist repeats the date and time, as if Hero hasn't inked it into her calendar with a vengeance, and beckons Hero in.

The door slams shut behind her.

June 11th, 4:38 p.m.

bea <3

> b
> why the hell was john talking to u

my hero
> He just wanted to apologize. It's no big deal. h

> b
> tell me u didn't say its ok

> Should I not have forgiven him...? h

June 11th, 4:52 p.m.

my hero
> Bea, I'm sorry if I was wrong. I can go take it back. h

June 11th, 5:13 p.m.

bea <3

> b
> u didnt do anythng wrong
> he shldnt have talked to u
> at least w out me there
> fuck him
> are u ok?

my hero
> I'm fine. It was no big deal. h

> b
> do u wnat to tlk about it

> h
> It really was fine. He just apologized and explained why he did it, and said thank you for the vigil. I'm glad he came home safe, it sucks that he was so scared that he ran away.

b of course he was scared
he totally fcked up ur life

b ur too sweet to him
what explanation is there even

Did Pedro ever tell you John moved
here because his mom died? h

b ...
what

Yeah. Mr. Donaldson cheated on Mrs. Donaldson
with John's mom. He was living in England with
her until she passed away, and then he was
uprooted to New Zealand h

b pedro managed to make johns life hell without any
of us looking twice at how we saw pedro. so why
would he be any different to u

Yeah. h

b shit

For daring to exist, too. They're working on it now,
he told me that much...I guess to make me feel
better that it won't happen again? But that's how
John knew Pedro would be so unreasonable about
cheating. He just didn't think Pedro would sully his
pristine reputation to mess with my life so publicly. h

b he couldve guessed. abt claudio at least

That Pedro would encourage Claudio to confront
me about "cheating" at my own birthday party
instead of talking to me in private? That students
would film Claudio calling me a whore and harass
me online for weeks? Listen to yourself, Beatrice. h

b so john made everyone think you cheated to teach
pedro that he wasnt as morally superior as he acted. except pedro was way worse than john expected

Yeah. h

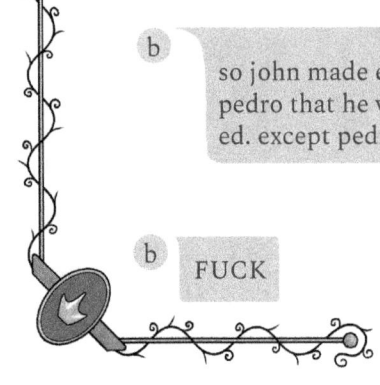

b FUCK

158

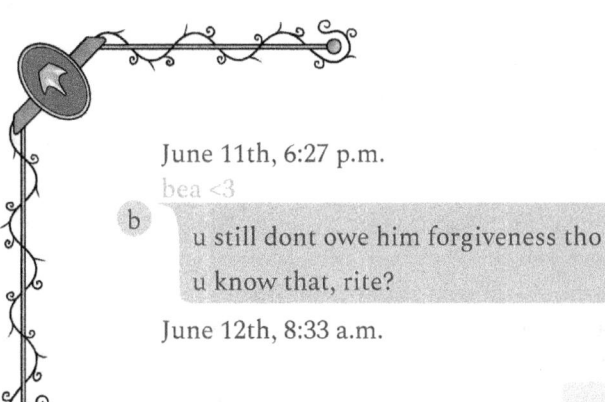

June 11th, 6:27 p.m.

bea <3

b

> u still dont owe him forgiveness tho
> u know that, rite?

June 12th, 8:33 a.m.

my hero

I found a new cookie recipe! Check your email!

h

June 12th, 3:48 p.m.

bea <3

b

> im coming over

Hero slams the door shut on her way out of the councilor's office. No amount of gentle valida-tion from her placid counselor can soothe Hero's rage. She sees John's hooded form slouch out the main exit as she turns into the loudly buzzing hallways of the administration building. The doors nearly close on her face when she rushes to catch him. It doesn't matter; Hero is quicker than he'll ever be.

"You take it back right fucking now."

John damn near trips over his own shock as he spins to catch her glare. "What?!" He waits. For what? For Hero to explain herself? To be reasonable in any capacity? She refuses. He continues, implacably and infuriatingly sensible. "Hero, could you explain what I need to take back?" He keeps his tone gentle, as if she's about to tip over the edge and shatter over a fight *she* started.

She's *not* delicate. She's *not* fucking fragile. She's not his to shield or shatter in the palm of his hands. She hates that he treats her like she's something to be carefully handled.

He can't handle her.

"You want my forgiveness because you can't forgive yourself, no matter how many people give you permission to." Her voice dips, cajolingly sweet, a mimicry of the person he taunts her for being. "You see yourself as a bad person, irrevocably tainted by the cruelty of your own design and terrified of the harm you can do. You didn't care that this would hurt me, or Meg, or anyone else we cared about. All you cared about was Pedro, and the way he made you hurt, and the way you wanted to hurt him back. Now you're chasing our forgiveness like a puppy, but the closure you need came six months ago, and you've ignored it in your own desperation."

Hero is nearly nose to nose with John, eyes bright with the irrefutable satisfaction of being right. John is half-feral, his teeth bared and his hair made to stick straight up by the force of his grasping fingers.

"And how often, in those six months, have you thought twice about putting yourself over some-one else?" he snarls. "Fight me if you want to! I haven't stopped you *once*. Instead, you held a vigil to bring me home, even when most of the school was dead convinced you were a liar, and a cheat, and a goddamn slut. Yet here you are, chasing after me, shoving closure in my face like it'll make you a hero to someone. It really doesn't, dude. It just makes you a martyr."

"Ha! As if rolling over and taking my words makes you any less of one. Forgive yourself. Fight back. I can take it. Don't you dare act like I *can't*."

159

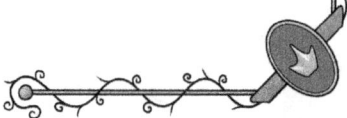

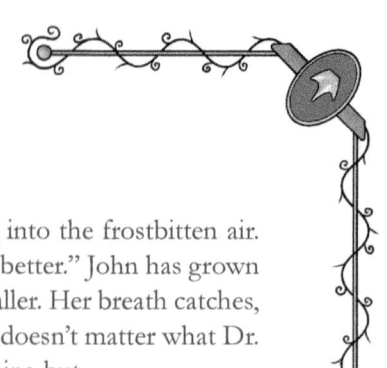

Because of you I've been through worse, she doesn't mention.

She doesn't have to.

John deflates. Righteousness slips away from his grasp and disappears into the frostbitten air. "You weren't wrong to date him, you know. You couldn't have known any better." John has grown small—shrunken into himself in an oversized hoodie—but Hero feels smaller. Her breath catches, and she pushes it down; she'll fight through a panic attack if she has to. It doesn't matter what Dr. Francis says. It *doesn't*. She wants Hero to tell the truth? Hero will say nothing but.

"And you couldn't have known your half-brother would hate your existence enough to cut off any support network you might have had here, even though the only reason you moved halfway across the world was because your family died. You still could've made better choices."

John recoils. "That's fucking different. I could've made better choices; you had no other choices to make. This was my fault."

You can't take my mistakes away.

But Hero can take *herself* away. She flees, retreating to a rooftop where the air is thin enough for her to be able to breathe through the terror in her chest. Somehow, this surrender feels like a victory.

March 30th, Boundaries Worksheet #2

You are on your way to the first day of your dream job. At the bus stop, your friend catches up to you and starts venting about their bad day. You feel deeply for her pain. However, your bus is pulling up to the stop, and if you miss it to let your friend finish her story, you will be late for work. How do you respond?

~~Why would she be at a bus stop if she's not getting on the bus?~~ I would ask her to ride the bus with me so we can keep talking, or call her from the bus if she needs to go somewhere else. I'd tell her I was going to work and that I love her, and make plans to call her again at lunch and meet up after work to take care of her, texting her throughout the day to help.

Dr. Francis: Thank you for your honest response, Hero. Please consider the long-term impacts of your decisions. This is your dream job, where you'd like to be regarded highly. Would a good friend demand your energy after a long day of work or ask you to sacrifice your attention during the day? Would you be a good friend if you allowed others to demand sacrifices from you? Specifically, recall how your friends supported you during your isolation after Claudio's public shaming. Beatrice is rather exceptional at carving out her own boundaries, even in times of crisis.

You are at an enjoyable party but need to leave early because you need to relax, and if you don't get enough sleep your exhaustion may affect your schoolwork. As you head out, the host catches you and starts chatting, excitedly making plans for later that night. How do you respond?

I would compromise by completing the plans the host makes with me before leaving. I would make a plan to study harder, organizing my notes to be more efficient. ~~I'd never go to a party if my grades were suffering. I'd make sure to have enough time at the party.~~ I would make sure to spend more time with the host later, since I've been neglecting our friendship to make them feel this way.

Dr. Francis: Interesting insight into your habits. The logistics of your answer are tightly packed, adding additional burdens when the scenario explicitly states that you must relax. This is reminiscent of your actions at the vigil which, as we've discussed, have left you resentful and overwhelmed.

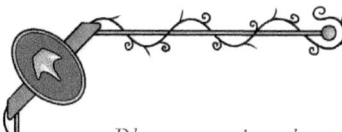

Please examine the trade-off you make here. What are you gaining that's different from the proposed options of leaving immediately or staying for the rest of the event? You mentioned feeling drained and exhausted from the frequent second-semester, free-from-college-apps parties. How can we make those enjoyable for you, rather than having them result in you sitting, miserable, on someone's porch?

You have blocked off today to hang out with a friend. However, as you chat, they repeatedly complain about their annoying coworker. You commiserate for an hour, but the conversation is starting to wear on you. You want to spend the day positively. You've tried to change the subject a few times, but your friend hasn't taken the hint. You're running out of ways to sympathize or deflect. How do you respond?

I would listen and ~~keep listening because I care about my friends, and gently~~ redirect the conversation to related, but more positive, subjects. ~~I don't fucking know I hate that this question is asking me to hurt my friends I hate this fucking worksheet and I hate that I don't know the right fucking answer to make it go away~~ I would propose an activity to change the mood of the hangout and distract my friend.

Dr. Francis: *I appreciate your frankness and ask you to remember there's no right answer. By changing the structure of the hangout, you cut off your friend's ability to rely on familiarity to keep complaining. An ingenious solution! I'd like to push you to answer the question, though: how would you progress if they still continued? Put yourself first, Hero.*

You have several projects due this week and haven't studied for Monday's final exam. You plan to cram on Sunday. At noon, your friend asks you to come over urgently. They're behind and need to turn in many projects on Monday. You've already done this work, so helping them would only take a few hours, but you wouldn't finish studying for your test on time. How do you respond?

~~Fucking FINALLY a question I can answer~~ I would bring my work and study at their place. With my project notes, they will work faster than they would on their own and I can help them get unstuck to prevent any stalling. Even if I don't finish all my studying, I would get most of it done and I've paid enough attention in class to get me through the rest. If possible, they can help me study for the test afterward.

Dr. Francis: *I see your chosen compromise here and applaud you for not fully sacrificing your own needs. Bravo, Hero! I'm glad to see you taking our discussions about healthy selfishness into consideration. Are you comfortable with this choice?*

You have several projects due this week and haven't studied for Monday's final exam. You plan to cram on Sunday, but a family emergency takes up your morning. At noon, you reach out to your friend to help you study, but they refuse because they're too tired. You know they're free and have most of the notes, but still need to finish studying. How do you respond?

I would let it go. It's not my place to push them and I would be a bad friend for asking at all.

Dr. Francis: *Hm, I'm concerned with your response and double standard here. Do you consider the friend in the previous scenario "bad" for asking? There's an interesting pattern to these answers. Let's discuss during your next appointment. I'd like to see what you really feel, not what you think you should be saying. Really, I'd like to see you*

forgive yourself. You've done nothing so wrong that you don't deserve the same friendship you offer others. See you soon.

The library air is thick and musty. The bookshelves loom over Hero and press her tighter into a space where she doesn't belong. No amount of arguing convinced her teacher to assign her a different partner, so now John's leg taps nervously a few inches away from her. Every few minutes, he flips a page and his sleeve brushes her bare arm.

Hero shivers. With the attitude that hangs between them, it's colder here than on any rooftop.

"We're supposed to write about Ophelia."

Hero doesn't bother to respond to John, merely glances pointedly at the assignment sheet. **Subject: Ophelia** is in bold at the top. How could either of them forget? John falters.

"Well, it's just, she doesn't do much?" he says.

Hero nearly screams, half-shoves the books off the table, and storms away in an awkward aborted motion, cut short when the librarian turns instinctively with a glare behind his glasses. Hero can't bear the censure. It itches at the seams of her shirt. Her sleeves are too tight. Has she sewn them wrong? She couldn't have; they'd been fine all day.

John lunges to catch a few papers teetering on the edge of the desk. Wild concern splashes across his wide eyes as he looks at Hero. She hates the softness and the way his gaze tracks her movements like he's worried about her. It's too bad she shouldn't make him mad—not here, not now.

"She's trapped," Hero blurts out. "It's that she can't do much, trapped by the burden of femininity and the role she has to play as a woman, right? No one is listening to her, yet she's the only person to trust Hamlet and speak to the man he used to be. She doesn't write his madness off as inevitable, but he writes *her* off as disposable, until Ophelia takes the only choice she has left and dies to make them listen!"

She's panting when she finishes, too loud by half for a library, but not as loud as she wishes to be. Hero squirms in her shirt and tugs at its hem.

When she looks up, John has pinned her with an unreadable look. "She was trapped by her lack of choices."

Hero flushes and looks away. After a long moment, John starts to write.

Silence reigns in the library, as it should. For once, Hero wants to break it.

"There were other choices I could've made."

John is careful, reserved: "What?"

"I could've been honest."

"Were you not?"

"Not really. I kept saying I wanted to, y'know? Like, I was supposed to want to kiss him. We were dating. I liked him, okay? I really did. I *did.*"

"Yeah?" His pen taps the desk, betraying his anxiety where his words don't.

"He thought I was cheating on him because of it." Hero pauses, then scrambles to clarify, "Because I didn't want to have sex. Or kiss him. I could've been honest. I could've told him I didn't want to. I think I might be ace, actually. I should've told him."

"Why are you telling me?" John asks so neutrally Hero can't work out what exactly he means to emphasize. She ponders which possible interpretation he intends—which version of the question he wants her to answer. Regardless, there's only one answer.

"I'm tired of being a liar and a cheat—what everyone thinks I am. I'm not."

He ignites, full of sudden horror, guilt, and emotion. "*I don—*"

"Shut up." She doesn't say it to be mean, but she means what she says. "I do care about you. I lied when I said I didn't, because I'm kind of a liar. I kind of hate you, but I'm also really fucking impressed by you." Hero breathes, because she's forgotten how, and she wants to marvel at how John looks slapped across the face by her words. "You're good at being angry, yeah, but you're also good at fixing what you fucking break. I'm not. I've never had to before, never had to do either of those. And I want *both*. But when I could've, I ran and hid. I lied instead of telling Claudio our relationship was too fucked-up to fuck."

John flicks through responses like catalogs, trying every style on his expression before he settles on the goofy, kind-of-vulnerable boy Hero misses painfully despite having never known John as that person. Has it been a year and a half and a world away since he's met this version of himself? It's like John left him behind during the move. He hasn't, Hero finds. He's still here.

"A lot of fuss over a feeling you never felt, huh! We really made much ado about nothing," he jokes, quirking a slanted grin at her.

"Shut up." Hero laughs. No amount of shoving papers at him hides the brightness in her voice.

May 2nd: Ophelia Partner Paper Assigned

May 3rd: Draft Thesis with John (3–4 p.m., Library)

May 5th: Paper Thesis Due

May 7th: ~~Outline with John (3–4 p.m., Library)~~ Outline with John (3:30–5 p.m., Library)

May 12th: Outline Due

May 13th: Research with John (12–2 p.m., Home)

May 15th: Therapy

May 20th: Write with John (1:30–5 p.m., Donaldson's)

May 24th: ~~Write with John (2–6:30 p.m., Donaldson's)~~ Write with John (2–8 p.m., Donaldson's)

May 27th: ~~Write with John (1–3:30 p.m., Park)~~ Study with John (1–10 p.m., Park)

May 28th: ~~Bake with John (12:30–2:30 p.m., Home)~~ Bake with John (12:30–9 p.m., Home)

May 29th: Hang Out with John (All Day, Donaldson's House)

May 30th: Therapy

May 31st: Paper Due

John finds Hero in the thick of a crowd, laughing and squirming in a vague imitation of dancing. The music pounds through the speakers and vibrates across the floors. Lights flash and dim. Cigarette smoke clouds the air. But Hero's unmistakable.

"Thought I might find you here," he calls when the crowd refuses to part enough to let him get closer.

She swivels to face him then lights up. She pushes past the people who wouldn't move for him; they part like double-doors for her. She doesn't notice, or care; in a moment she's tossed herself at him. Suddenly, he's too busy hugging her to care, either.

"We graduated!" she squeals. He can hardly hear her over the din, but he knows she's waited for this for months.

He bumps her hip as she drags him out to the porch, laughing off grasping hands and disappointed protests. "You're outta here, Hero. You made it out."

He looks back at the friends she's leaving behind, people he knows she made plans for tonight

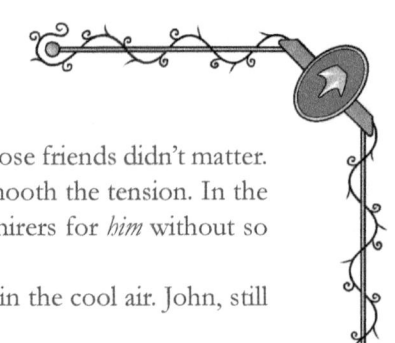

with. The Hero he'd ruined would never have left like this, laughing like those friends didn't matter. She would've walked away on a road paved with her own apologies to smooth the tension. In the moment it takes him to process this, that she's giving up a crowd of admirers for *him* without so much as a second glance, she's already pulled ahead.

"*We* made it out!" She calls back over her shoulder and skids to a halt in the cool air. John, still carried by the momentum of her thrill, nearly trips over her.

"Hey, Hero? I'm sorry."

"Yeah?" She's had time to learn the measured tone John loves to use. He should be disgruntled at how quickly she's picked up on his tricks. Instead, he swallows a grin.

"Just, you could've—*should* have—gotten to enjoy senior year, and you didn't. Because of me. So I'm…sorry?" John, awkward as ever, catches himself and clarifies: "I'm sorry. I'm sorry, as in a statement, not a question. I'm not confused about whether I'm sorry!" He nods decisively.

"You've already apologized," Hero reminds him gently. Her response surprises him, though it shouldn't have. He'd spilled out in a mess of words all the options he thought she should have, but Hero isn't limited to *should* anymore. She'd made her own choice when none of his appealed.

"Yeah, I just—but, y'know, 'cause—well, but I'm—"

Hero looks at him in a way she wouldn't have six months ago. "You offer forgiveness so easily, and yet refuse to take it for yourself? Ask me if you're forgiven, John Donaldson."

John stares at her, knuckles going white around his phone. Hero reaches out and plucks it from his hands. She's seen the way the cracks etch themselves into his skin when he's stressed. "C'mon, John."

"Am I forgiven?"

After the last few months, John knows that there is a version of Hero who wants to tell him what he wants to hear. There is a version of Hero still angry enough to tell him what he fears.

There is a version of Hero, right here, who wants to tell the truth. "Ask yourself, John Donaldson. Ask yourself."

He sinks down, sprawls out over the porch, and snags her wrist on his way down until she has no choice but to flop beside him with a gleeful laugh. The party thrums around them, flourishing, fading. The stars glimmer against a backsplash of darkness.

"We made it out, John," Hero whispers.

"Happy graduation," he whispers back.

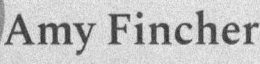

Amy Fincher
"I Had Rather Hear My Dog Bark at a Crow"

In the early 2000s, I saw a magical production of Much Ado About Nothing *at the Globe Theater, performed entirely by women. I wanted to capture some of that spark in my re-imagination of Beatrice and Benedick. I was also inspired by the beauty of the 1993 film adaptation, and paid homage to it with elements of the location and costuming. Finally, I chose a style and color palette meant to evoke the romance and nostalgia of an animated fairy tale. The line I kept thinking of while creating my illustration was "I would rather listen to my dog bark at a crow than hear a man swear that he loves me."*

INDEX

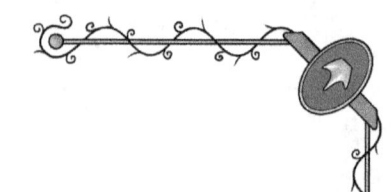

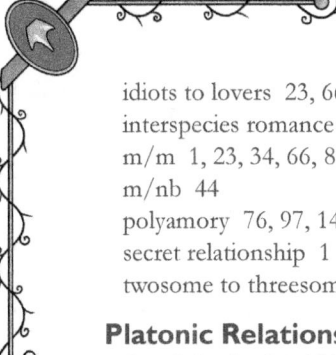

Source Information
for Casei Solus's Collage

Note: All images except the two invitations are creative commons, commercial use permitted (Attribution CC license), or used under fair use rules. Casei Solus made the Halloween invitation and Wedding invitation.

Aine. 2014. *New tattoo. Just a tiny practice one to remind me what it feels like, so I am ready for my next one. I was surprised how little it hurt.* Photograph. Flickr. September 28, 2014. https://flickr.com/photos/dainec/15353248156

Amazon.com. DESK TECH *Small Cork Bulletin Board with Wooden Frame, 12 x 18 inches, Beige.* Photograph. Amazon. Accessed September 10, 2021. https://www.amazon.com/Office-Works-Small-Board-inches/dp/B075R429RL

Aviatrix. 2018. *US Female F-16 Fighter Pilot Capt Brittany Trimble.* Photograph. Flickr. July 24, 2018. https://www.flickr.com/photos/136374834@N03/42900650464

Ball, David. 2006. *Close-up of a boutonniere.* Photograph. Wikimedia Commons. June, 2006. https://commons.wikimedia.org/wiki/File:Boutonniere-whitesuit.jpg

Crandell, Bradshaw. *Are you a girl with a star-spangled heart?* Join the WAC Now!, 1943. Uploaded by Heritage Auctions. Last Modified July 5, 2019. https://commons.wikimedia.org/wiki/File:Bradshaw_Crandell_-_Are_you_a_girl_with_a_star-spangled_heart.jpg

Dale, Timothy and Bob Vila. Embedded Photograph in "7 Types of Wall Texture and the Techniques Behind Them." Last Modified January 7, 2021. https://www.bobvila.com/articles/wall-texture-types/

G. G. Hesselgren Publishing Co. *The Castleton. Plan of First floor; Plan of upper floors.* In G. C. Hesselgren Pub. Co. Apartment houses of the metropolis. New York: G. C. Hesselgren Pub. Co. 1908. https://digitalcollections.nypl.org/items/510d47db-9f0e-a3d9-e040-e00a18064a99

jovino. 2010. *<3 (#28 & #29).* Photograph. Flickr. February 23, 2010. https://flickr.com/photos/jovino/4380885548

istolethetv. 2008. *stay puft French bulldog.* Photograph. Flickr. October 19, 2008. https://digitalcollections.nypl.org/items/510d47db-9f0e-a3d9-e040-e00a18064a99

Zimmerman, Bernard Embedded Photograph in an untitled article. *in-store savings coupon.* POS Solutions. Accessed September 10, 2021. https://www.possolutions.com.au/blog/discount-vouchers-update

Rosale Fashion Shops. *Rank insignia.* Photograph. Rosale. Accessed September 10, 2021. https://rosale.fashion-shops2021.ru/content?c=us%20army%20general%20insignia&id=32

Shebley, Cindy. 2017. *movie-tickets-psycho.* Photograph. Flickr. September 11, 2017. https://www.flickr.com/photos/cindyshebley/36383429994

Teich, Curt. *Greetings from Columbus, Mississippi, Army Flying School.* In Tenney, Fred, and Kevin Hilbert. Large Letter Postcards: *The Definitive Guide 1930s to 1950s.* Atglen, Pennsylvania: Schiffer Publishing, Ltd. 2009. https://www.flickr.com/photos/shookphotos/6002771596/

Walmart.com. *Unique Industries Assorted Colors Halloween Party Banner,* 108" x 6". Photograph. Walmart. Accessed September 10, 2021. https://www.walmart.com/ip/Glitter-Happy-Halloween-Banner-Orange-and-Black-9ft/975837389

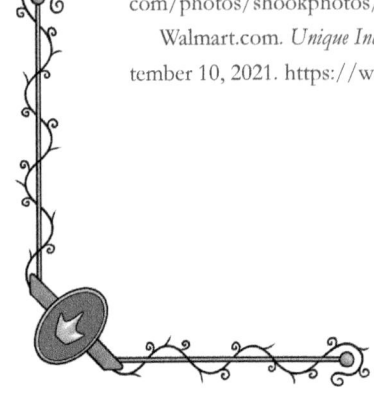

ABOUT THE CONTRIBUTORS

Aceriee

Hi! I'm Aceriee and I draw sometimes. I've been drawing all my life, but after falling into the Supernatural fandom in 2014 I've mostly focused on fanart.

Cris Alborja

I'm an illustration and comic artist from Spain. I've got a nursing degree, but I decided to pursue my passion. I have studied Illustration at EASD Pablo Picasso in A Coruña and comics at O Garaxe Hermético in Pontevedra. I have done cover art for an anthology called *Infiniteca* by Retranca Editorial and comics for *Altar Mutante*, *Nai dos Desterrados*, and *Abraxas en Cuarentena* fanzines, as well as in *Gaspariño 21* by Retranca Editorial.

Joshua Beeking

I'm Joshua Beeking, an illustrator from Québec City who works in both traditional and digital media. I have been working on sharpening my skills for over 10 years. I received formal education at Québec's O'Sullivan College, where I earned a diploma in 2D/3D Animation and Rendering in 2012. I won first place at the UQAM digital creation contest in 2011 for best character designs.

I'm currently a full-time freelance artist with more than 200 commissions completed over the years and aim to share my little touch of creativity with the world!

Liz Brooks

I'm a freelance artist currently living in Michigan with my boyfriend and my dog Ringus Mingus (aka Gus). I've been doing freelance work for a few years now and am currently working on making a webcomic series about gay Renaissance Faire knights. In my free time, I enjoy reading, playing video games poorly, and baking.

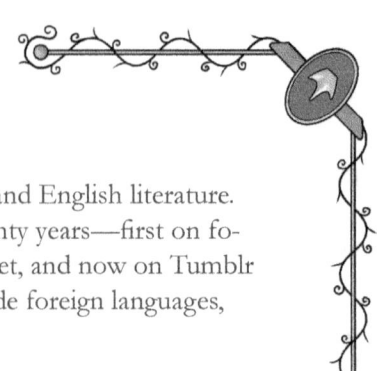

Juno Caster

Juno is a queer woman in her thirties living in France; she teaches ESL and English literature. She's been involved in fandom, mostly through writing fanfiction, for twenty years—first on forums and privately hosted websites, then on LiveJournal and FanFiction.net, and now on Tumblr and AO3. She's mostly into Asian dramas these days; other interests include foreign languages, true crime, and coffee.

Era J. M. Couts

Era has been writing for over 20 years.

She writes about characters and their development, about feelings and struggles, and about how complicated life can be even when it looks so simple. She loves to write epic, painful love stories that don't always have a happy ending. But most often they do.

She will, one day, write a dystopian series that she's been plotting for over a decade. One day, certainly one day. Aside from being a writer, Era is a casual reader, an opinionated mind, an Aries, an immigrant, a coffee lover, and a night owl who has been forced to conform to the social norm of waking up early only to become a "Morgenmuffel."

She is passionate, energetic, lazy, and sarcastic. She is a CrazyCatLady in the making, a food lover who cannot cook, the Man™ her grandma wanted her to marry, and a happy soul in her own shoes. And, above all, she is weird, queer, and so damn proud of it.

Aria L. Deair

Aria L. Deair is an author who has been writing and (while cursing her excessive comma usage) publishing fanfiction online for more than sixteen years. Freelance writer by day and author every other hour that she isn't sleeping, she spends her days courting carpal tunnel and "forgetting" to wear her wrist brace.

As a proud member of more fandoms than she can count, Aria can be found blogging about some of the writing that she is avoiding doing at arialerendeair.tumblr.com.

Like a dragon with her hoard, she can be found in her New Hampshire apartment, surrounded by notebooks (most of which are empty), half-filled mugs of tea, and some of the comfiest blankets that have ever existed. Disturb her at your own risk, especially during NaNo Season.

Amy Fincher

Amy Fincher (she/her) is a producer and artist with over a dozen years of experience in the video game and animation industries. She has contributed to various AAA and indie titles, including the *Civilization*, *XCOM*, and *Skylanders* series. When the mood strikes and time allows, she teaches art classes and takes on art commissions on the side. Her hobbies include learning aerial silks, collecting aesthetically pleasing empty containers, looking at shiny rocks, and taking very long naps.

Taylor C. Fischer

Taylor graduated from the Maryland Institute College of art in 2010. They believe that there are experiences and stories that can connect all of us with the aid of illustration and design.

Their previous projects include: Dauntless, Elderscrolls Online, Sid Meier's: Civilization, League of Legends, and XCOM.

Taylor continues to create personal work in their free time, and also enjoys raising farm animals, horseback riding, training horses, beekeeping, and living in their tiny house on wheels.

Preferred pronouns are They/Them.

Gio Guimarães

Giovanna, or simply Gio, she/her, is a Brazilian artist who has worked for a long time as illustrator, comic artist, and animator. Some of her works are the comics *Robocop* and *Green Hornet*, cards for *Avatar: The Last Airbender*, short animations for advertising and TV shows, and art for games. Since 2016, she's lived in São Paulo and worked for an American game company as Senior Illustrator. Besides the "official" work, she is always working on personal projects such as independent comics, short animations, illustrations, and fandom works.

Adrian Harley

Adrian Harley is an almost lifelong North Carolinian and a fantasy-fiction aficionado who didn't start delving deep into fandom until adulthood. They are an editor of research by day and an aspiring novelist, also by day. They go to bed early. They have short stories in OFIC Magazine and multiple Duck Prints Press anthologies. They live with their husband and a perfectly reasonable number of cats.

Joey Hazell

I've been drawing since my mom first put a crayon in my hand as a way to help me express my emotions. This resulted in bedroom walls getting covered in elaborate story-filled murals, and I haven't stopped since (though my choice of media has changed a bit). My pronouns are she/her, and currently I reside in the Toronto area, trying to figure out how to make this comic-making, illustration-drawing thing work. With a strong love for narratives, my primary focus is on making fanart for whatever fandom has me most recently captivated, and trying to create my own queer, nerdy works of fiction to put out in the world.

R. L. Houck

R. L. Houck (she/her) still has one of the first stories she ever wrote as a seven-year-old in elementary school. It was about flightless penguins reaching the sun, and a good indication of her boundless imagination and her love of animals. The latter became a full-time veterinary career; the former keeps her occupied with fanfiction and original fiction in between appointments.

Identifying as asexual herself, she is fond of exploring characters on the asexual spectrum in her writing. She has a tendency toward erotica, and her modus operandi could best be described as "smut with feelings." However, she also enjoys writing about found families and fluffy meet-cutes. Anything goes, and she is very grateful to Duck Prints Press for allowing her to place well-known and respected characters in flower shops and space...and officially publishing those exploits!

Outside of writing, she enjoys snuggling on the couch with her dog and four cats, watching zombie or other disaster movies or TV shows. A native New Yorker, she currently resides in Vir-

ginia but dreams of one day retiring to Portugal.

Lucy K. R.

Lucy K.R. (she/her) is technically in existence. Every time she is free, she writes. Sometimes when she is not free, she also writes. This has occasionally created problems. She is fortunate to be supported (read: enabled) by her enthusiastic fiancée Tomo, a loving OG family, and a lively found family as well.

Eager for a change after a decade of waitressing, Lucy K. R. took the chance in March of 2021 to make her first steps into the world of published work. Prior to the success of the largely fabricated German translation of the short-story found in the collection *die Karaoke-Königinnen*, she was best known for her work on *Mageling: Rise of the Ancient Ones* and in the Duck Prints Press anthologies *And Seek (Not) to Alter Me* and *She Wears the Midnight Crown*.

In her stories, Lucy enjoys writing evil ideas as gently as possible, portrayed through unexpected lenses. She would like to acknowledge that she has never written a biographical statement that did not turn out weird, beg your indulgence, and express her hope that you enjoy her work in this anthology. The people at Duck Prints Press have been a delight, and she is deeply grateful to be included!

Nickel J. Keep

Nickel (they/them) was born in the Dreamlands during a time period that cannot be completely explained. But for simplicity sake, they currently live in Pennsylvania with their three partners, their two children, the most terrifying pibble named Ink, and a fat, lazy chonk of a cat named Sphinx. When not writing, Nickel can be found drawing, playing video games, or running Magic: The Gathering tournaments as an L1 judge. They can frequently be found in various fandoms, including, but not limited to *Leverage, Haven, Mass Effect, Dragon Age*. and most horror podcasts (looking at you, *Old Gods*. Looking at you.).

Mikki Madison

Mikki Madison has been writing stories since she was seven years old. While she is most prolific in fanfiction and has works scattered among more than a dozen fandoms, she has been making strides into original fiction. Her favorite genres to read are romance, fantasy, and cozy mysteries.

When she isn't reading, writing, or falling headfirst into a new fandom, she can be found baking, doing puzzles, walking her foster dog, doting on her niblings, or playing Pokémon Go. She has also written under the name M. K. Mads.

Nova Mason

Nova Mason spent a significant portion of her childhood fantasizing about dragons, spaceships, and other worlds. She is now, allegedly, a grown-up, with two kids and more varied interests. Dragons, spaceships, and other worlds are still pretty high on the list, though.

Alicia Matheson

Alicia Matheson (she/her), bi-demisexual and Elder Millenial circa 1982! Southern California native, currently living in the Pacific Northwest; Alicia has been writing and doing digital and traditional art for decades. She also works as an author under the pen name Licie Laine.

Theo Neidlinger

Writer with a focus on LGBTQ+ themes. They/them.

nottesilhouette

Hi, I'm Notte (she/they)! I've been a writer for over a decade, which is when I started reading fanfiction and almost immediately felt compelled to write some too. I started in the Percy Jackson fandom, then moved through various media until my stories started becoming so AU they were practically my own.

When I'm not writing, I'm studying—any time left after that goes into reading as much as possible! I love talking to people who want to talk to me, and I will sleep anytime I'm presented with a soft surface to lie on (and sometimes even without).

Pimmy Oldham

A quirky, queer published artist and hobby writer, mainly working in digital media for the last five years, but often drifting back into traditional media out of nostalgia for my long-deserted youth. I hobby art predominantly in the Supernatural fandom. Heller to the end of my days.

My home is in the UK, my heart is in Europe, and my head is usually orbiting Pluto (she's still a planet to me). I usually have three or four cats vying to lie on me, my keyboard, or my graphics tab in no set order and live with them and my daughter in generally harmonious chaos.

Pallas Perilous

Pallas Perilous (she/they) is an illustrator, writer, and designer who has been creating work inside, outside, and adjacent to fandom for twenty years. In her professional life, she primarily creates graphic novels for young adults through traditional publishers, but she has also self-published half a dozen books, provided visual communications consulting for fancy tech companies, and done a lot of public speaking. She is active in several programs focused on mentorship and advocacy for emerging creators, especially those from fandom and marginalized communities.

Magnolia Porter

I'm an illustrator and painter who enjoys figure expression (both grand and sentimental), what it means to be a creature, and exploiting my exposure to the ideas of holiness and unholiness for symbolism material, especially while exploring a mixture thereof ("I'll tell you my sins so you can sharpen your knife," anyone?). I also dabble in creative writing, though it is not quite my breath and blood like art is. I daydream of fantasy worldbuilding, but unfortunately my troubles with plot have kept those worlds from expanding.

Jared Powell

I'm Jared, a gay trans artist, writer, and political scientist. I live in Colorado with my partner, my son, and our three cats. In my free time I enjoy leatherworking, puppeteering, reading, watching my shows, creating fanart and fanfic, listening to music, and baking.

Xanthe P. Russell

I'm Xanthe, she/they, a queer freelance artist based in the United Kingdom. I am primarily a portrait artist who specialises in using portraiture as a way of expressing my love for both the subject and the art world in general. I mainly work digitally, although I love to dabble in traditional art (such as pencils, paints, embroidery, etc), and I am constantly looking to push the boundaries of what my art can be! I recently graduated with a BA in History of Art, and often use artists of the past and present as inspirations for my work. My art has been featured in a few online magazines such as the *Kraze* and *MouthingOff*, along with some fanzine and independent projects.

My work is a mix of fanart and original character designs. I have a wide range of fandoms that I've been involved in over the years, but one that has remained consistent (and was also what got me interested in digital art back in 2013) is the K-pop fandom. Fandoms in general have been places where I've met a lot of talented and lovely people who have helped inspire and motivate me as a creative person! I also have a love for music and writing, and I have written a lot of music and stories in my spare time. Being creative has always been a big and happy part of my life, and I love being able to share that creativity with the world!

Vee Sloane

Vee Sloane has authored a novel, several short stories, some poetry, and twenty-two year's worth of fanfic. She lives with one lovely spouse, one rambunctious clever child, and one sleepy cat.

Casei Solus

Casei is a self-taught artist from Florida, USA. She is known for her impressionist fanart and her minimalist pride merch. For work, she designs and mocks up merch for clients. She doesn't care about her pronouns.

Theresa Tanner

She/her. My father's family was in newspaper journalism, and he taught me how to get to the heart of a story and how to proofread. My mom was an army doctor, and her family included many educators. I grew up to teach high school science and write stories, so I'd like to think both sides would be proud of me. When I retire from teaching, I plan to pursue writing as my second full-time career. When not teaching or writing, I enjoy playing with my cat, video games, knitting, listening to music, streaming TV, and, of course, reading. I live in West Texas now, but have lived in Maryland and Germany and have traveled through much of the United States and Western Europe.

I've written several novels with the help of NaNoWriMo, although none are yet published. I have several hundred works on Archive of Our Own, primarily in the *Supernatural* and *Yuri!!! on Ice* fandoms. I also enjoy *Miraculous Ladybug, Marvel Cinematic Universe, Boku no Hero Academia, Star Wars,*

Star Trek, *Mass Effect*, and *The Lord of the Rings*.

K. B. Vimes

K.B. Vimes lives in West Virginia with his wife and their six cats, four frogs, three lizards, and a number of fish. In his spare time he makes paper crafts, takes long walks with his wife, and visits state parks. He's been writing since he was old enough to hold a pencil, and for years has told stories to anyone willing to hold still long enough to listen.

Lyn Weaver

Lyn Weaver has been writing fanfiction for over a decade and original fiction for even longer. Her preferred genres are fantasy and horror, and her preferred tropes are "enemies to lovers" and anything to do with identity issues. She won't read a story if something bad happens to the cat.

A. A. Weston

Alex, a.k.a. foxymoley, (she/her) is best described as a jack of all trades but practices digital art more than anything else. She just wants to make things and change the world for the better.

Nicole Wilkinson

Nicole has been publishing her writing for the public since she first stumbled into fanfiction back in 2007, when a college friend introduced her to the concept through the world of *Final Fantasy VIII* slash fiction. Since then, it's been a roller coaster ride straight through dozens of fandoms, eventually leading to original content published through a variety of means. She's in her mid-thirties, uses she/her pronouns, and more recently has discovered an intense affection for playing Dungeons and Dragons.

OUR TOP-TIER
PATREON SUPPORTERS

Anonymous Backer
Sam Brown
Alex Gruendl
Tina Houck
jumblejen
Aria L.
A. Taylor
Karen Welborn

ABOUT DUCK PRINTS PRESS LLC

Duck Prints Press LLC is an independent publisher based in New York State. Our founding vision is to help fanfiction authors navigate the complex process of bringing their original works from first draft to print, culminating in publishing their work under our imprint. We are particularly dedicated to working with queer authors and publishing stories featuring characters from across the LGBTQIA+ spectrum.

Become a Duck Prints Press Patron by backing us on Patreon!

Find us online at our website, **duckprintspress.com**, or on social media:
Bluesky: duckprintspress
Dreamwidth: duckprintspress.dreamwidth.org
Facebook: duckprintspress
Instagram: duckprintspress
Mastodon: @dppunforth
Patreon: duckprintspress
Pillowfort: duckprintspress
Pinterest: duckprintspress
TikTok: @duckprintspress
Tumblr: duckprintspress

Goodreads: https://www.goodreads.com/user/show/129902473-duck-prints-press-llc
Storygraph: https://app.thestorygraph.com/profile/unforth